Five Nights at Freddy's
THE SILVER EYES

Five Nights at Freddy's

THE SILVER EYES

by
SCOTT CAWTHON
KIRA BREED-WRISLEY

Scholastic Inc.

Photo of tv static: © Klikk/Dreamstime

All rights reserved. Published by Scholastic Inc., *Publishers since 1920.* SCHOLASTIC and associated logos are trademarks and/or registered trademarks of Scholastic Inc.

The publisher does not have any control over and does not assume any responsibility for author or third-party websites or their content.

This book is a work of fiction. Names, characters, places, and incidents are either the product of the author's imagination or are used fictitiously, and any resemblance to actual persons, living or dead, business establishments, events, or locales is entirely coincidental.

Library of Congress Cataloging-in-Publication Data available

ISBN 978-1-338-13437-7

20 19   21 22 23 24

Printed in the U.S.A.   40

First edition, October 2016

Book design by Rick DeMonico

CHAPTER ONE

He sees me.

Charlie dropped to her hands and knees. She was wedged behind a row of arcade games, cramped in the crawl space between the consoles and the wall, tangled electrical cords and useless plugs strewn beneath her. She was cornered; the only way out was past the thing, and she wasn't fast enough to make it. She could see him stalking back and forth, catching flickers of movement through the gaps between the games. There was scarcely enough room to move, but she tried to crawl backward. Her foot caught on a cord. She stopped, contorting herself to carefully dislodge it.

She heard the clash of metal on metal, and the farthest console rocked back against the wall. He hit it again, shattering the display, then attacked the next, crashing against them almost rhythmically, tearing through the machinery, coming closer.

I have to get out, I have to! The panicked thought was of no help; there was no way out. Her arm ached, and she wanted to sob aloud. Blood soaked through the tattered bandage, and it seemed as though she could feel it draining out of her.

The console a few feet away crashed against the wall, and Charlie flinched. He was getting closer; she could hear the grinding of gears and the clicking of servos, ever louder. Eyes closed, she could still see the way he looked at her, see the matted fur and the exposed metal beneath the synthetic flesh.

Suddenly the console in front of her was wrenched away. It toppled over, thrown down like a toy. The power cords beneath her hands and knees were yanked away, and Charlie slipped, almost falling. She caught herself and looked up just in time to see the downward swing of a hook . . .

WELCOME TO HURRICANE, UTAH.

Charlie smiled wryly at the sign and kept driving. The world didn't look any different from one side of the sign to the other, but she felt a nervous anticipation as she passed it. She didn't recognize anything. Then again, she hadn't really expected to, not this far at the edge of town where it was all highway and empty space.

She wondered what the others would look like, who they were now. Ten years ago they'd been best friends. And then *it* happened, and everything ended, at least for Charlie. She hadn't seen any of them since she was seven years old. They had written all the time as kids, especially Marla, who wrote like she talked: fast and incoherent. But as they got older they had grown apart, the letters had grown fewer and further between, and the conversations leading up to this trip had been perfunctory and full of awkward pauses. Charlie repeated their names as though to reassure herself that she still remembered them: *Marla. Jessica. Lamar. Carlton. John. And Michael* . . . Michael was the reason for this trip, after all. It was ten years since he'd died, ten years since *it* happened, and now his parents wanted them all together for the dedication ceremony. They wanted all his old friends there when they announced the scholarship they were creating in his name. Charlie knew it was a good thing to do, but the gathering still felt slightly macabre. She shivered and turned down the air-conditioning, even though she knew it was not the cold.

As she drove into the town center, Charlie began to recognize things: a few stores and the movie theater, which was now advertising the summer's blockbuster hit. She felt a brief moment of surprise, then smiled at herself. *What did you expect, that the whole place would be unchanged? A monument to the moment of your departure, frozen forever in July 1985?* Well, that was exactly what she had expected. She looked at her watch. Still a few hours to kill before they all met up. She thought about going to the movie, but she knew what she really wanted to do. Charlie made a left turn and headed out of town.

Ten minutes later, she pulled to a stop and got out.

The house loomed up before her, its dark outline a wound in the bright-blue sky. Charlie leaned back against the car, slightly dizzy. She took a moment to steady herself with deep breaths. She had known it would be here. An illicit look through her aunt's bank books a few years before had told her that the mortgage was paid off and that Aunt Jen was still paying property taxes. It had only been ten years; there was no reason it should have changed at all. Charlie climbed the steps slowly, taking in the peeling paint. The third stair still had a loose board, and the rosebushes had taken over one side of the porch, their thorns biting hungrily into the wood. The door was locked, but Charlie still had her key. She had never actually used it. As she took it from around her neck and slid it into the lock, she remembered her father putting its chain around her neck. *In case you ever need it.* Well, she needed it now.

The door opened easily, and Charlie looked around. She didn't remember much about the first couple of years here. She had been only three years old, and all the memories had faded together in the blur of a child's grief and loss, of not understanding why her mother had to go away, clinging to her father every moment, not trusting the world around her unless he was there, unless she was holding tightly to him, burying herself in his flannel shirts and the smell of grease and hot metal and him.

The stairs stretched straight up in front of her, but she did not move directly to them. Instead she went into the living room, where all the furniture was still in place. She had not really noticed it as a child, but the house was a little too large for the furniture they had. Things were spread out too widely in order to fill the space: The coffee table was too far from the couch to reach, the easy chair too far across the room to carry on a conversation. There was a dark stain in the wooden floorboards near the center of the room. Charlie stepped around it quickly and went to the kitchen, where the cupboards held only a few pots, pans, and dishes. Charlie had never felt a lack of anything as a child, but it seemed now that the unnecessary enormity of the house was a sort of apology, the attempt of a man who had lost so much to give his daughter what he could. He'd always had a way of over-doing whatever he did.

The last time she was here the house had been dark and everything felt wrong. She was carried up the stairs to her bedroom although she was seven years old and could have gone quicker on her own two feet. But Aunt Jen had stopped on the front porch, picked her up, and carried her, shielding her face as though she were a baby in the glaring sun.

In her room, Aunt Jen set Charlie down and closed the bedroom door behind them. She told her to pack her suitcase, and Charlie had cried because all her things could never fit into that small case.

"We can come back for the rest later," Aunt Jen said, her impatience leaking through as Charlie hovered indecisively at her dresser, trying to decide which T-shirts to bring along. They had never come back for the rest.

Charlie mounted the stairs, heading to her old bedroom. The door was partially cracked, and as she opened it she had a giddy feeling of displacement, as though her younger self might be sitting there among her toys, might look up and ask Charlie, *Who are you?* Charlie went in.

Like the rest of the house, her bedroom was untouched. The walls were pale pink, and the ceiling, which sloped dramatically on one side to follow the line of the roof, was painted to match. Her old bed still stood against the wall beneath a large window; the mattress was still intact, though the sheets were gone. The window was cracked slightly open, and rotting lace curtains wavered in the gentle breeze from outside. There was a dark water stain in the paint beneath the window where the weather had gotten in over the years, betraying the house's neglect. Charlie climbed onto the bed and forced the window shut. It obeyed with a screech, and Charlie stepped back and turned her attention to the rest of the room, to her father's creations.

Their first night in the house, Charlie had been afraid to sleep alone. She did not remember the night, but her father had told her about it often enough that the story had taken on the quality of memory. She sat up and wailed until her father came to find her, until he scooped her up and held her and promised her he would make sure she was never alone again. The next morning, he took her by the hand and led her to the garage, where he set to work keeping that promise.

The first of his inventions was a purple rabbit, now gray with age from years of sitting in the sunlight. Her father had named him Theodore. He was the size of a three-year-old child—her size at the time—and he had plush fur, shining eyes, and a dapper red bow tie. He didn't do much, only waved a hand, tilted his head to the side, and said in her father's voice, "I love you, Charlie." But it was enough to give her a night watcher, someone to keep her company when she could not sleep. Right now Theodore sat in a white wicker chair in the far corner of the room. Charlie waved at him, but, not activated, he did not wave back.

After Theodore, the toys got more complex. Some worked and some did not; some seemed to have permanent glitches, while others simply did not appeal to Charlie's childish imagination. She knew her father took those back to his workshop and recycled them for parts, though she did not like to watch them be dismantled. But the ones that were kept, those she loved, they were here now, looking at her expectantly. Smiling, Charlie pushed a button beside her bed. It gave way stiffly, but nothing happened. She pushed it again, holding it down longer, and this time, across the room and with the weary creak of metal on metal, the unicorn began to move.

The unicorn (Charlie had named him Stanley for some reason she could no longer remember) was made of metal and had been painted glossy white. He trundled around the room on a circular track, bobbing his head stiffly up and down. The track squealed as Stanley rounded the corner and came to a stop beside the bed. Charlie knelt beside him on the floor and patted his flank. His glossy paint was chipped and peeling, and his face had given over to rust. His eyes were lively, gazing out of the decay.

"You need a new coat of paint, Stanley," Charlie said. The unicorn stared ahead, unresponsive.

At the foot of the bed, there was a wheel. Made of patched-together metal, it had always reminded her of something she might find on a submarine. Charlie turned it. It stuck for a moment, then gave way, rotating as it always did, and across the room the smallest closet door swung open. Out sailed Ella on her track, a child-size doll bearing a teacup and saucer in her tiny hands like an offering. Ella's plaid dress was still crisp, and her patent leather shoes still shone; perhaps the closet had protected her from the damage of the damp. Charlie had had an identical outfit, back when she and Ella were the same height.

"Hi, Ella," she said softly. As the wheel unwound, Ella retreated to the closet again, the door closing behind her. Charlie followed her. The closets had been built to align with the slant of the ceiling, and there were three of them. Ella lived in the short one, which was about three and a half feet tall. Next to it was one a foot or so taller, and a third, closest to the bedroom door, was the same height as the rest of the room. She smiled, remembering.

"Why do you have three closets?" John had demanded the first time he came over. She looked at him blankly, confused by the question.

"'Cause that's how many there are," she said finally. She pointed defensively to the littlest one. "That one's Ella's anyway," she added. John nodded, satisfied.

Charlie shook her head and opened the door to the middle closet—or tried to. The knob stopped with a jolt: It was locked. She rattled it a few times but gave up without much conviction. She stayed crouched low to the floor and glanced up at the tallest closet, her *big-girl closet* that she would someday grow into. *"You won't need it until you're bigger,"* her father would say, but that day never came. The door now hung open slightly, but Charlie didn't disturb it. It hadn't opened for her; it had only given way to time.

As she moved to stand, she noticed something shiny, half-hidden under the rim of the locked middle door. She leaned forward to pick it up. It looked like a broken-off piece of a circuit board. She smiled slightly. Nuts, bolts, scraps, and parts had turned up all over the place, once upon a time. Her father always had stray parts in his pockets. He would carry around something he was working on, set it down, and forget where it was, or worse, put something aside "for safe-keeping," never to be seen again. There was also a strand of her hair clinging to it; she unwound it carefully from the tiny lip of metal it was stuck on.

Finally, as though she had been putting it off, Charlie crossed the room and picked up Theodore. His back had not faded in the sun like the front of his body, and it was the same rich, dark purple she remembered. She pressed the button at the base of his neck, but he remained lifeless. His fur was threadbare, one ear hanging loose by a single rotting thread, and through the hole she could see the green plastic of his circuit board. Charlie held her breath, listening fearfully for something.

"I—ou—lie—" the rabbit said with a barely audible halting noise, and Charlie set him down, her face hot and her chest pinched tight. She had not really expected to hear her father's voice again. *I love you, too.*

Charlie looked around the room. When she was a child it had been her own magical world, and she was possessive of it. Only a few chosen friends were ever even allowed inside. She went to her bed and set Stanley moving on his track again. She left, closing the door behind her before the little unicorn came to a halt.

She went out the back door to the driveway and stopped in front of the garage that had been her father's workshop. Half-buried in the gravel a few feet away was a piece of metal, and Charlie went to pick it up. It was jointed in the middle, and she held it in her hands, smiling a little as she bent it back and forth. *An elbow joint,* she thought. *I wonder who that was going to belong to?*

She had stood in this exact spot many times before. She closed her eyes, and the memory overwhelmed her. She was a little girl again, sitting on the floor of her father's workshop, playing with scraps of wood and metal as though they were toy blocks, trying to build a tower with the uneven pieces. The shop was hot, and she was sweaty, grime sticking to her legs as she sat in her shorts and sneakers. She could almost smell the sharp, metallic odor of the soldering iron. Her father was nearby, never out of sight, working on Stanley the unicorn.

Stanley's face was still unfinished: one side white and shining and friendly, with a gleaming brown eye that seemed almost to see. The other half of the toy's face was all exposed circuit boards and metal parts. Charlie's father looked at her and smiled, and she smiled back, beloved. In a darkened corner behind her father, barely visible, hung a jumble of metal limbs, a twisted skeleton with burning silver eyes. Every once in a while, it gave an uncanny twitch. Charlie tried never to look at it, but as her father worked, as she played with her makeshift toys, her eye was drawn back to it again and again. The limbs, contorted, seemed almost mocking, the thing a ghastly jester, and yet there was something about it that suggested enormous pain.

"Daddy?" Charlie said, and her father did not look up from his work. "Daddy?" she said again, more urgently, and this time he turned to her slowly, as though not fully present in the world.

"What do you need, sweetie?"

She pointed at the metal skeleton. *Does it hurt?* She wanted to ask the question, but when she looked into her father's eyes she found she could not. She shook her head.

"Nothing."

He nodded at her with an absent smile and went back to his work. Behind him, the creature gave another awful twitch, and its eyes still burned.

Charlie shivered and drew herself back to the present. She glanced behind her, feeling exposed. She looked down, and her gaze fixed on something: three widely spaced grooves in the ground. She knelt, thoughtful, and ran her finger over one of them. The gravel was scattered away, the marks worn heavily into the dirt. *A camera tripod of some sort?* It was the first unfamiliar thing she'd seen. The door to the workshop was cracked open slightly, inviting, but she felt no desire to go inside. Quickly, she headed back to her car, but she stopped as soon as she settled into the driver's seat. Her keys were gone, having probably fallen out of her pocket some-where inside the house.

She retraced her steps, merely glancing into the living room and kitchen before heading up to her bedroom. The keys were on the wicker chair, beside Theodore the rabbit. She picked them up and jangled them for a moment, not quite ready to leave the room behind. She sat down on the bed. Stanley the unicorn had stopped beside the bed as he always did, and as she sat, she patted him absently on the head. It had grown dark while she was outside, and the room was now cast in shadows. Somehow, without the bright sun-light, the toys' flaws and deterioration were thrown into sharp relief. Theodore's eyes no longer shone, and his thin fur and hanging ear made him look like a sickly vagabond. When she looked down at Stanley, the rust around his eyes made them look like hollow sockets, and his bared teeth, which she had always thought of as a smile, became the awful, knowing grin of a skull. Charlie stood up, careful not to touch him, and hurried toward the door, but her foot caught on the wheel beside the bed. She tripped on the tracks and fell sprawling to the floor. There was a whir of spinning metal, and as she raised her head, a small pair of feet appeared under her nose, clad in shining patent leather. She looked up.

There above her was Ella, staring down at her, silent and uninvited, her glassy eyes almost appearing to see. The teacup and saucer were held out before her with a military stiffness. Charlie got up cautiously, taking care not to disturb the doll. She left the room, stepping carefully to avoid accidentally activating any other toys. As Charlie went, Ella retreated to her closet, almost matching her pace.

Charlie hurried down the stairs, seized by an urgency to get away. In the car, she fumbled the key three times before sliding it into place. She backed too fast down the driveway, running recklessly over the grass of the front yard, and sped away. After about a mile, Charlie pulled over on the shoulder and turned the car off, staring straight ahead through the windshield, her eyes focused on nothing. She forced herself to breathe slowly. She reached up and adjusted the rearview mirror so she could see herself.

She always expected to see pain, anger, and sorrow written on her face, but they never were. Her cheeks were pink, and her round face looked almost cheerful, like always. Her first weeks living with Aunt Jen, she heard the same things over and over when Aunt Jen introduced her: *What a pretty child. What a happy-looking child she is.* Charlie always looked like she was about to smile, her brown eyes wide and sparkling, her thin mouth ready to curve up, even when she wanted to sob. The incongruity was a mild betrayal. She ran her fingers through her light brown hair as though that would magically fix its slight frizziness and put the mirror back into position.

She turned the car back on and searched for a radio station, hoping music might bring her fully back to reality. She flipped from station to station, not really hearing what any of them were playing, and finally settled on an AM broadcast with a host who seemed to be yelling condescendingly at his audience. She had no idea what he was talking about, but the brash and annoying sound was enough to jar her back into the present. The clock in the car was always wrong, so she checked her watch. It was almost time to meet her friends at the diner they had chosen, near the center of town.

Charlie pulled back onto the road and drove, letting the sound of the angry talk radio host soothe her mind.

When she reached the restaurant, Charlie pulled into the lot and stopped, but did not park. The front of the diner had a long picture window all across it, and she could see right inside. Though she had not seen them for years, it took her only a moment to spot her friends through the glass.

Jessica was easiest to pick out from the crowd. She always enclosed pictures with her letters, and right now she looked exactly like her last photo. Even seated, she was clearly taller than either of the boys, and very thin. Though Charlie could not see her whole outfit, she was wearing a loose white shirt with an embroidered vest, and she had a brimmed hat perched on her glossy, shoulder-length brown hair, with an enormous flower threatening to tip it off her head. She was gesturing excitedly about something as she spoke.

The two boys were sitting next to each other, facing her. Carlton looked like an older version of his red-headed child-hood self. He still had a bit of a baby face, but his features had refined, and his hair was carefully tousled and held in place by some alchemical hair product. He was almost pretty, for a boy, and he wore a black workout shirt, though she doubted he'd ever worked out a day in his life. He slouched forward on the table, resting his chin in his hands. Beside him, John sat closest to the window. John had been the kind of child who got dirty before he even went outside: There would be paint on his shirt before the teacher handed out the watercolors, grass stains on his knees before they came near a playground, and dirt under his fingernails just after he washed his hands. Charlie knew it was him because it had to be, but he looked completely different. The grubbiness of childhood had been replaced by something crisp and clean. He was wearing a neatly pressed, light-green button-down shirt, the sleeves rolled up and the collar open, preventing him from looking too uptight. He was leaning back confi-dently in the booth, nodding enthusiastically, apparently absorbed in whatever Jessica was saying. The only concession to his former self was his hair, sticking up all over his head, and he had a five-o'clock shadow, a smug, adult version of the dirt he was always covered in as a kid.

Charlie smiled to herself. John had been something like her childhood crush, before either of them really understood what that meant. He gave her cookies from his Transformers lunchbox, and once in kindergarten he took the blame when she broke the glass jar that held colored beads for arts and crafts. She remembered the moment when it slipped from her hands, and she watched it fall. She could not have moved fast enough to catch it, but she would not have tried. She wanted to see it break. The glass hit the wood floor and shattered into a thousand pieces, and the beads scattered, many colored, among the shards. She thought it was beautiful, and then she started to cry. John had a note sent home to his parents, and when she told him "thank you" he had winked at her with an irony beyond his years and simply said, "For what?"

After that, John was allowed to come to her room. She let him play with Stanley and Theodore, watching anxiously the first time he learned to press the buttons and make them move. She would be crushed if he didn't like them, knowing instinctively that it would make her think less of him. They were her family. But John was fascinated as soon as he saw them; he loved her mechanical toys, and so she loved him. Two years later, behind a tree beside her father's workshop, she almost let him kiss her. And then *it* happened, and everything ended, at least for Charlie.

Charlie shook herself, forcing her mind back to the present. Looking again at Jessica's polished appearance, she glanced down at herself. Purple T-shirt, denim jacket, black jeans, and combat boots. It had felt like a good choice this morning, but now she wished she had chosen something else. *This is all you ever wear,* she reminded herself. She parked and locked the car behind her, even though people in Hurricane did not usually lock their cars. Then she went into the diner to meet her friends for the first time in ten years.

The warmth, noise, and light of the restaurant hit her in a wave as she entered. For a moment she was overwhelmed, but Jessica saw her pause in the doorway and shouted her name. Charlie smiled and went over.

"Hi," she said awkwardly, flicking her eyes at each of them but not fully making contact. Jessica scooted over on the red vinyl bench and patted the seat beside her.

"Here, sit," she said. "I was just telling John and Carlton about my glamorous life." She rolled her eyes as she said it, managing to convey both self-deprecation and the sense that her life was truly something exciting.

"Did you know Jessica lives in New York?" Carlton said. There was something careful about the way he spoke, like he was thinking about his words before he formed them. John was silent, but he smiled at Charlie anxiously.

Jessica rolled her eyes again, and with a flash of déjà vu Charlie suddenly recalled that this had been a habit even when they were children.

"Eight million people live in New York, Carlton. It's not exactly an achievement," Jessica said. Carlton shrugged.

"I've never been anywhere," he said.

"I didn't know you still lived in town," Charlie said.

"Where else am I going to live? My family has been here since 1896," he added, deepening his voice to mimic his father.

"Is that even true?" Charlie asked.

"I don't know," Carlton said in his own register. "Could be. Dad ran for mayor two years ago. I mean, he lost, but still, who runs for mayor?" He made a face. "I swear, the day I turn eighteen I am out of here."

"Where are you going to go?" John asked, looking seriously at Carlton.

Carlton met his eyes, just as serious for a moment. Abruptly, he broke away and pointed out the window, closing one eye as if to get his aim true. John raised an eyebrow as he looked out the window, trying to follow the line Carlton was pointing to. Charlie looked, too. Carlton wasn't pointing at anything. John opened his mouth to say something, but Carlton interrupted.

"Or," he said as he smoothly pointed in the opposite direction.

"Okay." John scratched his head, looking slightly embarrassed. "Anywhere, right?" he added with a laugh.

"Where's everyone else?" Charlie asked, peering out the window and searching the parking lot for new arrivals.

"Tomorrow," John said.

"They're coming tomorrow morning," Jessica jumped in to clarify. "Marla's bringing her little brother. Can you believe it?"

"Jason?" Charlie smiled. She remembered Jason as a little bundle of blankets with a tiny red face peeking out.

"I mean, who wants a baby around?" Jessica adjusted her hat primly.

"I'm pretty sure he's not a baby anymore," Charlie said, stifling a laugh.

"Practically a baby," Jessica said. "Anyway, I booked us a room at the motel down by the highway. It was all I could find. The boys are staying with Carlton."

"Okay," Charlie said. She was vaguely impressed by Jessica's organization, but she wasn't happy about the plan. She was loath to share a room with Jessica, who now seemed like a stranger. Jessica had become the kind of girl who intimidated her: polished and immaculate, speaking as though she had everything in life figured out. For a moment Charlie considered going back to her old house for the night, but as soon as she thought it, the idea repelled her. That house, at night, was no longer the province of the living.

Don't be dramatic, she scolded herself, but now John was speaking. He had a way of commanding attention with his voice, probably because he spoke less often than everyone else. He spent most of his time listening, but not out of reticence. He was gathering information, speaking only when he had wisdom or sarcasm to dispense. Often it was both at once.

"Does anyone know what's happening tomorrow?"

They were all silent for a moment, and the waitress took the opportunity to come over for their order. Charlie flipped quickly through the menu, her eyes not really focusing on the words. Her turn to order came much faster than she was expecting, and she froze.

"Um, eggs," she said at last. The woman's hard expression was still fixed on her, and she realized she had not finished. "Scrambled. Wheat toast," she added, and the woman went away. Charlie looked back down at the menu. She hated this about herself. When she was caught off guard she seemed to lose all ability to act or process what was going on around her. People were incomprehensible, their demands alien. *Ordering dinner shouldn't be hard,* she thought. The others had begun their conversation again, and she turned her attention to them, feeling like she had fallen behind.

"What do we even say to his parents?" Jessica was saying.

"Carlton, do you ever see them?" Charlie asked.

"Not really," he said. "Around, I guess. Sometimes."

"I'm surprised they stayed in Hurricane," Jessica said with a note of worldly disapproval in her voice.

Charlie said nothing, but she thought, *How could they not?*

His body had never been found. How could they not have secretly hoped he might come home, no matter how impossible they knew it was? How could they leave the only home Michael knew? It would mean really, finally giving up on him. Maybe that was what this scholarship was: an admission that he was never coming home.

Charlie was acutely aware that they were in a public place, where talking about Michael felt inappropriate. They were, in a sense, both insiders and outsiders. They had been closer to Michael, probably more than anyone in this restaurant, but, with the exception of Carlton, they were no longer from Hurricane. They did not belong.

She saw the tears falling on her paper placemat before she felt them, and she hurriedly wiped her eyes, looking down and hoping no one had noticed. When she looked up, John appeared to be studying his silverware, but she knew he had seen. She was grateful to him for not trying to offer comfort.

"John, do you still write?" Charlie asked.

John had declared himself "an author" when they were about six, having learned to read and write when he was four, a year ahead of the rest of them. At the age of seven, he completed his first "novel" and pressed his poorly spelled, inscrutably illustrated creation on his friends and family, demanding reviews. Charlie remembered that she had given him only two stars.

John laughed at the question. "I actually do my *Es* the right way these days," he said. "I can't believe you remember that. But I do actually, yeah." He stopped, clearly wanting to say more.

"What do you write?" Carlton obliged, and John looked down at his placemat, speaking mostly to the table.

"Um, short stories, mostly. I actually had one published last year. I mean, it was just in a magazine, nothing big." They all made suitable noises of being impressed, and he looked up again, embarrassed but pleased.

"What was the story about?" Charlie asked.

John hesitated, but before he could speak or decide not to, the waitress returned with their food. They had all ordered from the breakfast menu: coffee, eggs, and bacon; blueberry pancakes for Carlton. The brightly colored food looked hopeful, like a fresh start to the day. Charlie took a bite of her toast, and they all ate silently for a moment.

"Hey, Carlton," John said suddenly. "What ever happened to Freddy's anyway?"

There was a brief hush. Carlton looked nervously at Charlie, and Jessica stared up at the ceiling. John flushed red, and Charlie spoke hastily.

"It's okay, Carlton. I'd like to know, too."

Carlton shrugged, stabbing at his pancakes nervously with his fork.

"They built over it," he said.

"What did they build?" Jessica asked.

"Is there something else there now? Was it built over, or just torn down?" John asked. Carlton shrugged again, quick, like a nervous tic.

"Like I said, I don't know. It's too far back from the road to see, and I haven't exactly investigated. It might have been leased to someone, but I don't know what they did. It's all been blocked off for years, under construction. You can't even tell if the building is still there."

"So it could still be there?" Jessica asked with a spark of excitement breaking through.

"Like I said, I don't know," Carlton answered.

Charlie felt the diner's fluorescent lights glaring down on her face, suddenly too bright. She felt exposed. She had barely eaten, but she found herself rising from the booth, pulling a few crumpled bills from her pocket, and dropping them on the table.

"I'm going to go outside for a minute," she said. "Smoke break," she added hastily. *You don't smoke.* She chided herself for the clumsy lie as she made her way to the door, jostling past a family of four without saying "excuse me," and stepped out into the cool evening. She walked to her car and sat on the hood, the metal denting slightly under her weight. She took in breaths of the cool air as if it were water and closed her eyes. *You knew it would come up. You knew you would have to talk about it,* she reminded herself. She had practiced on the drive here, had forced herself to think back to happy memories, to smile and say, *"Remember when?"* She thought she was prepared for this. But of course she had been wrong. Why else would she have run out of the restaurant like a child?

"Charlie?"

She opened her eyes and saw John standing next to the car, holding her jacket out in front of him like an offering.

"You forgot your jacket," he said, and she made herself smile at him.

"Thanks," she said. She took it and draped it over her shoulders, then slid over on the car's hood for him to sit.

"Sorry about that," she said. In the dim lights of the parking lot she could still see him blush to the ears. He joined her on the car's hood, leaving a deliberate space between them.

"I haven't learned to think before I talk. I'm sorry." John watched the sky as a plane passed overhead.

Charlie smiled, this time unforced.

"It's okay. I knew it was going to come up; it had to. I just—it sounds stupid, but I never think about it. I don't let myself. No one knows what happened except my aunt, and we never talk about it. Then I come here, and suddenly it's everywhere. I was just surprised, that's all."

"Uh-oh." John pointed, and Charlie saw Jessica and Carlton hesitating in the doorway of the diner. She waved them over, and they came.

"Remember that time at Freddy's when the merry-go-round got stuck, and Marla and that mean kid Billy had to keep riding it until their parents plucked them off?" Charlie said.

John laughed, and the sound made her smile.

"Their faces were bright red, crying like babies." She covered her face, guilty that it was so funny to her.

There was a brief, surprised silence, then Carlton started laughing. "Then Marla puked all over him!"

"Sweet justice!" Charlie said.

"Actually, I think it was nachos," John added.

Jessica wrinkled her nose. "So gross. I never rode it again, not after that."

"Oh, come on, Jessica, they cleaned it," said Carlton. "I'm pretty sure kids puked all over that place; those wet floor signs weren't there for nothing. Right, Charlie?"

"Don't look at me," she said. "I never puked."

"We used to spend so much time there! Privileges of knowing the owner's daughter," Jessica said, looking at Charlie with mock accusation.

"I couldn't help who my dad was!" Charlie said, laughing.

Jessica looked thoughtful for a moment before she continued. "I mean, how could you have a better childhood than spending all day at Freddy Fazbear's Pizza?"

"I dunno," said Carlton. "I think that music got to me over the years." He hummed a few bars of the familiar song. Charlie dipped her head to it, recalling the tune.

"I loved those animals so much," Jessica said suddenly. "What's the proper term for them? Animals, robots, mascots?"

"I think those are all accurate." Charlie leaned back.

"Well, anyway, I used to go and talk to the bunny, what was his name?"

"Bonnie," Charlie said.

"Yeah," said Jessica. "I used to complain to him about my parents. I always thought he had an understanding look about him."

Carlton laughed. "Animatronic therapy! Recommended by six out of seven crazy people."

"Shut up," Jessica retorted. "I knew he wasn't real. I just liked talking to him."

Charlie smiled a little. "I remember that," she said. Jessica in her prim little dresses, her brown hair in two tight braids like a little kid out of an old book, walking up to the stage when the show was over, whispering earnestly to the life-size animatronic rabbit. If anyone came up beside her, she went instantly silent and still, waiting for them to go away so she could resume her one-sided conversations. Charlie had never talked to the animals at her father's restaurant or felt close to them like some kids seemed to; although she liked them, they belonged to the public. She had her own toys, mechanical friends waiting for her at home, that belonged only to her.

"I liked Freddy," said John. "He always seemed the most relatable."

"You know, there are a lot of things about my childhood that I can't remember at all," Carlton said, "but I swear I can close my eyes and see every last detail of that place. Even the gum I used to stick under the tables."

"Gum? Yeah, right; those were boogers." Jessica took a tiny step away from Carlton.

He grinned. "I was seven; what do you want? You all picked on me back then. Remember when Marla wrote 'Carlton smells like feet' on the wall outside?"

"You did smell like feet." Jessica laughed with a sudden outburst.

Carlton shrugged, unperturbed. "I used to try to hide when it was time to go home. I wanted to be stuck in there overnight so I could have the whole place to myself."

"Yeah, you always kept everyone waiting," said John, "and you always hid under the same table."

Charlie spoke slowly, and when she did everyone turned to her, as though they had been waiting.

"Sometimes I feel like I remember every inch of it, like Carlton," she said. "But sometimes it's like I hardly remember it at all. It's all in pieces. Like, I remember the carousel, and that time it got stuck. I remember drawing on the place-mats. I remember little things: eating that greasy pizza, hugging Freddy in the summer and his yellow fur getting stuck all over my clothes. But a lot of it is like pictures, like it happened to someone else."

They were all looking at her oddly.

"Freddy was brown, right?" Jessica looked to the others for confirmation.

"I guess you really don't remember it that well after all," Carlton teased Charlie, and she laughed briefly.

"Right. I meant brown," she said. *Brown, Freddy was brown.* Of course he was; she could see him in her mind now. But somewhere in the depths of her recall, there was a flash of something else.

Carlton launched into another story, and Charlie tried to turn her attention to him, but there was something disturbing, worrisome, about that lapse in memory. *It was ten years ago; it's not like you've got dementia at seventeen*, she told herself, but it was such a basic detail to have misremembered. Out of the corner of her eye, she caught John looking at her, a pensive expression on his face, as though she had said something important.

"You really don't know what happened to it?" she asked Carlton with more urgency in her voice than she intended. He stopped talking, surprised. "Sorry," she said. "Sorry, I didn't mean to interrupt you."

"It's okay," he said. "But yeah—or no, I really don't know what happened."

"How can you not know? You live here."

"Charlie, come on," said John.

"It's not like I hang around that part of town. Things are different; the town has grown," Carlton said mildly, seeming unruffled by her outburst. "And I honestly don't look for reasons to go around there, you know? Why would I? There isn't any reason, not anymore."

"We could go there," John said suddenly, and Charlie's heart skipped.

Carlton looked nervously at Charlie. "What? Seriously, it's a mess. I don't know if you can even get to it."

Charlie found herself nodding. She felt as though she had spent the whole day weighed down by memory, seeing everything through a filter of years, and now she felt suddenly alert, her mind fully present. She wanted to go.

"Let's do it," she said. "Even if there's nothing there. I want to see." They were all silent. Suddenly, John smiled with a reckless confidence.

"Yeah. Let's do it."

CHAPTER TWO

harlie pulled to a stop, feeling the soft give of dirt under her tires, and turned off the car. She got out and surveyed their surroundings. The sky was a rich, dark blue, the last trails of the sunset streaking off to the west. The parking lot was unpaved, and before them lay a sprawling monster of a building, a rising acre of glass and concrete. There were lamps in the parking lot that had never been used, and no lights shone out onto the lot. The building itself looked like an abandoned sanctuary, entombed in black trees amid the distant roar of civilization. She looked at Jessica in the passenger seat, who was craning her neck out the window.

"Is this the right place?" Jessica asked.

Charlie shook her head slowly, not quite certain what she was seeing. "I don't know," she whispered.

Charlie got out of the car and stood in silence as John and Carlton pulled up beside her.

"What is this?" John stepped out of the car cautiously and stared blankly at the monument. "Does anyone have a flashlight?" He looked at each of them.

Carlton held up his key chain and waved around the feeble glow of a penlight for a minute.

"Great," John muttered, walking away with resignation.

"Hold on a sec," Charlie said and went around to her trunk. "My aunt makes me carry around a bunch of stuff for emergencies."

Aunt Jen, loving but severe, had taught Charlie self-reliance above almost anything else. Before she let Charlie have her old blue Honda, she had insisted that Charlie know how to change a tire, check the oil, and know the basic parts of the engine. In the trunk, in a black box tucked in next to the jack, spare tire, and small crowbar; she had a blanket, a heavy police-issue flashlight, bottled water, granola bars, matches, and emergency flares. Charlie grabbed the flashlight; Carlton grabbed a granola bar.

Almost by silent agreement, they began to walk the building's perimeter, Charlie holding up the light in a steady beam in front of them. The building itself looked mostly finished, but the ground was all dirt and rock, uneven and soft. Charlie shone the light on the ground, where grass had grown patchy in the dirt, inches long.

"No one has been digging for a while," Charlie said.

The place was massive, and it took a long time to circumnavigate. It wasn't long before the rich blue of the evening was overtaken by a blanket of scattered silver clouds and stars. The surfaces of the building were all the same smooth, beige concrete, with windows too high up on the walls to see inside.

"Did they really build this whole thing and then just leave?" Jessica said.

"Carlton," said John, "you really don't know anything about what happened?"

Carlton shrugged expansively. "I told you, I knew there was construction, but I don't know anything else."

"Why would they do this?" John seemed almost paranoid, scouting the trees as though eyes might be looking back at him. "It just goes on and on." He squinted, gazing along the outside wall of the building, which seemed to stretch endlessly into the distance. He glanced back to the trees as if making sure they hadn't missed a building somehow. "No, it was here." He placed his hand on the drab concrete facing. "It's gone."

After a moment, he gestured to the others and began to walk back the way they came. Reluctantly, Charlie turned back, following the group. They kept going until they could see their cars again up ahead in the darkness.

"Sorry, guys; I hoped there would at least be something familiar," Carlton said exhaustedly.

"Yeah," Charlie said. She had known it would be, but seeing that Freddy's had been razed to the ground was still a shock. It was so paramount, sometimes, in her mind, that she wanted to get rid of it, wanted to scrub the memories—good and bad—from her head, as if they had never been. Now someone had scrubbed it from the landscape, and it felt like a violation. It should have been up to her. *Right,* she thought, *because you had the money to buy it and preserve it, like Aunt Jen did with the house.*

"Charlie?" John was saying her name, and it sounded like he was repeating it.

"Sorry," she said. "What were you saying?"

"Do you want to go inside?" Jessica asked.

Charlie was surprised they were only now considering this, but then again none of them was usually prone to criminal activity. The thought was a release, and she took a deep breath, speaking on her exhale. "Why not?" she said, almost laughing. She hefted the flashlight. Her arms were getting tired. "Anyone else want a turn?" She waved it back and forth like a pendulum.

Carlton grabbed it and took a moment to appreciate its weight.

"Why is this so heavy?" he said, passing it off to John. "Here you go."

"It's a police flashlight," Charlie said absently. "You can hit people with it."

Jessica wrinkled her nose. "Your aunt really wasn't kidding around, huh? Ever used it?"

"Not yet." Charlie winked and made a half-threatening glance at John, who returned an uncertain half smile, unsure how to react.

The wide entrances were sealed with hammered metal doors, no doubt intended to be temporary until construction was finished. Still, it wasn't difficult to find a way in, since many large mounds of gravel and sand scaled the walls, leading right up to the edges of the large, gaping windows.

"Not trying hard to keep people out," John said.

"What's anyone going to steal?" Charlie said, staring at the blank, towering walls.

They climbed the hills slowly, the gravel shifting and sliding beneath their feet as they went. Carlton reached the window first and peered through. Jessica looked over his shoulder.

"Can we drop down?" John asked.

"Yes," said Carlton.

"No," Jessica said at precisely the same time.

"I'll go," Charlie said. She felt reckless. Without looking through to see how far the fall was, she put her feet through the opening and let herself drop. She landed, knees bent; the impact rocked her, but it did not hurt. She looked up at her friends staring down. "Oh. Hang on!" Charlie called, pulling a short stepladder from a wall nearby and setting it under the window. "Okay," she said. "Come on!"

They dropped down one by one, and looked around them. Inside was an atrium, or maybe it would have become a food court, with metal benches and plastic tables scattered around, some bolted to the floor. The ceiling rose up high above them, with a glass roof where they could see the stars peering down at them.

"Very postapocalyptic," Charlie joked, her voice echoing in the open space.

Jessica sang a brief, wordless scale suddenly, startling them all into silence. Her voice rang out pure and clear, something beautiful in the emptiness.

"Very nice, but let's not call too much attention to ourselves," John said.

"Right," Jessica said, still very happy with herself. As they walked on, Carlton swept up and took her arm.

"Your voice is amazing," he said.

"It's just good acoustics," Jessica said, attempting humility but not meaning a word of it.

They walked the empty halls, peering into each of the massive cavities where a department store might have been. Some parts of the mall had been almost finished, while others were in shambles. Some hallways were littered with piles of dusty concrete bricks and stacks of wood; others were lined with glass-paneled storefronts, lights hanging in perfect rows above their heads.

"It's like a lost city," John said.

"Like Pompeii," said Jessica, "just without the volcano."

"No," Charlie said, "there's nothing here." The whole place had a sterile feel to it. It was not abandoned—it had never sustained life at all.

She looked in a store window across from her, one of the few with glass, wondering what would have been displayed. She imagined mannequins, dressed in bright clothing, but when she tried to picture them, all she could see was blank faces, concealing something. She suddenly felt out of place, unwelcomed by the building itself. Charlie began to feel restless, some of the luster wearing off the adventure. They had come; Freddy's was gone, and so was the shrine she had kept in her thoughts, where she could still find Michael playing where she last saw him.

John stopped suddenly, turning off the flashlight as carefully as he could. He put a finger to his lips, motioning for silence. He gestured back the way they had come. In the distance, they saw a small light bobbing in the darkness like a ship in the fog.

"Someone else is here," he hissed.

"A night guard, maybe?" Carlton whispered.

"Why would an abandoned building need a guard?" Charlie wondered.

"Kids probably come here to party," Carlton said, then grinned. "I would have come here to party, too, if I'd known about it, or if I partied."

"Okay, well, let's backtrack slowly," John said. "Jessica . . ." he started, then made a *zip-it* motion across his lips.

They continued down the hallway, this time with only the dimmer light of Carlton's key chain.

"Wait." Jessica stopped with a whisper, looking intently at the walls surrounding them. "Something's not right."

"Yeah, no giant pretzels. I know." Carlton seemed sincere. Jessica waved a hand at him impatiently.

"No, something isn't right about the architecture." She took several steps back, trying to see the whole of it. "Something is definitely not right," she repeated. "It's bigger on the outside."

"Bigger on the outside?" Charlie repeated, sounding puzzled.

"I mean there's a big difference between where the inside wall is and where the outside wall is. Look." Jessica ran along a length of wall between where two stores would have been.

"There would have been a store here and a store there." John pointed to the obvious, not understanding the problem.

"But there's something in the middle!" Jessica exclaimed, beating her hands against an empty portion of the wall. "This part juts out into the parking lot like the stores on each side, but there's no way into it."

"You're right." Charlie started walking toward Jessica, studying the walls. "There should be another entrance here."

"And"—Jessica dropped her voice so that only Charlie could hear her—"about the same size as Freddy's, don't you think?" Charlie's eyes widened, and she took a quick step back from Jessica.

"What are you two whispering about?" Carlton stepped closer.

"We're talking about you," Jessica said sharply, and they walked into one of the vacant department stores that seemed to sandwich the sealed space. "Come on," she said, "let's take a look." They started combing the wall as a group, clustered around the tiny light.

Charlie was not sure what to hope for. Aunt Jen had warned her about coming back. She didn't encourage Charlie to skip the memorial, not directly, but she wasn't pleased that Charlie was returning to Hurricane.

Just be careful, Aunt Jen had said. *Some things, some memories, are best left undisturbed.*

Is that why you kept Dad's house? Charlie thought now. *Is that why you kept paying for it, leaving it untouched like some kind of shrine, but never visiting?*

"Hey!" John was gesturing wildly, running inside to catch up to the rest of them. "Hide!"

The light was out in the hall again, bobbing up and down, and it was coming closer. Charlie glanced around. They were already too deep inside the massive store to get out in time, and there seemed to be nowhere to hide.

"Here, here!" Jessica whispered. There was a break in the wall beside a rig of scaffolding, and they hurried into it, squeezing past stacks of open boxes and sheets of plastic hanging from the ceiling.

They made their way down what appeared to be a make-shift hallway just on the other side of the department store wall. It was really more like an alley; it was incongruous with the rest of the mall, not shiny and new but dank and musty. One wall was made of the same concrete as the out-side of the building, though it was rough and unfinished, and the other was exposed brick, some parts faded smooth with age, others with the mortar crumbling, leaving chinks and holes. Heavy wooden shelves of cleaning equipment stood against the wall, listing to the side, their boards sinking under the weight of old paint cans and mysterious buckets. Something was dripping from uncovered pipes overhead, leaving puddles that they all stepped carefully around. A mouse scuttled by, almost running over Carlton's foot. Carlton made a strangled sound, hand over his mouth.

They crouched down behind one of the wooden shelving units, pressing up against the wall. Charlie doused the light and waited.

She took shallow breaths, perfectly still, watching and wishing she had picked a better position to freeze into. After a few minutes, her legs started to feel numb under her, and Carlton was so close that she could smell the light, pleasant scent of his shampoo. "That's nice," she whispered.

"Thanks," Carlton said, knowing immediately what she was referring to. "It comes in Ocean Breeze and Tropical Paradise. I prefer Ocean Breeze, but it dries the scalp."

"Hush!" John hissed.

Charlie wasn't sure why she was so worried. It was just a night guard, and at the worst they would be asked to leave, maybe yelled at a little. She had an overblown aversion to getting in trouble.

The bobbing light came closer. Charlie was acutely aware of her body, holding every muscle motionless. Suddenly she could make out a thin figure leaning in from the great room outside. He shone his light in a long beam down the hallway, sweeping it up and down the walls. *He's got us,* Charlie thought, but inexplicably he turned and went, apparently satisfied.

They waited another few minutes, but there was nothing. He was gone. They all moved slowly out of their crouched positions, stretching limbs that had gone to sleep. Carlton shook one foot vigorously until he could stand on it. Charlie looked down at Jessica, who was still hunched over, as if frozen in time.

"Jessica, are you okay?" she whispered.

Jessica looked up, smiling.

"You won't believe this."

She was pointing at the wall, and Charlie leaned over to see. There, etched in the worn brick, were clumsy letters, almost illegible in a child's handiwork:

Carlton smells like feet.

"You have to be kidding me," John whispered in awe, turning to face the wall and placing both hands against it. "I recognize these bricks." He laughed. "These are the same bricks!" His smile faded. "They didn't tear it down; they built around it."

"It's still here!" Jessica unsuccessfully tried to keep her voice down. "There has to be a way in," she added, her eyes wide with an almost childish excitement.

Charlie shone the flashlight up and down the hallway, playing the light off each wall, but there was no break, no door.

"There was a back door to Freddy's," John said. "Marla wrote that right next to the back door, right?"

"Why didn't they just knock it down?" Charlie pondered.

"Does this hallway just lead nowhere?" Jessica said, puzzled.

"It's the story of my life," Carlton said lightly.

"Wait . . ." Charlie ran her fingers along the edge of a shelf, peering through the odds and ends crammed onto it. The wall behind it looked different; it was metal, not brick.

"Right here." She stepped back and looked at the others. "Help me move it."

John and Jessica pressed against one side in a unified effort, and she and Carlton pulled on the other. It was immensely heavy, laden with cleaning supplies and large buckets of nails and tools, but it slid farther down the hall almost easily, without incident.

Jessica stepped back, breathing hard. "John, give me the big light again." He handed it over, and she turned it back on, aiming where the shelf had stood. "This is it," she said.

It was metal and rusting, spattered with paint, a stark contrast to the walls around it. There was only a hole where the handle had been; someone must have removed it so the shelf could lie flush against the door.

Silently Charlie handed the flashlight back to John, and he held it above her head so she could see. She slipped around the others and tried to squeeze her fingers into the hole where the doorknob once was, trying to pull it open to no avail.

"It's not going to open," she said. John was behind her, peering over her shoulder.

"Just a second." He squeezed himself into the space beside her and knelt carefully. "I don't think it's locked or anything," he said. "I think it's just rusty. Look at it."

The door extended all the way to the floor, its bottom ragged and unfinished. The hinges were on the other side, and the edges were caked in rust. It looked as though it had not been opened in years. John and Charlie pulled on it together, and it moved a fraction of an inch.

"Yay!" Jessica exclaimed, almost shouting, then covered her mouth. "Sorry," she said in a whisper. "Containing my excitement."

They took turns pulling on it, leaning over one another, the metal scraping their fingers. The door held for a long moment, and then it came loose under their weight, swinging open slowly with an unearthly screech. Charlie looked nervously over her shoulder, but the guard did not appear. The door opened only about a foot wide, and they went one by one, until all four were through.

Inside, the air changed, and they all stopped short. Ahead of them was a dark hallway, familiar to them all.

"Is this . . . ?" Jessica whispered, not taking her eyes from the dark expanse.

It's here, Charlie thought. She held out her hand for the flashlight, and John handed it to her wordlessly. She shone the light ahead of them, sweeping the walls. They were covered in children's drawings, crayon on yellowing, curling paper. She started forward, and the others followed, feet shuffling on old tile.

It seemed to take forever to traverse the hall, or perhaps it was just that they were moving slowly, with methodical, deliberate steps. Eventually the hallway opened up into a larger expanse—the dining room. It was just as they remembered it, completely preserved. The flashlight beam bounced off a thousand little things reflective, glittered, or topped with foil ribbon.

The tables were still in place, covered in their silver-and-white checked cloths; the chairs were pulled up to them haphazardly, some tables with too many and others with too few. It looked as though the room had been abandoned in the middle of the lunch hour: Everyone had gotten up expecting to return, but never did. They walked in cautiously, breathing cold, stale air that had been trapped inside for a decade. The whole restaurant gave off a sense of abandonment—no one was coming back. There was a small merry-go-round barely visible in the distant corner, with four child-size ponies still at rest from their last song. In an instant, Charlie froze in place, as did the others.

There they were. Eyes stared back from the dark, large and lifeless. An illogical panic pulsed through her; time held still. No one spoke; no one breathed, as though a predatory animal was stalking them. But as the moments passed, the fear waned, until she was back again, as a child, and with old friends, separated from one another for far too long. Charlie walked toward the eyes in a straight line. Behind her the others were motionless; hers were the only footsteps. As Charlie walked, she touched the cold back of an old party chair without looking at it, guiding it out of her path. She took one final step, and the eyes in the dark became clear. It was them. Charlie smiled.

"Hi," she whispered, too soft for the others to hear.

Before her stood three animatronic animals: a bear, a rabbit, and a chicken, all standing as tall as adults, maybe taller. Their bodies were segmented like artists' models, each limb made of distinct, squarish pieces, separate at the joints. They belonged to the restaurant, or maybe the restaurant belonged to them, and there had been a time when everyone knew them by name. There was Bonnie, the rabbit. His fur was a bright blue, his squared-off muzzle held a permanent smile, and his wide and chipped pink eyes were thick-lidded, giving him a perpetually worn-out expression. His ears stuck up straight, crinkling over at the top, and his large feet splayed out for balance. He held a red bass guitar, blue paws poised to play, and around his neck was a bow tie that matched the instrument's fiery color.

Chica the Chicken was more bulky and had an apprehensive look, thick black eyebrows arching over her purple eyes and her beak slightly open, revealing teeth, as she held out a cupcake on a platter. The cupcake itself was somewhat disturbing, with eyes set into its pink frosting and teeth hanging out over the cake, a single candle sticking out the top.

"I always expected the cupcake to jump off the plate." Carlton gave a half laugh and cautiously stepped up to

Charlie's side. "They seem taller than I remember," he added in a whisper.

"That's because you never got this close as a kid." Charlie smiled, at ease, and stepped closer.

"You were busy hiding under tables," Jessica said from behind them, still some distance away.

Chica wore a bib around her neck with the words LET'S EAT! set out in purple and yellow against a confetti-covered background. A tuft of feathers stuck up in the middle of her head.

Standing between Bonnie and Chica was Freddy Fazbear himself, namesake of the restaurant. He was the most genial looking of the three, seeming at ease where he was. A robust, if lean, brown bear, he smiled down at the audience, holding a microphone in one paw, sporting a black bow tie and top hat. The only incongruity in his features was the color of his eyes, a bright blue that surely no bear had ever had before him. His mouth hung open, and his eyes were partially closed, as though he had been frozen in song.

Carlton drew closer to the stage until his knees pressed against the rim of it. "Hey, Freddy," he whispered. "Long time no see."

He reached out and grabbed at the microphone, wiggling it to see if he could get it loose.

"Don't!" Charlie blurted, looking up into Freddy's fixed gaze as though making sure he hadn't noticed.

Carlton pulled his hand back like he had touched something hot. "Sorry."

"Come on," John said, cracking a smile. "Don't you want to see the rest of the place?"

They spread out across the room, peering into corners and carefully trying doors, acting as though everything might be breakable to the touch. John went over to the small carousel, and Carlton disappeared into the dark arcade off the main room.

"I remember it being a lot brighter and noisier in here." Carlton smiled as though at home again, running his hands over the aging knobs and flat plastic buttons. "I wonder if my high scores are still in there," he muttered to himself.

To the left of the stage was a small hallway. Half hoping no one would notice where she had gone, Charlie started down it silently as the others occupied themselves with their own curiosities. At the end of the short, plain corridor was her father's office. It had been Charlie's favorite place in the restaurant. She liked to play with her friends in the main area, but she loved the singular privilege of coming back here when her father was doing paperwork. She paused outside the closed door, her hand poised over the knob, remembering. Most of the room was filled with his desk, his filing cabinets, and small boxes of uninteresting parts. In one corner was a smaller filing cabinet, painted a salmon color that Charlie had always insisted was pink. That had been

Charlie's. The bottom drawer held toys and crayons, and the top had what she liked to call "my paperwork." It was mostly coloring books and drawings, but occasionally she would go over to her father's desk and try to copy down whatever he was writing in a childish, crayoned hand. Charlie tried the door, but it was locked. *Better this way,* she thought. The office was personal, and she did not really want it opened tonight.

She headed back into the main dining room and found John looking pensively at the merry-go-round. He eyed her with curiosity but did not ask where she had gone.

"I used to love this thing." Charlie smiled, approaching warmly. Yet now the painted figures seemed odd and lifeless to her.

John made a face, as though he knew what she was thinking.

"Not the same," he said. He rubbed his hand over the top of a polished pony as though to scratch it behind the ear. "Just not the same," he repeated, removing his hand and gazing elsewhere. Charlie glanced over to see where the others were—in the arcade, she could see Jessica and Carlton wandering among the games.

The consoles stood still and unlit like massive tombstones, their screens blank. "I never liked playing the games," Jessica said, smiling. "They moved too fast, and just when I'd start to figure out what to do, I'd die and it would be someone else's turn." She wiggled a joystick that squeaked from neglect.

"They were rigged anyway," Carlton said with a wink.

"When's the last time you played one of these?" Jessica asked, peering closely into one of the screens to see what image was burned into it from too many years of use. Carlton was busy rocking a pinball machine back and forth, trying to get a ball to come loose.

"Uh, there's a pizza place I visit sometimes." He set the table back on four legs carefully and glanced at Jessica. "But it's no Freddy's," he added.

John was roaming through the dining room again amid the tables, flicking the stars and spirals hanging overhead. He plucked a red party hat from the table, stretched the rubber band hanging loosely from its base, and snapped it around his head, red-and-white tassels hanging down over his face.

"Oh, let's check out the kitchen," he said. Charlie followed as he bounded off toward it.

Although the kitchen had been off-limits to her friends, she'd spent a lot of time there, so much so that the chefs chased her out by name, or at least by the name they heard her father call her: Charlotte. John overheard someone calling her Charlotte one day when they were in kindergarten and persisted in teasing her with it constantly. He could always get a rise out of her with that. It wasn't that Charlie didn't like her full name, but Charlie was who she was to the world. Her father called her Charlotte, and it was like a secret between them, something no one else was allowed to share. The day she left Hurricane for good, the day they said good-bye, John had hesitated.

"Bye, Charlie," he said. In their cards, letters, and phone calls, he had never called her Charlotte again. She never asked why, and he never told her.

The kitchen was still fully stocked with pots and pans, but it held little interest for Charlie in the midst of her memories. She headed back out into the open space of the dining room, and John followed. At the same time, Jessica and Carlton stumbled out of the arcade, tripping into each other as they crossed the thresholds between rooms in the dark.

"Anything interesting?" John asked.

"Uh, a gum wrapper, thirty cents, and Jessica, so no, not really," Carlton said. Jessica playfully gave him a punch in the shoulder.

"Oh, have we all forgotten?" Jessica gave an evil smile, pointing to another hallway on the opposite side of the din-ing room. She headed toward it swiftly before anyone could answer, and they followed her. The hallway was long and narrow, and the farther they went, the less the flashlight seemed to illuminate. At last the passage opened out into a small room for private parties, set up with its own tables and chairs. As they entered, there was a collective hush. There in front of them was a small stage, the curtain drawn. A sign was strung across the front. OUT OF ORDER, it read in neat, handwritten letters. They stood still for a minute, then Jessica went up to it and poked the sign.

"Pirate's Cove," she said. "Ten years later and it's still out of order."

Don't touch it, Charlie thought.

"I had one birthday back here," John said. "It was out of order then, too." He took hold of the edge of the curtain and rubbed the glittered fabric between his fingers.

No, Charlie wanted to say again, but stopped. *You're being silly*, she chided herself.

"Do you think he's still back there?" Jessica said playfully, threatening to make the reveal with one giant swing on the curtain.

"I'm sure he is." John gave a false smile, seeming uncomfortable for the first time.

Yes, he's still there, Charlie thought. She stepped back cautiously, suddenly becoming aware of the drawings and posters surrounding them like spiders on the wall. Charlie's flashlight carefully inched from picture to picture, all depicting different variations of the same character: a large and energetic pirate fox with a patch over one eye and a hook for a hand, usually swinging in to deliver a pizza to hungry children.

"This is the room where you were the one hiding under tables," Jessica said to Charlie, trying to laugh. "But you're a big girl now, right?" Jessica climbed up on the stage unsteadily, almost losing her footing. John reached out a hand to steady her as she righted herself. She giggled nervously, looking down at the others as though for guidance, than grabbed hold of the tasseled edge of the fabric. She waved her other hand in front of her face as dust fell from the cloth.

"Maybe this isn't a good idea?" She laughed, but there was an edge to her voice, like she really meant it, and she looked down at the stage for a moment, as though poised to climb back down. Still, she didn't move, taking the edge of the curtain again.

"Wait," John said. "Can you hear that?"

They were all dead quiet, and in the silence Charlie could hear them all breathing. John's breaths were deliberate and calm, Jessica's quick and nervous. As she thought about it, her own breathing began to feel odd, like she had forgotten how to do it.

"I don't hear anything," she said.

"Me neither," Jessica echoed. "What is it?"

"Music. It's coming from—" He gestured back the way they had come.

"From the stage?" Charlie cocked her head to the side. "I don't hear it."

"It's like a music box," he said. Charlie and Jessica listened carefully, but their blank expressions didn't change. "It stopped, I guess." John returned his gaze forward.

"Maybe it was an ice cream truck," Jessica whispered.

"Hey, that wouldn't be so bad right now." John appreciated the levity.

Jessica turned her attention back to the curtain, but John began to hum a tune to himself. "It reminded me of something," he mumbled.

"Okay, here I go!" Jessica announced. She did not move. Charlie found her eyes drawn to Jessica's hand on the curtain, her pink, manicured nails pale against the dark, glittery fabric. It was almost like the hushed moment in a theater crowd, when the lights went dark but the curtain had not yet risen. They were all still, all anticipating, but they were not watching a play, no longer playing a game. All the mirth had gone out of Jessica's face; her cheekbones stood out stark in the shadows, and her eyes looked grim as though the simple thing she was about to do might be of terrible consequence. As Jessica hesitated, Charlie realized her hand hurt; she was making a fist so tight her nails dug into her flesh, but she could not force her grip to loosen.

A crash sounded from back the way they came, a cascading, clanging noise ringing out and filling the whole space. John and Charlie froze, meeting each other's eyes in sudden panic. Jessica dropped the curtain and leaped off the stage, bumping into Charlie and knocking the light out of her hands.

"Where's the way out?!" she exclaimed, and John came over to help. They hurriedly searched the walls, and Charlie chased the light beam spiraling across the floor. Just as they were all back to their feet, Carlton came trotting in.

"I knocked over a bunch of pots in the kitchen!" he exclaimed, an apology amid the panic.

"I thought you were with us," Charlie said.

"I wanted to see if there was any food left," Carlton said, not making it clear if he'd found anything or not.

"Seriously?" John laughed.

"That guard might have heard," Jessica said anxiously. "We have to get out of here."

They started for the door, and Jessica started running. The rest took off after her, picking up speed as they reached the hallway until they were racing as though something were behind them.

"Run, run!" John called out, and they all burst into giggles, the panic feigned but the urgency real.

They squeezed back through the door one by one and pushed it shut with the same painful squeal, Carlton and John leaning on it until it sealed. They all took hold of the shelf, hefting it back into place and replacing the tools so that it appeared undisturbed.

"Look good?" Jessica said, and John tugged her arm, guiding her away.

They made their way quickly but carefully back the way they came using only Carlton's penlight, back through the empty hallways and the open atrium to the parking lot. The guard's light did not appear again.

"Little anticlimactic," Carlton said with disappointment, checking back one more time in hopes they were being chased.

"Are you kidding?" Charlie said as she went to her car, already pulling the keys free from her pocket. She felt as though something locked deep inside her had been disturbed, and she was not sure if that was a good thing or not.

"That was fun!" John exclaimed, and Jessica laughed.

"That was terrifying!" she cried.

"It can be both," Carlton said, grinning widely. Charlie began to laugh, and John joined in.

"What?" Jessica said. Charlie shook her head, still laughing a little.

"It's just . . . we're all exactly the same as we were. I mean, we're totally different and older and everything. But we're the same. You and Carlton sound exactly like you did when we were six."

"Right," Jessica said, rolling her eyes again, but John nodded.

"I know what you mean," he said. "And so does Jessica, she just doesn't like to admit it." He glanced back at the mall. "Is everybody sure that guard didn't see us?"

"We can outrun him now," Carlton said reasonably, his hand resting on the car.

"I guess," John said, but he did not sound convinced.

"You haven't changed, either, you know," Jessica said with a certain satisfaction. "Stop looking for problems where there aren't any."

"Still," John said, glancing back again. "We should get out of here. I don't want to push our luck."

"See you all tomorrow, then?" Jessica said as they parted ways. Carlton gave a little wave over his shoulder.

Charlie's heart sank a little as Jessica settled herself into the passenger seat, tidily buckling herself in. She had not been looking forward to this. It wasn't that she didn't like Jessica, just that being alone with her was uncomfortable. She still wasn't much more than a stranger. Yet Charlie was still exhilarated from the night's adventure, and the lingering adrenaline gave her a new confidence. She smiled at Jessica. After tonight, they suddenly had something very much in common.

"Do you know which way the motel is?" she asked, and Jessica nodded and reached for the purse down at her feet. It was small and black with a long strap, and on the drive to the construction site Charlie had already seen her remove a lip gloss, a mirror, a pack of breath mints, a sewing kit, and a tiny hairbrush. Now she pulled out a small notebook and pen. Charlie smiled.

"Sorry, how much stuff do you have in that thing?" she asked, and Jessica looked at her with a grin.

"The secrets of The Purse must not be disclosed," she said playfully, and they both laughed. Jessica started reading Charlie the directions, and Charlie obeyed, turning left and right without paying much attention to her surroundings.

Jessica had already checked in, so they went straight to their room, a small beige box of a room with two double beds covered in shiny brown spreads. Charlie set her bags on the bed closest to the door, and Jessica went to the window.

"As you can see, I splurged on the room with the view," she said and flung the curtains open dramatically to reveal two Dumpsters and a dried-out hedge. "I want to have my wedding here."

"Right," Charlie said, amused. Jessica's prim demeanor and fashion-model looks made it easy to forget that she was smart as well. As a child she remembered being slightly intimidated every time they got together to play before realizing after the first few minutes how much she liked Jessica. She wondered if it was hard for Jessica to make friends, looking the way she did, but it wasn't the kind of thing you could really ask someone.

Jessica flopped down on the bed, lying across it to face

Charlie. "So tell me about you," she said confidentially, mocking a talk-show host or someone's nosy mother.

Charlie shrugged awkwardly, put on the spot. "What does that mean?" she said.

Jessica laughed. "I don't know! What an awful thing to ask, right? I mean, how do you answer that? Um, how about school? Any cute boys?"

Charlie lay down across the bed, mimicking Jessica's position. "Cute boys? What are we, twelve?"

"Well?" Jessica said impatiently.

"I don't know," she said. "Not really." Her class was too small. She had known most of the people in it since she moved in with Aunt Jen, and dating anyone, liking them "like that," seemed forced and altogether unappealing. She told Jessica as much. "Most of the girls, if they want to date, they date older guys," she said.

"And you don't have an older guy?" Jessica teased.

"Nah," Charlie said. "I figured I'd wait around for our batch to grow up."

"Right!" Jessica burst out laughing before quickly thinking of something to share. "Last year there was this guy, Donnie," she said. "I was gaga for him, like, really. He was so sweet to everyone. He wore all black all the time, and he had this black curly hair so thick all I could think about when I sat behind him was burying my face in it. I was so distracted I ended up with an A minus in trig. He was super artistic, a poet, and he carried around one of those black leather notebooks, and he was always scribbling something in it, but he would never show anybody." She sighed dreamily. "I figured if I could get him to show me his poetry, I would really come to know his soul, you know?"

"So did he ever?" Charlie said.

"Oh yeah," she said, nodding emphatically. "I asked him out finally, you know, 'cause he was shy and he was never gonna ask me, and we went to the movies and made out a little, and then we went and hung out on the roof of his apartment building and I told him all about how I want to study ancient civilizations and go on archaeological digs and stuff. And he showed me his poems."

"And did you come to know his soul?" Charlie said, excited to be included in girl talk, something she felt like she'd never really gotten to participate in before. Charlie nodded eagerly. *But not too eagerly.* She calmed herself as Jessica scooted forward on the bed to whisper.

"The poems were *awful.* I didn't know it was possible to be both melodramatic and boring at the same time. I mean, like, just reading them made me embarrassed for him." She covered her face in her hands. Charlie laughed.

"What did you do?"

"What could I do? I told him it wasn't gonna work out and went home."

"Wait, right after you read his poetry?"

"I still had the notebook in my hand."

"Oh no, Jessica, that's awful! You must have broken his heart!"

"I know! I felt so bad, but it was like the words just came out of my mouth. I couldn't stop myself."

"Did he ever speak to you again?"

"Oh yeah, he's perfectly nice. But now he takes statistics and economics and wears sweater vests."

"You broke him!" Charlie threw a pillow at Jessica, who sat up and caught it.

"I know! He'll probably be a millionaire stockbroker instead of a starving artist, and it's all my fault." She grinned. "Come on, he'll thank me someday."

Charlie shook her head. "Do you really want to be an archaeologist?"

"Yeah," Jessica said.

"Huh," said Charlie. "Sorry, I thought—" She shook her head. "Sorry, that is really cool."

"You thought I'd want to do something in fashion," Jessica said.

"Well, yeah."

"It's okay," Jessica said. "I did, too. I mean, I do, I love fashion, but there's only so much to it, you know? I think it's amazing to think about how people lived a thousand years ago, or two thousand, or ten. They were just like us, but so different. I like to imagine living in other times, other places, wonder who I would have been. Anyway, what about you?"

Charlie rolled over onto her back, looking up at the ceiling. The tiles were made of loose, stained Styrofoam, and the one above her head was askew. *I hope there aren't any bugs up in there,* she thought.

"I don't know," she said slowly. "I think it's really cool that you know who you want to be, but I have just never had that kind of a plan."

"Well, it's not like you have to figure it out now," Jessica said.

"Maybe," Charlie said. "But I don't know, you know what you want to do, John's known since he could hold a pencil that he wanted to be a writer and he's already getting published, even Carlton—I don't know what he has planned, but you can just see that there's a scheme brewing behind all his kidding around. But I just don't have that kind of direction."

"It really doesn't matter," Jessica said. "I don't think most people know at our age. Plus, I might change my mind, or not get into college, or something. You never know what's going to happen. Hey, I'm gonna get changed. I want to get some sleep."

She went into the bathroom, and Charlie stayed where she was, gazing at the sorry-looking ceiling. She supposed it was becoming a defect, her earnest refusal to consider the past or future. *Live in the present moment,* her Aunt Jen said often, and Charlie had taken it to heart. *Don't dwell on the past; don't worry about things that may never happen.* In eighth grade she had taken a shop class, vaguely hoping the mechanical work might spark something of her father's talent, might unleash some inherited passion lying latent within her, but it had not. She had made a clumsy-looking birdhouse for the backyard. She never took another shop class, and the birdhouse only attracted one squirrel who promptly knocked it down.

Jessica came out of the bathroom wearing pink striped pajamas, and Charlie went in to get ready for bed, changing and brushing her teeth hurriedly. When she came out again, Jessica was already under the covers with the light by her bed turned off. Charlie turned hers off, too, but the light from the parking lot still shone in from the window, somehow filtering past the Dumpsters.

Charlie stared up at the ceiling again, her hands behind her head.

"Do you know what's going to happen tomorrow?" she asked.

"I don't really know," Jessica said. "I know it's a ceremony at the school."

"Yeah, I know that," Charlie said. "Are we going to have to do anything? Like, do they want us to speak?"

"I don't think so," Jessica said. "Why, do you want to say something?"

"No, I was just wondering."

"Do you ever think about him?" Jessica asked.

"Sometimes. I try not to," Charlie said half-truthfully. She had sealed off the subject of Michael in her mind, locked him tight behind a mental wall she never touched. It wasn't an effort to avoid the subject; in fact, it was an effort to think of him now. "What about you?" she asked Jessica.

"Not really," she said. "It's weird, right? Something happens, and it's the worst thing you can ever imagine, and it's just burned into you at the time, like it's going to go on forever. And then the years go by, and it's just another thing that happened. Not like it's not important, or terrible, but it's in the past, just as much as everything else. You know?"

"I guess," Charlie said. But she did know. "I just try not to think about those things."

"Me too. You know I just went to a funeral last week?"

"I'm sorry," Charlie said, sitting up. "Are you okay?"

"Yeah, I'm fine," Jessica said. "I barely even knew him; he was just an old relative who lived three states away. I think I met him once, but I hardly remember it. We mostly went for my mom's sake. But it was at an old-fashioned funeral parlor, like in the movies, with an open coffin. And we all walked by the coffin, and when it was my turn I looked at him, and he could have been sleeping, you know? Just calm and restful, like people always say dead people look. There was nothing that I could have pointed out that made me think *dead*, if you asked me; every feature of his face looked the same as if he were alive. His skin was the same; his hair was the same as if he were alive. But he wasn't alive, and I just knew it. I would have known it immediately, even if he wasn't, you know, in a coffin."

"I know what you mean. There is something about them when they're . . . ," Charlie said softly.

"It sounds stupid when I say it. But when I looked at him, he looked so alive, and yet I knew, just *knew* that he wasn't. It made my skin crawl."

"That's the worst thing, isn't it?" Charlie said. "Things that act alive but aren't."

"What?" Jessica said.

"I mean things that look alive but aren't," Charlie said quickly. "We should get some sleep," she said. "Did you set the alarm?"

"Yes," Jessica said. "Good night."

"Night."

Charlie knew sleep was still a long way off. She knew what Jessica meant, probably better than Jessica did. The artificial shine in eyes that followed you as you moved, just like a real person's would. The slight lurch of realistic animals who did not move the way a living thing should. The occasional programming glitch that made a robot appear to have done something new, creative. Her childhood had been filled with them; she had grown up in the strange gap between life and not-life. It had been her world. It had been her father's world. Charlie closed her eyes. *What did that world do to him?*

CHAPTER THREE

Thud. Thud. Thud.

Charlie startled out of sleep, disoriented. Something was banging on her door, trying to force its way in.

"Oh, for goodness' sake," Jessica said grumpily, and Charlie blinked and sat up.

Right. The motel. Hurricane. Someone was knocking on the door. As Jessica went to answer it, Charlie got out of bed and looked at the clock. It was 10:00 a.m. She looked out the window at the bright new day. She had slept worse than usual, not nightmares, but dark dreams she could not quite remember, things that stuck with her just beyond the back of her mind, images she could not catch.

"Charlieeeee!" someone was screeching. Charlie went to the door and found herself immediately enveloped in a hug,

Marla's plump arms gripping her like a vise. Charlie hugged her back, tighter than she meant to. When Marla let go, she stepped back, grinning. Marla's moods had always been so intense they were contagious, spreading out to whoever was in her path. When she was gloomy, a pall fell over all her friends, the sun gone behind her cloud. When she was happy, like now, it was impossible to avoid the lift of her joy. She was always breathless, always slightly scattered, always giving the impression that she was running late, though she almost never was. Marla was wearing a loose dark-red blouse, and it suited her well, setting off her fair skin and dark-brown hair.

Charlie had kept in better touch with Marla than the others. Marla was the type who made it easy to stay friends, even at a distance. Even as a little kid she was always sending letters and postcards, undeterred if Charlie didn't respond to every one. She was resolutely positive and assumed that everyone liked her unless they made it clear otherwise, using the proper expletives. Charlie admired it about her—she herself, though not shy, was always calculating: *Does that person like me? Are they just being polite? How do people tell the difference?* Marla had come to visit her once when they were twelve. She had charmed Charlie's aunt and made fast friends with her school friends while still making it abundantly clear that she was *Charlie's* friend, and she was there only to see Charlie.

Marla's gigantic smile turned serious as she studied Charlie, peering at her as if trying to spot the differences since they last met. "You're as pale as ever." She took Charlie's hands in her own. "And you're all clammy. Don't you ever get warm?" She dropped Charlie's hands and proceeded to study the motel room skeptically, as though uncertain exactly what it was.

"It's the luxury suite," Jessica said without expression as she searched for something in her bag. Her hair was sticking up in all directions, and Charlie stifled a smile. It was nice to see something about Jessica in disarray for once. Jessica found her hairbrush and held it up triumphantly. "Ha! Take that, morning frizz!"

"Come on in," Charlie said, realizing she and Marla were still in the doorway, the door wide open. Marla nodded.

"One sec. JASON!" she shouted out the door. No one emerged. *"JASON!"*

A young boy came trotting up from the road. He was short and wiry, darker-skinned than his half sister. His Batman T-shirt and black shorts were made for someone twice his size. His hair was cut close to his head, and his arms and legs were streaked with dirt.

"Were you playing in the road?" Marla demanded.

"No?" he said.

"Yes, you were. Don't do that. If you get yourself killed, Mom's gonna blame me. Get inside." Marla shoved her little brother inside and shook her head.

"How old are you now?" Charlie asked.

"Eleven," Jason said. He went to the TV and started fiddling with buttons.

"Jason, stop it," Marla said. "Play with your action figures."

"I'm not a little kid," he said. "Anyway, they're in the car." But he stepped away from the television and went to look out the window.

Marla rubbed her eyes. "We just got here. We had to leave at six this morning, and *someone*," she said pointedly, glancing over her shoulder at Jason, "wouldn't stop fiddling with the radio. I am *so* tired." She didn't seem tired, but then she never did. At their sleepovers as kids, Charlie remembered her bouncing around like a maniac while the rest of them were winding down for the night—then falling asleep abruptly, like a cartoon character who'd been hit over the head with a rolling pin.

"We should get ready," Jessica said. "We're supposed to meet the guys at the diner in an hour."

"Hurry!" Marla said. "We have to change, too. I didn't want to get all gross while we were driving."

"Jason, you can watch TV," Charlie said, and he looked at Marla. She nodded, and he grinned and turned it on, starting to flip through channels.

"Please just pick a channel," Marla said. Charlie headed into the bathroom to get dressed while Jessica fussed with her hair.

A little less than an hour later, they pulled into the diner parking lot. The others were already there, in the same booth they'd been in the night before. When they got inside, Marla performed a second round of squeals and hugs, only slightly quieter now that they were in public. Overshadowed by her enthusiasm, Lamar stood and waved at Jessica and Charlie, waiting until Marla sat down.

"Hi, guys," he said at last. He was wearing a dark tie and a dark gray suit. He was tall and thin, black, with his hair shaved close to his head; his features were sharp and attractive, and he looked just a little older than the rest of them. It could have been the suit, but Charlie thought it was something about the way he stood, holding himself like he would be comfortable wherever he was.

They had all dressed up a little for the ceremony. Marla had changed at the motel, and she and Jessica were both wearing dresses. Jessica's was knee-length and covered in pastel flowers, a light fabric that moved as she walked. Marla's was simple, white with big sunflowers splashed over it. Charlie hadn't thought to bring a dress, and she hoped she didn't look out of place in black pants and a white button-down shirt. John was wearing a light-purple shirt today, though he'd added a matching tie in a slightly darker color, and Carlton seemed to be wearing an identical outfit as before, still all in black. They all sat down.

"Well, don't we all look nice," Marla said happily.

"Where's Jason?" Jessica craned her head from side to side.

Marla groaned. "I'll be right back." She scooted out of the booth and hurried out the door.

"Lamar, what have you been up to?" Charlie asked. Lamar grinned.

"He's an Ivy League–man," Carlton said, teasing. Lamar looked briefly down at the table, but he was smiling.

"Early acceptance," was all he said.

"Which one?" Jessica said.

"Cornell."

"Wait, how did you already apply to college?" Charlie said. "That's not till next year. I don't even know where I want to go."

"He skipped sixth grade," John said. There was a brief flicker of something across his face, and Charlie knew what it was. John liked being the clever one, the precocious one. Lamar had been kind of a goof-off when they were kids, and now he had leaped ahead. John forced a grin, and the moment passed. "Congratulations," he said, with no hint that it was not entirely sincere.

Marla came bursting in again, this time towing Jason behind her, holding on to his upper arm. At the hotel she had made him change into a blazer and khakis as well, though he was still wearing his Nikes.

"I'm coming. Stop it," he whined.

"Is that Jason?" Carlton asked.

"Yeah," Jason said.

"Do you remember me?" Carlton said.

"I don't remember any of you," Jason said unapologetically.

"Sit there," Marla said, pointing to the next booth over.

"Okay," he grumbled.

"Marla, he can sit with us," Jessica said. "Jason, come on over."

"I want to sit here," he said and sat down behind them. He pulled a video game out of his pocket and was oblivious to the world.

The waitress came over and they ordered; Marla told her to put Jason's breakfast on their check. When their food came, Charlie checked her watch.

"We don't have a lot of time," she said.

"We'll get there," Carlton said. "It's not far." A small piece of food fell out of his mouth as he gestured down the road.

"Have you been back to the school?" Lamar asked, and Carlton shrugged.

"I pass it sometimes. I know this is a nostalgia trip for all of you, but I just live here. I don't exactly go around reminiscing about kindergarten all the time."

They were all quiet for a second, the beeps and pings of Jason's video game filling the silence.

"Hey, did you know Lamar's going to Cornell next year?" Jessica said to Marla.

"Really? Well, aren't you ahead of the pack," she said. Lamar looked down at his plate. When he looked up, he was a little flushed.

"All part of the five-year plan," he said. They laughed, and his blush deepened. "It's kind of weird to be back here," he said, hastily changing the subject.

"I think it's strange that I'm the only one who still lives here," Carlton said. "Nobody ever leaves Hurricane."

"Is it strange, though?" Jessica said thoughtfully. "My parents—you remember, my mom's from New York originally; she used to joke about going back. *When I go back to New York*, but it might as well have been *When I win the lottery*; she didn't mean it. And then right after Michael's . . . right after, she stopped joking about it, then three months later we were all on a plane to visit her sister in Queens, and we never came back. My dad's father died when I was nine, and they came back to Hurricane for the funeral without me. They didn't want me coming back here, and honestly I didn't want to go. I was kind of anxious the whole time they were gone. I kept looking out the window, hoping they would come back early, like something bad was going to happen to them if they stayed."

They looked at one another, considering. Charlie knew they had all moved, all but Carlton, but she had never thought about it—people moved all the time. Carlton was right, though. People didn't leave Hurricane.

"We moved because my dad got a new job, the summer after third grade," John said. "That's not exactly mysterious. Lamar, you left in the middle of the semester that year."

"Yeah," he said. "But that's because when my parents split, I went with my mom to Indianapolis." He frowned. "But my dad moved, too. He's in Chicago now."

"My parents left because of Michael," Marla said. They all turned to her. "Afterward, my mom couldn't sleep. She said spirits were stirring in the town, unquiet. My dad told her she was being ridiculous, but we still left as fast as we could." Marla looked around at her friends. "What?" she said defensively. "*I* don't believe in ghosts."

"I do," Charlie said. She felt like she was talking from a great distance; she was almost surprised they could hear her. "I mean, not ghosts, but . . . memories. I think they linger, whether there's someone there or not." The house, her old house, was imbued with memory, with loss, with longing. It hung in the air like humidity; the walls were saturated, like the wood had soaked in it. It had been there before she came, and it was there now; it would be there forever. It had to be. There was too much, too great and vast a weight, for Charlie to have brought it with her.

"That doesn't make any sense," Jessica said. "Memory is in our brains. Like, literally stored in the brain; you can see it on a scan. It can't exist outside of someone's mind."

"I don't know," John said. "Think of all the places that have . . . atmosphere. Old houses, sometimes, places where you walk in and you feel sad or nostalgic, even though you've never been there before."

"That's not other people's memories, though," Lamar said. "That's subconscious cues, stuff we don't realize we're noticing, that tells us we should feel some way. Peeling paint, old-fashioned furniture, lace curtains, details that tell us to be nostalgic—mostly things we pick up from movies, probably. I got lost at a carnival when I was four. I never got so scared in my life, but I don't think anybody's feeling suddenly desperate for their mom when they pass that Ferris wheel."

"Maybe they are," Marla said. "I don't know, sometimes I have little moments where it's like there's something I forgot, something I regret, or that I'm happy about, or something that makes me want to cry, but it's only there for a split second. Then it's gone. Maybe we're all shedding our fear and regret and hope everywhere we go, and we're catching traces of people we've never met. Maybe it's everywhere."

"How is that different from believing in ghosts?" Lamar asked.

"It's totally different," Marla said. "It's not supernatural, and it's not, like, the souls of dead people. It's just . . . people leaving their mark on the world."

"So it's the ghosts of living people?" Lamar said.

"No."

"You're talking about people having some kind of essence that can hang around a specific place after the person is gone," Lamar said. "That's a ghost."

"No, it's not! I'm not saying it right," Marla said. She closed her eyes for a minute, thinking. "Okay," she said at last. "Do you all remember my grandmother?"

"I do," said Jason. "She was my grandmother, too."

"She was my dad's mom, not yours," Marla said. "Anyway, you were only a year old when she died."

"I do remember her," Jason said quietly.

"Okay," Marla said. "So she collected dolls from the time she was a kid. She and my grandfather used to travel a lot after he retired, and she'd bring them back from all over the world—she had them from France, Egypt, Italy, Brazil, China, everywhere. She kept them in their own special room, and it was full of them, shelves and shelves of dolls, some tiny and some almost as big as I was. I loved it; one of my earliest memories is playing in that room with the dolls. I remember my dad would always warn me to be careful, and my grandmother would laugh and say, 'Toys should be played with.'

"I had a favorite, a twenty-one-inch red-haired doll in a short, shiny white dress like Shirley Temple. I called her Maggie. She was from the 1940s, and I loved her. I told her everything, and when I was lonely, I would imagine myself in that room, playing with Maggie. My grandmother died when I was six, and when my dad and I went to see my grandfather after the funeral, he told me I should pick a doll to keep from the collection. I went to the room to get Maggie, and as soon as I walked through the door, something was wrong.

"It was as though the light had changed, become darker, harsher than it used to be. I looked around, and the lively, playful poses of the dolls now seemed unnatural, disjointed. It was as though all of them were staring at me. I didn't know what they wanted. Maggie was in the corner, and I took a step toward her, then stopped. I met her eyes, and instead of painted glass I saw a stranger. I turned and ran. I raced down the hall as though something might be chasing me, not daring to look back until I reached my father's side. He asked if I had picked a doll, and I just shook my head. I never went back in that room."

Everyone was silent. Charlie was transfixed, still seeing little Marla running for her life.

"What happened to the dolls?" Carlton asked, only half breaking the spell.

"I don't know. I think my mom sold them to another collector when my grandfather died," Marla said.

"Sorry, Marla," Lamar said, "it's still just tricks of the mind. You missed your grandmother, you were frightened of death, and dolls are inherently freaky."

Charlie broke in, wanting to head off the argument. "Is everybody done eating? We have to go soon."

"We still have plenty of time," Carlton said, looking down at his watch. "It's, like, five minutes away." Something else fell out of his mouth, landing next to the first dropped bit of food.

John looked around the table, from person to person, as though he were waiting for something.

"We have to tell them," he said, looking at Charlie.

"Oh yeah, we totally do!" Jessica said.

"Tell us what?" Jason piped up, peeking over the back of Marla's seat.

"Shh," Marla said halfheartedly. She was looking at John. "Tell us what?"

John dropped his voice, forcing everyone to lean in closer. Charlie did it, too, eager to hear, even though she knew exactly what he was going to say.

"We went to Freddy's last night," he said.

"Freddy's is still there?" Marla exclaimed, too loud.

"Shhh!" Jessica said, making frantic hand movements.

"Sorry," Marla whispered. "I just can't believe it's still there."

"It's not," Carlton said, raising his eyebrows and grinning enigmatically at Lamar.

"It's hidden," John explained. "They were supposed to knock it down to build a mall, but they didn't. They just . . . built around it."

"Entombed it," John corrected.

"And you got in?" Lamar said. Charlie nodded confirmation. "No way."

"What was it like?" Marla asked.

"Exactly the same," John said. "It was like . . ."

"It was like everyone vanished," Charlie said softly.

"I want to go, too! You have to take us," Marla said. Jessica cleared her throat hesitantly, and they all looked at her.

"I don't know," she said slowly. "I mean, today? Should we?"

"We have to see it," Lamar said. "You can't tell us this and not let us see it."

"I want to see it," Jason chimed in. "What's Freddy's?" They ignored him. His eyes were wide, and he was hanging on to every word.

"Maybe Jessica's right," John said with reluctance. "Maybe it's disrespectful to go tonight." There was a moment's pause, and Charlie knew they were waiting for her to talk. She was the one they were really afraid of offending; they needed her permission.

"I think we should go," she said. "I don't think it's disrespectful. It's almost a way of honoring . . . what happened." She looked around the table. Jessica was nodding. Charlie wasn't sure it was much of an argument, but they didn't need to be convinced. They wanted an excuse.

Marla twisted herself to look back at Jason's plate. "Are you done eating?" she asked.

"Yup," he said. Marla pointed to the game in his hand.

"You know you can't play with that during the ceremony," she said.

"Yup."

"I'm serious, Jason. I'm locking it in the car."

"Why don't you just lock me in the car," he muttered.

"I'd love to," Marla said under her breath as she turned back to the group. "Okay, we can go."

They headed to the school in a caravan, the boys in Carlton's car, Marla following, and Charlie bringing up the rear.

"We should have carpooled," Jessica said idly, staring out the window. It hadn't occurred to Charlie.

"I guess," she said.

"On the other hand, I'm not sure I want to ride with Marla and Jason," Jessica said plainly.

"They are kind of intense," Charlie agreed.

When they arrived, the parking lot was already jammed full. Charlie parked on a side street in what she hoped was a legal spot, and they walked to the school along the familiar sidewalk.

Jessica shivered. "I've got goose bumps."

"It is weird to be here," Charlie said. The school looked unchanged from the outside, but the fence was new and slick, a black, plastic-coated chain link. The whole town was like this, a mix of old and new, familiar and not. The things that had changed seemed out of place, and the things that had remained the same made Charlie feel out of place. *It must be so strange for Carlton to live here*, she thought. *"I know this is a nostalgia trip for all of you, but I just live here,"* he had said. Somehow, Charlie was not sure she believed that.

When they got to the playing field behind the school, the bleachers were already full. Rows of folding chairs had been laid out in front of them to add more seating, and Charlie spotted Marla and the boys at the front.

"Oh, great," she said. "I don't want to sit in the front row."

"I don't mind," Jessica said. Charlie looked at her.

Of course you don't, she wanted to say. *You're . . . you.*

"Yeah," she said instead, "no big deal. Half the town must be here," she observed as they made their way to the group, where two seats had been saved. There was one open in the front row, next to Carlton, and one right behind it, beside Marla. Jessica winked at Charlie and sat down next to Carlton. She leaned toward him, and they started whispering. Charlie repeated herself to Marla: "There's a lot of people here."

"Yeah," Marla said. "I mean, it's a small town, you know?

Michael's . . . it was a big deal. Plus, his parents still live here. People remember."

"People remember," Charlie echoed softly. There was a small raised stage set up in front of them, with a podium and four chairs. Behind the chairs a screen was suspended; projected on it was a larger-than-life picture of Michael. It was a close-up, just his face. It was not the most flattering picture: His head was thrown back at an odd angle, his mouth open in laughter, but it was perfect—a joyful moment, snatched up and kept, not curated. He looked happy.

"Darn it," Marla said softly. Charlie looked at her. She was dabbing at her eyes with a tissue. Charlie put an arm around her.

"I know," she said.

The sound system came on suddenly with a whine that slowly faded. Four people walked onstage: a heavyset man in a suit who went straight to the microphone, an elderly woman, and a couple, a man and a woman. The man in the suit stepped up to the podium, and the elderly woman sat down in one of the four chairs. The couple stayed back, but they did not sit. Charlie knew they must be Michael's parents, but she did not recognize them. When she was young they had just been parents, a species that was for the most part unremarkable. She realized suddenly that she didn't even know their names; Michael's parents had not gone out of their way to interact with their son's friends, and Charlie had literally spoken to them as "Michael's mom," and "Michael's dad," as if those were appropriate forms of address.

The man at the podium introduced himself as the school's principal. He said a few things about loss and community and the fleeting preciousness of youth. He talked briefly about Michael's kindness, his artistic talent, and the impression he made, even as a small child, on everyone he met. It was true, Charlie reflected. Michael had been an unusually charismatic child. He wasn't exactly a leader, but they all found themselves wanting to please him, to make him smile, and so they often did the things they knew he wanted to do, just to make him happy.

The principal finished and introduced Michael's parents, Joan and Donald Brooks. They stood at the podium awkwardly, each looking from face to face in the crowd, as if they were not sure how they had gotten here. Finally Joan stepped forward.

"It feels strange to be up here," was the first thing she said, and a murmur of something like agreement swept quietly through the crowd. "We are so grateful to all of you for coming, especially those of you who came from out of town." She looked directly at the front row, talking to Charlie and the others. "Some of Michael's friends have come from all over, and I think that is a testament to who he was that ten years later, with your lives on new paths, moving on to a whole new stage of life—" So close to the stage, Charlie could see she was about to cry, tears wavering in her eyes, but her voice was steady. "We are grateful you are here. We wanted to give Michael a legacy with this scholarship, but it is clear that he has already left one, all on his own." Marla grabbed Charlie's hand, and Charlie squeezed back.

"I want to say," Joan continued, "something about the families who are not here. As we all know, Michael was not the only child lost during those terrible few months." She read out four more names, two girls and two boys. Charlie glanced at Marla. They all knew there had been other children, but Michael's death had loomed so great in all their lives that they had never even talked about the other victims. Now Charlie felt a pang of guilt. To someone, those little girls and boys had been as vital as Michael. To someone, their losses had meant the end of the world. She closed her eyes for a moment. *I can't mourn everyone,* she thought. *No one can.*

Joan was still talking. "Although their families have moved on to other places, those young boys and girls will always have a place in our hearts. Now I would like to call to speak a young man who was particularly close to my son. Carlton, if you would?"

They all watched in surprise as Carlton stood and climbed up behind the podium. Joan hugged him tightly and stayed close behind him as he pulled a crumpled piece of paper from his pocket. He cleared his throat, looking over the heads of the crowd, then crumpled the paper up again and put it back in his pocket.

"I don't remember as much about Michael as I should," he said finally. "Too much of those years is a blur; I know we met when we were still in diapers, but I don't remember that, thankfully." There was a soft titter through the crowd. "I do know that as far back as I have memories, Michael is in them. I remember playing superheroes; drawing, which he was much better at than me; and as we got older I remember . . . well, playing superheroes and drawing. What I really remember, though, is that my days were always more exciting when he was in them. He was smarter than me; he was the one always coming up with new ideas, new ways to get in trouble. Sorry about those lamps, by the way, Mrs. Brooks. If I had jumped the way Michael said, I probably would only have broken one."

Donald laughed, a gulping, desperate sound. Charlie shifted uncomfortably and pulled her hand from Marla's with an apologetic half smile. Their grief, naked, was too much to watch. It was raw, an open wound, and she could not stand to look.

Carlton came back down to sit with them. Michael's grandmother spoke, and then his father, who had recovered enough to share a memory of taking his son to his first art class. He told the crowd about the scholarship, for a graduating senior who has demonstrated both excellence and passion in the arts, and announced the winner of the first one, Anne Park, a slight Korean girl who came quickly up to the stage to accept her plaque and hugs from Michael's parents. It must have been strange for Anne, Charlie thought, her honor so overshadowed by its origins. But then, she realized, Anne must have known Michael, too, however much in passing.

After the ceremony, they went to say hello to Michael's parents, hugging them and making sounds of condolence. *What do you say to someone who has lost a child? Can it be any easier? Can ten years make a difference, or do they wake up each morning as fresh with grief as the day he died?* On a long cafeteria table by the stage, pictures and cards were collecting slowly—people had brought flowers, notes to Michael's parents or to him. Things they remembered, things they wished they had said. Charlie went over and browsed through the notes. There were pictures of her and the others as well as of Michael. It shouldn't have surprised her—they were all together constantly, as a group or in rotating groups of two and three. She saw herself in the middle of a pose: Michael, John, and she, all covered in mud, with Jessica beside them, still perfectly clean, refusing to go near them. Charlie smiled. *That looks about right.* In another, a five-year-old Marla struggled to support the weight of her newborn little brother, with Lamar peering suspiciously at the tiny thing over her shoulder. Some of Michael's drawings were there, too, crayon scribbles professionally, incongruously framed.

Charlie picked one up, a drawing of what she supposed was a *T. rex* stomping through a city. It was actually, she realized now, almost amazing how talented he was. While she and the others were scribbling stick figures, Michael's drawings looked realistic, sort of.

"That's really good," John said over her shoulder. Charlie startled.

"You scared me," she said.

"Sorry."

Charlie looked back at the drawing. Whatever it was, it was better than she could draw now. Suddenly her chest tightened, gripped with loss and rage. It wasn't just that Michael died young, it was what that truly meant: He had been stopped in his tracks, years, decades of life snatched and torn violently from him. She felt herself well up with youthful indignation as if she were a child again, wanting only to whine, *It's not fair!*

Taking a deep breath, Charlie set the picture back down on the table and turned away. The gathering was continuing, but she needed to leave. She caught Marla's eye, and Marla, as scarily intuitive as always, nodded and caught Lamar's sleeve. From their various vantage points, they all headed for the parking lot. No one seemed to notice their departure, which made sense. Except for Carlton, they were all strangers here.

In the lot, they stopped by Marla's car. She had somehow called down a miracle and found a space right next to the school.

"Can I play my game now?" Jason said immediately, and Marla found her keys in her purse and handed them over.

"Don't drive away," she warned. Suddenly, Marla grabbed her brother and pulled him close, hugging him to her for a long minute.

"Jeez, I'm only going to the car," he muttered when she let him go.

"Yeah, maybe I should let you drive away," she said, giving him a little push. She cleared her throat. "So are we going to Freddy's?" she said. They all looked at one another.

"Yeah," Charlie said. "I think we should." Somehow, following this, going back to Freddy's seemed like more than a game. It felt right. "Let's meet there at sunset," she said. "Hey, Jessica, can you catch a ride with the guys or something? I'm gonna go for a walk."

"You can come with us," Marla said. "I promised Jason I'd take him to the movies."

Charlie headed down the road without waiting to hear the rest of the discussion. A dozen feet from the lot, she realized she was being followed. She turned around.

"John?"

"Do you mind if I come? You're going to your old house, right?"

"How did you know that?"

"It's the only interesting thing out this way. Anyway, I went to see my old place, too. It was painted blue, and there was a garden in the yard. It was weird. I know it wasn't blue when I lived there, but I couldn't remember what color it was supposed to be. Everything's so different."

Charlie didn't say anything. She wasn't even sure she wanted John to come with her. Her house, her father's house, it was private. She thought of the first time John had seen the toys, his fascination, an interest that was all his, that had nothing to do with pleasing her. She relented.

"Okay, you can come."

"Is it . . ." He hesitated. "Is it different?"

"It's really not," Charlie said. It wasn't quite true, but she wasn't sure how to explain the thing that had changed.

They walked together for the better part of three miles, away from town and down old roads, first paved, then gravel. As they neared the place they left the roads, ascending the steep incline of a hill overrun with brush and trees that should have been trimmed or cut down ages ago. Three rooftops peeked over the leaves, scattered widely over the hill, but no one had lived in these houses in a long time.

At last they walked up the driveway, and John stopped short, staring up at the house.

"I thought it would be less intimidating," he said softly. Impatient, Charlie took his arm for a second and pulled him away, leading them around the side of the house. It was one thing for him to be here with her, but she was not quite ready to let someone else inside. She wasn't even sure she wanted to go inside again anyway. He followed her without protest, as if aware that they were in her territory and she would decide where they went.

The property was large, more than a lawn. There were woods surrounding the wide space of the backyard, and as a child Charlie had often felt like she was in her own little realm, ruler of all she surveyed. The grass had gone wild, weeds growing feral and up to their knees. They walked the perimeter. John peered into the woods, and Charlie was struck by her old childhood fear, like something out of a fairy tale. *Don't go into the woods alone, Charlotte,* her father warned. It was not sinister, just a parent's warning, *don't get lost,* like telling her not to cross the street without holding someone's hand or not to touch the stove when it was hot, but Charlie took it more seriously. She knew from her storybooks, as all children did, that the woods contained wolves, and more dangerous things. She caught John's sleeve.

"Don't," she said, and he pulled back from the woods, not asking why. Instead, he went to a tree in the middle of the yard and put a hand on it.

"Remember that tree?" he asked, smiling, something a little wicked in his voice.

"Of course," Charlie said, walking over. "It's been here longer than I ever was." But he was looking at her, waiting for more, and suddenly she remembered.

It had been a sunny day, springtime; they were six years old, maybe. John was visiting, and they were playing hide-and-seek, half supervised by Charlie's father, who was in his garage workshop, absorbed in his machines. The door was open so he would notice if someone screamed, but short of that, the outdoors was their own. John counted to ten, eyes covered, facing the tree that was home base. The yard was wide and open; there were not many places to hide, so Charlie, buoyed up by the excitement of the game, dared to hide beyond the forbidden edge of the woods, just barely past the tree line. John searched the other places first: behind her father's car, in the corner where one part of the garage jutted out, the space beneath the porch where a child could just barely crawl. He realized where she must be, and Charlie braced herself to run as he began to walk the edges of the yard, darting into the woods and out again, looking behind trees. When at last he found her, she took off, tearing across the lawn to the home base tree. He was just behind her, so close he could almost touch her, and she sped on, staying just out of reach. She hit the tree, almost slamming into it, and John was right behind her, bumping into her a second later, too fast to stop. They were both giggling hysterically, and then they stopped at the same moment, still gasping to catch their breath.

"Hey, Charlotte," John said, stressing her name in the mocking tone he always used.

"Don't call me that," Charlie said automatically.

"You ever see grown-ups kiss?" He picked up a stick and started digging at the tree bark, like he was more interested in that than in her answer. Charlie shrugged.

"Yeah, I guess so."

"Wanna try it?" He still wasn't looking at her; his face was streaked with dirt, like it often was, and his hair was sticking out in all directions, a twig caught in it above his forehead.

"Gross," Charlie said, wrinkling her nose. Then, after a moment, "Yeah, okay."

John dropped the stick and leaned toward her, his hands behind his back. Charlie closed her eyes, waiting, still not entirely sure what she was supposed to do.

"Charlotte!" It was her father. Charlie jumped back. John's face was so close to hers that she banged into him with her forehead.

"Ow!" he yelled, clapping a hand to his nose.

Charlie's father came around the side of the tree. "What are you up to? John?" He pried John's fingers away from his nose. "You're not bleeding. You'll be fine," he said. "Charlotte, closer to the house, please." He then pointed his finger, directing them forward. "John, it looks like your mom is here anyway." He walked ahead of them, toward the driveway where her car had just pulled in.

"Yeah, okay." John trotted off toward the driveway, turning once to wave at Charlie. He was grinning like something wonderful had happened, although Charlie was not quite sure what it was.

"Oh my," Charlie said now, covering her face, sure it was bright red. When she looked up again, John was grinning that same satisfied, six-year-old grin.

"You know, my nose still hurts when it rains," he said, touching a finger to it.

"It does not," Charlie said. She leaned back against the tree. "I can't believe you tried to kiss me. We were six!" Charlie stared at him accusingly.

"Even the littlest heart wants what it wants," John said in a mock romantic voice, but there was an edge of something real in it, something not well enough hidden. Charlie realized, suddenly, that he was standing very close to her. "Let's go see your dad's workshop," John said abruptly, too loud, and Charlie nodded.

"Okay." She regretted it as she said it. She did not want to open the workshop door. She closed her eyes, still leaning against the tree. She could still see it; it was all she could see when she thought of that place. The twitching, malformed, metal skeleton in its dark corner, with its wrenching shudders and its blistering silver eyes. The image welled up in her head until it was all there was. The memory radiated a cutting anguish, but she did not know who it belonged to: to the thing, to her father, or to herself.

Charlie felt a hand on her shoulder and opened her eyes. It was John, frowning at her like he was worried.

"Charlie, are you okay?"

No.

"Yes," she said. "Come on, let's go see what's in the workshop."

It was not locked, and there was no real reason it should be, Charlie thought. Her eyes went first to the dark corner. The figure was not there. There was a weathered apron hanging in its place, the one her father had worn for soldering, and his goggles next to it, but there was no sign of that uncanny presence. Charlie should have felt relief, but she didn't, only a vague unease. She looked around. There seemed to be almost nothing left of the workshop: The benches were there, where her father had assembled and tweaked his inventions, but the materials, the blueprints, and the half-finished robots that were once crammed onto every surface had disappeared.

Where are they? Had her aunt had them carted away to a junkyard to rust and crumble among other discarded, useless things? Or had her father done it himself, so no one else would have to? The concrete floor was littered here and there with scraps; whoever had done the cleanup had not been thorough. Charlie knelt and picked up an oddly shaped scrap of wood, then a small circuit board. She turned it over. *Whose brain were you?* she wondered, but it did not matter, not really. It was battered and worn, the etched copper too badly scratched to repair, even if someone wanted to.

"Charlie," John said from across the workshop. He was in the dark corner; if the skeleton had been there, it could have reached out to touch him.

But it's not there.

"What?"

"Come see what I found."

Charlie went. John was standing beside her father's tool-box, and he stepped away as she came over, giving her space. Charlie knelt down before it. It looked as if it had just been polished. It was made of dark, stained wood, glossy with some kind of lacquer. She opened it gently. Charlie picked up an awl from the top tray and held it for a moment, the rounded wooden handle fitting into the palm of her hand as if it had been made for her to use. Not that she knew how. The last time she had picked it up, she could barely fit her fingers around its base. She picked up the tools one after another, lifting them from their places. The tool-box had wooden spaces carved out to fit the precise shape of each item. All the tools were polished and clean, their wooden handles smooth and their metal unrusted. They looked as though they had been used just that morning, wiped down and put away meticulously. Like someone still cared for them. She looked at them with a fierce, unexpected joy, as if something she had fought for was returned to her. But her joy felt wrong, misplaced; looking at her father's things set her off-balance. Something in the world was not as it should be. Seized suddenly with an unfounded fear, she thrust the awl back into its place in the box, dropping it like something burning. She closed the lid, but she did not stand.

Memory overtook her, and she closed her eyes, not fighting against it.

Her feet were wedged in the dirt, and two large and callous hands covered her eyes. Suddenly there was a bright light, and Charlie squinted, squirming impatiently to see what was before her. Three complete and gleaming figures towered over her, motionless, the sun reflecting off every edge and contour. They were blinding to behold.

"What do you think?" She heard the question but could not answer it; her eyes hadn't adjusted. The three masses of standing metal all looked similar in structure, but Charlie had grown accustomed to seeing more than was there, imagining the final result. For a long time now there had been three empty suits, hanging like carcasses from a rafter in the attic. Charlie knew that they had a special purpose, and now she understood what it was.

Two long beams protruded from the top of the head of one of the hulking masses. The head itself was solid and skull-like; the beams looked as if they had been violently thrust there.

"That's the rabbit!" Charlie squealed, proud of herself.

"You aren't scared of him?" the voice asked.

"Of course not. He looks like Theodore!"

"Theodore. That's right."

The figure in the middle was more clearly rendered: Its face was chiseled, its features distinct. It was clearly a bear, and a single metal beam stuck out from the top of its head as well. Charlie was puzzled for a moment, then smiled. "For the top hat," she said with confidence.

The last form was perhaps the most frightening; a long, metal clamp protruded from its empty face, in the place where a mouth might go. It was holding something on a platter, a metal structure that looked like a jaw, wires running like strewn spaghetti up and down the frame and in and out of sockets.

"That one's scary," she admitted hesitantly.

"Well, this part will look like a cupcake!" Her father pressed down on the top, and the jaw snapped shut, making Charlie jump, then giggle.

Suddenly, her laughter stopped. She had been so distracted she'd forgotten. *I'm not supposed to stand here. I don't stand here!* Her hands were trembling. How could she have forgotten?

The corner. She looked at the ground, unable to lift her eyes, unable to move. One of her shoes was untied. There was a screw next to her foot and an old piece of tape, opaque with dirt. There was something behind her.

"Charlie?"

It was John.

"Charlie!"

She looked up at him.

"Sorry. Just lost. This place . . ." She stood and took a step forward, positioning herself in the place she remembered. She glanced behind her as if the memory might manifest. The corner was empty; there was nothing. She knelt again and put her hand on the ground, fishing around until she found a small screw in the bare dirt. She palmed it, then looked closer; there were small holes in the ground, exposed when she moved the loose dirt. Charlie ran her fingers over them, thoughtful.

"Charlie, I have to tell you something." There was something urgent in John's voice. Charlie looked around the workshop and stood up.

"Can we go outside?" she said. "I can't breathe in here."

"Yeah, of course," he said. He followed her out into the yard and back to the hide-and-seek tree. She was tired, a wrung-out exhaustion deep inside. She would be fine in a minute, but she wanted a place that held only silly childhood memories. She sat down in the grass, leaned against the trunk, and waited for John to talk. He settled himself cross-legged in front of her, a little stiffly, smoothing his pants, and she laughed.

"Are *you* worried about getting dirty?"

"Times change," he said with a wry smile.

"What do you have to tell me?" she asked, and his face grew serious.

"I should have said something a long time ago," he said. "I just—when something happens like that, you don't trust your memory, don't trust your own mind."

"What are you talking about?" Charlie asked.

"Sorry." He took a deep breath. "I saw someone that night, the night Michael disappeared."

"What do you mean?"

"Remember when we were sitting at the table by the stage, and the animals started going crazy?"

"I remember," Charlie said. It had been bizarre, their movements upsetting. They were moving too fast, bending and spinning, cycling through their limited, programmed moves over and over. They seemed frantic, panicked. Charlie was mesmerized. She should have been afraid of them, but she was not; she saw, in their juddering motion, a kind of desperation. She was reminded, for a moment, of dreams of running, dreams when the world depended on her going just ten steps forward, yet her body could only move in slow motion. Something was wrong, terribly wrong. Chaotically, violently, the animatronic animals onstage thrashed robotic limbs in all directions, their eyes rolling in their sockets.

"What did you see?" Charlie said to John now, shaking her head as though she could rid it of the image.

"There was another mascot," he said. "A bear."

"Freddy," Charlie interrupted without thinking.

"No, not Freddy." John took her hands as if trying to calm them both, but he let go before he spoke again. "It was standing right near us, next to our table, but it wasn't looking at the stage like everyone else was. That technician came over, remember, and even he was just watching the animatronics—I guess he was trying to figure out what was happening. I looked over at the mascot, and it looked back at me . . ." He stopped.

"John, what?" Charlie said impatiently.

"Then the animatronics onstage stopped moving, and I looked over at them, and when we all turned back around, Michael was gone. And so was the mascot."

Charlie stared at him in disbelief.

"You saw the kidnapper," she said.

"I didn't know what I saw," John said. "It was all chaos. I didn't even think about it; I didn't make the connection; it was just another animal at Freddy's. I didn't think about who might have been inside it. I was . . . I was a kid, you know? You figure that the grown-ups already know everything you know."

"Yeah," Charlie said. "I know. Do you remember anything? What the person looked like?" John was staring up at the sky, as if he were seeing something Charlie could not.

"Yes," he said. His voice was deliberate, steady. "The eyes. They were all I could see, but I still see them sometimes, like they're right there in front of me. They were dead."

"What?"

"They were dead, just dull and flat. Like, they still moved and blinked and saw, but whatever was behind them had died a long time ago." He fell silent.

It was growing dark. There was a bright, almost unnatural streak of pink across the western sky, and Charlie shivered.

"We should go get the car," she said. "It's almost time to meet everyone."

"Yeah," John said, but he didn't move right away, still staring into the distance.

"John? We have to go," Charlie said. He seemed to come back to himself slowly.

"Yeah," he said. "We should go." He got up and brushed off his pants, then grinned at Charlie. "Race you?" he said and took off running. Charlie chased after him, her feet pounding the asphalt, and her arms swinging free.

harlie and John were the last ones to the mall. When they pulled up, the others were gathered tight in a circle in front of Marla's car, as if sharing a conspiracy.

"Come on," Marla said before they had walked all the way to the group. She was bouncing on the balls of her feet as if she were ready to run for the door of the abandoned building. Everyone but Charlie and John had changed their clothing, wearing jeans and T-shirts, things more suited for exploration, and she had a brief moment of feeling out of place. *At least I didn't wear a dress*, Charlie thought.

"Let's go," she said. Marla's impatience seemed to be contagious, or maybe it just gave Charlie an excuse to let her real feelings come to the surface. She wanted to show Freddy's off to the others.

"Hold up," John said. He looked at Jessica. "Did you explain everything?"

"I told them about the night guard," she said. "What else is there?" He looked thoughtful for a moment.

"I guess nothing," he said.

"I brought more lights," Carlton said and held up three flashlights of varying sizes. He tossed one to Jason, a small one with an elastic headband attached. Jason turned it on, fixed it around his head, and began moving enthusiastically in waves and circles, making the light bob and dance.

"Shh," Charlie said, even though he was not making any sound.

"Jason," Marla whispered, "turn it off. We can't attract attention, remember?"

Jason gleefully ignored them, spinning off into the parking lot like a top.

"I told him if he's not good he has to wait in the car," Marla told Charlie quietly. "But now that we're here, I'm not sure which place is creepier." She eyed the bare branches overhead raging in the wind, threatening to reach down and grab them.

"Or we can feed him to Foxy." Charlie winked. She went to her trunk and hefted out the police flashlight, but she did not turn it on. Instead Carlton switched on two of his smaller lights and handed one to Jessica.

They headed into the mall. Knowing where they were going and what was waiting for them there, Charlie, John, Jessica, and Carlton moved through the empty spaces with a sense of purpose, but the others kept stopping to look around.

"Come on," Jessica said impatiently as Lamar gazed up at the atrium dome.

"You can see the moon," he said and pointed. Next to him, Marla nodded, mimicking his posture.

"It's beautiful," she said, although she could not see it.

From a distance, they heard footsteps echo in the emptiness.

"Hey, hey, over here!" John hissed, and they hurried as quietly as they could. They could not run for fear of making noise, and so they walked, fast but careful, hugging the walls. They entered the black void of the department store, creeping along in the shadows until they reached the break in the wall. John held back the hanging plastic obscuring the opening as the others maneuvered around the scaffolding. Jason was slow, and Charlie put a hand on his shoulder to hurry him up. As she steered him to the opening, a strong beam of light swept into the room, scanning up and down the walls. They all ducked through the plastic and ran down the alley to where the others were crouched down against the wall.

"He saw us!" Jason whispered, alarmed, running straight to his sister.

"Shh," Marla said.

They waited. Charlie was next to John this time, and after that moment by the tree, whatever it was, she was very, almost uncomfortably, aware of him. They were not quite touching, but she seemed to know exactly where he was, an awkward sixth sense. She glanced at him, but his eyes were fixed on the opening to the hallway. They could hear the guard's footsteps now, clear in the empty space, each one distinct. He was moving slowly, deliberately. Charlie closed her eyes, listening. She could tell where he was from the sound, she thought, getting closer, then farther, crisscrossing the open room like he was hunting for something. The steps came right up to the entrance of the alley and stopped. They all held their breaths.

He knows, Charlie thought. But the steps started again, and she opened her eyes and saw the light receding. He was going away.

They waited, still motionless, until they could no longer hear the tapping of his hard-soled shoes. She and John both stumbled a little as they stood, and she realized they had been leaning against each other without realizing it. She didn't look at him; instead she set to work taking the heaviest things off the wooden shelf.

"Will I be needing this?" Lamar asked, as Charlie handed him a bucket with a saw sticking out of it.

"We have to move the shelf," Jessica said. "Come on."

Jessica, Charlie, Carlton, and John got back into place and moved the shelf. Lamar tried to find a place to help, but there was not really room. Marla just waited.

"I'm better suited to supervising," she said when Charlie mock-glared at her.

This time the screaming of the metal door was not as loud, as if it no longer protested their entrance quite so strongly. Still, Marla and Jason covered their ears.

"You think *that's* not going to bring the guard?" Marla hissed.

Charlie shrugged. "Didn't last time," she said.

"I know he saw us," Jason said again. The others ignored him. "His flashlight went right over me," he insisted.

"It's really okay, Jason," Jessica said. "We thought he saw us last night, too, but it was fine." Jason looked dubious, and Lamar bent over to his eye level.

"Hey, Jason," he said. "What do you think the guard would do if he saw us?"

"Shoot us?" Jason whimpered, eyeing Lamar warily.

"Worse," Lamar said gravely. "Community service."

Jason wasn't sure what it meant, but he held his eyes open wide as though it was something terrible.

"Will you leave him alone?" Marla whispered, amused.

"He didn't see us," Jason reassured himself, though clearly unconvinced. Charlie turned on the big light and shone it down the hallway.

"Oh my!" Marla gasped as the first light streaked across the interior of the pizzeria. Suddenly it became real, and her face flushed with awe and fear.

They went in one by one. The temperature seemed to drop as soon as they walked into the hall, and Charlie shivered, but she did not feel ill at ease. She knew where they were now, and she knew what they would find. When they got to the dining room, Carlton spread his arms wide and twirled.

"Welcome . . . to Freddy Fazbear's Pizza!" he said in a booming announcer's voice. Jessica giggled, but the melodrama did not actually seem out of place. Marla and Lamar gaped at the room, awestruck. Charlie set the large flashlight on the ground, the beam facing up, and it lit up the main room in a dim and ghostly illumination.

"Cool," Jason said. His eyes fell on the merry-go-round, and he raced for it and jumped onto the back of a pony before anyone could stop him. He was too big for it, his sneakers dangling all the way to the ground. Charlie smiled. "How do I make it go?" he shouted.

"Sorry, buddy," John said. Jason climbed off, disappointed.

"The arcade is over this way!" Carlton said, motioning to anyone who might follow. Marla went with him, while Jason fiddled hopefully with the carousel's control box. Lamar had walked to the stage and was standing transfixed, staring up at the animals. Charlie went over to him.

"I can't believe they're still here," he said as she walked up.

"Yeah," she said.

"I'd forgotten this was a real place." Lamar smiled, for the first time resembling the little boy Charlie had once known.

Charlie smiled back. There was something surreal about the place; she had certainly never told any of her school friends about it. She would not have known where to begin; worse, she would not have known where to stop. Jessica poked her head out from the retracted curtain at the side of the main stage, and they both startled.

"What are you doing?" Lamar asked.

"Exploring!" she said. "There's nothing back here but a bunch of wires, though." She disappeared into the folds of cloth again. After a moment they heard a thud as she jumped to the ground, and she came strolling over.

"Do they work?" Lamar asked, pointing at the animals.

"I don't know," Charlie said. Truthfully, she had no idea how they worked. They had always just *been,* set to intermittent life by whatever alchemy her father performed in his workshop. "It doesn't look like anything is missing. They *should* work," she reluctantly added, though in her head she questioned the idea of trying to turn them on.

"Hey!" Jessica exclaimed. She was kneeling by the stairs to the stage. "Everybody come here now!"

Charlie went over, and Lamar followed.

"What is it?" Charlie asked.

"Look," Jessica said, shining her little light. Though well hidden along the grain of the wood, there was a door inset into the wall of the stage.

"How did we not see that?" Charlie wondered.

"We weren't looking," John said, staring intently at the small door. The whole group had gathered, and now Jessica looked around at them with a grin, put her hand on the little doorknob, and pulled.

Magically, it opened. The door revealed a small, sunken room. Jessica shone the light around it. It was full of equipment; one wall was covered in TV screens.

"Must be CCTV," Lamar said.

"Come on." Jessica handed her flashlight to Charlie and swung her legs through the door. There was one deep step leading down into the room, which was no bigger than a large refrigerator turned on its side.

"That's a little too cramped for me; I'll keep looking around out here." John saluted, then turned as though to stand guard.

"This is like a clown car," Marla remarked as she jostled against Charlie. The space was too cramped for all of them, but they crowded together; Jason sat on the step, feeling more comfortable by the exit. There were eight of the television screens across the wall, each with its own little panel of buttons and knobs, and sticking out beneath them was a panel, almost a table, covered in buttons. They were large and black, unlabeled, and spaced in an irregular series. The other wall was blank except for a single large switch by the door.

"What's this do?" Jason said and put his hand on the switch. He hesitated just long enough for someone to stop him, then pulled it.

The lights came on.

"What?" Carlton looked to the others frantically.

They all stared at one another in confused silence. Jason climbed up and poked his head out into the main room.

"They're on out here, too, some of them, at least," he said too loudly.

"Why is there power?" Jessica whispered, reaching over Jason to pull the door closed again.

"How is that possible?" Charlie said. "This place hasn't been open in ten years."

"Cool." Marla leaned forward, studying the monitors as though expecting some sort of answer to be revealed.

"Turn on the TVs," Jason said suddenly. "I can't reach." Jessica flipped on the first TV, and static crackled across the screen.

"Nothing?" Charlie asked impatiently.

"Just a sec." She twisted a dial, wiggling it back and forth until an image emerged. It was the stage, centered on Bonnie.

The other animals weren't visible. Jessica turned on the rest of the TVs, adjusting them until the pictures became clear, although most were still poorly lit.

"They still work," Charlie said almost under her breath.

"Maybe," Jessica said. "Hey, someone go out there. See if the camera is live."

"Okay," Marla said after a brief hesitation, wriggling her way to the exit and awkwardly climbing over Jason. A moment later she appeared on camera, onstage beside Bonnie. Marla waved. She appeared multicolored as the stage lights bathed her in purple, green, and yellow from different sides.

"Can you see me?" she asked.

"Yeah," Carlton shouted. Lamar was staring at the buttons.

"What do these do?" he said with a wicked grin, pressing one.

Marla screamed.

"Marla, are you okay?" Charlie shouted. "What happened?"

Marla was standing still on the stage, but she had backed away from Bonnie and was staring at him as if he might bite.

"He moved!" Marla yelled. "Bonnie moved! What did you do?"

"Marla," Jessica yelled, laughing, "it's okay! We pushed a button!"

Lamar pressed the button again, and they all watched the screen this time. Sure enough, Bonnie turned stiffly to one side. He pressed it again, and the rabbit swiveled back to face the absent audience again.

"Try another one," Carlton said.

"Go ahead," Lamar said and climbed out of the little room to join Marla onstage. He crouched down to inspect Bonnie's feet. "They're attached to a swiveling panel," he called.

"Yeah?" Jessica called back, not really listening.

Carlton started pressing buttons as the rest of them watched the cameras. After a moment, Charlie left the room as well.

"It's too stuffy in here," she explained. Jessica's perfume and Carlton's hair gel, both of which smelled nice enough out in the open, were starting to form a sickly miasma. She stepped out into the open to watch them experiment with the animals onstage. Most of the dining room was still dark. There were three colored spotlights suspended from the ceiling, aiming beams of purple, yellow, and green at the stage. The animals were cast now in unnatural colors, and dust in the beams of light shone like tiny stars, so many that it was difficult to see through them. The floor beneath the long tables was dusted with glitter that had fallen from the party hats, and as she looked around she noticed again the drawings that lined the walls of the place, all at the height of children's eyes.

They had always been there, and Charlie wondered now where her father had gotten the first ones when the restaurant opened. Had he used her own childish scribblings, or had he made them himself and stuck them up, forgeries to encourage actual children to display their art? The thought of her father hunched over his workbench, gripping an unsteady crayon with hands accustomed to manipulating microchips, made her want to giggle. She noticed the flashlight still on in the center of the room and went to switch it off. *Don't waste the battery*, she said in her head, in chorus with Aunt Jen's voice.

She turned her attention to the stage. It looked like the others had gotten Chica and Bonnie to go through a series of small, specific movements. They could each swivel their entire bodies back and forth, and their hands, feet, and heads could be moved in various directions, but each movement was separate.

Charlie went back to the control room and stuck her head in. "Can you make them do the dance?" she asked.

"I don't know how," Carlton said, leaning back away from the monitors. "All of this must have been used to program the dances. I don't think someone was in here manually controlling everything during the shows." He shook his head with certainty. "That would have been impossible."

"Huh," Charlie said.

"Everyone, quiet," Marla called out, and they all fell silent.

For a long moment there was no sound, then Lamar said, "What?"

Marla frowned, tilting her head to the side, listening for something. "I thought I heard something," she said finally. "It was like . . . pings of a music box?" Her mouth barely moved as she spoke. "It's gone."

"Why isn't Freddy moving?" Charlie asked.

"I don't know," Carlton said. "I can't find the controls for him."

"Hmm," Jessica said, tapping the monitors. "These cameras don't show the whole place."

Charlie peered at them, but they were mixed up, in no logical order. She couldn't piece together a picture of the whole restaurant.

"There's three cameras on the stage, one on each animal, but there should be one on the whole thing," Jessica was saying. "There's the entrance to the kitchen, but not the kitchen itself, and you can't see the hallway and the room with the little stage we were at last night."

"Maybe the cameras are just in the main room?" Carlton suggested.

"Nope," said Jessica. "There are cameras everywhere out there."

"So?" Carlton said.

"So there's got to be another control room!" Jessica said triumphantly. "Maybe down the hall by the other stage."

Charlie went back out into the main room again. She was feeling restless, less excited by the discoveries than the others, though she was not sure why. She watched the stage. Carlton was still playing with the buttons, Bonnie and Chica jerking in small, disjointed motions as Freddy Fazbear remained motionless, his eyes half-closed and his mouth slack, slightly open.

"Hey," Lamar said suddenly. "Marla. The music. I hear it now." Everyone was silent again, then Marla shook her head.

"Creepy," she said, more excited this time, rubbing her hands together as though they were sharing campfire stories. Lamar looked thoughtfully at Freddy.

"Let's go find the other control room," Jessica said, emerging with a determined look on her face.

"Okay!" Marla jumped from the stage to join them, and they started scanning the rest of the stage, looking for a second door.

"I'm staying in here," Jason called from the first room. "This is so cool!" Chica swiveled back and forth rapidly on the stage as he pushed her button repeatedly. Lamar went to join Jason.

"Okay, my turn," he said, leaning on the door. He went in, not waiting for Jason's response.

Charlie stayed where she was, still staring at Freddy, frozen in the middle of his act. John came up next to her, and she felt a flash of irritation; she did not want to be cajoled into joining in the search. He stood there for a moment, looking at Freddy, then leaned in close to her and whispered, "I'm counting to one hundred. You'd better hide."

Surprised out of her thoughts, she looked at him for a moment, her irritation broken. He winked at her, then covered his eyes. It was absurd, it was childish, and in that moment it was the only thing she wanted to do. Slightly giddy, Charlie took off, looking for a place to hide.

Jason pushed the series of buttons again with increasing frustration. "I'm bored now," he announced.

"How can you be bored?" Lamar said, wide-eyed.

"They aren't working anymore." Jason continued to press buttons, no longer watching the monitors.

Lamar studied the monitor. Bonnie's head was up and turned to the side, his eyes appearing to watch the camera. "Well, go find your sister then," he told Jason.

"I don't need her permission to be bored!" Impatiently, Jason climbed up and out of the control room.

"Everyone is so sensitive," Lamar muttered, suddenly realizing he was alone in the control room. He climbed out, but Jason was already gone.

Jessica was leading the exploration party, heading toward the little stage they had discovered the night before. Marla looked back and saw Jason skipping to catch up just before they disappeared into the long hall.

"Hey, be careful!" she called over her shoulder as Jason branched off in his own direction. Lamar caught up to the group and followed them on their way into the hall. The main dining room was empty now, though Jason could hear Charlie's and John's playful shouts echoing from the party rooms that extended off the main building. Left alone, Jason headed straight for the arcade.

It was more dimly lit than the rest of the place, and without power the arcade machines appeared as towering black monoliths in a forgotten graveyard. The air was stale and thin. Jason went to the nearest console and pressed a few buttons, some stuck with age, but nothing happened.

Plug it in, duh. He ducked behind the games to check, but even though the mounds of wires seemed impossibly tangled, it looked like they were plugged in. *Maybe there's a switch for the whole room?* He started checking the walls.

There was no obvious switch, but as Jason scanned the walls, he became distracted by the children's drawings taped in clusters. Jason was too young to have any memories of his own from being at Freddy's; even Hurricane itself was no more than a hazy set of impressions. But something about the pictures brought up a sense of nostalgia. They were all the same, really, the kinds of drawings he and every other kid had done—figures with circles for bodies and sticks for arms, in a multitude of colors. Only a few details showed which figures were the animals: Chica with her beak, Bonnie with his ears. It seemed like there had been a bit more attention paid to the drawings of Freddy Fazbear. They were a little better; the children had been a little more careful to make the details right. Jason found himself looking at one drawing in particular. It was the same as the others, maybe a little better: Bonnie the Bunny hugging a child. There was no name at the bottom. Jason took the picture off the wall, uncertain why this one in particular interested him so much.

John burst into the room with a wide grin and a deep breath, but then, seeing that it was only Jason inside, he quickly returned to a stoic demeanor. "What's up?" He nodded his head, playing it cool, then casually stepped away before silently returning to a sprint.

Playing hide-and-seek like babies, Jason thought. *I hope I never fall in love.*

He looked back down at the drawing and squinted as though not seeing correctly. The child was now facing away from Bonnie. Jason stared for a long moment. *Wasn't he hugging Bonnie before?* He looked out at the main room, but Marla was out of sight, looking for the control room. Jason folded the drawing carefully and put it in his pocket. It was suddenly apparent how quiet it had become outside. Jason stepped out timidly and peeked into the dining room. "Guys?" he whispered, looking back once, then ventured out to find the group.

★   ★   ★

Jessica, Lamar, Carlton, and Marla were still creeping slowly through the other half of the building. The spotlights from the dining room didn't reach this far, only accenting edges and corners or specks of glitter. Jessica scanned the wall with her flashlight, looking for breaks in the plaster, and motioned to Marla to do the same.

"We have to check for a hidden door," she said.

"The last one wasn't really hidden," Carlton pointed out.

"Yeah," Jessica conceded, but she kept her light on the wall, clearly not ready to give up the hunt. They passed two bathrooms they had not noticed the night before.

"Do you think the plumbing still works?" Carlton said. "I really need to pee."

"What are you, five years old? I don't want to hear that." Jessica rolled her eyes and walked faster.

When they got to the room with the little stage, everyone stopped. Marla and Lamar went closer to the stage, drawing together slightly as if unaware they were doing it. Even though Carlton and Jessica had been here the night before, it was as though they were seeing it anew through Marla's and Lamar's eyes. They still had not seen what was behind the curtain, Carlton realized suddenly.

"I remember these posters," Lamar said.

"I remember this, too," Marla said, pointing to the sign that read OUT OF ORDER strung across the stage. "My whole life I've felt uneasy when I've seen that phrase, even if it's just at a vending machine." She laughed insincerely.

"I know what you mean," Lamar said softly, but before he could go on, Carlton interrupted.

."Found it."

"Maybe," Jessica amended. There was a door, close-set into the wall like the one below the stage—not quite hidden, but not meant to be noticed. It was painted black, like the walls of the room. Jessica turned the knob and pulled, but it was stuck tight.

"Locked?" Lamar said.

"I don't think so."

"Let me try," Marla said. She grabbed the knob and yanked, and it came open, sending her stumbling back.

"Impressive!" Lamar said.

"Yeah, well, taking care of Jason makes me tough." Marla grinned as she knelt down to squeeze through the small door.

It was almost the same as the first room: a set of eight TV screens and a large panel of unmarked black buttons. Carlton fumbled to find the master switch, reaching his hand into a dark corner. Then, with a click, the power came on, and a soft buzzing sound filled the room. Rich, bizarre reds and blues began streaming in under the door from the stage lights outside. Jessica and Carlton began switching the televisions on; they fiddled with the knobs until they were showing pictures, though most were very dark. From here they could see a long shot of the main stage, just as in the other room, but the rest of the cameras were showing other places and angles. While the first control room had only shots of the main dining room, here they could see into other areas of the restaurant—the private party rooms, which were set up with glittery decorations for events that would never happen; hallways; an office; and even what looked like a storage closet. The room behind them was visible as well, the camera trained on the OUT OF ORDER sign, now lit with otherworldly shades, and the curtain behind it. On one screen they could see Jason ducking back into the arcade.

"Maybe I should go get him," Marla said, but no one responded.

Carlton started pressing buttons. Spotlights appeared and vanished on the stage in the main dining room as he did, illuminating first one animal and then another, lighting up empty spaces where someone might once have stood. He flipped a switch, and it seemed for a moment that nothing happened. Then Lamar started laughing, pointing at one of the screens. The pizza decorations lining the walls were spinning wildly, as though they might leap off and go rolling away.

"I forgot they used to do that," Lamar said as Carlton brought them slowly to a halt.

There was a large black dial to one side of the buttons, and Carlton spun it, but it seemed to do nothing.

"Let me try," Lamar said. He elbowed Carlton to the side and pressed another button. There was a high-pitched whine; they all jumped, and it quickly faded down to a static hum. Lamar pressed the button again, and the sound was gone.

"I guess we know what turns the speakers on," Carlton said.

"I bet we could figure out how to play the music," Jessica said. She reached forward and pushed something else, and stage lights popped up while the main lights dimmed. The figures on the main stage suddenly stood out a little, commanding attention. She pushed it again, and the lights faded back to normal.

"I love that," Carlton said.

"What?" asked Marla.

"Stage lights," he said. "One switch, and it's like a whole 'nother world up there."

Another button flickered the stage lights on and off in the room behind them, while another started and stopped the little merry-go-round, its tinkling music grinding too slowly, like the ride itself was trying to remember how the song went. They managed to get the speakers on again without the feedback whine, but there was still only static.

"I have an idea," Jessica said, pushing to the front of the group. She switched on the static again, then started turning the knob back and forth. The hum grew lower in pitch, then higher, responding to her adjustments.

"Progress," Carlton said.

"It's still just static," Marla said, unimpressed. Jessica turned it lower again, then snatched her hand from the dial like she had been bitten and punched the button, shutting the speakers off.

"What?" Marla asked.

Jessica remained motionless, her hands still suspended in the air.

"What happened? Did it shock you?" Carlton asked.

"It sounded like a voice," Jessica answered.

"What did it say?" Marla asked, apparently interested again.

"I don't know. Let me try again."

She turned the speaker on again, calling forth the static, and lowered the hum as they all listened, intent on the sound. As it sank to a lower register, just below the range of a human voice, they all heard it: grinding and broken words, almost too slow and distorted to be considered speech. They looked at one another.

"What on earth?" Marla said.

"No, it's just random static," Lamar said. He reached for the controls and dialed the pitch back up slowly. For another fleeting moment, there was a purposeful sound.

"That sounded like singing," Carlton said.

"No," Lamar said, sounding more unsure this time.

"Do it again," Marla said. Lamar did, but this time the static was empty.

"Is that Charlie?" Marla suddenly became focused on a blurry figure moving down the dark hall toward them, sliding along the wall as though to remain unnoticed.

Charlie was hurrying, almost skipping, and trying to find another place to hide. She glanced behind her, vaguely suspecting that John might be cheating. She moved through the darkness and toward the colorful glow of the small stage curtain, which was throwing eerie reds and blues onto the tables and party hats. Going down this passage had always felt like a long and perilous journey, one not to be made alone. She kept her gaze fixed behind her, letting the wall beside her guide her step. She knew John was close, probably creeping up on her in the dark. Suddenly she backed into something, stopping short. She had been moving faster than she thought, or more likely the hall was not as long as she remembered.

She saw his shadow at the end of the hall—if he turned his head, he would see her. Without thinking, Charlie climbed up onto the platform that she had bumped into and ducked behind the curtain, tucking herself between the wall and a large, bulky prop, trying not to breathe.

"Charlie?" he called, still far away. *"Charlie!"* Charlie felt her heartbeat quicken. There had been boys she liked, now and then, but this was something different. She wanted him to find her, but not quite yet. As she waited, her eyes adjusted to the darkness, and she was able to make out the shape of the curtain and the edge of the stage. She looked up at the object in front of her.

No. Her body shuddered, then froze.

It was standing over her. It was the thing from her father's workshop, the misshapen thing that hung in the corner, shaken by random convulsions as its eyes burned silver. *Does it hurt?* Now it was still, and its eyes were blank and dull. It was staring straight ahead, insensate, and its arm with its hook hung useless at its side. She recognized his eyes, but he was somehow worse now, encased in hollow body parts and matted with red fur, with a stench of oil and glue. He had a name now; they called him Foxy. But she knew better.

Charlie shrank away, pressing against the wall. Her heart was racing, and her breath was shallow, too fast. Her arm had been touching its leg, and now she felt a sudden itchiness from it, like she had been contaminated. She wiped her hand violently against her shirt as she began to panic.

Run.

She sprang away from it, pushing off the wall to get away, to move before it saw her, but the edge of the stage caught her foot. She stumbled forward, momentarily becoming entangled in the curtain. She struggled to get free when suddenly the thing's arm jerked up, and the hook slashed at her arm. She ducked away too late, and it cut her. The pain was shocking, like freezing water. She tripped backward and felt herself falling for long seconds, and then she was caught.

"Charlie? Are you okay?"

It was John; he had caught her. She tried to nod, but she was shaking. She looked at her arm. There was a cut above the elbow, almost four inches long. It was bleeding freely, and she covered it with her hand, the gaps between her fingers welling over as her own blood leaked through.

"What happened?" Marla asked, rushing up behind her. "Charlie, I'm so sorry, I must have hit a button that caused it to move. Are you okay?"

Charlie nodded, a little less shaky. "I'm fine," she said. "It's not that bad." She moved her arm around experimentally. "See? No nerve damage," she said. "I'll be fine."

Carlton, Jessica, and Lamar came hurrying out of the control room.

"We should take her to the E.R.," Carlton said.

"I'm fine," Charlie insisted. She stood up, refusing John's help, and braced herself on the stage for a moment. She heard her Aunt Jen's voice in her head: *How much blood have you lost? You don't need to go to a hospital.* She could move her arm just fine, and she would not bleed to death from this. She felt dizzy, though.

"Charlie, you look like a ghost," John said. "We need to get you out of here."

"Okay," she said. Her thoughts were scattered, and the injury hurt less than it should have. She took deep breaths as they headed for the exit, grounding herself. John handed her a piece of cloth, and she put it to the cut to slow the bleeding.

"Thanks," she said, looking at him. Something was missing. "Was that your tie?" she asked, and he shrugged.

"Do I look like a tie person?"

She grinned. "I thought it looked good on you."

"Jason!" Marla yelled as they passed the arcade. "Move it, or I'm leaving you behind!"

Jason ran to catch up.

"Is Charlie okay?" he said anxiously. Marla caught her breath and put her arm around him.

"She's fine," she reassured him.

They walked briskly down the same corridor that they entered through. Jason looked back as he was being guided out, studying the pictures on the wall once more before losing sight of them. The colored lights from the stage were fading, and the flashlight was throwing shapes and shadows on everything, making the drawings difficult to see, but Jason could swear he saw the figures moving in the pictures.

They all hurried back through the empty building and out to the parking lot, not keeping watch for the guard. When they made it out to the car, Lamar, who had grabbed the big flashlight, flipped it on and shone it at Charlie's arm. She looked down at the cut.

"Do you need stitches?" Marla asked. "I am so sorry, Charlie."

"We were all being careless. It's not your fault," Charlie said. She knew she sounded annoyed, but she didn't mean to; her voice was tight and clipped with pain. The shock had worn off, but that meant the wound had begun to hurt. "It's fine," Charlie said, and after a long moment the others gave in somewhat reluctantly.

"We should at least get you some stuff to clean that up and bandage it," Marla said, wanting to do something to atone, however small.

"There's a twenty-four-hour drugstore just off the main road," Carlton offered.

"Charlie, why don't you go with Marla, and I'll drive your car back to the motel?" Jessica said.

"I'm fine," Charlie protested halfheartedly, but she handed Jessica the keys. "You're a good driver, right?"

Jessica rolled her eyes. "People from New York know how to drive, Charlie."

John lingered a moment as Charlie was getting into Marla's car. She smiled at him.

"I'm fine," she said. "I'll see you tomorrow." He looked at her like there was something more he wanted to say, but he just nodded and left.

"Okay," Marla said. "To the drugstore!"

Charlie twisted in her seat to look at Jason. "Did you have fun?" she asked.

"The games don't work," he said, obviously preoccupied.

The drugstore was only a few minutes away. "You stay in the car," Marla commanded to Jason as they pulled to a stop.

"Don't leave me out here," Jason pleaded.

"I told you to stay," she repeated, a little confused by the fear in his voice. He didn't answer, and she and Charlie headed inside.

As soon as they were gone, Jason pulled the drawing out of his pocket. He held it up under the faint lights of the parking lot to examine. It had not changed back: Bonnie the Bunny was reaching toward a child, who was facing away from him. Curious, Jason scraped at the crayon lines with his fingernail. The wax came off easily, leaving its trace on the paper.

As soon as Marla passed into the fluorescent-lit, air-controlled drugstore, she sighed and put her hands to her temples. "Oh, he's such a little brat," she said.

"I like him," Charlie said honestly. She was still using John's tie to stanch the bleeding, and now, in brighter light, she peeled it back to see the cut. The bleeding had almost stopped; it was not as bad as it had first appeared, though the tie was irreparably ruined. "Hey," she said. "How come you brought Jason, anyway?"

Marla didn't answer right away, setting her sights on the first-aid aisle and heading for it.

"Here we are," she said. "What do you think, gauze?"

"Sure, but don't call me Gauze." Charlie leaned into Marla but was ignored.

"Antiseptic," Marla continued, grabbing the items. "The thing is," she said, "so Jason's dad and our mom have been married since before he was born. I mean, obviously. And they're probably getting divorced. I know about it, but Jason doesn't."

"Oh no," Charlie said.

"They're fighting all the time," Marla went on, "and it scares him, you know? I mean, my dad left when I was still a little kid, so I grew up with that; I was used to it. Plus, I got to have a great stepdad. But for him, it's gonna feel like the end of the world. And they're sure not doing anything to make it easier—they're fighting right in front of us. So I didn't want to leave him alone with that for a week."

"I'm so sorry, Marla," Charlie said.

"Yeah, it's okay," Marla said. "I'm leaving in a year anyway. I'm just worried about the brat out there."

"He's really not a brat," Charlie said, and Marla grinned.

"I know; he's pretty great, right? I kinda like having him around."

They paid for the supplies. The clerk, a teenage boy, didn't bat an eye at Charlie's moderately blood-spattered appearance. Outside, they sat on the hood of the car. Marla started to open the bottle of antiseptic, but Charlie held out a hand for it.

"I can do it myself," she said. Marla looked like she was about to argue, but she swallowed whatever she was about to say and handed Charlie the bottle and a piece of gauze. As Charlie awkwardly cleaned her arm, Marla smiled impishly.

"Speaking of people we like having around, are you having fun with John?"

"Ow! That stings. And I don't know what you mean," Charlie said primly, suddenly putting all her attention on her task.

"You do, too. He's following you around like a little puppy, and you are loving it."

Charlie bit back a smile. "How about you and Lamar?" she retorted.

"Me and who now?" Marla said. "Here." She held out a hand for the bloody gauze, and Charlie handed it to her, reaching for a clean strip. "You're going to have to let me tape it," Marla said. Charlie nodded and held the gauze in place as Marla reached for the tape.

"Come on," Charlie went on. "I see the way you look at him."

"Nope!" Marla smoothed down the last piece of tape and put everything back in the bag.

"Seriously," Charlie said as they got back into the car. "You're adorable together. And your names are anagrams of each other. Marla and Lamar! It's meant to be!" Both laughing, they headed back to the motel.

CHAPTER FIVE

When they got to the motel, Jessica was already there—and so was John. He stood up when Charlie walked in.

"I was worried about you. I thought maybe I could sleep on the floor?" He waited nervously for her reaction, as though he had realized only upon seeing her that he might have overstepped her boundaries.

On another day, in another place, Charlie might have been annoyed by his excessive concern. But here, in Hurricane, she was glad to have it. *We should all be together,* she thought. *It's safer.* She wasn't really afraid, but unease still clung to her like cobwebs, and John's presence had been a calming one ever since they arrived. He was still looking at her, waiting for a response, and she smiled at him.

"As long as you don't mind sharing the floor with Jason," she said.

He grinned. "Just let me have a pillow and I'll be fine." Marla tossed him one, and he stretched elaborately, set it on the ground, and lay down.

They all went to bed almost immediately. Charlie was exhausted; now that her injury had been cleaned and bound, the adrenaline of the night left her body all at once, leaving her drained and a little shaky. She didn't even bother changing into pajamas; she just collapsed on the bed next to Jessica and was asleep in seconds.

Charlie woke just after dawn, when the sky was still pale and a little pink. She looked around the room. The others wouldn't be up for hours, she suspected, but she was too alert to try to fade back into sleep. She grabbed her shoes and, stepping over Jason's and John's sleeping bodies, went outside. The motel was set a little way back off the road, trees spread thickly around and behind it. Charlie sat down on the curb to put her shoes on, wondering if she could go for a walk in the woods without getting lost. The air was crisp, and she felt renewed and energized by the brief night's sleep. Her arm hurt, a dull and pulsing pain that kept drawing her attention, but it had not bled through the bandages. Charlie usually found it easy to ignore pain when she knew she was not in danger from it. The woods were inviting, and she decided to risk getting lost.

As she was about to stand, John sat down beside her.

"Morning," he said. His clothes were rumpled from his night on the motel floor, and his hair was a mess. Charlie held back a laugh. "What?" he said. She shook her head.

"You look a little like your old self today," she said. He looked down at himself and shrugged.

"Clothes don't make the man. What are you doing up so early?"

"I don't know, couldn't sleep. What about you?"

"Somebody stepped on me."

Charlie winced. "Sorry," she said, and he laughed.

"I'm just kidding. I was awake."

"I was going to go for a walk," she said, pointing at the tree line. "Out there, somewhere. Do you want to come?"

"Yeah, definitely."

They headed into the woods, and John hung back for a moment and surreptitiously retucked his shirt, trying to smooth out the wrinkles. Charlie pretended not to notice.

There was no path, and so they made their way through the trees at random, glancing back now and then to be sure they could still make out the motel parking lot. John stumbled over a fallen branch, and Charlie reached out with her good arm to catch him before he fell.

"Thanks," he said. "Strong arm, too."

"Well, you caught me yesterday, so it's only fair that I catch you back. Now we're even," she said. She looked around. The motel was scarcely in sight, and she felt concealed, made safe by the woods. She could say anything here, and it would be all right. She leaned back against a tree, picking idly at the bark behind her. "You know Freddy's wasn't the first restaurant?" She said it abruptly, surprising herself, and John looked at her quizzically, like he had not quite heard her. She didn't want to say it again, but she forced herself to. "Freddy's, it wasn't my dad's first restaurant. There was a diner, a little one. It was before my mom left."

"I had no idea," John said slowly. "Where was it?"

"I don't know. It's one of those memories from when you're a little kid, you know? You only remember the things that are right around you. I remember the linoleum on the kitchen floor; it was this black-and-white diamond pattern, but I don't remember where the restaurant was, or what it was called."

"Yeah," John said. "We took a vacation to a theme park when I was, like, three, and all I remember is the backseat of the car. So were *they* there?" His voice dropped a little quieter when he said it, almost reflexively. Charlie nodded.

"Yeah. There was a bear and a rabbit, I think. Sometimes the details get mixed up in my head. They're not like normal memories," she said, needing him to understand the story's defects before she told him the rest. "It's like when you have a realistic dream, and in the morning you're not sure if it really happened or not. It's just impressions, little snatches of time. It's . . ." She trailed off. She wasn't explaining it right; she was choosing all the wrong words. She was reaching back too far in her memory, to a time when she did not yet speak. It was a time when she did not have the words to name the things she saw, and so now, when she tried to recall them, the words could never be right.

She looked at John. He was watching her patiently, waiting for her to go on. She wanted to tell him this story from her life that she had never told. It was not even a story, not really, just something that nagged at the edge of her mind, something flashing by randomly in the corner of her eye. She was not entirely certain it was real, and so she told no one. She wanted to tell John, because she wanted to speak it to another person, because he looked at her with trusting eyes and she knew he would listen to and believe her. Because he had cared for her a long time ago, because he had caught her when she fell, and he had come here to sleep and keep watch all night. And, thought a pragmatic, slightly cruel part of her, because he was not part of her real life. She could tell him this, tell him anything, and when she returned home, it would be as though it had never happened. She wanted suddenly to touch him, have confirmation that he was really there, that this was not another dream. She reached out her hand to him, and, surprised but glad, he took it. He stayed where he was, as if afraid that moving in closer would scare her. They stayed that way for a moment, and then she let go, and she told him the story the way she spoke it in her head, the memories of a small child mixing with the things she had come to understand as she grew older.

There was another restaurant, rustic and small, with red checkered cloths on the tables, and a kitchen you could see into from the dining area, and they all were there together. Her father and her mother and *us*. When Charlie was very, very young, she was never alone. There was Charlie, and there was a little boy, a little boy so close to Charlie that remembering him was like remembering a part of herself. They were always together; she learned to say *we* before she learned to say *I*.

They played together on the floor of the kitchen, sometimes drawing pictures while hiding under a hardwood table. She remembered the shuffling of feet and the shadows of customers walking by. Light was broken by a slowly turning fan and thrown across the floor in ribbons. She remembered the smell of an ashtray and the hearty laughter of adults lost in a good story while their children played.

Very often she would hear her father's laugh echoing from a distant corner as he talked with customers. When Charlie pictured him laughing like that now it was with a little ache, a sucking feeling in the center of her chest, because his eyes were bright and his smile was easy and because he wanted them all to be a part of the restaurant, to share his work freely. Because he was not afraid to let his children roam and explore. He was yet untouched by grief, and so while he looked a little like the father she truly remembered, he was not the same man at all.

Charlie was looking down at the ground as she talked, at the dirt and stones and cracked remains of leaves, and her hand was at her back, stripping bark from the tree. *Does that hurt the tree?* she thought, and forced her hands away, knotting them in front of her.

The restaurant was open until late at night, and so when they began to falter, Charlie and the little boy would crawl into the pantry with blankets and soft toys to sleep until it was time to close. She remembered using sacks of flour as pillows, big bags almost as long as they were tall. They would snuggle down together and whisper words of nonsense that meant deep things only to the two of them, and Charlie would drift into sleep, half listening to the warm sounds of the restaurant, the clank of dishes and the murmur of grown-up talk, and the sound of the bear and the rabbit as they danced to their chiming tunes.

They loved the animals, the yellowish-brown bear and the matching rabbit, who wandered the restaurant, dancing and singing for the customers, and sometimes just for Charlie and the little boy. They sometimes moved stiffly and mechanically, and sometimes with fluid, human movements, and while the boy liked the animals best when they acted like people, Charlie liked them the other way. Their stilted movements, their lifeless eyes, and their occasional glitches fascinated her: They acted alive, but were not. The narrow yet bottomless chasm between those things, alive and not-alive, enthralled her, though she would never have been able to explain why.

"I think they were costumes," Charlie said now, still looking down at the ground. "The animals weren't always robots; the bear and the bunny were costumes, and sometimes people wore them, and sometimes my father put it onto one of his robots, and you could always tell which it was by the way they danced."

Charlie stopped. There was more, but she could not bring herself to speak. There was something else that made her lock down her mind and force the memory away, the part that made her unwilling to ask Aunt Jen for answers, because she was afraid of what those answers might be. Charlie had not dared to look at John the whole time she was talking, staring only at the ground, at her hands, at her sneakers. Now she did look at him, and he was rapt, seeming almost to be holding his breath. He waited, not wanting to speak until he was sure she was finished.

"That's all I remember," she said at last, even though it was a lie.

"Wait, who was the little boy?" John said.

Charlie shook her head, frustrated that he had not understood.

"He was mine," she said. "I mean, he was my brother. We were the same." She was speaking childishly, as if the memory had taken hold of her, forcing her to regress. She cleared her throat. "Sorry," she said, speaking more slowly, trying to choose her words with care. "I think he was my twin brother."

She saw John open his mouth, about to ask the question, *What happened to him?* But there must have been something in her face, something warning, because he held it back and said instead, "Do you think that place was around here? I mean, I guess it could have been anywhere. Another state, even."

"I don't know," Charlie said slowly, looking over her shoulders, then up at the trees. "This all feels the same. It feels like I could walk around any corner and it could be there." Her voice began to break. "I want to find it," she added suddenly, and as soon as she said it, it was what she wanted to do.

"Well, what do you remember about it?" John said enthusiastically, almost lunging forward like an eager dog on a lead. He must have been dying to go looking from the moment she mentioned the place. Charlie smiled but shook her head.

"I really don't remember much," she said. "I don't know how much help I can actually be; like I said, the things I remember are just little scraps, they're not information. It's like a picture book." She closed her eyes, trying to see the place in her mind's eye. "The floor would shake." She lifted her head as the thought became clear. "A train?" she asked as though John would know. "I remember this thunderous sound every day; it was the biggest sound I'd ever heard. I don't mean loud, I mean you could feel it in your whole body, like it was rumbling right through your chest."

"It must have been close to some tracks, then, right?" John said.

"Yeah," Charlie said with a spark of hope. "There was a tree out in front," she went on. "It looked like an old, angry monster, hunched forward and wizened, with two giant, gnarled branches reaching out like arms. Whenever we left for the night, I hid my face in my father's shirt so I wouldn't have to see it as we walked by."

"What else?" John said. "Were there stores, or other restaurants?"

"No. I mean, I don't think so. I'm sorry." She scratched her head. "It's gone."

"It's not enough," John said, a little frustrated. "It could be anywhere, a train and a tree. There must be something else you can remember. Anything?"

"No," Charlie said. The more she pushed herself to remember, the harder it got. She was grasping blindly, and it was like trying to get hold of living creatures, as if the memories saw her coming and slipped away.

She tossed out fragments as she managed to catch them: the tablecloths, red-and-white checked, and made of real cloth, not plastic. She remembered grabbing at one, unsteady on her feet, and the whole table setting falling down on top of her, plates and glasses shattering around her as she covered her head. *Charlotte, are you okay?* Her father's voice seemed clearer than ever.

There was a squeaky floorboard in the corner of the diner that Charlie liked to push on, making it sing as if it made music. There was a picnic table out back where they used to sit in the sun, one leg of it sinking in the soft ground. There was the song her parents used to sing in the car whenever they came home from a trip; they would burst into it when they were a little way from home, and then they'd start laughing as if they had done something clever.

"It's nothing helpful," Charlie said. "Just kid stuff." She felt a little light-headed. She had spent so many years avoiding these memories; her mind shied away as if from snakes. Having done it, she felt strange and a little guilty, like she had done something wrong. But she also felt something that might have been joy, in the things she never allowed herself to think of. The memories of that time were unsafe, there were traps and snares wrought into their very substance, but there were precious things among them.

"Sorry," she said. "I can't remember more."

"No, that's really impressive. I can't believe you remember that far back at all," he said. "I didn't mean to push you," he added a little sheepishly, then looked thoughtful. "What was the song?"

"I think it was the same one they dance to at Freddy's," Charlie said.

"No, the one your parents sang in the car."

"Oh," she said. "I don't know if I remember it. It wasn't really a song, you know? It was just a little line." She closed her eyes, picturing the car, trying to envision the backs of her parents' heads as though she were still in the backseat. She waited, trusting her mind to give it up, and after a moment, it did. She hummed it, just six notes.

" 'We're back in harmony,' " she sang. "And they'd, you know, harmonize," she added, embarrassed by her parents even now. John's expression was blank for a moment as the words at first seemed meaningless, but then his eyes lit with promise.

"Charlie, there's a town north of here called New Harmony."

"Huh," was all she said for a moment. She listened to the words in her head, wanting them to set off an inspiration, trip a memory, but they did not.

"I feel like that should ring a bell, but it doesn't," she said. "Sorry. I mean, it doesn't sound wrong, but it doesn't sound *right*, either." She was disappointed, but John still had that thoughtful look on his face.

"Come on," he said, extending his hand. Charlie wiped her cheek and took a shaky breath, then looked to him. She nodded with an exhausted smile and got to her feet.

"Should we wait for everyone to wake up?" John said as they emerged into the parking lot after a brisk walk back.

"No," Charlie said with unexpected vehemence. "I don't want everyone there for this," she added in softer tones. Just the thought of the whole group going along made her anxious. It was too risky, too private; she had no idea what they might find or what it might do to her, and she couldn't abide the thought of making those discoveries with an audience.

"Okay," John said. "Just us, then."

"Just us."

Charlie went inside and grabbed her car keys, moving slowly so as not to disturb the others. As she was heading back to the door, Jason stirred and opened his eyes, looking up at her like he wasn't quite sure who she was. She put a finger to her lips.

He nodded sleepily and closed his eyes again, and she hurried out the door. She tossed the keys to John and got in on the passenger's side.

"There's a map in here," she said, jostling open the glovebox door. The map fell out amid a pile of hand warmers and emergency food rations.

"Your aunt strikes again." John smiled.

Charlie held the map just a few inches from her face. New Harmony was close, only about half an hour away.

"Think you can navigate?" he asked.

"Aye, Cap'n!" Charlie said. "Turn left out of the lot."

"Thanks," he said wryly.

They drove back through the town and out the other side, the houses farther and farther between as they went. Each one stood solitary, connected only by sagging power lines. Charlie watched the telephone poles and the dipping wires repeating hypnotically as if they would go on forever, then blinked, breaking the spell. Ahead of them the mountains rose up ancient and dark against the clear blue sky; they looked more solid than anything else around them, more real, and maybe they were. They had been here, watching, long before the houses, long before the roads, and they would be here long after they were all gone.

"Nice day," John said, and she looked at him, tearing her gaze from the view.

"Yeah," Charlie said. "I kind of forgot how beautiful it is out here."

"Yeah," he said. He was quiet for a moment, then looked at her sideways, and Charlie couldn't tell if he was being shy or just keeping his eyes on the road.

"It's weird," he said at last. "When I was a kid, the mountains kind of scared me, especially when we were driving in the dark. They were like some monstrous beasts looming over us." He laughed a little, but Charlie did not.

"I know what you mean," she said, then grinned at him. "I think they're pretty much just mountains, though. Hey," she said suddenly, "you never told me what your story was about."

"My story?" He flicked his eyes at her again, a little nervous.

"Yeah, you said you got a story published. What was it about?"

"I mean, it was just a little magazine, just local," he said, still reluctant. Charlie waited, and finally he continued. "It's called 'The Little Yellow House.' It's about a boy," he said. "He's ten years old. His parents are fighting all the time, and he's afraid they're going to get divorced. They fight, and he overhears them saying awful things to each other, and he hides in his room with the door shut, but he can still hear them.

"So he starts looking out the window, at the house across

the street. They sort of keep their curtains open just enough that he can glimpse inside. He watches them go in and out of the house, this family, and he starts making up stories about them, imagining who they are and what they do, and after a while they start feeling more real to him than his own family."

He glanced at Charlie again, as if trying to gauge her reaction, and Charlie smiled. He went on.

"So summer comes, and his family goes away for a week, and it's miserable, and when they get back, the family in the house across the street has moved away. There's nothing left, just a FOR SALE sign hanging in front."

Charlie nodded, waiting for him to continue, but he looked at her a little sheepishly.

"That's the end," he said.

"Oh," she said. "That's really sad."

He shrugged. "I guess. I'm working on something happy now, though."

"What's that?"

He grinned at her.

"It's a secret."

Charlie smiled back. It felt good to be out here, good to just be driving out into the horizon. She cranked the window down and put her arm out into the air, enjoying the feel of the rushing wind. *It's not wind rushing, it's us,* she thought.

"What about you?" John said.

"What about me?" Charlie said, still happily playing against the wind.

"Come on, what's the life of Charlie like these days?"

Charlie smiled at him and pulled her arm back into the car. "I don't know," she said. "Pretty boring." There was a part of her that did not want to tell him for the same reason she wanted him with her now: She did not want her new life to mix with the old. But John had told her something real, something personal, and she felt like she owed him the same in return.

"It's all right," she said at last. "My aunt is cool, even if she does sometimes look at me like she's not quite sure where I came from. School's fine, I have friends and all that, but it feels so temporary. I have another year, but I feel like I'm already gone."

"Gone where?" John asked, and Charlie shrugged.

"I wish I knew. College, I guess. I'm not sure what comes next."

"Nobody ever knows what comes next, I guess," he said. "Do you—?" He stopped himself, but she prodded him.

"Do I what?" she said teasingly. "Do I ever think of you?" He flushed, and she instantly regretted the words.

"I was going to say, do you ever see your mom," he said quietly.

"Oh," she said. "No, I don't." It exhausted Charlie to think of her mother, and she thought her mother felt the same. Too much hung between them—not quite blame, because neither of them were to blame for what had happened, but something close to it. Their pain, individual, radiated off them both like auras, pushing at each other like magnets with the poles reversed, forcing them apart.

"Charlie?" John was saying her name, and she looked over at him.

"Sorry," she said. "I drifted for a second."

"You got any music in this car?" he asked, and she nodded eagerly, seizing on the diversion. She bent over, picked up cassettes scattered on the floor, and started reading labels. He made fun of her tapes, she argued back, and after some playful bickering, she shoved a tape into the player and settled back again to stare out the window.

"I think this is where the map's usefulness ends." John gestured to the road ahead. "The whole area's pretty much blank; I think what we're looking for isn't going to be on this map." He folded the map and tucked it neatly to the side of the seat, craning his neck out the window to see what they were passing.

"Yeah," she said. It looked like they had returned to civilization. Single houses littered the fields, and dirt roads branched off in all directions. The landscape was mostly bushes and short trees, the whole area nestled between rows of low-lying mountains.

John looked at Charlie, hoping she would notice something that would point them in the right direction.

"Nothing?" he said, though her blank stare had already given him the answer.

"No," she said plainly. She didn't want to elaborate.

The houses became fewer and more scattered, and the fields of dry brush seemed to stretch wider, giving the whole area a feeling of desertion. John found himself glancing over at Charlie at short intervals, waiting for a signal, half expecting her to tell him to stop and turn around, but Charlie just stared into the distance, her eyes fixed on nothing, resting her cheek in her hand.

"Let's go back," she said finally, sounding resigned.

"We could have missed something," John said. He slowed the car, looking for a spot to make a U-turn. "We missed a lot back there; maybe it's down one of those dirt roads."

Charlie laughed.

"Really? You think we missed a lot?" She grew thoughtful. "No, none of this feels right. Nothing rings a bell." She felt a tear spill onto her cheek, and she swiped it away before John could notice.

"Okay, no worries," Charlie said abruptly, pulling herself back from reverie. "Let's grab a bite, just you and me." John smiled, still checking his mirrors for a place to turn. Charlie shivered. Then something caught her eye. She almost jumped in her seat, sitting straight up.

"STOP!" she shouted. John slammed on the brakes and the car skidded, dust billowing up all around the car. When they stopped, Charlie sat silently as John checked the rearview mirror again, his heart racing.

"Are you okay?" he said, but Charlie was already out of the car. "Hey!" he called after her, scrambling out of his seat belt and rushing to lock the car behind him.

Charlie was running back toward the town, but her eyes were on the field beside the road. He caught up quickly, trotting along beside her without asking questions. After a few minutes, Charlie slowed and began shuffling her feet on the ground, peering down as though she had lost something small and valuable in the dirt.

"Charlie?" John said. Until this moment he had not thought about what it was they were doing. It was an adventure, a chance to be alone with Charlie, to run off after a clue, but now she was starting to worry him. He brushed his hair back from his face. "Charlie?" he said again, his voice touched with concern, but Charlie did not look at him; she was intent on whatever she had found.

"Right here," she said. She made a sharp turn toward the edge of the road, where something protruded and snaked across the ground. John knelt carefully, brushing some of the loose dirt with his hand and exposing a flat metal beam. He kept going, uncovering a track that stretched across the road and went off into the field in both directions. It took him a moment to speak; it was as though the earth itself had tried to conceal it from them. *Be careful*, he thought with a minor pang of alarm, but he brushed aside the feeling. "I think we found your tracks," he said, looking up at Charlie, but she was nowhere in sight. "Charlie?" He took a quick look up and down the road, but there were no cars. "Charlie!" he called again, waving the dust away from his face and racing to catch up. When he reached her, he hung back a little, afraid to disturb her intense focus.

There was a cluster of trees up ahead, gathered together as though around a campfire, tall and short or thick and scraggly. Charlie dragged her foot along the track as she walked, as if it might vanish if she ceased to touch it.

"What is that, an old station?" John asked, squinting and blocking the sun with his hand. There was a long building nestled in the trees, its color blending in with the small grove, making it difficult to spot.

The tracks veered away, heading off toward the mountains, and Charlie stopped dragging her foot along them, letting them go. John finally caught up, and they walked through the dry grass together toward the grove of trees, not far away now.

"There has to be a road." Charlie strayed almost randomly, heading away from the building. John hesitated.

"But . . ." He gestured toward the building, then followed her, looking back to make sure he knew the way back to the car. Before long, the ground leveled out beneath their feet. Old pavement, broken with weeds and mounds of crumbling rock, stretched across the field in a narrow, almost hidden path, leading once again toward the small building.

"This is it," Charlie said softly. John approached her carefully, then stood at her side. They walked the road together, dodging around the pillars of grass that shot up from the breaks and holes. The tree was there, the one with reaching arms and ghastly face, but it was no longer frightening, no longer as Charlie remembered. It must have already been dead when she was a child, she realized. Its limbs had fallen off, leaving jagged holes where they had been, and they lay where they fell, rotting into the ground. The tree seemed a frail and weak shade of its former self, only recognizable by the stumps and bulges on its side that had made its face. Now even the face looked tired.

The building itself was long and dilapidated. It was a single story, with a dark roof and weather-beaten walls. The place had once been painted red, but time and sun and rain had won out over the paint; it was peeled and curling, whole long strips of it gone and the wood beneath showing, dark with what might be rot. Its foundation was overgrown with tall grass, and Charlie thought it looked as if it were sinking, as though the whole structure was slowly being swallowed by the earth. Charlie grabbed John's arm as they neared it, then let it go and straightened her back. She felt as though she were preparing for a fight, as if the building itself might attack if it sensed weakness.

Charlie went warily up the few steps to the door, sticking to the edges and testing the wood before she let down her full weight. The stairs held, but there were soft, splintered patches in the middle she didn't want to try. John didn't follow her right away, sidetracked by something nearly hidden in the grass.

"Charlie." He held it up: a battered metal sign with the painted words FREDBEAR'S FAMILY DINER in red script.

Charlie gave a gentle smile. *Of course this is it. I'm home.*

John came up the stairs behind her and set the sign down carefully by the door, and they went inside. The door swung open easily. Light streamed in through the windows on all sides, revealing emptiness and decay. Unlike Freddy's, this place had been cleaned out. The wooden floors seemed intact, but they were warped from weather. Sunlight was streaming in, unobstructed, and went where it wanted without furniture or people to block its path. Charlie looked up at the ceiling fan; it was still there, but one of its blades was missing.

There were double doors to their right with circular windows. Unlike the dining area, which was breached with sunlight and the sounds of the outside, the room behind the double doors was still pitch black. John was more interested in this than Charlie, and he carefully peered into one of the windows, obviously tempted to nudge it open and see what was inside. Charlie left him to his curiosity and walked farther into the dining room, which she only knew as the dining room through memory. Now it was a vacant and lonely room, stretching long and narrow, at least fifty feet, growing darker as it went. There was a slightly elevated stage at the end of the room, and Charlie realized as she looked around that the place had probably once been a dance hall, and the long desk by the entrance that her parents had used for a cash register had probably been a bar. She went over to it and saw that she was right: There were even grooves and scratches in the wood floor where barstools had once dug their feet. She tried to picture it, a dark bar with a country-western band playing on the stage, but she could not.

When Charlie looked at the stage, she could still see two animatronic animals in shadow, moving in unnatural twists and turns. She could hear echoes of carnival music and distant laughter. She could still smell the cigarette smoke in the air. She hesitated before going farther, as though the ghosts she remembered might linger on the stage. She tried to catch a glimpse of where John was. He finally had the door to the kitchen half-open and was sticking his head inside. Charlie turned her attention back to the stage and walked toward it across the creaking floor. Even the smallest sound was deafening, accompanied by faint whistles as the wind slipped through cracks in the windows and walls. Strips of wallpaper had peeled down and hung flat against the wall, inert until a breeze lifted them up, and they wagged like thin fingers pointing at Charlie as she walked.

Charlie stood at the base of the stage, studying the floor carefully for traces of what might have stood there before. All that remained were holes where bolts had once been. The corners looked blackened, with the shapes of coils and wires etched into dirt and wood.

Everything is gone.

Her head jerked toward the corner to her right; there was another door. *Of course there is another door. This is why you are here.* She stood still, looking at the door, but not ready to touch it. She was grasped with a strange and illogical fear, as though spiders and boogeymen might come rushing out.

The door was ajar. Charlie looked back toward John again, hesitant to go on without him. As though he heard her calling to him, he leaned out of the kitchen door with a wide-eyed expression. "This is really creepy." He was obviously enjoying himself, like a kid in a haunted house.

"Can you come with me?" Charlie's plea came as a surprise to John, who seemed pleased but irritated at the same time, having been enjoying his own adventure on the other side of the building. "Two seconds," he promised, then disappeared again.

She rolled her eyes, disappointed but not surprised that his childish curiosity would take priority. She rested the back of her hand against the aged wooden door and gently guided it open, bracing herself against whatever might be inside.

Whatever she had been expecting, this wasn't it. It was a closet, the inside extending off to her left about eight or nine feet into darkness. There were horizontal poles mounted along the walls where hangers had once been. Square shapes imprinted in the dust filled her mind with images of boxes, maybe speakers.

As she stepped inside, she pushed the door open all the way, trying to let in as much light as possible. As she walked farther in, she let her hand drag along the wall. Although nothing was there now, she could feel heavy cloth, coats, and sweaters hanging.

No. These were costumes.

Costumes had hung here in the dark, hiding their colors but allowing themselves to be felt by every cheek and small hand that passed through. Rubber-padded palms and fingers swayed this way and that. Reflections on false eyes passed overhead.

Charlie reached the end and turned to look back. She crouched down, looking up at the empty space. It didn't feel empty. She could still feel the costumes; they were hanging all around her. There was someone else in the closet with her, kneeling down at her own height. It was her friend, the little boy.

My little brother.

They were both playing and hiding together as they always did. *This time was different.* The little boy looked up toward the door suddenly as though they had been caught doing something they shouldn't have been doing. Charlie looked up as well. There was a figure in the door. It looked like one of the costumes was standing on its own, but it was motionless, so still that Charlie wasn't sure what she was seeing.

It was the rabbit, the yellowish-brown rabbit they loved, but it did not dance or sing, just stood there and stared at them, unblinking. They began to squirm under its gaze, and the little boy screwed up his face to wail. Charlie pinched his arm, seized with an instinctual sense that they must not cry. The rabbit looked back and forth from one to the other with those all-too-human eyes, ponderous, as though weighing and measuring them in some way that Charlie could not understand, like it was making a momentous decision. Charlie could see its eyes, its human eyes, and she was cold with terror. She felt the fear in her brother as well, felt it echoing between them, reverberating and growing because it was shared. They could not move, they could not scream, and finally the creature inside that patchwork, ragged yellow rabbit suit reached forward for the boy. There was a moment, one single moment, when the children still clung together, gripping hands, but the rabbit snatched the boy to his breast, yanking them apart, and fled.

From that moment the entire memory shattered with piercing and unrelenting screams, not her brother's, but her own. People rushed to help, her father picked her up and held her, but nothing could console her; she screamed and screamed, louder and louder. Charlie snapped back from her dream, the sound still high and painful in her ears. She was crouched down in silence. John stood at the door, not daring to interrupt.

She did not remember much of what had happened next; everything was dark. It was all a blur of images and facts she had pieced together later, things she might remember and others she might have imagined. She was never in the restaurant again. She knew her parents shuttered the doors immediately.

Then they moved to the new house, and Charlie's mother left a little while after that. Charlie did not remember her saying good-bye, although she knew her mother must have. Her mother would not have left without a good-bye, but it was just lost in the mist of time and grief like so much else. She remembered the first time she stood in the doorway of her father's workshop, the first day they were alone in everything. It was the day he began to build her a mechanical toy, a little dog who tilted its head from side to side. She smiled when she saw it finished, and her father looked at her the way he would look at her for the rest of his life, as though he loved her more than life itself and as though his love made him unbearably sad. She knew even then that something vital inside him had broken, something that could never be repaired. Sometimes he seemed to look right through her, as if he couldn't see her even when she was standing right in front of him.

Her father never again spoke her brother's name, and so Charlie learned not to speak it, either, as though to speak it would send them back to that time and unravel them both. She woke in the mornings and looked for the little boy, having forgotten in her dreams that he was gone. When she turned to where he would be and saw only her stuffed toys she would cry, but she would not say his name. She was afraid to even think it, and she trained her mind to shrink from it until she truly forgot, but deep inside she knew it: Sammy.

A rumbling sound rose, loud and low like a train passing, and Charlie startled.

"A train?" She looked around her, eyes wide; she was disoriented, not sure if she was in the past or present.

"It's okay. I don't think it's anywhere near here. Might just be a big truck." John took Charlie's arm and pulled her to her feet. "Did you remember something?" he whispered. He was trying to catch her gaze, but she was focused elsewhere.

"A lot." Charlie put her hand to her mouth, still staring into the darkness as if she could see the scene. John's hand on her arm was an anchor, and she clung fast to it. *This is real. This is now*, she thought, and she turned to him, seized by a fierce gratitude that he was there with her. She buried her face in his chest as if his body could shield her from what she had seen, and she let herself cry. John hugged her tight, one hand on her head, cautiously stroking her hair. They stayed that way for long moments, and at last she calmed, her breathing deep and even again. John loosened his grip on her, and as soon as he did, Charlie stepped back, suddenly aware of how close they had been.

John's hands were still suspended in midair from where Charlie had been. After a moment of shock, he lowered one and used the other to scratch his head.

"So . . ." He hoped for an answer to fill the silence.

"A rabbit," Charlie said calmly, looking toward the doorway. "A yellow rabbit." Her voice became graver as the image was still fresh in her mind.

"The one I saw the night Michael disappeared, the bear, I'm pretty sure he was yellow, too."

"I thought you said it was like the others," Charlie said.

"I thought it was. When everybody said Freddy was brown, that night we first met up, I just thought I was remembering it wrong. I mean, I really don't have a great memory for back then, you know? I didn't even remember what color my old house was. But then you said he was yellow, too."

"Yeah, they were yellow." She nodded; it was the answer he was expecting.

"I think it's connected—the animals from here, and the one I saw at Freddy's."

And the one that took my brother, Charlie thought. She took a final look around the place.

"Let's go back," she said. "I want to get out of here."

"Okay," John said.

As they headed to the door, a small object caught Charlie's eye, and she snatched it up. It was a twisted piece of metal, and as John watched, close by, she stretched it out, then let it snap back together with a loud *crack*, like a whip. John jumped.

"What is that?" he said, composing himself.

"I'm not sure," she said, but she slipped it into her pocket. John was watching her like there was something he wanted to say. "Let's go," Charlie said.

They began the trek back to the car. *Sammy, then years later Michael and the other kids—of course it's connected*, Charlie thought. *Lightning might strike twice, but not murder.*

"Can you drive again?" she asked after a long period of silence. The only sounds so far had been their shoes crunching through the dry grass.

"Yeah, of course," he said.

John managed to get the car turned around in the constricted space, and Charlie settled against the window, her eyes half-closed already. She watched the trees fly by outside her window and felt herself beginning to doze. The metal object in her pocket was digging into her leg, keeping her awake, and she repositioned it, thinking dreamily of the first time she saw one of the things.

She was sitting with Sammy in the restaurant, before it opened for the day; they were under a window, in a dusty beam of light, playing some invented game she could no longer remember, and their father came over, grinning. He had something to show them.

He held up the piece of twisted metal and showed them how it opened, then let it snap back in his hand. They both cried out in surprise, then started giggling and clapping their hands.

Their father did it again. "I could snap off your nose!" he said, and again they laughed, but quickly his face turned serious. "I mean it," he said. "This is a spring lock, and I want you to know how it works because it's very dangerous, and I don't ever want you touching these. This is why we never put our hands in the animal costumes; it's very easy to trigger these if you don't know what you're doing, and you could get hurt. It's like touching the stove—do we ever touch the stove?"

They shook their heads with a solemnity beyond their years.

"Good. Because I want you both to grow up with all your noses!" he cried, and he swept them up, one in each arm, swinging them around as they laughed. Suddenly there was a loud *snap*.

Charlie jolted out of sleep.

"What was that?"

"What was what?" John said. The car was off. Charlie looked around; they were back at the motel.

Charlie took a moment to reorient herself, then gave a reluctant smile. "Thanks for driving."

"What were you dreaming about?" John said. "You looked happy."

Charlie shook her head.

"I don't remember."

CHAPTER SIX

The other car was gone from the lot, and when they went into the room, there was a note on Charlie's pillow, written in Marla's big, loopy handwriting.

We're meeting for dinner at 6:30, and then going to you-know-where! she had written. *See you two soon—don't forget about the rest of us! XOXO Marla*

She had drawn a smiley face and a heart below her name. Charlie smiled to herself, folding the note and slipping it into her pocket without showing it to John.

"What does it say?" he asked.

"We have to meet them at the diner in"—she checked her watch—"an hour." John nodded. He was still standing in the doorway, waiting for something. "What?" Charlie said.

"I need to go change," he said, gesturing at the rumpled

clothing he was wearing. "Can I take your car?" He held up the keys and jangled them.

"Oh, yeah, of course. Just come back for me," Charlie said with a grin.

He smiled. "Of course," he added with a wink.

When the door closed behind him, Charlie let out a sigh. *Alone at last.* She was unaccustomed to so much company; she and Aunt Jen moved in their own orbits, meeting gladly from time to time throughout the day, but with the assumption that Charlie could take care of her own needs or would speak up if she could not. Charlie never spoke up. She could feed herself, get to school and back, and maintain her high grades and casual friendships. What could Aunt Jen do about nightmares? About questions she did not really want the answers to? What could Aunt Jen tell her that was not even more horrific than what she already knew? So she was not used to the sustained presence of other people, and it was a little tiring.

She showered quickly and pulled on new clothes, jeans and a black T-shirt, then lay back on the bed, staring up at the ceiling. She had a vague sense that her mind should be racing with excitement or horror at their discoveries, going over and over the memories she had awakened, searching for something new. Instead, she just felt blank. She wanted to be alone, to push the memories to the back of her mind where they belonged.

After what seemed like only a few short minutes, there was a knock on the door, and Charlie sat up, checking her watch. More time had passed than she realized; it was time to leave. She let John in.

"I have to put on my shoes," she said. She looked up at him as she knotted the laces. He had changed, this time into jeans and a T-shirt, a contrast with the formal clothes she had gotten used to. His hair was still wet, and there was something fresh and bright about him. She smiled a little.

"What?" he said when he noticed.

"Nothing," she said. "You still look dirty," she joked as she pushed past him. They got in the car. This time she drove, and when they reached the diner, Charlie turned off the engine and hesitated, not moving to leave the car.

"John," she said. "I don't want to tell anyone about Fredbear's."

"But—" He stopped himself. "Yeah," he said. "I think we forget this is your life and not just some adventure. It's fine; I can keep a secret."

"It's all our lives," she said. "We were all there. We can tell them later; I just want to sort some of it out for myself right now."

"You got it," he said, and he looked a little pleased. Charlie knew why—it was a secret between them, something she entrusted only to him.

When they went inside, everyone was already halfway

through dinner. Charlie realized with a sharp pang that she had not eaten all day, and she found herself suddenly starving. The waitress spotted them as they sat down and came over immediately. They talked intermittently: Lamar, Jason, and Marla had gone to a movie, and Carlton and Jessica had played video games at his house. But their conversation was cursory, just filling the time as they ate. Charlie barely listened, and she had the feeling that even those who were talking were paying little attention to their own words. There was an agitated energy among the group; they were all just waiting, their minds already focused on Freddy's.

"What about you two?" Jessica asked, looking at Charlie and John.

"Yeah, what about you two?" Marla echoed with a twinkle in her eye.

"We just went for a drive," John said quickly. "Got lost for a while."

"I bet you did," Carlton muttered into his burger, grinning slyly even though his mouth was full.

After dinner, the group hurried through the mall and toward the restaurant, hushed and cautious. As they passed through the atrium, their shoes made only soft sounds on the tiled floor, and no one spoke. Charlie had left the big flashlight in the car. They knew their way well enough by now, and the guard had almost seen them the night before; there was no reason to risk drawing extra attention. They came to the end of the hall, and Lamar, at the front of the group, stopped short. Charlie bumped into Marla before she realized what was happening, and she murmured an apology, then froze.

The night guard was blocking the alley behind Freddy's, his arms folded across his chest. He had no flashlight, and so he had been invisible, hidden in the darkness until they were almost upon him.

"I had a feeling you wouldn't leave it alone," he said with an odd, uneven smile.

Marla whispered something unpleasant under her breath.

"I could have you arrested for trespassing," he said. "Saw you here last night, but I couldn't see where you got to. I guess now I know," he added with a smirk.

There was something almost immediately off-putting about the man. He was tall and slightly too thin for his uniform, which bagged at the shoulders and waist, as if he had once been a more robust man but had lost his form somehow to illness or tragedy; his name tag, reading DAVE, hung askew on his chest. His skin was sallow, and his eyes were undercut by heavy lines, adding to the impression of longstanding ill health.

"What were you all doing back here anyway?" he demanded. "You kids partying? Drugs? I could have you arrested right now, you know." Charlie and John glanced at each other.

"We're sorry," Lamar said quickly. "We'll go. We don't have any drugs."

"Says who? Says you?" The guard wore an odd expression, and his words were harsh and fast; he seemed not to be responding to what they were saying. He looked angry, but his mouth kept quirking up at the corners, like he was trying not to smile.

"What do we do?" Jessica whispered.

"Probably the most action he's ever had out here," Carlton said with a hint of disdain, and Charlie remembered suddenly that Carlton's father was a cop. She remembered him in his uniform, tilting down his dark sunglasses at them with a mock-glare, then smiling, revealing the joke. The guard, however, looked like he meant it.

"We'll go," Lamar said again. "Sorry."

Charlie looked at the man, considering him: the ill-fitting uniform, his peaky, almost exhausted-looking features. He really could kick them off the property or even have them arrested for trespassing, but still, she could not really fear him. His inadequacy shone through him like a kind of negative charisma. He would always be shoved to the back of a crowd, always shouted down in an argument, always picked last, forgotten, ignored in favor of those who were simply more vital, more vigorously attached to life. Charlie frowned at herself. It was an unusual train of thought for her—she did not usually assume she could read the lives of strangers through the lines on their faces. But it gave her an idea.

"Why don't you come with us?" she said. "We just want to explore a little bit more, then we'll leave. You know your way around better than any of us," she added, hoping that some of the flattery would stick.

"And then we'll never come back again," Carlton said. The guard did not immediately dismiss the idea, and the others quickly chimed in with their own assurances. The guard peered at them one by one, fixing his gaze on each in turn. When he looked at Charlie, she looked away, not wanting to meet his eyes, as if she would be giving something away if she let him look too deeply. Once he had inspected them to his satisfaction, he nodded.

"Sure," he said. "Only because I've always wanted to take a walk in there myself." He jerked a thumb behind him, and, catching the surprise that must have shown on their faces, added, "I'm not an idiot. I've been working here for years, walked this building inside and out every night. You think I don't know what's back there?" Charlie felt herself flush; she had somehow assumed their discovery was unique. The guard looked down at his name tag suddenly, then pointed to it. "Name's Dave," he said.

"I'm Jason," Jason said, and, a little warily, the others recited their own names in turn. They stood there, looking at one another awkwardly for a moment, no one wanting to be the first to move, then Jessica shrugged.

"Come on," she said. She walked quickly to the scaffolding that hid the alley to Freddy's and pulled back the plastic, revealing the break in the wall, and they all filed through, squeezing past the piled boxes. Dave hung back politely, letting them all go first. He motioned to Charlie to go ahead.

I don't want you behind me, Charlie thought. She looked at Jessica, who wasn't moving, either.

"Please, go ahead," Charlie said with an edge in her voice, and Dave ducked his head shyly and went. Charlie followed him, and Jessica tucked the plastic carefully back where it was, concealing their passing even though there was no one left to catch them. As they made their way down the dank alley, Charlie touched her fingers to the brick wall, dragging her hand along it as if to guide her. The flashlights seemed a little dimmer now, though she knew it could only be her imagination.

They led the guard to the heavy wooden shelf that hid the entrance, and Lamar, John, and Jessica dragged it out of the way, revealing the door. Charlie expected their new companion to be impressed, but he just nodded, as if he had suspected this all along.

One by one, they entered the hall to the restaurant, and again Charlie lagged back from the group. She caught Carlton by the arm as he passed her.

"Carlton," she whispered. "Have you ever seen this guy?"

Carlton shook his head. "It's not *that* small a town; I don't know everybody."

Charlie nodded absently, her eyes still on the newcomer as they made their way down the long hallway into Freddy's main dining room. She had invited the guard because it seemed like the only way to get back in, but now she was beginning to regret it. Letting a stranger into Freddy's was like letting him into her home, like giving something up.

"What happened to the restaurant?" Lamar said, his tone carefully even, forcing a friendliness he could not have felt. "Why is it boarded up? And why is the mall abandoned anyway?" His voice sounded thin in the narrow hallway, a little muted.

"You don't know?" Dave said. "This town needs money, jobs, revenue, things like that, and one thing we've got a lot of is space. So they decided to build a big mall, try and attract businesses, maybe even tourists. They built up around where Freddy Fazbear's was, but when it came to it, no one would lease the restaurant, you know, because of what happened. So someone had the bright idea of sealing the whole place up, intact; someone who had a sentimental attachment to it, perhaps. I don't think they even tried to clear it out. But it wasn't enough. Something about that place spilled over into the rest of the building, maybe right down into the soil. No one wanted to bring their business here. Sometimes business owners, franchisers from outside the town, would come and look at the place, but they never signed the papers. Said it just didn't feel right. I think it's got an aura, a mystical energy, maybe, if you believe in that sort of thing." Dave wiggled his fingers in the air as though casting a spell.

"I don't believe in that sort of thing," Lamar said shortly, but the guard did not seem to notice his tone.

"To each his own," he said. "All I know is, no one ever wanted their stores here, and they abandoned the construction before the building was even finished. Now nobody comes up here except kids wanting to screw around. And me," he added with what sounded like pride. He must have felt possessive, Charlie thought, the only one who ever came here for years and years. It must have felt like it belonged to him, this strange, half-finished building. To him, they must be the invaders.

They came to the end of the hallway, and the space opened up before them. Jessica ran ahead to the control room beneath the stage, her flashlight bobbing merrily ahead of her. She disappeared for a moment, then hit the light switch, and all at once the room was warm and bright. Charlie stopped, blinking in the sudden light. Dave brushed past her, and as he did something caught her eye: There was a scar on his neck, curved and ugly, almost a perfect half-moon. The tissue was knotted and white—the cut that made it must have been a deep one. Only a few feet away, Dave turned in a circle, taking in the restaurant, awed, and as he did, Charlie saw that the scar had a twin; the same half-moon, in the same place on the other side of his neck. She shivered a little. The marks were too clean, too perfectly placed; they almost looked deliberate.

The group fanned out. Carlton, for some reason, headed toward the kitchen, and Jason wandered away toward the arcade again.

"Be careful!" Marla called after him, but she was already following Lamar to the control room to join Jessica. Charlie hung back, and John stayed with her. There was something different in the air, Charlie thought. It felt thinner, like she had to breathe deeper to get enough oxygen. *It's just a guy*, she told herself, but that was the problem. They had brought an outsider in with them, and now the restaurant felt less secure, no longer hidden away. Freddy's had been breached. Freddy, Bonnie, and Chica had begun to jerk in their stiff, single movements. Charlie looked at Dave, but he did not appear surprised. *He's been here before*, she thought. Then: *Of course he's been here before. The whole town used to come here back then.*

John motioned her on, and reluctantly she went with him to the control room, Dave tagging along behind them like a stray.

In the booth, Jessica was hunched over, pressing buttons, and Lamar was studying the control board, trying to make sense of it. Dave peered intently over their shoulders, watching. He was nodding slightly to himself, wrapped up in some private calculation, and when Jessica stepped back and stretched, he cleared his throat.

"Um," he said. "Could I try?" He drew himself up a little, extending his arm graciously.

Jessica and Lamar exchanged glances, then shrugged.

"Why not?" Jessica said. They shuffled around so that he could reach the board, and he stared down at it for a long moment without moving, then touched a short series of buttons. A hum rose from the speakers, a long, low tone that did not waver.

"Whoa," Jessica said and pointed to the monitors. Charlie saw movement on the screen and backed out of the control room to look for herself. Onstage, the animals were dancing. Crudely, awkwardly, without the grace or complexity Charlie remembered, but they were moving in sequences, not just one motion at a time.

Charlie went back to the control room but did not go beyond the door.

"How did you do that?" she snapped, not caring if it was rude. Dave raised his hands in the air.

"Beginner's luck," he said. "I just pressed some buttons."

"Right," Charlie said. She rubbed her temples. "Can someone please turn off the speakers?"

Lamar darted forward and flipped a switch, and the sound died. Despite the silence, Charlie felt as if she could still hear it, whining away inside her head. She closed her eyes for a moment, and when she opened them, Jessica and Lamar had gone back to working the controls, but there was a caution to their movements, and they glanced at each other every few seconds as if seeking reassurance. Charlie looked at John. His arms were folded across his chest, and his eyes were trained on the back of Dave's head.

In the arcade, Carlton pressed some random buttons on a game console, knowing nothing would happen, then turned around, finding himself the subject of an eleven-year-old's resentful stare.

"What?" he said.

"I'm not a baby," Jason said. "You don't have to watch me."

"What? Jason, I'm not watching you, I'm just hanging out with you. I'm not Marla. Go stick your tongue in an electric socket, for all I care." He waggled his eyebrows comically, and Jason laughed.

"Okay, then, maybe I will," he said. He scanned the baseboards for a socket, briefly considering calling Carlton's bluff, but when he glanced back, Carlton had already wandered off. Jason bit his lip and rocked on his heels, feeling foolish. After a moment, he went back to the drawings on the wall. There were too many drawings to peruse each one in turn, but Jason suspected he would not need to. As they had the night before, the drawings would come to him. They *wanted* to be found. All Jason had to do was look.

The drawings in the arcade gave up nothing: They were just children's grubby art, faded with age. He went back out into the dining room, still hugging the walls and scanning them, hunting for something that was more than crayon.

"What're you up to, Jason?" Lamar was suddenly behind him. Jason turned around and studied him for a moment, considering. He liked Lamar, even if his friendliness could be traced easily to his interest in Marla. Lamar had bent down so his head was almost level with Jason's, and Jason leaned toward him and whispered, "The drawings are moving."

Lamar drew back, and for a moment a look of real alarm crossed his face, but it was fleeting. Jason bit his lip, waiting, and Lamar grinned at him, then reached out to pat him on the head.

"Okay, Jason. We'll get you the help you need," he said heartily, and Jason laughed and slapped Lamar's hand away.

"Shut up, seriously," Jason said with a hint of sheepishness, and Lamar patted his head again and headed off. As soon as Lamar was a few feet away, Jason rolled his eyes. *What do you think I am, your pet?* He gave his hair a violent tussle as if he could shake loose whatever Lamar had done to him, then went back to the wall, concentrating.

He had made his way all along one wall and was turning the corner when it happened: a flicker, just out of the corner of his eye, almost a shimmering. He stopped. *Which one was it?* He scanned the drawings again, going up and down the wall carefully, around the place he thought he had seen movement, but there was nothing. He started over, stopping to look at each crayon scribble, and then it happened again. He seized on it this time, his eye finding the drawing just as the shimmer of movement stopped, and just as he did, he saw another, so brief he would have ignored it, just a trick of the light, had he not been watching for it. It was above the first and maybe two feet to the left; his eyes darted back and forth, trying to see both at once. Suddenly, there was a third movement in a drawing between the two, this one more noticeable. This time he almost, almost saw the drawing shift before it was still again. Sitting back on his heels, Jason looked at the three drawings, each in turn. The crayon was black, and they all looked like they had been drawn by the same kid, all with two figures in the foreground: a child and a rabbit.

Jason glanced around the room. His sister and the others still seemed to be engaged by the stage; Lamar had gone back to join them. Jason pulled the drawing he had found the night before from his pocket. He smoothed it out, pressing it to the surface of the floor, then, slowly, he peeled its linty tape out flat and stuck the paper to the wall just at his eye level. He stared at the wall, waiting.

Nothing happened.

Jason frowned. He had been so certain these would tell him something, but they were just drawings. The child and the bunny stood in the middle of the paper, in one close together, in another far apart. But there was nothing there that could be called a story. *Oh well.* He started to look over at the others again—and the highest one began to move.

This time he saw the shift: The crayon lines twisted and slid on the page, moving of their own accord, too fast to follow. When the first stopped moving, another started, they continued one after the other until the last, the one he had just put back, was finished. Jason watched, eyes wide, his heart pounding, but by the time he realized what was happening, it was over. The figures were fixed in place, and now they did tell a story. In the first, a child was sitting alone. In the second, Bonnie appeared behind the child. In the next, Bonnie had snatched the child, lifting it off the ground.

In the last, the child was screaming.

His eyes wide and his heart racing, Jason stepped back. He was transfixed: His body suddenly felt leaden, too heavy to run. A sound arose, like wind rustling the pages on the wall, though they hung motionless before him. The sound rushed

and grew, louder and louder until wind gave way to screaming. Jason clapped his hands over his ears as pages began to
drop from the walls, landing with loud crashes, as if they
were made of something far heavier than paper. As he
watched, the fallen pages turned a dark red, soaking through
with color as they touched the floor. Jason turned to run, but
his path was blocked as pages tumbled from the ceiling in a
torrent. One landed on his shoulder, another on his back and
then another, and they clung to him, wrapping around him
as if they would suffocate him. Jason felt his legs buckle
under the weight, dropping at last to one knee.

As he braced himself under the storm of paper, the room
began to shake violently. Jason gritted his teeth, trapped—
and suddenly it was over. The red-soaked papers were gone,
there was nothing on his back, and Marla had him by the
shoulder and was staring at him, wide-eyed.

"Jason, what on earth is wrong with you?"

Jason scrambled to his feet, brushing himself off as if he
were covered with invisible insects.

"The pictures were falling on me," he said urgently, still
panicked, but as he looked back at the wall, he realized that
the room was silent and still. A single picture had fallen from
its place. Marla looked down at it, then back to her brother,
and shook her head. She leaned close and hissed into his ear,
"You embarrass me." She let loose her grip after a moment,
her face almost blank, and walked away. Jason stumbled as he

got to his feet but followed as quickly as he could, keeping his eyes trained on the walls as they went.

In the control room, Dave had his hands on the buttons, his fingers wandering lightly over them without pressing anything. The movement looked careless, instinctual, like a habit. Charlie leaned close to John.

"He's been here before," she whispered. "Look at the way he touches the controls."

"Maybe he's just good with computers," John offered, not sounding convinced.

"Can you make them dance again?" Jessica asked. Dave barely seemed to acknowledge the question. His mouth hung slightly open, and he seemed to be staring at something none of them could see. In the bright lights, they could all see that his uniform was grubby and torn in places, his face poorly shaven and his eyes a little unfocused. He looked less like a guard than a vagrant, and he looked at them all as if he had wandered in ages ago and they were the newcomers. It took him a moment to register the question.

"Sure, let's see what we can do," he said. He smiled at her, his mouth askew. His eyes were a little too intent on her face, holding her gaze just a little too long. Jessica swallowed, seized with an instinctive revulsion, but she smiled back politely.

"All right," Dave said. "I've been here a few times before; I think I can work some magic."

Charlie and John exchanged glances.

"You've been here before?" John said in a careful, even tone, but Dave ignored him, or did not hear.

There was a keypad to the far left of the control board that no one had touched yet, as it did not appear to be connected to anything. Now Dave reached for it and began to press the buttons quickly, as if he had done it a hundred times before. He gave Jessica a conspiratorial glance. "For special occasions, you can request a dance." He smiled at her again with that crooked intensity.

"Great," Jessica said, breathing a sigh of relief. Anything to get out of such forced proximity to this man. She looked at Lamar. "I'm going to go look. Will you take over?"

"Yeah, sure," he said, scooting forward to fill the vacancy as Jessica and Dave made their way out to the show area.

Onstage, the lights were flashing in patterns, accompanying music that no longer played, and Bonnie's mouth was moving as though in song. His eyelids closed for long blinks, then opened again with loud clicks, his glass eyes moving from side to side. One large blue hand rose and fell, strumming exaggeratedly on the red guitar whose strings had long since gone missing.

"Lamar, how much of this are you doing?" Carlton said, suitably impressed.

"Not much!" Lamar called back. "Most of it seems preprogrammed."

Bonnie turned to them, and Jessica startled as he seemed to look right at her. But he turned away just as quickly to face the rows of empty seats, lifting his head to sing.

"It's strange seeing them like this," Jessica said, taking a step back to get a better view. Bonnie's foot tapped along in rhythm, and his mouth opened and closed with song. There was no voice; there was no music. There was only a strange humming coming from the speakers and an orchestra of mechanical snaps and squeaks. Bonnie sped up, strumming and tapping faster. His eyes suddenly seemed out of sync, looking left while the head went right, then rolling back into his head.

Dave approached the stage with deliberate steps. "Nervous little fella, aren't you?" He smiled, seemingly unbothered as the rabbit moved faster and faster.

"Hey, Lamar, can you take it down a notch?" Jessica called.

Bonnie's arms began convulsing violently, his mouth open but stuttering, his eyes throwing their gaze in seemingly random directions.

"Lamar! Something's wrong!" Jessica cried.

Bonnie's foot jerked upward with a sound like a gunshot, yanking free the bolt that anchored him to the stage.

"Lamar!" Carlton climbed onto the stage and hurried to Bonnie, trying to search the rabbit for an off button as he ducked its erratic swings.

"Carlton, get down, you idiot!" Jessica ran to the stage.

Bonnie was moving too fast, out of control as if his program had hit a glitch. He was no longer following the dance sequence they all remembered so well. He began to convulse and thrash. Carlton scrambled back, trying to get away, but Bonnie's arm broke away from the guitar, swinging out and hitting Carlton across the chest, knocking him off the stage. He landed on his back and stayed down, gasping for breath.

"Lamar!" Jessica shouted. "Lamar, turn it off!"

"I don't know how!" he yelled back.

Jessica knelt down beside Carlton, looking helplessly at him. She tapped his shoulder insistently.

"Carlton, are you okay? Carlton? Look at me!"

Carlton gave a small laugh that sounded more like a cough, then grabbed her hand and pulled himself up to sit.

"It's okay," he said. "Just got the wind knocked out of me." Jessica still looked worried. "I just need a minute," he assured her, the words still coming in little wheezes.

In the control room, Lamar pressed button after button frantically, but on the screens he could still see Bonnie moving wildly and at random, not responding to anything he did. Charlie rushed in, pushing him out of the way, but it took her only seconds to see that the buttons were powerless. She locked eyes with Lamar for a moment. *We aren't in control,* she thought. As one, they rushed from the control room to help the others.

Jessica screamed, a short, high-pitched sound, and Marla and John ran to her, Charlie and Lamar arriving seconds later. All the animals were moving now in that same fitful way, cycling through their programmed movements at random with a desperate, panicked air. The lights began to pulse, flickering rapidly on and off. The stage lights did the same, the colors appearing and disappearing so that the whole space was washed first in bright gold, then a sickly green, then a bruised and vicious purple. They blinked like strobes, and the effect was nauseating. The speakers blared brief bursts of static, cutting in and out like the lights, and beneath the static was the same sound they had heard the night before, the growling of a voice too low to be human, too indistinct to be speaking words.

The group came together cautiously, not quite trusting their own senses. The lights throbbed savagely, and as Charlie walked toward her friends, she could not be sure how far away they were or what was right in front of her. They huddled in the middle of the floor, staring at the animals as they rattled and rocked as if with their own agenda. Carlton got to his feet; Jessica watched him with concern, but he waved her off.

"I told you, I'm fine," he said, shouting to be heard over the intermittent noise.

Charlie stood fixed in place, unable to take her eyes off the animals. *They're trying to get away*, she thought. It was a child's thought, and she tried to dismiss it, but it clung as she watched them, scarcely noticing the fitful flickering of the lights and sound. The animatronic creatures didn't look like they were glitching; their movement seemed not mechanical but hysterical, like there was something they needed desperately to do but, horribly, could not.

"Where's Dave?" John said suddenly. Charlie met his eyes with a rising dread. *Oh no.* They all looked around, but the guard was nowhere in sight.

"We have to find him," Charlie said.

"He probably left already; who cares?" Marla said, her voice high and frightened.

"I'm not worried about him," she said grimly. She turned to John. "Come on," she said, setting off toward the hallway to the right of the stage. He glanced at the rest of the group over his shoulder, then followed Charlie at a brisk pace.

"We should find the other control room and see if we can stop all this from there," Jessica said crisply, taking charge. "You and Jason go look for Dave," she told Marla.

"I'll go with them," Lamar said quickly.

"Control room?" Carlton said, looking at Jessica.

"Control room," she confirmed. They all set off, moving slowly. The strobing lights distorted the space in front of them, seeming to throw up obstacles that were not there, obscuring the ones that were. The effect was disorienting, a constantly shifting maze of light and noise.

"Ow!" Marla shouted, and everyone stopped short.

"Are you okay?" Carlton yelled.

"Yeah, I just bumped into this stupid merry-go-round," she called back. The speakers were momentarily noiseless, but they shouted across the small distance as if there were a canyon between them.

In another hallway, Dave was moving toward a goal. Without the others there to watch, he moved fast, scuttling almost sideways and darting his eyes back over his hunched shoulders from time to time to see he was not followed. There was a large key ring at the belt of his uniform, but only a few keys hung from it. He selected one, opened a door, and let himself into the restaurant's office. He closed the door quickly behind him, cushioning it against noise even though the group would never hear it this far away or note it between their own shouts and the blaring of the speakers. He turned on the overhead light; it was steady, illuminating the room without a flicker. On the far wall, there was a tall closet flat against the wall, and he used another key on his ring to open it. Dave stood still in the open door for a long moment, breathing deeply. As he did, his back straightened and his hollow chest seemed to expand, drawing an uncharacteristic confidence from what he saw. An odd, thin smile on his lips,

Dave reached out with his fingertips, savoring the moment, and brushed yellow fur.

Jessica and Carlton hurried away down the hall toward the second control room, but Marla and the two boys moved more slowly, sticking their heads into the party rooms, then the arcade. The rooms appeared empty, but in the constantly changing light, Jason thought as they moved on, it would be easy to miss just about anything. Having checked the area, Marla and Lamar headed back into the main room.

"Where are Jessica and Carlton?" Lamar shouted over another burst of garbled sound. Jason stopped and looked back, and in a fleeting instant he saw it: a rabbit, outlined in the hall for a split second as the lights flashed on him, then vanishing and appearing again in his place in the party room they had just left.

"Marla!" Jason shouted. "MARLA!" His voice was shrill, agitated.

She whirled around. "What? Are you okay?"

"I saw Bonnie! He was there!"

"What?" Marla's eyes went automatically to the stage. Bonnie was still there, moving back and forth in the same odd, spastic movements. "Jason, look, he's there. He can't move off the stage."

Jason looked. Bonnie was there. *I saw him*, he thought, looking back down the hallway, but it was empty.

Jessica came running up, out of breath.

"Is everyone okay? I heard screaming."

"We're fine," Lamar said. "Jason thought he saw something."

"Where's Carlton?" Marla said. She rubbed her temples. "Ugh, this light is giving me such a headache."

"He's still fighting with the controls," Jessica said. "We should find Charlie and John; I think we need to get out of here."

"I think they went that way," Lamar said, pointing to the hall at the far end of the room, just past the stage.

"Come on," Jessica said. Jason followed as the group crossed the main dining room again, maneuvering cautiously around tables and chairs. He looked back as they reached the hall. Suddenly, Bonnie appeared again, darting out from the arcade and ducking into the hall that led to Pirate's Cove. Jason watched his sister and the others file through the doorway, then slipped away before they could see him go. He ran across the room, intent on following the rabbit, then slowed his pace when he reached the dark hallway.

The lights in the little hall were completely out, and though he could see nothing, it was a minor relief from the pulsing strobes. Jason hugged the wall as he moved, trying to scan ahead of him for signs of movement, but it was too dark; his eyes had not adjusted. After what seemed like ages, he came out of the hall and into Pirate's Cove. From a distance, he could hear his sister's voice, calling his name. *Guess they noticed I'm gone*, he thought wryly. He ignored it. Crossing the room, he peered down the other hallway—the one that led to more party rooms—but it was so dark that he could scarcely see more than a few feet ahead.

Turning back, he approached the little stage, the OUT OF ORDER sign still strung across it. *As if anything in this place is in order.* Suddenly, the curtain moved, and Jason froze. The curtain began pulling back. Jason couldn't bring himself to run. All went dark, then the lights came on suddenly to reveal Carlton standing in front of him, having emerged from behind the curtain.

"What are you doing back here by yourself? Come on, let's go," Carlton greeted him with a warm smile.

Awash with relief, Jason took a step forward, opening his mouth to speak—and stiffened, struck still with fear.

Bonnie suddenly broke through the darkness, appearing beneath the stage lights before them. But it was not Bonnie; this rabbit's yellow fur was almost blinding in the light. He rushed at them, and before Jason could cry out, the giant rabbit had a hold of Carlton from behind, smothering his face with a giant, matted paw and wrapping his other great arm around Carlton's chest, gripping tightly. Carlton struggled silently, hitting and kicking, but the creature barely seemed to notice. He screamed into the rabbit's paw, but the sound was swallowed whole. As he fought, the rabbit slunk back the way he came, dragging Carlton with him like a prize from the hunt.

Jason watched them go, agape. His heart raced, and his breath was shallow; the stifling air around him made him light-headed. A noise came from behind him, the grinding screech of rusted metal beginning to move, and he leaped forward and turned, moving just in time to avoid a hook as it plunged swiftly downward. Foxy's eyes flashed in synchrony with the lights above, and for a dizzy moment it seemed to Jason that those eyes were the controlling force behind it all, that if Foxy closed his eyes, every light might go out. The animal did not move like the others. It slowly, purposefully, rose between the gap in the curtains, its gleaming eyes reaching a staggering height.

"Jason!" It was Charlie's voice, he knew, but he kept staring back and forth, first at Foxy, then at the place where Carlton had been stolen away. "Jason!" she called again, and then she and John were beside him, touching him, shaking him out of his ghastly reverie. John grabbed his hand and pulled him into a run. In the main room, the others were already halfway down the hallway to the outside door, all but Marla, who was waiting anxiously at the entrance, her face flooding with relief when she saw Jason.

"Marla, Bonnie, he took Carlton!" Jason yelled, but she just put a hand on his back and pushed him through the door and into the hall.

"Go, Jason!"

"But I saw Bonnie take Carlton!" he cried, but he ran, afraid to stop.

They ran down the hall to the outside door, all bouncing with a frightened impatience as they filed through to the alley one by one; there was no way to go faster. When they were all through, Charlie looked down the hallway for a long moment, but there was no one coming. She shoved the door closed and stepped out of the way as Lamar and John wrestled the shelf back into place, blocking it off.

"No one saw Dave," Charlie said. It was not a question. They all shook their heads. "He must have taken off when the lights started going haywire," Lamar offered, but he did not sound convinced.

"Carlton!" Jason cried out again. "Carlton is still in there! Bonnie took him!"

They all glanced around. Carlton was not with them.

"Oh no," Jessica said. "He's still inside."

"Bonnie took him!" Jason said, choking out the words one by one, his voice shaking. "I saw it. Bonnie was there, he was in Pirate's Cove, and he grabbed Carlton and carried him away. I couldn't stop him." He scrubbed a sleeve across his eyes, wiping tears.

"Oh, sweetheart . . ." Marla hugged him, and he clung to her, hiding his face in her shirt. "No, it was a trick of the light. Bonnie couldn't do that; he's just a robot. He was onstage when we left."

Jason closed his eyes. He had only glanced for a second at the main stage as they were leaving, but it was true: Bonnie had been there, moving in strange and clumsy twists and bends, stuck in place. He pulled away from his sister's arms.

"I saw it," he insisted, more weakly. "Bonnie took him."

The others exchanged glances above his head. Charlie looked at Marla, who shrugged.

"We have to go back in," Charlie said. "We have to get him." Jessica was nodding, but John cleared his throat.

"I think we need help," he said. "It's not safe in there."

"Let's get Carlton's dad," Marla said. "I'm not taking Jason back in there."

Charlie wanted to protest, but she bit her tongue. They were right; of course they were right. Whatever had just happened was beyond them. They needed help.

CHAPTER SEVEN

They made their way back through the corridors of the abandoned mall, not bothering to be cautious with their footsteps or the beams of their lights.

"So much for being sneaky," Charlie said darkly, but no one responded. By silent consensus their pace quickened steadily; by the time they reached the parking lot they were almost running. Spotting her car as they came out the front door, Charlie felt an almost physical relief to see it, like it was an old friend.

"Someone should stay here," she said, pausing with her hand on the door handle. "We can't leave Carlton."

"No," Marla said firmly. "We're leaving now." They looked at her in surprise for a moment—suddenly, she was talking to them all the way she talked to Jason: *Sister knows best*. Lamar and Jason exchanged glances, but no one said anything. "We're going into town. All of us," she added, giving Charlie a warning look, "and we're finding help."

They hurried into their cars. As Charlie took the wheel, John got into the passenger seat, and she smiled tightly at him. Jessica climbed into the back a moment later, and Charlie felt a minor disappointment; she had wanted to talk to him alone. *We're running for help, it's not a date,* she scolded herself, but that hadn't really been the point. He felt safe, a touchstone amid the strange things that were happening all around them. She looked over at him, but he was staring out the window. They pulled out of the lot, following Marla's car as she sped into the darkness.

When they reached the town, Marla yanked her car to the side of the main street and stopped, and Charlie followed suit. Before the car had fully come to a halt, Jessica leaped out of the backseat and started running. Marla followed a step behind. They stopped in front of the movie theater, and only then did Charlie see that there was a cop in uniform beneath the marquee, leaning back against his black-and-white car. His eyes widened at the sight of the young women barreling toward him, and he took an involuntary step back as Marla started talking without pausing for breath.

". . . Please, you've got to come," Marla was finishing as the others caught up.

The cop looked a little bewildered. He had a shiny pink face, and his hair was so short it was entirely covered by his hat. He was young, maybe midtwenties, Charlie realized, and he was looking at them skeptically.

"Is this an actual emergency?" he said. "You may not realize it, but pranks can get you into real trouble."

Jessica rolled her eyes and stepped forward, closing the distance between them.

"We're not playing a prank," she said crisply, and Charlie suddenly remembered how tall she was. "Our friend is trapped in that abandoned shopping mall, and it's your job to help us."

"The shopping mall?" He seemed confused, then looked in the direction they'd come from. "THAT shopping mall?" His eyes widened, then he frowned at them reproachfully, looking remarkably like a disappointed parent despite his youth. "What were you doing up there in the first place?"

Charlie and Marla exchanged glances, but Jessica didn't blink.

"Deal with us later. He's in danger, and you have to help us, Officer—" She leaned in and peered at his name tag. "Officer Dunn. Do you want me to go to the fire department?"

Despite her fear, Charlie almost laughed. Jessica said it as if she were in a store, threatening to take her business elsewhere. It was so absurd it should have gotten her no more than a puzzled glance, but Dunn reached for his radio hastily.

"No," he said. "Hang on."

He pressed a button, and the radio emitted a short burst of static. Charlie felt a brief chill at the sound, and as she looked around, she saw John stiffen and Jason take a tiny step closer to Marla. Not seeming to notice their reactions, Dunn barked incomprehensible sounds into his radio, talking in cop code, and Charlie suddenly had a flash of memory, of running around the yard, whispering into walkie-talkies with Marla. They could never understand each other on the cheap toys her father had found in the drugstore bargains bin, but they didn't mind; actual communication was never the point.

"Charlie, come on!" Jessica shouted at her, and Charlie came back to herself. Everyone was heading toward the cars and piling back in. Marla pulled out in front, and the cop followed her, with Charlie bringing up the rear.

"Why doesn't he have the siren on?" Jessica said. Her voice was thin and brittle, as if her only choices were a sharp tongue or tears.

"He doesn't believe us," John said softly.

"He should have the siren on," Jessica said, and this time it was almost a whisper. Charlie's knuckles were white on the steering wheel as she stared straight ahead at the cop's red taillights.

When they got back to the mall, Jessica dashed ahead, forcing the rest of them to run behind her. Charlie didn't mind; it felt good to run, purposeful. Lamar was talking to the cop as they ran, shouting over the noise of their thudding feet.

"The restaurant is all boarded up, but there's a door left open," he said, the words broken by his uneven breathing. "Behind the plastic—you move it—dark alley—Carlton smells like feet." Officer Dunn's step stuttered briefly, but he regained his stride. When they reached the alley, they slowed their pace, moving more cautiously down the narrow hall until they came to the door.

"Right here," John said, and Dunn moved forward to help with the shelf. They drew it back too fast, the contents rattling and wobbling. The shelf pitched backward, and tools, cables, and paint cans full of nails crashed to the floor.

"Ow!" John yelled as a hammer bounced off his foot. They all watched as the things scattered, some rolling away and vanishing down the dark corridor.

"What?!" Jason wailed, and they all looked up from the spill. He was pointing at the door.

"What is this?" Marla gasped. The door had chains strung across it from top to bottom, three enormous padlocks holding them all together. The links were bolted into the metal frame of the door, and they were heavy, too heavy to cut without special tools. It was all rusty; the whole thing looked as though it had been there for years. Charlie walked up to the door and touched a chain, as if to be sure it was real.

"This wasn't here," she said, the words sounding inane even as she spoke.

"We have to get him out!" Jason cried haltingly, his hands covering his eyes. "Bonnie is going to kill him, and it's my fault!"

"What's he talking about?" the police officer said, looking at them with renewed suspicion. "Who is Bonnie, and why is she going to hurt your friend?"

"He's—it's a robot," Charlie said quickly. "The robots from Freddy Fazbear's are still there, and they still work."

"Freddy Fazbear's." Dunn's face flushed, and he looked at the door again. "I used to go there as a kid," he said softly, his tone caught between nostalgia and fear. He caught himself quickly and cleared his throat.

"He came to life," Jason insisted, no longer making the effort to hide his tears. Dunn bent down to his height, his tone softening.

"What's your name?" he asked.

"We have to get him out," Jason repeated.

"His name is Jason," Marla said, and Jason glared at her.

"Jason," Dunn said. He put a hand on Jason's shoulder, glancing at the others with an obvious suspicion. *He thinks we made him say that*, Charlie realized. Jason wriggled in Dunn's grasp, but the officer did not let him go, looking him in the eye to ask the next question: "Jason, did they tell you to say this? What's going on here?"

Irritated, Jason pulled free and took a large step back.

"That's what really happened," he said firmly.

Officer Dunn exhaled, a long, slow vent of frustration, then got to his feet, shedding his kid-friendly act. "So, the robots took your friend," he said. *I know what you're trying to pull*, said his tone.

"We were in there," Charlie stated flatly, keeping her voice level, as if saying it calmly and plainly enough might convince him that they were not telling lies. "Our friend didn't make it out."

The officer looked again at the chains.

"Look," he said, apparently deciding to give them the benefit of the doubt. "I don't know how you got in there in the first place, and right now I don't want to know. But the machinery in there is old; it hasn't been touched in ten years. Chances are it's pretty spooky. Heck, I wouldn't want to go in there. So even though I can't blame you for being freaked out, I can guarantee you those robots in there aren't moving by themselves. That place is dead, and it needs to be left alone," he said with a forced chuckle. Jason set his jaw, but he didn't say anything. "I think you all need to go home," Dunn finished, the statement sounding more like a threat than advice.

They looked at one another.

After a moment of uncomfortable silence, Jessica looked to Charlie. "These chains weren't here before. Right?" she faltered, looking back at her friends for confirmation like she was beginning to doubt her own memory.

"No," Charlie said instantly. "They weren't. We aren't leaving, and we need your help."

"Fine," Dunn said shortly. "What's his name?" He produced a notebook seemingly from nowhere.

"Carlton Burke," Jessica said. She was about to spell it for him, when suddenly Officer Dunn put down his pen and closed his eyes, his nostrils flaring.

He glared at them, no longer looking quite so young. "I'm going to give you one more chance. Tell me exactly what happened." He spoke slowly, emphasizing the spaces between his words. He was in control again, no longer out of his depth, like he suddenly understood everything.

They tried to explain all at once, talking over one another. Jessica's voice was loudest and calmest, but even she could not keep her anxiety from bleeding through. Charlie hung back, quiet. *Tell me exactly what happened.* Where were they supposed to start? With the night? With the week? With

Michael? With the first time her father picked up a circuit board? How was anyone ever to respond to something like "tell me what happened"? The cop was nodding, and he picked up the radio again, but this time he spoke comprehensibly.

"Norah, call Burke. It's his kid. I'm up at the old mall site." There was an answering burst of static, and the officer turned his attention back to them. "Come on," he said.

"Come on where?" John said.

"Off the property."

Marla started to protest, but Dunn interrupted. "I'm escorting you off the property," he said. He pulled the baton from his belt and pointed with it.

"Come on," Lamar said. Jason was still staring sullenly at the ground, and Lamar gave him a gentle nudge on the shoulder. "Jason, come on. We have to do what he says now, okay?"

"But Carlton!" Jason said loudly, and Lamar shook his head.

"I know. It's okay, we'll find him, but we have to go now." He guided Jason toward the mouth of the alley, and everyone followed. The police officer walked behind, following Charlie a little too closely. She sped up, but so did he, and she resigned herself to being shadowed.

When they got to the parking lot, he directed them to wait by the car and walked off a few paces, speaking into the radio again, too far away to hear.

"What's going on?" Jason said. He was beginning to whine; he heard the tone in his voice and tried to modulate it. *I am not a little kid*, he reminded himself. No one answered, but Marla rubbed his back absently, and he did not move away.

Long minutes passed in silence. Jessica sat on the hood of the car, facing away from the rest of the group. Charlie wanted to go to her, but she did not. In her distress, Jessica was closing down, going stiff and cold and snippy, and Charlie did not think she had what it took to break through that without breaking down herself.

"Was he talking about Carlton's dad?" Charlie asked, but no one had time to answer. Headlights appeared, and a car pulled in beside them. The man who got out was tall and thin, and his light hair could have been either blond or gray.

"Carlton's dad," Marla whispered, a late answer to Charlie's question. The man smiled as he approached.

"Carlton's dad," he confirmed. "Though since you're all grown up now, you'd better call me Clay." They all muttered it, half in greeting, half just to test it out. Jason covered his mouth self-consciously, tonguing the invisible gap in his molars.

"I thought our days of mischief would be behind us, no?" Clay said, his expression good-humored.

Jessica slid off the hood of Charlie's car, her face drawn.

"I'm so sorry; he's missing," she said tightly. "I don't know what happened; he was right with us!"

"Bonnie kidnapped him!" Jason burst out. "I saw! The rabbit took him!"

Clay started to smile, then stopped himself when he saw their faces.

"Oh, kids, I'm sorry. You haven't been around in a while. I'm afraid Carlton is playing a joke on you, ALL of you."

"What?" Lamar said.

"Oh, come on. With you guys back in town, he couldn't resist," Clay said. "Whatever happened, I guarantee he set it up. He'll probably pop out of the bushes any minute now."

There was a silence as they all waited against probability. Nothing happened.

"Well," Clay said at last. "That would have been too much to ask! Come on, why don't you come back to our place? I'll make you all some hot chocolate, and when Carlton finally shows up, you can tell him he's grounded!"

"Okay," Charlie said, without waiting for the consent of the others. She wanted to believe Clay, wanted to believe that Carlton was all right and would show up laughing. But, almost as badly, she wanted to go somewhere where an adult was in charge, someone who would make hot chocolate and assure them there was no such thing as monsters. Her father had never made that claim. Her father could never have told her that lie.

No one objected, and so they started up their caravan again, trailing Clay home. They all settled into their accustomed places: Charlie, John, and Jessica in Charlie's car, and Marla, Jason, and Lamar in Marla's. In the rearview mirror, Charlie saw Officer Dunn's car, still right behind them. *Is he just going this way, or is he making sure we go where we're told?* she wondered, but it didn't really matter. They weren't planning on flight.

At Carlton's house they filed in through the front door. Charlie looked back in time to see the police car drive on by. *He was following us.* As they climbed the steps, John leaned in to whisper in her ear.

"I didn't realize how rich they were when I was a kid!" he said, and she stifled a laugh. It was true; the house was enormous. It was three stories high, and it sprawled out into the woods that surrounded it, so wide that Charlie thought there must have been whole rooms where all you could see out the window was trees. Clay showed them to the living room, which looked well used, the furniture mismatched and the rugs, dark and durable, made to take stains.

"Carlton's mom—who you can call Betty now—is asleep," Clay said. "The soundproofing is pretty good. Just don't shout or crash around."

They chorused promises, and he nodded, satisfied, and vanished through a doorway. They dispersed themselves over the furniture, sitting on couches and chairs. Charlie sat on the rug between Jessica's chair and Lamar's. She wanted them all to stay close together. John sat down beside her and gave a little smile.

"Did we get pranked?" Marla asked.

"I guess maybe. I'm not sure what else would explain it," Jessica said listlessly, staring into the empty fireplace. "I mean, none of us even knows each other that well, not really. Maybe he would do something like that." They all shifted uncomfortably. It was true; they had been behaving as if their time apart were just a little break, like they could just fill one another in on what they had been up to, and it would be just like it was, just like their group had never split up. But ten years was too long for that to be true, and deep down everyone knew it. Charlie darted her eyes at John. She felt a little embarrassed, but she could not have expressed why.

Clay came back in, carrying a tray of steaming mugs and a bag of little marshmallows.

"Here you are!" he said jovially. "Hot chocolate for everyone, even me." He set the tray down on the coffee table and took a seat in a battered green armchair that seemed to fit him like a coat, as accustomed to his body as he was to its form. They reached forward and took the cups; only Jason reached for the marshmallows. Clay looked around from face to face.

"Look," he said. "I know you don't believe me, but Carlton does things like this—although I have to admit, this is probably the weirdest. It's not right, making you relive all that stuff from when you were kids." He stared into his mug for a long moment. "I need to have another talk with him," he said quietly. "Believe me, my son has a strange sense of humor," he went on. "You know, for high school we sent him to a place in the next town over. No one knew him. He managed to convince his classmates *and* his teachers that he had a twin brother at the school for the first month of class. I don't know how on earth he managed it, but I didn't find out until he got tired of the act and I started getting calls from school that one of my sons had gone missing."

Charlie smiled weakly, but she was not convinced. This was different.

"This is different," Marla said, as if reading Charlie's thoughts. "Jason saw him disappear. He was terrified. It's cruel, if it's a prank." Marla shook her head with anger and scratched her nails against the porcelain cup. "If it's a prank," she repeated in a softer tone. She looked at Charlie, her face stormy, and Charlie knew that if Carlton had, in fact, set all of this up, Marla would never speak to him again. Their happy reunion was over.

"Yes," Clay said, "I know. But he doesn't see it that way." He took a sip of cocoa, searching for words. "The twins, they had totally different personalities. Shaun was this outgoing, cheerful guy. He was on the debate team. He played soccer, for goodness' sake! Carlton had never gotten near a sports game without being forced. I don't know how he kept it up."

"Still," Marla said, but she sounded less convinced.

"The worst part was," Clay went on, talking more to himself now than to the teenagers, "Shaun had a girlfriend. She really liked him, too, but he was just playing the part. Poor girl had been dating a guy who didn't even exist. I think he was surprised when he realized how upset people were. He gets carried away and just assumes everyone is having as much fun as he is."

Charlie looked at John, and he met her glance anxiously. *We don't know each other, not really.*

"Maybe he did set it up," she said aloud.

"Maybe," Jessica echoed.

"I saw him!" Jason said loudly. Before anyone could respond, he stormed out of the room, disappearing through a doorway. Marla stood automatically and moved to follow him, but Clay put up a hand.

"Let him go," he said. "He needs some time to himself. And I want to talk to the rest of you." He set his mug down and leaned forward. "I know you were just kidding around, but I don't want to hear you kids joking about Freddy Fazbear's. You know, I wasn't the chief back then. I was still a detective, and I was working on those disappearances. To this day, it was the worst thing I've ever had to see. It's not something to joke about." He looked at Charlie. His gray eyes were hard, and the lines of his face were immobile; he was no longer the friendly father figure, but the police chief, staring as if he could see right through her. Charlie had a sudden urge to confess, but she had nothing to confess to.

"I'm especially surprised at you, Charlie," Clay said quietly.

Charlie blushed, shame rising up in her with the flush of heat. She wanted to protest, to explain herself, to say anything that might soften the eyes that seemed to bore into her skull. Instead she ducked her head and muttered an indistinct apology.

Lamar broke the silence.

"Mr. Burke—Clay—did they ever find out who did it? I thought they arrested somebody."

Clay didn't respond for a long moment. He was still looking at Charlie, and she felt as if he were trying to tell her something, or else read something in her face.

"Clay?" Marla said, and he seemed to come back to himself. He looked around the group, his expression dark.

"Yes," he said quietly. "We did arrest someone. I did, in fact, and I am as sure now that he was guilty as I was then."

"So what happened?" Lamar asked. There was a hush among the group, as if something very important was about to happen.

"There were no bodies," Clay Burke said. "We knew it was him; there was no doubt in my mind. But the children had disappeared. They were never found, and without their bodies . . ." He stopped talking, staring off into the middle distance as if scarcely aware that they were there.

"But kidnapping," Charlie said. "They disappeared!" She was suddenly furious, appalled at the obvious injustice. "How can this man be walking around somewhere? What if he does it again?" She felt Marla's hand on her arm, and she nodded, settling back, trying to calm down. But the anger was still there inside, seething under the surface of her skin. Clay was looking at her with something like curiosity in his eyes.

"Charlie," he said, "justice penalizes the guilty, but it must also protect the innocent. It means that sometimes the guilty get away with terrible things, but it is the price we pay." He sounded grave, his words weighty. Charlie opened her mouth to argue. *But this was* my *price*, she wanted to say, but before she spoke she looked at his face. He had a grim conviction about him; what he was saying mattered very much to him, and he believed it utterly. *It's how you sleep at night*, she thought with an uncharacteristic bitterness. They locked eyes for a long moment, then Charlie sighed and nodded, giving up the challenge. Intellectually, she didn't even disagree with him. Clay sat up suddenly in his chair.

"So," he said brightly, "I think it's a bit too late for you girls to be driving back to that motel. Why don't you spend the night here? We have two more guest rooms. And you can scold Carlton for his little prank in the morning," he added with a grin.

Lamar and John showed Charlie, Marla, and Jessica up to the bedrooms, and Jason reemerged as they headed up the stairs, joining the group like he had never been gone.

"So Jason and I will take one," Marla said, "and Jessica, you and Charlie can have the other."

"I want to stay with Lamar," Jason said instantly, and Lamar grinned widely before he could help himself.

"Yeah, okay," he said. He glanced at Marla over her brother's head, and she shrugged.

"Take him," she said. "Keep him if you want! So that means someone gets her own room," she went on, "or we could all stay together. I know everything is fine, but I kind of feel like we should stay together." She was voicing Charlie's precise thoughts from only a little while before, but now Charlie jumped in.

"I'll take the other room," she said.

Marla gave her a dubious look, and even John looked a little surprised, but Charlie just looked at them and said nothing.

When the door closed behind her, Charlie sighed with relief. She went to the window; it was as she imagined, nothing in view but the trees. The house seemed completely isolated, though she knew that the driveway and the road were just on the other side. From outside she could hear nocturnal birds and the rustling of other, larger creatures on the ground below. She felt suddenly restless, wide awake. Looking out the window, she almost wanted to go outside, to slip into the woods and see what they concealed. She looked at her watch. It was long past midnight, so with reluctance she took off her shoes and lay down on the bed.

It was, like everything else in Carlton's house, well worn, the kind of furniture only owned by people who have been wealthy for generations, whose ancestors could afford things of such high quality that they lasted for a hundred years. Charlie closed her eyes in what she assumed would be a futile effort to find rest, but as she lay there, listening to the sound of the woods and Jessica and Marla gossiping and laughing in the next room, she felt as if she were sinking into the mattress. Her breath deepened, and she was soon asleep.

She woke suddenly, startled from sleep. She was a little girl again, and her father was asleep in the next room. It was summer, and the windows were all open; it had started to rain, and the wind rushed into the room in great gusts, blowing her bedroom curtains in a frenetic dance and ushering in a fine mist. But that was not why she awoke. There was something in the air, something unshakable that gripped her. Something was very wrong.

Charlie climbed out of bed, lowering herself carefully onto the floor. Beside her bed stood Stanley the unicorn, patient and deactivated, staring at her with lifeless eyes. She patted his nose, as if giving him comfort might bring it to her as well. Quietly, she snuck past him and out into the hallway, uncertain what compelled her. She crept down the hallway, past her father's room to the stairs, and ducked down beside the wooden bannister as if its open slats could protect her from anything at all. She held fast to it as she made her way down the staircase, letting the rail take her weight as she avoided the boards that creaked. One by one she took the steps; it felt like ages, like years might pass before she reached the bottom, and when she arrived she might be an old woman, her whole life spun out in the descent of these stairs.

At last Charlie reached the end of the stairs, and she looked down to see that she had changed. Her body was no longer small, nightgown-clad and barefoot, but her teenage body, tall, strong, and fully clothed. When she straightened from her fearful crouch, she stood taller than the bannister, and she looked around at her childhood home, startled. This is me, *she thought.* Yes. This is now.

Something banged in front of her. The front door was wide open and thudding irregularly against the wall, caught by the wind. The rain was whipping in, soaking the floor and lashing the coatrack that stood beside it, rocking it back and forth like it weighed nothing at all. Leaves and small branches were scattered on the floor, ripped from the trees and swept in, but Charlie's eyes went to her old, familiar shoes, her favorites. They were placed neatly beside the mat, black patent leather with straps, and she could see the rain pooling inside and ruining them. Charlie stood still for a moment, transfixed, too far for the rain to reach but close enough for the haze to slowly wet her face. She ought to go to the door and close it.

Instead, Charlie backed away slowly, not taking her eyes from the border of the storm. She took a step, then another—and her back hit something solid. She whirled around, startled, and saw it.

It was the thing from her father's workshop, the terrible, twitching thing. It stood on its own, bent and twisted, with a narrow, reddish, canine face and an almost human body. Its clothing was rags, its metal joints and limbs stark and exposed, but Charlie registered only its eyes, the silver eyes that flashed at her, on and off, over and over, blinking in and out of existence. Charlie wanted to run, but her feet would not move. She could feel her pulse in her throat, choking her, and she struggled to breathe. The thing convulsed, and in slow, jerking motions its hand rose up and reached out to touch her face. Charlie drew in a shaking breath, unable to duck away, and then it stopped, the hand only inches from her cheek.

Charlie braced herself, her breath shallow and her eyes screwed shut, but the touch of metal and ragged cloth on her skin did not come. She opened her eyes. The thing had gone still, and the silver light in its eyes was dimmed, nearly out. Charlie backed away from it, watching warily, but it did not move, and she began to wonder if it had shut down, run out of the finite current that powered it. Its shoulders were hunched forward, hapless, and it stared dully past her as if it were lost. Charlie felt a sudden stab of sorrow for this creature, that same feeling of lonely kinship she felt in her father's workshop so many years ago. Does it hurt? *she had asked. She was old enough now to know the answer.*

All at once, the thing lurched to life. Charlie felt her head go light as it took an awkward step toward her, hurtling its body forward as if it had only just learned to walk. Its head turned frantically from side to side, and its arms jerked up and down with dangerous abandon.

Something shattered. It was a lamp, the thing had knocked over a ceramic lamp, and the sound of it bursting on the wooden floor shook Charlie from her stupor. She turned and ran up the stairs, scrambling as fast as her legs would carry her to her father's door, too scared to even call out for him. As she clambered up the steps some small part of her realized that they were too big, that she was nearly on all fours, tripping barefoot over the hem of her nightgown. She was a little girl again, she realized in a bursting moment of awareness, and then it was over, and being a little girl was the only thing she could remember.

She tried again to scream for her father, but he was already there. She did not need to call him. He was standing in the hall, and she grabbed at his shirttails as she crouched behind him. He put a hand on her shoulder, steadying her, and for the first time, her father's touch did not make Charlie feel that she was safe. Peeking out from behind his back, Charlie could see the thing's ears, then its face, as it climbed the stairs in its fitful, jerking steps. Her father stood calm, watching it, as it climbed the final stair, and then Charlie's father grasped her hand and disentangled it, gently forcing her to let him go. He went forward to meet the thing in large, even strides, but as he reached out to it, Charlie could see that his hands were shaking. He touched the thing, put his hands on either side of its face for a long moment, as if he were caressing it, and its limbs stopped, head still moving gently from side to side. It looked almost bewildered, as if it, too, had awakened to something strange and frightening. Charlie's father did something she could not see, and the thing stopped moving; its head drooped, defeated, and its arms fell to its sides. Charlie backed up toward her room, feeling her way along the wall behind her, not daring to look away from the thing until she was safely behind her door. As she looked out one last time into the hallway, she could just barely see the glint from its eyes, cast down at the floor. Suddenly, the little silver lights flickered. The head did not move, but in a slow, calculated arc the eyes swung to meet Charlie's gaze. Charlie whimpered, but she did not look away, and then the head snapped up with a crack like something breaking—

Charlie startled out of sleep, an involuntary shudder running through her. She put a hand to her throat, feeling her heartbeat there, too quick and too hard. She darted her eyes around the room, putting together where she was one piece at a time. *The bed.* Not her own. *The room.* Dark; she was alone. *The window.* The woods outside. *Carlton's house.* Her breath slowed. The process had only taken seconds, but it disturbed her to be so disoriented. She blinked, but the afterburn of those silver eyes was still with her, glowing behind her eyelids as if they had been real. Charlie stood and went to the window, thrust it open, and leaned out, desperate to breathe in the night air.

Did that happen? The dream felt like memory, felt like something that had happened just moments ago, but that was the nature of dreams, wasn't it? They felt real, and then you woke up. She closed her eyes and tried to catch the thread, but it was too difficult to tell what was the dream and what was not. She shivered in the breeze, though it was not cold, and brought herself back inside. She looked at her watch. Only a couple of hours had passed, and it was still hours more until daylight, but sleep felt impossible. Charlie put on her shoes and shuffled quietly through the hall and down the stairs, hoping not to wake her friends. She went out to the porch, sitting down on the front steps and leaning back to look up at the sky. There were traces of clouds overhead, but the stars still shone through, scattered overhead, uncountable. She tried to lose herself in them as she had as a child, but as she gazed up at the pinpoint lights, all she could see were eyes, looking back at her.

There was a noise behind her, and she jumped, whirling to press her back against the railing. John was standing behind her with a startled look on his face. They stared at each other for a moment like strangers, and then Charlie found her voice.

"Hey, sorry, did I wake you up again?"

John shook his head and came to sit beside her.

"No, not really. I heard you go out, or I figured it was you. I was awake, though—Jason snores like a guy about three times his size."

Charlie laughed.

"I had a weird dream," she said. John nodded, waiting for her to go on, but she did not. "What did people think of my father?" she asked instead. John leaned back and looked at the stars for a moment, then pointed.

"That's Cassiopeia," he said, and she squinted in the direction of his finger.

"It's Orion," she corrected. "John, I'm serious. What did people think about him?"

He shrugged uncomfortably.

"Charlie, I was a little kid, you know? Nobody told me anything."

"I was a little kid once myself," she said. "Nobody tells you anything, but they talk in front of you like you're not there. I remember your mom and Lamar's mom talking, making bets on how long Marla's new stepdad would stick around."

"What did they come up with?" John said, amused.

"Your mom was banking on three months; Lamar's mom was more optimistic," Charlie said, grinning, but then her face grew serious again. "I can tell you know something," she said quietly, and after a moment he nodded.

"Some people thought he did it, yeah," he admitted.

"What?" Charlie was aghast. She stared at him, eyes wide, scarcely breathing. "They thought *what*?" John glanced at her nervously.

"I thought that's what you were asking," he said. Charlie shook her head. *Some people thought he did it.*

"I—no, I meant what did they think of him as a person. Did they think he was odd, or kind, or . . . I didn't know . . ." She trailed off, lost in the magnitude of this new truth. *People thought he did it.* Of course they did. It was *his* restaurant. The first child to vanish was *his* child. In the absence of a confession or a conviction, who else would anyone think of? Charlie shook her head again.

"Charlie," John said hesitantly, "I'm sorry. I just assumed. You must have known people would think that, though—if not then, then now."

"Well, I didn't," she snapped. She felt a hollow satisfaction when he drew back, hurt. She took a deep breath. "I know it sounds obvious," she said in more even tones. "But it just never, ever occurred to me that anyone would think he was responsible. And then afterward, after he committed—" *But that would have only reinforced their suspicions*, she realized as she said it.

"People thought it was because of the guilt," John said, almost to himself.

"It was." Charlie felt anger welling up inside her, the dam about to break, and she held it back, biting off words in short, sharp bursts. "Of course he felt guilt, it was *his* restaurant. *His* life's work, *his* creations, and it was all turned into a massacre. Don't you think that's enough?" Her voice sounded vicious, even to her own ears. *Apologize*, she thought, but she ignored it.

People thought he did it. He wouldn't, he couldn't. But if he had, how would she even have known? *I knew him*, she thought fiercely. But did she? She loved him, trusted him, with the blind devotion of a seven-year-old girl, even now. She understood him with the knowing and not-knowing that comes of being a child. When you focus on your parent as if they are the center of the earth, that thing on which your survival depends, only later do you realize their flaws, their scars, and their weaknesses.

Charlie had never had the dawning moments of realization as she grew older that her father was only human; she had never had the chance. To her he was still mythic, still larger than life, still the man who could deactivate the monsters. *He was also the man who made them.* How well did she really know him?

The rage was gone, had ebbed back to wherever it rose from, and she was empty of it, her insides dry and vacant. She closed her eyes and put a hand to her forehead.

"I'm sorry," she said, and John touched her shoulder for a brief moment.

"Don't be," he said. Charlie put her hands over her face. She did not feel like crying, but she didn't want him to see her face. She was thinking of things that were too new, too awful, to think in front of someone else. *How would I have known if he did?*

"Charlie?" John cleared his throat and repeated her name. "Charlie, you know he didn't do it, right? Mr. Burke said they knew who did, but they had to let him go. He got away with it. Remember?"

Charlie didn't move, but something like hope stirred inside her.

"It wasn't him," John said again, and she looked up.

"Right. Right, of course it wasn't," she whispered. "Of course it wasn't him," she said at a normal pitch.

"Of course not," he echoed. She nodded, bobbing her head up and down like she was gathering momentum.

"I want to go back to the house one more time," she said. "I want you to come with me."

"Of course," he said. She nodded again, then turned her face back up to the sky.

harlie!" Someone was at the door, knocking loud enough to rattle the old hinges. Charlie roused slowly, her eyes sticky with sleep, but this time at least she knew where she was.

She had left the window open, and now the air coming in had a fresh, heavy smell: It was the scent of coming rain, mossy and rich. She got up and looked out the window, inhaling deeply. Unlike most of the world, the woods outside looked almost the same in the morning as they had in the dark. Charlie and John had gone back to bed soon after they finished talking. John had looked at her like there was more he wanted to say, but she had pretended not to notice. She was grateful to him for being there, for giving her what she needed without having to ask, because she would never have asked.

"Charlie!" The banging came again, and she gave in.

"I'm up, Marla," she shouted back.

"Charlie!" Now Jason was joining in the game, knocking and rattling, and Charlie groaned and went to the door.

"I said I'm up," she said, mock-glaring out at them.

"Charlie!" Jason shouted again, and this time Marla shushed him. He grinned up at Charlie, and she laughed and shook her head.

"Believe me, I'm awake," she said. Marla was fully dressed, her hair a little damp from the shower, and her eyes were bright and alert. "Are you always like this?" Charlie said, her grumpiness only half-invented.

"Like what?"

"Chipper at six in the morning," she said and rolled her eyes at Jason, who copied her, happy to be included.

Marla smiled brightly. "It's eight! Come on, there's been talk of breakfast."

"Has there been talk of coffee?"

Charlie followed Marla and Jason down the stairs to the kitchen, where she found Lamar and John already seated around a high, modern-looking wood table. Carlton's father was at the stove, making pancakes.

"It smells like rain," Charlie said, and Lamar nodded.

"There's a thunderstorm coming," he said. "It was on the news earlier, he told us." He jerked a thumb at Clay.

"It's a big one!" Clay exclaimed in response.

"We're supposed to leave today," Jason said.

"We'll see," Marla said.

"Charlie!" Clay cried, not taking his eyes off his work. "One, two, or three?"

"Two," Charlie said. "Thanks. Is there coffee?"

"Help yourself. Mugs in the cupboard," Clay said, gesturing to a full pot on the counter. Charlie helped herself, waving off offers of milk, cream, half-and-half, sugar, or fake sugar.

"Thanks," she said quietly as she settled herself beside Lamar, meeting John's eyes briefly. "Did Carlton come in?"

Lamar shook his head, a tight jerk to the side.

"He hasn't turned up yet," Clay said. "Probably isn't awake yet, wherever he is." He placed a full plate in front of Charlie, who dug in, not realizing how hungry she was until she was already chewing. She was about to ask where Carlton was likely to be when Jessica appeared, yawning, her clothes unrumpled, unlike Charlie's.

"You're late," Marla teased, and Jessica stretched elaborately.

"I don't get out of bed until the pancakes are ready," she said, and with impeccable timing Clay slapped one onto a plate, fresh off the pan.

"Well, you're just in time," he said. Suddenly, his expression changed, wavering somehow between apprehension and relief. Charlie turned in her seat. There was a woman standing behind her, dressed in a gray skirt suit, her blonde hair shellacked against her head as if she were a plastic toy.

"Are we a Waffle House now?" she asked. She looked around the kitchen briefly.

"Pancakes," Jessica corrected, but no one responded.

"Betty!" Clay cried. "You remember the boys, and this is Charlie, Jessica, and Marla. And Jason." He pointed to each in turn, and Carlton's mother gave each of them a nod, like she was tallying them up.

"Clay, I have to be in court in an hour."

"Betty's the D.A. for the county," Clay went on as if he had not heard her. "I catch the crooks; she puts 'em back out on the streets!"

"Yes, our family is a full-service operation," she said dryly, pouring herself coffee and settling down at the table beside Jessica. "Speaking of which, where's our young felon-to-be?"

Clay hesitated. "Another one of his pranks," he said. "He'll be back home later, I'm sure." Their eyes met, and something private passed between them. Betty broke away with a laugh that sounded a little forced.

"Oh, Lord, what is it this time?" There was a moment's pause. In the morning light, the story sounded insane, and Charlie had no idea where to begin. With a nervous clearing of his throat, Lamar started to explain.

"We, uh—we went up to the mall construction site, to go see what was left of Freddy Fazbear's."

At the name, Betty's head jerked up, and she gave a quick nod.

"Go on," she said, her voice suddenly cold and clipped.

Lamar explained, awkwardly, and Marla and Jason jumped in with details. After a few minutes, Carlton's mother had a messy version of the truth. As she listened, her face hardened until it looked like plaster; she was a statue of herself. She shook her head as they finished, small, rapid movements, and Charlie thought she looked like she was not just trying to deny what they were saying, but to shake the knowledge entirely from her mind.

"You have to go get him, Clay, right now," she demanded. "Send someone! How could you wait all night?"

She set her coffee on the table more forcefully than she should have, spilling a little, then went to the phone and started dialing.

"Who are you calling?" Clay said, alarmed.

"The police," she snapped.

"I *am* the police!"

"Then why are you here instead of finding my son?"

Clay opened and closed his mouth helplessly for a moment before finding his bearings.

"Betty, it's just another joke. Remember the frogs?"

She set the phone back on its hook and turned to face him, her eyes smoldering. Charlie could suddenly see her standing righteous before a jury, wreaking the wrath of the law.

"Clay." Her voice was low and steady, a dangerous calm. "How could you not wake me up? How could you not tell me this?"

"Betty, you were asleep! It's just Carlton being Carlton. I didn't want to disturb you."

"Did you think I would be less disturbed when I woke up and found him missing?"

"I thought he would be back by now," Clay protested.

"This is different," she said with finality. "It's *Freddy's*."

"I don't understand Freddy's? I know what happened there, what happened to those kids," he retorted. "*I don't understand?* For goodness' sake, Betty, I saw Michael's blood, streaked across the floor where he was dragged from—" He stopped, realizing too late that he was surrounded by the teenagers. He looked around at them, near panic, but his wife had not noticed—or, Charlie thought, she just did not care.

"Well, you didn't see *him*," Betty snapped. "Do you remember what you told Carlton? Be tough? Be brave, little soldier? So he was brave, he was a little soldier for you. He was shattered, Clay! He had lost his best friend, had Michael snatched away right in front of him. Let me tell you something, chief: That boy has thought about Michael every single day of his life for the last ten years. I have seen him stage jokes so elaborate they deserve to be mounted as performance art pieces, but there is no way on earth that Carlton would desecrate Michael's memory by making Freddy's a joke. Call someone right now."

Clay looked slightly shocked, but he gathered himself quickly and left the room. Charlie heard a door slam shut behind him. Betty looked around at the teenagers, breathing hard as if she had been running.

"Everything is going to be fine," she said tightly. "If he is trapped in there, we will get him out. What do you kids have planned for the day?" The question was inane, as if they were all going to hang out at the park or go to a movie while Carlton might be in danger.

"We were supposed to leave today," Marla said.

"Obviously we won't," Lamar said hastily, but Betty did not seem to be listening to them.

"I'll have to call in to work," she said distractedly and went to the phone to make the call. Charlie looked at John, who jumped to the rescue.

"We were going to go to the library," he said. "We had some things we wanted to investigate—research!" He blushed faintly when he said it, and Charlie knew why. It was absurd to be talking like this, about cases and disappearances and murders. But Marla was nodding.

"Yeah, we'll all go," she said, and Charlie's heart sank. There was no reason she couldn't just tell them all that she wanted to go back to her old house, just her and John. No one would be hurt. But that wasn't the problem—even sharing the knowledge felt too much like exposure. Carlton's mother hung up the phone, done with her call.

"I hate this," she announced to the room in general, her careful, controlled voice almost shaking. *"I hate this!"* Charlie and the others jumped in unison, startled by the sudden outburst. "And now, like always, I get to sit here by myself hoping and praying that everyone will be okay."

Charlie looked at Marla, who shrugged helplessly. Lamar cleared his throat nervously. "I think we'll stick around for another day," he said. There was a pause, then Marla and Jessica jumped in to help.

"Yeah, traffic is *crazy* out there," Jessica said, high-pitched and forced.

"Yeah, and also because of the storm, and it's not like we're going to have fun knowing he's missing," Marla said.

"I guess you're stuck with us." Jessica flashed an anxious smile at Carlton's mother, who did not seem to register it.

"Come on," John said before anyone else could speak. He and Charlie hurried out of the house and got into the car.

Charlie heaved a sigh of relief as she started the engine. "That was awful," she said.

"Yeah." He gave her a worried look. "What do you think? About Carlton?"

Charlie didn't answer until she was safely backed out of the driveway. "I think his mom is right," she said, pulling into gear. "I think last night we all let ourselves believe what we wanted to believe."

Officer Dunn pulled to a stop in the mall parking lot, responding to Chief Burke's order to return. In the light of day it was just an abandoned construction site, an ugly blemish on the flat desert landscape. *You can't tell from looking if it's being built up or torn down*, Dunn thought. *Can't tell creation from destruction at a distance.* He liked the phrase; he turned it over in his head for a moment, staring at the place. On impulse, he radioed dispatch.

"Hey, Norah," he said.

"Dunn," she answered crisply. "What's going on?"

"Back at the mall for another look," he said.

"Ooh, bring me back a soft pretzel," she teased. He laughed and broke the connection.

As he walked briskly through the mall, Dunn was at least grateful the children were not there this time. As the youngest member of the Hurricane Police Department, Dunn always took care to think of teenagers as children, even though he knew how small the gap between them was. If he could bring them to believe he was a responsible adult, hopefully at some point he would believe it, too.

Dunn flipped on his flashlight as he reached the entrance

to the narrow alleyway that led to Freddy Fazbear's. He swept the beam up and down the walls ahead of him, but the alley was empty of life. He took a deep breath and went in. Dunn kept to the wall, his shoulder brushing lightly against the rough brick as he tried to avoid the puddles that pooled beneath leaky pipes. The bright beam of his flashlight illuminated the alley almost as well as overhead bulbs, but somehow the light was not comforting—it only made the place look stark and grim, the shelves of tools and rejected paint cans now woeful and exposed. As he moved toward the door to the restaurant, something tiny and cold landed on his head, and he startled, swinging his light up like a weapon and pressing his back against the wall as defense against the threat. Another cold drop of water landed on his cheek. He took deep breaths.

When at last he reached the outer door to the restaurant, the shelf that had blocked it was gone. The chains that had seemed so permanently fixed in place were hanging loose, and the door was cracked open slightly. The immense, rusted padlock lay in the dirt, its shackle hanging open. Dunn kicked it away from the door. He dug his fingers into the gap, prying until he could get a grip on it, then pulled at the door with both hands until it screeched open wide enough for him to enter. He crept down the inner passage with his light held out in front, hugging the wall tight to one side. The air seemed to change as he moved closer to the interior of the restaurant, and Dunn felt a crawling chill that penetrated his uniform and fed his growing anxiety.

"Don't freak out, Dunn," he said out loud, then felt instantly foolish.

He reached the main dining area and stopped, sweeping the light over each wall in turn. The light seemed dimmer inside, swallowed by the space. The room was empty, but it was just as he remembered from when he was a kid. He had been ten when the tragedies started, eleven when they ended. His birthday party was supposed to be at Freddy's, but after the first disappearance his mother had cancelled it, invited his friends to his house, and hired a clown, which proved equally terrifying. *Smart move, Mom*, Dunn thought. The beam played over the little carousel, which he had never ridden, claiming he was too old for it. Just before the beam of light reached the stage, Dunn stopped, swallowing hard. *The rabbit took him*, the kid had said. Dunn shook himself and played the light across the stage.

The figures were there, just as he remembered, and, unlike the carousel, they did not seem diminished in size. They were exactly as he recalled, and for a moment an almost painful nostalgia swelled in his chest. As he gazed at them, remembering, he noticed that their eyes were all fixed oddly forward like they were watching something on the far side of the room. The flashlight trained in front of him, Dunn approached the stage until he was standing only a few feet from it, and he stared up at each of the animals in turn. Bonnie was holding his guitar jauntily, as if he might begin strumming whenever the mood struck him, and Chica and her cupcake seemed to be sharing some arcane secret. Freddy, with his microphone, stared out into the distance, unblinking.

Something moved behind him, and Dunn whirled around, his heart racing. The flashlight found nothing, and he swept it nervously from side to side, revealing only empty tables. He glanced back nervously at Bonnie, but the rabbit was still frozen in his own inscrutable reverie.

Dunn took shallow breaths, holding himself completely still, and listened, his senses kicked into high gear with adrenaline. After a moment the noise came again—a shuffling sound, this time coming from off to the right. He swept the light instantly toward it. There was an open doorway, and beyond it a hall. Crouching down, Dunn made his way down the hall, keeping to the side as though something might come running past. *Why am I here alone?* He knew the answer. His sergeant hadn't taken the search seriously—in truth, neither had Dunn. After all, it was just the chief's son again, making trouble. *It's probably just Carlton*, Dunn reminded himself.

He reached the end of the hall, where a door stood ajar. With one hand Dunn gave the door an inward push, dropping low and to the side as he did. The door swung inward, and nothing happened. He pulled the nightstick from his belt. Its heft was unfamiliar—he had never had much need for it in Hurricane. Now, though, he gripped its hard rubber handle like a lifeline.

The office was not quite empty; there was a small desk, and a folded-up metal chair leaned against it. A large cabinet stood against one wall, its door open just a crack. There were no exits other than the one Dunn was standing in. He swept the light up and down the length of the cabinet and took a deep breath. He bounced his nightstick lightly in his hand, reassuring himself of its presence, and carefully assessed the small space. Standing to the side, he used the stick to open the door, moving slowly. It came open easily, and again, everything was still. Relieved, Dunn looked inside. The cabinet was empty—except for a costume.

It was Bonnie, or rather it wasn't. The face was the same, but the rabbit's fur was yellow. It was slumped lifelessly against the back wall of the cabinet, its eyes dark, gaping holes. *The rabbit took him.* The kid hadn't been lying, then; Carlton must have gotten someone to dress up in this outfit to help him play his trick. Still, Dunn's unease did not abate; he did not want to touch the thing. He lowered his light and stuck his nightstick back in his belt, intending to go.

Before he could turn, the costume pitched forward, landing on Dunn with the lifeless weight of a heavy corpse. For a moment it did not move, then all at once it was writhing violently, grabbing at him with strong, inhuman hands. Dunn screamed, a desperate, high sound, struggling as the rabbit gripped his shirt, then his arm. Dunn felt a sudden, vicious pain, and a small, detached part of his mind thought, *He broke it; he broke my arm.* But the pain was washed numb by terror as the rabbit swung him around and slammed him into the cabinet door, taking Dunn's weight easily as if he were a child. Dunn struggled to breathe; the rabbit's arm was pressed against his neck so tightly that every movement choked him. Just when he thought he was on the brink of passing out, the pressure lifted, and Dunn gasped with relief, clutching his throat. Then he saw the knife.

The rabbit held a slim silver blade. Its big, matted paws should have been too clumsy, but Dunn knew as he stared down at it that the rabbit had done this before and would easily do it again. Dunn screamed, an indistinct shriek. He had no hope that he would be heard; it was only a guttural, despairing noise. He breathed deep and did it again, a bestial sound, his whole body vibrating with it, as if this could somehow be defense against what happened next.

The knife went in. Dunn felt it tear through skin and muscle, felt it sever things he could not name to plant itself deep in his chest. As he seized with pain and terror, the rabbit pulled him close, almost in an embrace. Dunn's head went light; he was losing consciousness. As he looked up, he could see two rows of smiling teeth, horrid and yellow, the costume peeling at the edges of the mouth. The two gaping holes for eyes looked down at him. They were dark and hollow, but the creature drew near enough that Dunn could see smaller eyes peering back at him from deep within the mask. They held Dunn's gaze patiently. Dunn felt his legs go numb, his vision clouding. He wanted to scream again, to somehow voice his final outrage, but he could not move his face, could not raise the breath to cry out. The rabbit held him upright, supporting his weight, and its eyes were the last thing Dunn ever saw.

Charlie unlocked the front door to her old house and looked back down the front steps.

"You coming?"

John was still standing on the bottom step, staring up at the house. He shivered a little before hurrying to join her.

"Sorry," he said sheepishly. "I just had a weird feeling for a second." Charlie laughed without much humor.

"Just for a second?"

They went inside, and John stopped again, looking around the front room like he had just stepped into a sacred place, somewhere that merited a humbling pause. Charlie bit her tongue, trying not to be impatient. It was how she had felt as well; she might have felt that way now if she were not overwhelmed by a sense of urgency, the feeling that the answer to everything, the answer to how to get Carlton back, must be somewhere in this place. Where else could it possibly be?

"John," she said, "it's okay. Come on."

He nodded and followed her up the stairs to the second floor. He stopped again briefly halfway up, and Charlie saw his eyes fixed on the dark stain that marred the wood floor of the living room.

"Is—" he began to say, then swallowed it and started over. "Is Stanley still there?"

Charlie pretended not to notice the lapse.

"You remember his name!" she said instead, grinning. John shrugged.

"Who doesn't love a mechanical unicorn?"

"Yeah, he's still there. All the toys still work. Come on." They hurried the rest of the way to her room.

John knelt down beside the unicorn and pressed the button that set him on his track, watching raptly as he made his squeaky way around the room. Charlie hid a smile behind her hand. John was watching intently, his face serious as if something very important were happening. For a moment he looked just like he had so many years ago, his hair falling into his face, his whole attention fixed on Stanley like nothing in the world was more important than this robotic creature.

Suddenly his attention was called upward, and his face lit up as he pointed.

"Your big-girl closet! It's open!" he exclaimed, getting back to his feet and approaching the tallest of the three closets, which was hanging open slightly. He pulled it open all the way, then leaned in, finding it empty. "So what was in it all those years?" he asked.

"Not sure," Charlie said with a shrug. "I sort of remember Aunt Jen bringing me back at some point, but I could be wrong. Maybe it was full of clothes that I was finally big enough to wear. Aunt Jen was always thrifty—why spend money on new clothes if you don't have to, right?" She smiled.

John glanced briefly at the smaller closets, but he left them alone.

"I'm going to see if I can find any photo albums or paperwork," Charlie said, and she nodded absently as Stanley rattled back to his starting point. As she left the room, she heard him starting up again, making another round on the track.

The room that had been her father's was next to Charlie's. It was at the back of the house, and it had too many windows. In the summer it was too hot, and in the winter the cold dribbled in like a persistent leak, but Charlie had known without being told why he used it. From here you could see the garage and his workshop. It had always made sense to Charlie; that was his place, like a part of him always lived there, and he did not like to be too far away from his touchstone. A wave from her dream came to her for a moment, not even an image, just a strange, evocative gesture of memory. She frowned, looking out the window at the closed, silent garage door.

Or maybe he just wanted to be sure nothing got out, she thought. She broke away from the window, shrugging her shoulders and shaking her hands, sloughing off the feeling. She looked around the room. Like her own, it was all but untouched. She did not open the drawers to his dresser, but for all she knew, it might still have been filled with shirts and socks, clean, folded, and ready to wear. His bed was made crisply, covered in the plaid blanket he used as a bedspread after Charlie's mother left, when there was no one to insist on white linen. There was a large bookcase against one wall, and it was still stuffed with books. Charlie went over and began scanning the shelves. Many were textbooks, engineering tomes whose titles meant nothing to her, and the rest were nonfiction, a collection that would have seemed eclectic to anyone who did not know the man.

There were books on biology and anatomy, some on human beings and others on animals; there were books about the history of the traveling carnival and of the circus. There were books about child development, about myths and legends, and about sewing patterns and techniques. There were volumes that claimed to be about trickster gods, about quilting bees, and about football cheering squads and their mascots. On the very top shelf were stacks of file folders, and the bottom shelf was empty except for a single book: a photo album, leather-bound and as pristine as time and dust could allow. Charlie grabbed it, and it stuck for a moment, almost too tall for the low shelf it had been given. After a minute it came free, and she headed back to her bedroom, leaving the door open with the sudden sense that if it closed she might never get back in.

John was sitting on the bed when she returned, looking at Stanley with his head tilted to the side.

"What?" Charlie said, and he looked up, still pensive.

"I was wondering if he's been lonely," he said, then shrugged.

"He's got Theodore," Charlie said, pointing to the stuffed rabbit with a smile. "It's Ella who's all alone in the closet. Watch." She placed the album beside John on the bed and went to its foot, then turned the wheel that set Ella on her track. She sat down beside him, and they watched together, spellbound as of old, as the little doll came out in her crisp, clean dress to blankly offer tea. Neither of them spoke until the smallest closet door closed behind her. John cleared his throat.

"So what's in the book?"

"Photos," Charlie said. "I haven't looked at them yet." She picked up the album and opened it at random. The top picture was of her mother holding a baby, maybe a year old. She held the child above her head, flying it like an airplane, her head thrown back in the midst of a laugh, her long brown hair swinging out in an arc behind her. The baby's eyes were wide, its mouth open in delight. John smiled at her.

"You look so happy," he said, and she nodded.

"Yeah," she said. "I guess I must have been." *If that's me,* she did not add aloud. She opened to another page, where the only picture was a large family portrait, stiffly posed at a studio. They were dressed formally: Charlie's father was wearing a suit; her mother was in a bright-pink dress with padding that lifted her shoulders almost to her ears, and her brown hair was straightened flat in place. Each of them was holding a baby, one in a white frilly dress and one in a sailor suit. Charlie's heart skipped, and beside her she heard John take a sharp, quick breath. She looked at him with a feeling like the floor was dropping away beneath them.

"It was real," she said. "I didn't imagine him."

John said nothing in response, just nodded. He put a hand on her shoulder briefly, and then they turned back to the photo album.

"We all looked so happy," Charlie said softly.

"I think you were," John said. "Look, you had such a goofy smile." He pointed, and Charlie laughed.

The whole book was like that, the first memories of a happy family who expected there to be many more. They were not arranged chronologically, so Charlie and Sammy appeared as toddlers, then as newborns, then at various stages in between. Except on formal occasions when Charlie was put into a dress—of which there seemed to be few—it was impossible to tell which baby was which. There were no traces of Fredbear's Family Diner.

Near the back of the book, Charlie came to a Polaroid of her and Sammy together, infants bright red and squalling on their backs, wearing nothing but diapers and hospital wristbands. On the white space below the picture someone had written, "Momma's Boy and Daddy's Girl."

The rest of the pages were blank. Charlie went back again, opening at random to find a strip from a photo booth, four shots of her parents alone. They smiled at each other, then made faces at the camera, then laughed, missing the chance to pose and blurring their faces. Lastly they smiled into the lens. Her mother was beaming happily at the camera, her face alight and flushed, but her father was staring into the distance, a smile fixed on his face like he had left it there by mistake. His dark eyes were intense, remote, and Charlie resisted a sudden urge to look behind her, as if she might see whatever it was he was looking at. She peeled back the cellophane from the album's page and took the strip out, then folded it in half, careful to place the crease between pictures, leaving them intact. She slipped the pictures into her pocket and looked at John, who was watching her again as if she were some kind of unpredictable creature he needed to be careful around.

"What?" she said.

"Charlie, you know I don't think he did it, right?"

"You said that."

"I'm serious. It's not just what Carlton's dad said. I knew him, as well as a kid can know some other kid's dad—he wouldn't do it. I wouldn't believe it." He spoke with calm certainty, like someone who believed that the world was made out of facts and tangible things and that there was such a thing as truth. Charlie nodded.

"I know," she said. She took her next breath slowly, gathering the words she would speak with it. "But I might." His eyes widened, startled, and she looked up at the ceiling for a minute, briefly trying to remember if all the cracks had been there when she was a child.

"I don't mean I think he did it; I don't think that," she said. "I don't think about it at all. I can't. I shut the whole thing off in my mind the day I left Hurricane. I don't think about Freddy's. I don't think about what happened, and I don't think about him."

John was looking at her like she was monstrous, like what she was saying was the worst thing he had ever heard.

"I don't understand how you can say things like that," he said quietly. "You loved him. How can you even consider the possibility that he would do something so terrible?"

"Even the people who do terrible things have people who love them." Charlie was looking for words. "I don't think he did it; I'm not saying that," she said again, and again the words hit the air as flimsy as paper. "But I remember him dressing up for us in the yellow Freddy suit, doing the dances, miming along with the songs. It was so much a part of him. He *was* the restaurant; there was no one else. And he was always so distant, like in that picture; there was always something else going on beneath the surface. It was like he had a real life and a secret life, you know?"

John nodded and looked about to speak, but Charlie rushed on before he could.

"*We* were the secret life. His real life was his work; it was what mattered. We were his guilty pleasure, the thing he got to love and sneak away to have time with, something he kept hidden away from the dangers of what he did in his *real* world. And when he was with us, there was always a part of him that was back in reality, whatever that was for him."

Again John opened his mouth, but Charlie snapped the photo album shut, stood up, and left the room. John didn't follow right away, and as she traversed the short hall to her father's bedroom, she could almost hear him making up his mind. Not waiting for him, she went to the bookshelf, wanting to get the book out of her hands, like maybe if it were closed up and put away, her mind, too, would return to its normal order. The book would not fit, and she dropped to her knees to get a better angle, trying to jam the thing back where it belonged, get it out of her hands. The shelf seemed to have shrunk, sunk down while she was gone, so that it could never be returned, never put right.

With a cry of frustration, Charlie shoved the photo album in as hard as she could. The shelf rocked back and then forward, and a sudden mass of papers and file folders tumbled from above her. Charlie began to cry as pages drifted down around her, covering the floor like snow as she wept. Swiftly, John was there.

He knelt down with her in the delicate wreckage, clearing papers away as quickly as he could without tearing them. He put a hand on her shoulder carefully, and she did not move away. He pulled her close and held her, and she hugged him back, gripping so tight she knew she must be hurting him, but she could not let go. She sobbed harder, as if being held, being contained, made it safe to let go. Long minutes passed; John stroked her hair, and Charlie still cried, her body shaking with the force of it, shuddering like she was possessed. She was not thinking of what had happened, not flitting from one memory to the next to mourn for them all—her mind was all but blank. She held nothing, *was* nothing, but this feeling of racking sobs. Her face was sore with tension, her chest hurt like all her pain was being forced out through its wall, and still she cried as if she would cry forever.

But forever was an illusion. Slowly her breathing calmed, and finally Charlie returned to herself and pushed away from John's shoulder, exhausted. Once again John was left with his arms partially suspended in the air, caught off guard by their sudden emptiness. He tried to move out of the awkward pose without calling attention to himself. Charlie sat back against the side of her father's bed, leaning her head against it. She felt wrung out, stretched thin and aged, but she felt a little better. She gave John a tiny smile, and she saw relief pass over his face at this first sign that she might be all right.

"I'm okay," she said. "It's just this place; it's all this." She felt silly trying to explain, but John scooted back to sit with her.

"Charlie, you don't have to explain. I know what happened."

"Do you?" She looked at him searchingly, not sure how to put the question. It seemed too crude, too graphic, to say it outright. "Do you know how my dad died, John?"

He looked immediately nervous. "I know he killed himself," he said hesitantly.

"No, I mean—do you know *how*?"

"Oh." John looked down at his feet as if he could not meet her eyes. "I thought he stabbed himself," he said quietly. "I remember hearing my mom and dad talk—she said something about a knife, and all the blood."

"There was a knife," Charlie said. "And there was blood." She closed her eyes and kept them shut as she talked. She could feel John's eyes on her face, watching every movement, but she knew if she looked at him she would not be able to finish.

"I never saw it," she said. "I mean, I never saw the body. I don't know if you remember, but my aunt came to get me at school in the middle of the day." She stopped, waiting for confirmation, her eyes shut tight.

"I remember," John's voice said from the darkness. "It was the last time I ever saw you."

"Yeah. She came and got me, and I knew something was wrong—you don't go home from school in the middle of the day because everything's fine. She took me outside to her car, but we didn't get in right away. She picked me up and set me on the hood of the car, and she told me she loved me."

"I love you, Charlie, and everything is going to be okay," Aunt Jen said, and then she destroyed the world with the next words she spoke.

"She told me that my father had died, and she asked if I knew what that meant."

And Charlie nodded, because she did know, and because, with an awful prescience, she was not surprised.

"She said I was going to stay with her for a couple of days, and we would go get some clothes from the house. When we got there, she picked me up like I was a little kid, and as we went through the door, she covered my face with her hand so I wouldn't see what was in the living room. But I did see."

It was one of his creatures, one she had never seen, and it was facing the stairs; its head was bowed a little so that Charlie could see that the back of its skull was open, the circuits exposed. The limbs and joints lay bare, a skeleton of naked metal strung with twisting wires of bloodless circulation, and its arms were outstretched in a lonesome facsimile of an embrace. It was standing in the middle of a dark, still pool of some liquid that seemed, though it must have been imperceptible, to be spreading. She could see its face, if it could be called a face—its features were scarcely formed, crude and shapeless. Even so, Charlie could see that they were contorted, almost grotesque; the thing would be weeping, if it could have wept. She stared at it for ages, though it could have been less than seconds, no more than a glimpse as Aunt Jen swept her up the stairs. Yet she had seen it so many times since then, when she slept, when she woke, when she unguardedly closed her eyes. It would appear to her, the face pressing its way into her mind as it had pressed into the world. Its blind eyes were only raised bumps like the eyes of a statue, seeing nothing but its own grief. In its hand, almost an afterthought, was the knife. When Charlie saw the knife, the whole thing snapped into focus. She knew what the thing was, and she knew what it had been built for.

John was staring at her, horror creeping in.

"*That's* how he . . . ?" He trailed off.

Charlie nodded. "Of course." He made a move to comfort her again, but it was the wrong thing to do. Without thinking, Charlie moved slightly, slipping out of reach, and his face fell.

"Sorry," she said quickly. "I just—sorry."

John shook his head quickly and turned to the jumble of papers on the floor.

"We should look through these, see if there's anything here," he said.

"Sure," she said brusquely, dismissing his attempts at reassurance.

They began randomly; everything had fallen in such a mess that there was no other way to begin. Most of the papers were engineering blueprints and pages of equations, incomprehensible to them both. There were tax forms, which John took up eagerly, hoping for information about Fredbear's Family Diner, but he gave up with a sigh after fifteen minutes, flinging the papers down.

"Charlie, I can't figure this out. Let's check through the rest, but I don't think puzzling at it is going to turn us into mathematicians or accountants."

Stubbornly, Charlie kept picking through the papers, hoping for something she would understand. She picked up a sheaf of paper, trying to straighten the next stack, and a photograph fell out from the pile. John snatched it up.

"Charlie, look," he said, suddenly excited. She took it from his hand.

It was her father, in his workshop, wearing the yellow

Freddy Fazbear costume. The head was tucked under his arm, staring sightlessly into the camera, but Charlie's father was smiling, his face pink and sweaty as if he had been in the costume for a long time. Beside him was a yellow Bonnie.

"The yellow rabbit," Charlie said. "Jason said there was a yellow rabbit."

"But your father is in the bear costume."

"The rabbit must be a robot," Charlie said. "Look at the eyes, they're red." She peered closer. The eyes were glinting red, but they weren't glowing, and in a moment she saw why. "It's not red eyes, it's red eye! There's a person in there!"

"So who . . . ?"

". . . who is in the suit?" Charlie finished the question for him.

"We have to go to the library," John said, jumping to his feet. Charlie stayed where she was, still staring down at the picture. "Charlie?"

"Yeah," she said. He held out a hand to pull her up.

As they descended the staircase, John hung back briefly, but Charlie did not turn around. She knew what he was imagining, because she was picturing it, too: the stain on the floor, slowly spreading.

Charlie drove fast to the library, a grim urgency hanging over her. The promised storm was in the air, the smell of it rising like a warning. In a strange way, the worsening weather satisfied something in Charlie. Storms inside, storms outside.

"I've never been this eager to get to the library," John joked, and she smiled tightly, without humor.

The main library in Hurricane was next to the elementary school where they had gone for the memorial ceremony, and as they got out of the car, Charlie glanced at the playground, envisioning children screaming and laughing as they ran circles, immersed in their games. *We were so young.*

They hurried up the few steps to the library together, a square, modern brick building that looked as if it had come paired with the school beside it. She only remembered the library vaguely from her childhood; they had gone infrequently, and Charlie had spent all her time there sitting on the floor in the children's section. Being able to see over the information desk was slightly disconcerting.

The librarian was young, Charlie thought, an athletic-seeming woman in slacks and a purple sweater. She smiled brightly.

"What can I do for you?" she said. Charlie hesitated. The woman was maybe in her late twenties; Charlie realized that ever since she returned to Hurricane she had been paying attention to age, scrutinizing each face and calculating how old they had been when *it* happened. This woman would have been a teenager. *It doesn't matter,* she thought. *You still have to ask.* She opened her mouth to ask for information about Fredbear's, but what came out instead was, "Are you from Hurricane?"

The librarian shook her head. "No, I'm from Indiana." Charlie felt her body relax. *She wasn't here.*

"Do you have any information on a place called Fredbear's Family Diner?" Charlie asked, and the woman frowned.

"Do you mean Freddy Fazbear's? They used to have one of those here, I think," she said vaguely.

"No, that's not the one," Charlie said, ready to be endlessly patient with the librarian, who was, thankfully, probably the only person in town who was somehow unaware of her history.

"Well, for town records, things like incorporation and licensing, you would have to go to City Hall, but it's—" She checked her watch. "It's after five, so not today anyway. I have newspapers all the way back to the 1880s, if you want to look at microfilm," she said eagerly.

"Yeah, okay," Charlie said.

"I'm Harriet," the woman said as she led them to a door at the back of the building. They recited their names dutifully, and she chattered on like a child about to display her favorite toy.

"So you know what microfilm is, right? It's because we can't keep stacks and stacks of papers here. There's no room, and eventually they would rot, so it's a way to preserve them.

They take pictures and save the film; it's almost like a movie reel, you know? Very small. So you need a machine to see it."

"We know what it is," John cut in when she paused. "We just don't know how to use it."

"Well, that's what I'm here for!" Harriet declared and threw the door open. Inside was a table with a computer monitor. The monitor sat on top of a little box with a small wheel on each side. Two handles stuck out in front. Charlie and John looked at it bemusedly, and Harriet grinned.

"You want the local paper, right? What years?"

"Um . . ." Charlie counted backward. "1979 to 1982?" she hazarded. Harriet beamed and left the room. John bent forward to peer at the machine, rattling the handles a little. "Careful," Charlie warned jokingly. "I think she might be lost without that thing." John raised his hands to his shoulders and stepped back.

Harriet reappeared with what looked like four small movie reels and held them up.

"What year do you want to start with?" she said. "1979?"

"I guess," Charlie said, and Harriet nodded. She went to the machine and threaded the film through expertly. She flipped a switch and the screen came to life; a newspaper appeared.

"January 1, 1979," John announced, leaning forward to read the headlines. "Politics, somebody won a sports game, and there was some weather. Also there was a bakery giving away free cookies to celebrate the New Year. Sounds like now, except no cookies."

"You use these to see more," Harriet said, manipulating the controls. "Let me know if you need help switching the reels. Have fun, you two!" She winked conspiratorially and closed the door behind her as she left.

Charlie positioned herself in front of the machine, and John stood behind her, his hand on her chair. It felt good to have him close, like he would stop anything that tried to sneak up on her.

"This is pretty cool," he remarked, and she nodded, scanning the paper for answers.

"Okay, let's narrow it down," he said grimly. "What's the thing most likely to make the papers?"

"I was looking for an opening announcement," Charlie said.

"Yeah, but what's going to make the papers? Sorry," he added. "I didn't want to say it, but we have to."

"Sammy," Charlie said. "We should have started with Sammy. We moved to the new house when I was three; it's got to be 1982."

Carefully, they switched the reel. Charlie eyed the door as they did, as if nervous that Harriet might catch them making a mistake.

"When's your birthday?" John said, sitting to take her place.

"Don't you know?" she teased. He screwed up his face in an exaggerated mime of thinking.

"May thirteenth," he said at last. She laughed, startled.

"How did you know?"

He grinned up at her. "Because I know things," he said.

"But why does it matter?"

"You remember being three when you moved, but you didn't turn three until May, so we knock out five months. Do you remember anything about the restaurant the night Sammy disappeared?"

Charlie felt herself flinch with an almost physical pain.

"Sorry," she said. Her face felt too hot. "Sorry, you startled me. Let me think." She closed her eyes.

The restaurant. The closet, hung full with costumes. She and Sammy, there safe in the dark, until the door opened, and the rabbit appeared, leaning over them with its awful face, its human eyes. Charlie's heart was racing. She slowed her breathing and held out a hand; John took hold of it. She held on tight, as if he could anchor her. *The rabbit leaning over them, the yellow teeth beneath the mask, and behind the rabbit . . . what was behind the rabbit? The restaurant was open; she could hear voices, people. There were more people in costumes—other performers? Robots? No . . .* She almost had it. Scarcely breathing, Charlie tried to coax out the thought, scared to frighten it away. Move slowly; speak softly. She had it, snatched it from the depths of her mind and held it wriggling in her fingers. Her eyes snapped open.

"John, I know when it was," she said.

Earlier that night, when they were still wide awake, the closet opened, and her mother looked in. She was haloed by the light from behind her, smiling down at her twins, radiant in her long, elegant dress, her flowing hair, her gleaming tiara. Mommy's a princess, *Charlie murmured sleepily, and her mother bent down and kissed her cheek.* Just for tonight, *she whispered, and then she left them in the dark to sleep.*

"She was a princess," she said excitedly.

"What? Who?"

"My mother," Charlie said. "She was dressed up as a princess. It was a Halloween party. John, go to November first."

John struggled briefly with the controls, and then it was there. The headline was small, but it was on the front page of the paper on Monday, November 1: TODDLER SNATCHED. Charlie turned away. John began to read aloud, and Charlie cut in, stopping him.

"Don't," she said. "Just tell me if it has anything useful."

He was quiet, and she stared anxiously at the door, waiting, tracing the knots in the false wood with her eyes.

"There's a picture," he said finally. "You need to look."

She leaned over his shoulder. The story had continued over an entire page inside, with pictures of the restaurant, of the family all together, and of her and of Sammy, though neither of the twins were named in the article. In the bottom left corner, there was a picture of her father and another man. Their arms were slung around each other's shoulders, and they were grinning happily.

"John," Charlie said.

"It says they were joint owners," John said quietly.

"No," Charlie said, unable to take her eyes from the picture, from the face they both knew.

Suddenly the door behind them erupted in pounding from outside, and they both jumped.

"CHARLIE! JOHN! ARE YOU IN THERE?"

"Marla," they said as one, and Charlie rushed to the door and threw it open.

"Marla, what is it?"

She was red-faced and breathless, and Harriet was anxiously hovering behind her. Marla's hair was wet; water dripped down her face, but she did not wipe it away or even seem to notice. *I guess the rain started*, Charlie thought, the mundane reflection drifting unbidden into her head despite her alarm.

"He's gone! Jason's gone," Marla cried.

"What?" John said.

"He's gone back to Freddy's; I know he has," she said. "He kept saying we should go back, that we shouldn't just be hanging around all day. I thought he was in another room, but I looked everywhere. I know that's where he is!" She said it all in one breath and ended gasping, a faint, whining hum resonating under her breathing, a keening sound she seemed unable to stop making.

"Oh no," Charlie said.

"Come on," Marla pressed. She was jittering, vibrating; John put a hand on her shoulder as if to comfort her, and she shook her head. "Don't try to calm me down, just come with me," she insisted, but there was no anger, only desperation. She turned and almost ran to the door, and John and Charlie followed with an apologetic look for the bemused librarian they left behind them.

CHAPTER NINE

arlton opened his eyes, disoriented, his head stuffed tight with a massive, pulsing ache. He was half sitting, stiffly propped against a wall, and he found he could not move his arms. His body was covered in little, random places of sharp pain and tingling numbness; he tried to shift away from the discomfort, but he was restrained somehow, and the little moves he could make just made new places hurt. He looked around the room, trying to get his bearings. It looked like a storage room: There were boxes along the walls, and discarded cans of paint and other cleaning supplies littered the floor, but there was more. There were piles of furry fabric everywhere. Carlton peered at them sleepily. He felt muzzy, like if he closed his eyes he could just fall back asleep, so easily . . . *No.* He shook his head hard, trying to clear it, and yelped. "Oh no," he groaned as the throbbing in his head demanded attention and his stomach flipped. He clenched his jaw and closed his eyes, waiting for the pounding and nausea to recede.

Eventually they did, fading back to something almost manageable, and he opened his eyes again, starting over. This time his mind had cleared a little, and he looked down at his body to see his restraints. *Oh no.*

He was wedged inside the heavy, barrel-shaped torso of a mascot costume, the headless top half of some kind of animal. His arms were trapped inside the torso section, pinned to his sides in an unnatural position by some sort of framework. The arms of the costume hung limp and empty from the sides. His legs stuck out incongruously from the bottom, looking small and thin in contrast. He could feel other things inside the mascot's torso, pieces of metal that pressed against his back and poked into him. He could feel raw patches on his skin, and he could not tell if the thing he felt trickling down his back was sweat or blood. Something was pressing into the sides of his neck; when he turned his head, whatever it was dug into his skin. The costume's fur was dirty and matted, a faded color that might once have been a bright blue but was now only a bluish approximation of beige. He could see a head of the same color a few feet away, sitting on a cardboard box, and with a flicker of curiosity he looked at it, but he could not tell what it was supposed to be. It looked as if someone had been told "make an animal" and had done just that, careful not to make it look like any specific *type* of animal.

He looked around the room, comprehension dawning. He knew where he was. The piles of fabric had faces. They were empty costumes, mascots from the restaurant, deflated, collapsed, and staring empty-eyed at him, like they wanted something.

He looked around, trying to assess calmly, though his heart was fluttering alarmingly in his chest. The room was small, a single bulb overhead lighting it dimly and flickering ever so slightly, giving the place a disquieting impression of movement. A small metal desk fan, brown with rust, gently oscillated in the corner, but the air it blew was heavy with the stale sweat of costumes left unwashed for a decade. Carlton was too hot; the air felt too thick. He tried to stand, but without his arms he could not brace himself, and as he moved he felt another violent wave of nausea, and a sudden, angry surge of pain in his head.

"I wouldn't do that," a raspy voice muttered. Carlton looked around, seeing no one, then the door opened. It moved slowly, and somewhere beneath his terror Carlton felt a twinge of impatience.

"Who is it? Let me out of this!" he said in panicked desperation.

The door squealed like an injured animal as it glided open, almost of its own accord, the frame empty. After a moment's pause, a yellow rabbit poked its head around the corner, its ears tilting at a jaunty angle. It was still for a moment, almost posing, then it came in with a bouncing walk, graceful, with none of the stiff, mechanistic movements of the animatronic animal. It did a small dance step, spun, and took a deep bow. Then it reached up and took off its own head, revealing the man inside the costume.

"I guess I shouldn't be surprised," Carlton said, his nerves triggering an automatic wisecrack. "Never trust a rabbit, I say." It didn't make sense, it wasn't funny, but the words were coming out of his mouth without any input from his brain. He still felt sick, his head still ached, but he had a sudden, visceral clarity: *This is what happened to Michael. You are what happened to Michael.*

"Don't speak," Dave said. Carlton opened his mouth to answer back, but the smart remark died on his tongue when he saw the guard's face. He had seemed somehow faded when they met, depleted and ineffectual. But now, as he stood over Carlton in his absurd-looking rabbit costume, he looked different. His face was the same, technically—his gaunt features and sunken eyes, his skin that seemed to have worn thin, ready to snap from strain—but now there was a mean, undeniable strength in him, a rodentine vitality that Carlton recognized.

It had occurred to Carlton years before that there were two types of nasty people: There were the obvious ones, like his sixth-grade English teacher who yelled and threw erasers, or the kid in fifth grade who picked fights with smaller children after school. That type was easy, their offenses public, brutal, and undeniable. But then there was the other kind of petty tyrant, those who grew spiteful with their small scraps of power, feeling more and more abused by the year—by family who did not appreciate them, by neighbors who slighted them in imperceptible ways, by a world that left them, somehow, lacking something essential.

Before him stood someone who had spent so much of his life fighting like a cornered rat that he had taken on the mantle of bitter sadism as an integral part of himself. He would strike out against others and revel in their pain, feeling righteously that the world owed him his cruel pleasures. The guard's face, with its malevolent delight in Carlton's pain and fear, was one of the most terrifying things he had ever seen. He opened and closed his mouth, then, valiantly, found his voice.

"What kind of a name for a serial killer is Dave?" he said. It came out as a trembling croak, lacking even the echo of bravado. Dave did not seem to hear him.

"I told you not to move, Carlton," he said calmly. He set the rabbit's head down on a plastic crate and began fiddling with the fastenings at the back of his neck. "It's not an order, it's a friendly warning. Do you know what I've put you in?"

"Your girlfriend?" Carlton said, and Dave made a thin curve of a smile.

"You're amusing," he said with distaste. "But no. You're not wearing a costume, Carlton, not precisely. You see, these suits were designed for two purposes: to be worn by men like me"—he gestured fluidly toward himself, with something that might have been pride—"and to be used as working animatronics like the ones you see on the stage. Do you understand?"

Carlton nodded, or began to, but Dave's raised eyebrow stopped him.

"I said don't move," he said. The neck of his costume came open, and he began to undo a second fastening at his back as he talked. "You see, all of the animatronic parts in that suit are still in it; they are simply held back by spring locks, like this."

Dave went to the pile of costumes and selected one, bringing the fuzzy green torso, headless, over to Carlton. He held out the costume, waggling two twisted pieces of metal that were attached to the sides of the neck.

"*These* are spring locks," he said, bringing the piece of metal so close to Carlton's face he almost could not focus his eyes on it. "Watch." He did something, touched some piece of the lock so imperceptibly that Carlton could not see what he had done, and it snapped shut with a sound like a backfiring car. Carlton stiffened, suddenly taking the order not to move deathly seriously.

"That's a very old costume, one of the first ones Henry made. You can trip these spring locks very, very easily if you don't know what you're doing," Dave went on. "It takes almost no movement at all."

"Henry?" Carlton said, trying to focus on what he was being told. He could still hear the snap, as if it had lodged in his head like a song that kept repeating. *I'm going to die*, he thought for the first time since waking. *This man will kill me, I will die, and then what? Will anyone even know?* He set his jaw and met Dave's eyes. "Who's Henry?"

"Henry," Dave repeated. "Your friend Charlie's father." He looked surprised. "Did you not know that he made this place?"

"Oh, right, well," Carlton said confusedly. "I just always thought of him as 'Charlie's dad.'"

"Of course," Dave said, the kind of polite murmur people made when they didn't care. "Well, that's one of his first suits," he said, gesturing at Carlton. "And if you trigger those spring locks, two things will happen: First, all the locks will snap right into you, making deep cuts all over your body, and a split second later all the animatronic parts they've been holding back, all that sharp steel and hard plastic, will instantly be driven into your body. You will die, but it will be slow. You'll feel your organs punctured, the suit will grow wet with your blood, and you will know you're dying for long, long minutes. You'll try to scream, but you will be unable to. Your vocal cords will be severed, and your lungs will fill with your own blood until you drown in it." There was a faraway look in his eyes, and Carlton knew with chilling certainty that Dave wasn't predicting. He was reminiscing.

"How—" Carlton's voice broke, and he tried again. "How do you know that?" he said, managing a raspy whisper. Dave met his eyes and smiled widely.

"How do you think?" He set down the costume he was holding and reached up to undo the final piece of his own. It took time; Carlton watched for several minutes as Dave romanced whatever mechanisms lay under the collar. He took the costume torso off with a flourish, and Carlton made an involuntary sound, a helpless and frightened mewl.

Dave had been shirtless under the costume, and now his bare chest was clearly visible even in the dim, flickering light. His skin was horribly scarred, with raised white lines that scored his flesh in a symmetrical pattern, each side of his body mirroring the other. Dave saw him looking and laughed, a sudden, happy sound. Carlton shivered at it. Dave raised his arms out from his body and turned slowly in a circle, giving Carlton ample time to see that the scars were everywhere, covering his back like a faint lace shirt, stretching to the waist of the rabbit pants as if they continued all the way down. On the back of his neck, where they were largest and most visible, two scars like parallel lines were etched from the nape of his neck all the way up to his scalp, disappearing into his hair. Carlton tried to swallow. His mouth was so dry he could not have spoken, even if there had been anything to say.

Dave smiled unpleasantly.

"Don't move," he said again.

"He's here; he has to be here!" Marla cried, staring despairingly at the door to Freddy's. She was clasping and unclasping her hands, the knuckles going white. Charlie watched her helplessly. There was nothing to say. The door was no longer covered in chains; instead it was simply no longer a door. It had been welded over; the metal was melted seamlessly into the frame, and the hinges were gone, covered in crude, patchy solder. They all stared, not fully able to comprehend what they were looking at. Charlie shifted her feet. She had stepped in a puddle as they hurried from the car, and now her shoes and socks were soaked and freezing. It seemed unforgivable to be focused on her own discomfort in such a moment, but she could not stop her attention from drifting to it.

"This is insane," Marla said, her mouth agape. "Who does this?" She threw up her hands in frustration. "Who does something like that?" She was almost shouting. "Someone did that! Someone welded this shut. What if Jason is in there?"

Marla put her hands over her face. Jessica and Lamar stepped forward to comfort her, but she waved them away.

"I'm fine," she said tightly, but she did not move, still staring at the place in the wall that had once been a door. She looked smaller, lesser; the panicked energy that had been driving her was gone, leaving her empty and without purpose. She looked at Charlie, ignoring the others, and Charlie met her eyes uncomfortably.

"What do we do?" Marla asked. Charlie shook her head.

"I don't know, Marla," she said uselessly. "If he's in there, we have to get him out. There has to be a way."

"There has to be another way in," John agreed, though he sounded surer than Charlie felt. "Freddy's had windows, a service door, right? There must have been fire exits. There has to be something!"

"Stop!" Marla cried, and they all froze in place. She was pointing at the floor.

"What is it?" Charlie asked, coming up next to her.

"It's Jason's footprint," Marla said. "Look, you can see the imprint; it's those silly shoes he spent a year's allowance on."

Charlie looked. Marla was right; there was a muddy footprint about Jason's size, still fresh. Marla's face was alive again, fiery and determined.

"He must have just been here," Marla said. "Look, you can see the tracks turn and leave again. The door must have been already welded when he got here. He's probably still here somewhere. Come on!"

Jason's tracks were heading farther down the alley, into the darkness, and the group crouched low to the ground, following his trail. Charlie hung back, not really helping but keeping an eye on the bobbing flashlight ahead. There was something she was forgetting, something she should know. Something about Freddy's. Noticing that she was apart, John let the others move ahead.

"You okay?" he asked in a low voice, and Charlie shook her head.

"I'm fine," she said. "Go ahead." He waited for her to say more, but she was staring ahead into the dark. *Another way in.*

"Found it!" Jessica's voice pierced the dark, and Charlie came back to herself and jogged to catch up to the others. Lamar had the flashlight again, and he was aiming it at an air vent close to the ground.

The vent was old and rusty, and its covering lay flat on the ground amid scattered footprints and clumps of mud.

"Jason, what are you doing?" Marla gasped and knelt beside the vent. "What are you thinking?" There was an edge to her voice, something teetering between panic and relief. "We have to go after him," she said.

Charlie watched, dubious, but said nothing. It was John who spoke up.

"It's too small," he said. "I don't think any of us will fit."

Marla looked down at herself, then around at the others one by one, calculating.

"Jessica," she said decisively. "Come on."

"What?" Jessica looked to the side as if there might be another of her. "I don't think I'll fit, Marla."

"You're the skinniest," Marla said shortly. "Just try, okay?"

Jessica nodded and went to the vent, kneeling in the muddy concrete that was the alley's floor. She studied the hole in the wall for a moment and tried to squeeze in, but her shoulders barely cleared the space, and after a moment she pulled back out, out of breath.

"Marla, I can't fit, I'm sorry," she said.

"You can fit!" Marla said. "Please, Jessica."

Jessica looked back at the others, and when Charlie saw her face it was almost white, harshly expressionless. *She's claustrophobic*, Charlie thought, but before she could speak, Jessica was back at the air vent, twisting herself, trying again to fit.

"Please," Marla said again, and Jessica shot back out like something had bitten her.

"I can't, Marla," she said, her breathing shallow and fast, as if she had been running full-out. "I don't fit!"

"There has to be another way in." Charlie stepped in, reaching her arm between Marla and Jessica as though breaking up a fight.

Charlie closed her eyes, trying again to remember. She pictured the restaurant, trying to see it not as they had the last few days, but as it had been years before. The lights were bright; it was full of people. "It used to get hot, stuffy," she said. "In summer it smelled like pizza and old french-fry grease and sweaty kids, and my dad would say . . ." *That's it.* "He would say, 'Whose brilliant idea was it to put a skylight in a closet?'" she finished triumphantly, relieved. She could picture the little supply room with the open roof. She and Sammy would sneak away and sit in there for a few minutes, enjoying the small stream of fresh air that filtered down from outside.

"So that's it. Let's get to the roof," John said, breaking Charlie's drift into memory.

"What roof?" Marla said, studying the top of the closed hall. She was no longer in a full-blown panic, reassured by evidence that Jason was still alive, but her anxiety was still palpable. Her glance darted constantly around the little group, as if her little brother might suddenly appear from the shadows.

"It's been covered over, like everything else," Lamar chimed in.

"Maybe not," Charlie said. "The roof of the mall is pretty high. I bet there's a crawl space, at least."

"A crawl space?" John said excitedly. "You mean a crawl space between the roof of Freddy's and the roof of the mall? Up there?" He stared up into the darkness for a moment. "A crawl space?" he repeated, his voice a little meeker.

Charlie was busy studying the ceiling of the corridor, measuring it in her head against what they had seen of the outside of the building. It was different—she was sure of it.

"This isn't the roof to the mall. It's not high enough," she said, feeling a spark of encouragement. She set off briskly down the hall, not waiting for the others. They followed, trailing behind her, and the space above her suddenly became illuminated as Lamar caught up and cast the beam of the flashlight upward. Charlie was going back and forth, looking from wall to ceiling and back again while trying to picture the space outside.

"The ceiling of this hall is probably level with the roof of Freddy's." Jessica's voice came from behind Charlie, who startled briefly. She had been so intent on her pursuit she had lost track of her friends.

"We have to get up there," Charlie said, turning back to the group expectantly. They looked blankly at her for a second. Then Lamar's arm moved reflexively, like he was about to raise his hand. He caught himself and cleared his throat instead.

"I hate to point out the obvious, but," Lamar said, gesturing. About ten feet ahead of them, a maintenance ladder rested against the old brick. Charlie grinned and hurried to the ladder, waving for John to follow. They grabbed it together; it was heavy, metal, and covered with spatters of paint, but it was manageable to carry. When Charlie had a firm grip on one side of the ladder, she turned her face back to the ceiling, searching.

"There is probably a hole, or a hatch, or something," she said.

"A hole, or a hatch, or something?" John echoed with a half smile as he lifted the other end of the ladder.

"Do you have a better idea? Now come on." She jerked the ladder forward so hard John stumbled and almost fell.

They moved slowly. With only one flashlight, they could not see where they were going and examine the walls at the same time, so every few yards they stopped for Lamar to run the light back and forth across the place where the brick wall met the dripping ceiling of the makeshift hallway. Though it slowed them down, Charlie was grateful for the breaks; the ladder, industrial metal, was heavy. She could have asked the others to switch off, but it felt essential somehow that she be part of the physical process. She wanted to help.

Marla's agitation was growing as they went, and after a few rounds of move-and-scan she started calling Jason's name softly.

"Jason! Jason, can you hear me?"

"He's inside," John said shortly. "He can't hear you." His voice was strained with the weight of the ladder—he had the wider end—and he sounded almost snappish. Marla glared at him.

"You don't know that."

"Marla, stop it," Jessica said. "We're doing everything we can."

Marla didn't answer. A few minutes later, they came to the end of the alley.

"So now what?" John said.

"I don't know," Charlie said, puzzled. "I was positive that we would find something."

"Is that the way life usually works for you?" John teased, raising an eyebrow at her.

From down the hall, Lamar let out a triumphant cry.

"Found it!"

Marla took off toward him at a run, and Jessica followed a little more cautiously behind, wary of obstacles in the dark.

Charlie gave John a wink and picked up the ladder again. He hurried to lift his side, and they lugged it back the way they came.

When Charlie and John caught up to the rest of the group, all three were looking up at the ceiling. Charlie mimicked their posture; sure enough, there was a square trapdoor, big enough for an adult to pass through, its edges barely visible in the darkness. Without speaking, they set up the ladder; it was perhaps ten feet high and rose close enough to the ceiling to access the door easily. Marla climbed up first as Lamar steadied the ladder on one side, Jessica on the other.

John and Charlie watched as Marla ascended.

"So the trapdoor there . . ." John pointed up at it. "The trapdoor of this hallway is right next to Freddy's. That will get us onto the roof of Freddy's, which is under the roof of the mall, in a crawl space. And on Freddy's roof, there's a skylight, which we will find while crawling through the crawl space." He drew an invisible diagram in the air with his finger as he spoke, and his tone was edged with skepticism. Charlie did not respond. Marla's footsteps on the ladder sounded through the hall, heavy, tinny thuds that echoed unsteadily all around them.

"Once we find the skylight in the crawl space," John went on, not certain if Charlie was even listening, "we are going to drop down through the skylight and into Freddy's, possibly with no way of getting back out."

At the top of the ladder, Marla fiddled with something on the ceiling that the others could not see, making little mutters of frustration.

"Is it locked?" Charlie called up.

"Okay, sure," John said, aware by now that he was talking only to himself. "This makes sense."

"The bolt is just stuck," Marla said. "I need—ha!" A dull snapping sound rang out. "Got it!" she cried. She raised her hands over her head and pressed upward, and slowly the door opened above her until it tipped over and fell with a thud.

"So much for sneaking in," John said drily.

"It doesn't matter," Charlie said. "We still have to go. Besides, do you really think whoever is in there doesn't know we're coming?"

Above them, Marla was navigating her way up through the door. She braced her arms on either side of the space and pushed up off the ladder. It swayed dangerously, and Lamar and Jessica clutched it, trying to stabilize it, but it was not necessary. Marla was already up and through, on the roof. They waited for her to say something.

"Marla?" Jessica called finally.

"Yeah, I'm fine," Marla said.

"What do you see?" Charlie called.

"Throw me the light." Marla's arm emerged from the trapdoor, flapping impatiently. Lamar got a bit closer and carefully lobbed the flashlight up. Marla snatched it out of the air, and immediately the beam vanished—the light had gone out.

In the crawl space, Marla sat in the dark trying to fix the flashlight. She shook it, rattling the batteries, and flipped the switch on and off uselessly. As she unscrewed the top of the light and blew into the battery cage, she felt a rising panic. Since realizing Jason had gone, Marla's entire being had been focused on him. It was only now, alone in the darkness, that she began to think about the danger she herself might be in. She screwed the top back onto the flashlight, and it came on instantly. The light flashed in her eyes, briefly clouding her vision. She pointed it away, then carefully swept it in a circle around her, revealing a sprawling void in all directions. It was the roof of Freddy Fazbear's Pizza.

"What do you see?" Charlie called again.

"You were right: There's space, but not much. It's so dark, and it smells awful up here." Her voice sounded shaky even to her own ears, and suddenly she was desperate not to be alone in this place. "Hurry, don't leave me up here by myself!"

"We're coming," Jessica called up to her.

"Me next," Charlie said, stepping forward. The ladder was rusty, and it made squeaking complaints as she climbed, protesting her weight as she moved from step to step. But it felt sturdy, and quickly she reached the trapdoor and did as Marla had done. She stood on the top step so she was head and shoulders through the door, braced her arms on either side, and pushed off the ladder, almost jumping, to land on Freddy's roof. There was not room to stand, scarcely room to sit—the space between the restaurant's roof and the mall's roof above it was less than a yard. Something was rattling above them, as if stones were falling overhead, and it took Charlie a moment to realize that it was the rain thundering on the uninsulated tin. Water dripped in on her head, and when she looked up she saw a place where the metal's seams had not been joined, two corrugated sheets simply lined up next to each other, allied by circumstance. She wiped her palms on her jeans; the shingles of the roof were wet, and her hands were covered in grit, dust, and something slick and more unpleasant.

She looked toward Marla, who was a few feet away.

"Here, come on. Get out of their way," Marla said, motioning her over, and Charlie hurried on her hands and knees. Jessica's head appeared in the trapdoor, and carefully she made her way up into the crawl space. Safely on the roof, Jessica looked around as if gauging something. Concerned, Charlie remembered her fear in the air vent, but Jessica took a long, deep breath.

"I can handle this," she said, though she did not sound as if she believed her own words. A moment later Lamar was next to them. He quickly reclaimed the flashlight and aimed it back toward the trapdoor. After a moment, John scrambled up into the crawl space—and something banged loudly beneath them, the sound repeating. Everyone but John startled at the sound.

"Sorry," he said. "That was the ladder."

"Charlie, which way?" Marla asked.

"Oh." Charlie closed her eyes again, retraced her steps as she had while they'd searched for a way in. "Straight across,

I think," she said. "As long as we get to the far side, we'll find it." Without waiting for responses, she started crawling in the direction she thought was right. A second later, light appeared ahead of her.

"Thanks," she called back softly to Lamar, who was steadying the flashlight, trying to anticipate where Charlie would go.

"I don't have anything else to do," he whispered.

The crawl space was wide. It should have felt spacious, but there were support beams and pipes strewn at random, intersecting the space or running across the roof below them so that it was a little like navigating a very cramped forest, ducking vines and climbing over fallen trees. The roof of Freddy's had a shallow upward slope; they would have to go down again once they reached the middle. The shingles beneath their hands and feet were soggy in a deep, swollen way that suggested they had not been truly dry in years, and a moldy smell rose from them. Every once in a while Charlie wiped her hands on her pants, knowing they would only be clean for a moment. From time to time, she thought she heard something skitter by, sounds a little too far away to be coming from their group, but she ignored them. *They have more right to be here than we do*, she thought, though she was not certain what species "they" might be.

The roof above them followed a bizarre pattern, sloping up and down without regard to the roof beneath, so that at one point it opened four feet above their heads, then at another plunged downward so close that it grazed their backs, forcing them to duck their heads and wriggle awkwardly through. Jessica was right behind Charlie, and from time to time she could hear her friend make soft, frightened noises, but every time she looked back, Jessica just nodded, stone-faced. They continued until they reached the wall that marked the edge of the roof.

"Okay," Charlie called, half turning behind her. "It should be near here. Let's spread out and look."

"No, wait. What's that?" Marla said, pointing. Charlie could not see what Marla had spotted, but she followed the direction until she came to it.

The skylight was a flat glass pane in the roof framed like a small window, a single panel with no visible handles, hinges, or latches. They leaned over it, trying to see into the room below, but the glass was too covered in grime for anything to show through. John reached forward and tried to clean it with his sleeve. He came away with the arm of his shirt black, but it had done no good—at least half the dirt was on the other side, and the skylight was still opaque with filth.

"It's just a closet; it's okay," Charlie said.

"But is anyone *in* the closet?" Lamar said.

"It doesn't matter," said Marla. "We don't have a choice."

Everyone looked at Charlie, who thoughtfully studied the skylight.

"It swings in," she said. "You pull down on this side"—she pointed—"and it swings. There's a latch on the inside, right there." She touched the side of the skylight, thinking. "Maybe if we—" She pushed on it, and it gave way almost instantly, jolting her with a sudden, panicked sense of falling, even though her weight was solidly on the roof.

"That's kind of narrow," John said. The skylight did not open all the way; the glass just tilted inward a little, barely enough for a person to slip through.

"I didn't build it," Charlie said, slightly irritated. "This is it, so if you're going, go."

Without waiting for a response, she swung her legs over the sill and lowered herself down, dangling for a moment in the dark. Closing her eyes and hoping the floor was not as far away as she remembered, she let go and fell.

She landed. The shock of impact ran through her legs, but it passed quickly.

"Bend your knees when you land!" she called up as she got out of the way. Marla dropped through, and Charlie went to the door, trying to find a light switch. Her fingers stumbled across the switch, and she flipped it up. The old fluorescent lights clicked and buzzed, and then slowly a dim and unreliable glow filled the space.

"All right," she whispered with a thrill of excitement. She turned around, and as something brushed her face, she had a fleeting impression of big plastic eyes and broken yellow teeth. She screamed and leaped back, clutching for balance at shelves that swayed as she grabbed them. The head she had touched, an uncovered wire frame for a costume with nothing but eyes and teeth to decorate it, wobbled precariously on the shelf beside Charlie, then fell to the ground. Her heart still pounding, Charlie brushed at herself roughly as if she were covered in spiderwebs, her legs unsteady as she moved back and forth with agitation. The head rolled across the floor, then came to rest at her feet, looking up at her with its cheerful, sinister smile.

Charlie jerked back from the ghastly grin, and something grabbed her from behind. She tried to yank free, but she was stuck, a pair of metal arms wrapped around her. The bodiless limbs clung to her shirt, their hinges biting into the cloth, and as she tried to wrest herself away her hair was caught, too, tangling her deeper into the wire until she felt like she would be consumed. Charlie screamed again, and the arms reached out farther, seeming to grow as she struggled against them. She fought back with all her strength, fueled by terror and a base, frantic fury that this thing would hurt her.

"Charlie, stop!" Marla cried. "Charlie!"

Marla grabbed her arm, trying to stop her frantic movement, using one hand to disengage Charlie's hair from the metal frame.

"Charlie, it's not real, it's just . . . robot parts," she said, but Charlie pulled away from Marla, still in a panic, and smacked her head into a cardboard box. She cried out, startled, as the box overturned. Eyes the size of fists fell to the ground like rain, showering down with a clatter and rolling everywhere, covering the floor. Charlie stumbled and stepped on one of the hard plastic orbs, sending her feet out from under her. She grabbed at a shelf, missed, and fell on her back, landing with a thud that took the wind out of her.

Stunned and gasping, she looked up. There were eyes everywhere, not just on the floor, but in the walls. They looked out at her from the dark, deep-socketed, shadowed eyes peering down from the shelves all around her. She stared, unable to look away.

"Charlie, come on." Marla was there, kneeling anxiously over her. She grabbed Charlie's arm again and pulled until Charlie was upright. Charlie still did not have her breath back, and as she inhaled thinly, she began to cry. Marla hugged her tightly, and Charlie let her.

"It's okay, it's okay," Marla whispered as Charlie tried to calm herself, looking around the storeroom for distraction.

It's not real, she told herself. They were in a storeroom, just a closet, and these were all spare parts. The air was thick with dust, and it tickled at her nose and throat as it poured off the shelves restlessly. The rest of the group dropped through the skylight one by one; John came last, landing in the middle of the room with a thump. Jessica sneezed.

"You okay?" John said as soon as he saw Charlie.

"Yeah, I'm fine." Charlie disentangled herself from Marla and crossed her arms, still collecting herself.

"You know we can't get back up through there," John said, looking up at the skylight.

"We just need something to stand on," Charlie said. "Or we can climb a shelf."

Jessica shook her head.

"No, look at the way it's opened."

Charlie looked. The skylight opened downward, so the pane of glass sloped in at a gentle angle, just enough to have let them through. To get out, they would have to—

"Oh," she said. There would be no getting out. However close they got to the skylight, the pane of glass would always be in the way, sticking out into the precise space they needed to pass through. If anyone tried to get a grip on the roof, they would have to lean so far over the glass that they would fall from the ladder.

"We might be able to break the glass," John started. "But the metal frame is going to be dangerous to climb over, even more dangerous with shards of broken glass." He fell silent and thought it through again, his face grim.

"It doesn't matter," Charlie said. "We'll find another way out. Let's start looking."

They peered cautiously out into the hallway. Lamar had turned off the flashlight, but it was easy enough to see their surroundings now with the light from the closet seeping into the hall. *At least nothing's dripping from the ceiling,* Charlie thought, wiping her hands on her pants again. The floor was black-and-white tile, as glossy as if it had just been polished. There were children's drawings on the walls, rustling with the air from the open skylight. Charlie remained motionless, more than aware of how much noise she had just made. *Does it know we're here?* she wondered, realizing as she did that by "it" she meant the building itself. It felt as if Freddy's was conscious of their presence, as if it reacted to them like a living, breathing thing. She reached out to brush her fingers against its wall, tracing lightly as if she were petting it. The plaster was still and cold, inanimate, and Charlie pulled her hand back. She wondered what Freddy's would do.

They wound around one corner, then another, and then stopped at the entrance to Pirate's Cove, hanging back from the doorway. *Pirate's Cove. I have my bearings again.* Charlie gazed at the little stage, no longer lit, and the curtain that hid its sole performer.

A few small lights flickered on the sides of the stage then came on, illuminating the space with a pale-gray glow. Charlie looked around and saw Lamar standing by the doorway with his hand on a switch.

"We don't have a choice," he said defensively, gesturing to his flashlight; its light was failing. Charlie nodded resignedly, and Lamar switched off the dying flashlight.

"I want to take a look in this control room," Marla said, pointing to the small door nearby. "Lamar, come with me. The rest of you try the other one. If we each take one set of cameras, we can see the whole restaurant. If Jason's in this place, we'll see him."

"I don't think we should split up," Charlie said.

"Wait," said Lamar. He passed John the dead light, freeing his hands. From his pockets he produced two walkie-talkies; they were large, black, boxy things Charlie had only seen attached to police officers' belts.

"Where did you get those?" she asked.

Lamar smiled mysteriously. "I'm afraid I can't tell you that," he said.

"He stole them from Carlton's house," Jessica stated plainly, taking one from his hand and examining it.

"No, they were in the garage. Mrs. Burke told me where to find them. They work, I tested."

Mrs. Burke knew we would come here? Charlie thought. Marla just nodded; maybe she had already known, or maybe nothing could surprise her anymore.

"Come on," Marla said and walked between the tables in front of Pirate's Cove, careful not to disturb anything. Lamar leaned over Jessica to show her how to use the walkie-talkie.

"It's this button," he said, indicating it, and then he took off after Marla.

After a startled moment, the rest of them followed. Something clutched in Charlie's stomach, the reality that both Jason and Carlton might truly be in danger seizing her. It was not that she had forgotten, but while they were outside, trying to solve the puzzles, it was possible to gain some distance from what was happening. She watched Marla stalking toward the control room with a bleak authority. Marla crouched at the small door before turning to Charlie.

"Go," she said, nodding toward the hall that led to the main dining area. They went, Charlie taking the lead as they crept down the hall, heading for the main stage.

Marla looked at Lamar, who nodded. She grasped the doorknob, clenched her teeth, and forced the door open all in one motion.

"Marla!"

Marla jumped, barely suppressing a scream. Jason was huddled in the space beneath the monitors, his eyes wide and terrified, staring at the door like a frightened mouse.

"Jason!" Marla crawled into the control room and swooped him into her arms. Jason hugged her back, for once grateful, even desperate, for her intense affection. She held on tight, crushing him to her until he began to worry that he might, in fact, be crushed.

From outside Marla's consuming embrace, Jason heard brief static. He looked over Marla's shoulder to see Lamar studying the walkie-talkie, preparing to speak into it.

"Jessica? We found him. He's okay," he said.

More static and words Jason did not quite catch came from the radio. The first wave of relief had worn off, and his ribs were starting to hurt.

"Marla?" He tapped her on the shoulder, first gently, then harder. "Marla!"

She let him go but took hold of his shoulders for a moment, peering into his eyes as if to be sure it was really him, that he had not been somehow replaced, or irrevocably damaged.

"Marla, cool it," he said as casually as he could, managing to keep his voice from shaking. Marla let go of his shoulders, giving him a playful shove, and began to scold him as she pulled him the rest of the way out from under the control panel.

"Jason, how could you—" Marla was interrupted as Lamar descended the rest of the way into the small room.

"Through the vent? Really?" Lamar laughed.

"You could have been killed, crawling through the air duct like that!" Marla added, grasping his shoulders.

Jason fought free, flailing his arms until she let him go.

"Okay!" he exclaimed. "Everybody missed me, good, glad to know I'm important."

"You *are* important," Marla said fiercely, and Jason rolled his eyes theatrically.

The little room lit up as Lamar flipped a switch, bringing the screens to life. Marla looked at Jason thoughtfully, then turned her attention to the security cameras. "Okay, let's see what we can see."

Lamar looked from screen to screen. The top middle screen showed the main dining room and the stage, and as they watched, Charlie, Jessica, and John appeared, crossing the room in a V formation, Charlie at the front.

"Look," Marla said suddenly, pointing to the screen at the lower right. "Look."

The night guard was there; though they could not make out his face, his baggy uniform and sagging shoulders told them that it was the same man. He was in the hall near the restaurant's entrance, walking past the party rooms and the arcade with a slow, purposeful gait.

"Lamar, warn them," Marla ordered urgently.

Lamar spoke into the walkie-talkie. "Jessica, the guard is somewhere around there. Hide!"

There was no response from the radio, but onscreen the group of three froze. Then, as one, they made for the control room under the stage, squeezing in and closing themselves in just as the guard appeared in the doorway.

★　　★　　★

Voices. People moving around.

Carlton did not allow himself to sigh in relief—a rescue wouldn't do him any good if he got his insides punctured by a hundred tiny robot parts first. Instead he continued with what he had been doing, inching his way across the floor and into the view of the security camera that perched near the ceiling just above the door. Each movement was so scarce it felt like nothing, but he had been doing this for over an hour, and he was almost, *almost* there. He kept his breathing steady, using his trapped hands to lift his body a tiny bit, move to the side, and let himself down again, just a little farther to the right. His fingers were cramping and his head still ached, but he kept going, relentless.

Although he was still afraid, still painfully aware of how easily he could trigger his own death, at some point the fear had dulled, or perhaps he had just become accustomed to it. Panic could not last forever; eventually the adrenaline had run out. Now, at least, the need for slow, precise movement took precedence over everything else. It was all there was. Carlton made one final movement and stopped, closing his eyes for a moment. He had made it.

Can't stop now.

The others were here. It had to be them, and if they were looking for him, they would check the cameras. He stared up into the lens, willing himself to be seen. He could not wave or jump up and down. He tried rocking back and forth a little, but no matter how stiffly he held himself, he felt the press of spring locks, ready to give. He bit his lip in frustration.

"Just see me!" he whispered to no one, but all at once he felt as if he had been heard, felt the inexplicable sense of someone else's presence in the room. His heart began to race again, the adrenaline that had given out finding its second wind.

Carefully, slowly, he looked around, until something caught his eye.

It was only one of the costumes, slumped empty in the shadows, half-hidden in the corner of the room. It was motionless, but its face was pointed directly at him, staring. As Carlton looked back, he realized that deep within the recesses of the costume's eye sockets were two tiny glints of light. He felt little muscles twitch, a restrained shudder running through his body, not quite enough to get him killed. He did not look away.

As Carlton held the creature's gaze, he felt himself begin to calm. His heart's pounding eased, and his breath grew even. It was as though suddenly he was safe, though he knew the suit he was wearing was still only one flinch, one startled jump, from killing him. Carlton kept looking at those two pinpoints of light, and as he did, he heard a voice. In a gasping instant, all the air was sucked from his lungs. As the voice spoke, that voice he would have known anywhere, that voice he would have given anything to hear again, Carlton began to weep, using all his will to keep his body from shaking. The eyes in the dark were intent on his face as the voice went on, speaking secrets to Carlton in the ringing silence, telling him things that he dreaded, things that someone had to hear.

CHAPTER TEN

The screens all lost their pictures and flipped to static.

"Hey!" Marla cried. She banged against the side of a monitor, and the image lurched, distorted, then sputtered and went out again. She hit it again, and with another spasm of static the image slowly cleared; as it resolved, the stage appeared.

"Something's wrong," Lamar said, and all three leaned forward, trying to get a better look.

"Bonnie," Jason said in a grave tone.

"Bonnie," Marla echoed, looking at Lamar with alarm. "Where's Bonnie?" Lamar hit the button on the walkie-talkie.

"Charlie," he said urgently. "Charlie, don't leave the control room."

*　　★　　★

In the control room under the stage, Charlie and Jessica peered at the monitors, scanning for signs of life. "It's too dark; I can't see anything on these," Jessica complained.

"There!" Charlie said, pointing. Jessica blinked.

"I can't see anything," she insisted.

"It's Carlton, right there. I'm going to get him." Not waiting for a response, Charlie crawled toward the exit.

"Charlie, wait," John said, but she was already out the door. It slammed shut behind her, and all three of them heard the dull metal thud of the drop lock falling into place. "Charlie!" John yelled again, but she was already gone.

"It's bolted shut," John grunted as he pulled on the door. The walkie-talkie sputtered, and Lamar's voice came choppily from the little box.

"Ch-lie, don't leave—r-m." Jessica and John exchanged a glance, and John picked up the radio.

"Too late," he said, looking to Jessica as he lowered the walkie-talkie.

Charlie made her way unsteadily between chairs, but after only moments she realized she had gotten herself turned around. The lighting had changed; now a single blinding blue light was strobing on and off above the stage. Over and over, the room flashed with a blinding burst, like lightning, then was instantly dark again. Charlie covered her eyes, trying to remember what she had bumped into first. Metal chairs and foil party hats pulsed like beacons in the dark with each burst of light, and Charlie's head began to throb.

She squinted, trying to orient herself, but beyond the tables surrounding her, all she could see were a thousand afterimages burned into her retinas. She had no idea which way to go to find Carlton. She leaned against a nearby chair and pressed her hand tightly over her forehead.

A table screeched against the floor briefly, and Charlie knew that it hadn't been her. She turned around, but the light had gone dark. When it flashed again she was looking directly at the stage—where there should have been three sets of eyes, she saw only two. Freddy and Chica stared down at her, their plastic gazes catching the light, twinkling with the strobe. Their heads seemed to follow her as she moved along the table.

Bonnie was gone.

Suddenly she felt exposed, all at once noticing just how many places there were in the open room for something to hide, just how visible she was to anyone—anything—that might be watching. She thought briefly of the little control room she had just left and felt a pang of regret. *Coming out here might have been very stupid . . .*

Another screech sounded, and she whirled around to see the table behind her moving slowly away. She turned to run, but she slammed into something before she could take a step. She jerked up her hands in the darkness to shield herself and touched matted fur. The strobe threw its light out again, and this time garbled noise blared from the gaping mouth in front of her. *Bonnie.* Bonnie stood only inches from her, his mouth opening and closing rapidly and his eyes rolling wildly in his head. Charlie jerked away, then backed up slowly. The rabbit did not try to follow, just continued his bizarre and silent incantation, his eyes aimlessly ricocheting in his head. Her foot caught on the leg of a metal folding chair; she fell back, landing hard on her bottom. She started to crawl, staying low, hurrying to get away from Bonnie. A spotlight flashed from the stage, this one clearly aimed at her. She raised her hand to see who was there, but the light blinded her. All she could make out were two sets of following eyes.

Charlie screamed and scrambled to her feet. She took off running, not looking back, and made it across the room and to the hallway that led to Pirate's Cove. She ducked into the bathroom along its wall. The door echoed when it shut behind her; the room was empty, with nothing but three sinks and three stalls. Only one of the fluorescent lights was on, and just barely, only enough to color the room dark gray instead of black. The metal walls of the stall dividers looked flimsy, and Charlie had a sudden vision of Bonnie, larger than life, grabbing the metal frame with his paws and ripping it up from the ground, the bolts tearing right out of the floor. She banished the thought and ran into the farthest stall from the door, slipping the lock—so small it looked almost delicate—into place. She sat on top of the toilet tank, her feet pulled up onto the seat and her back pressed against the blue tile wall of the bathroom. In the empty room, Charlie could hear her own breath echoing. She forced it to slow and closed her eyes, telling herself to be silent, to hide.

"Charlie?" John was still pounding on the little door of the control room. "Charlie! What's going on out there?"

Jessica sat quietly, still rattled from the screams and crashes outside.

"She can take care of herself," John said, easing his grip on the door.

"Yeah," Jessica said. He did not turn around to look at her.

"We have to get out of here," John said. He rattled the door again—the top swayed a little as he pulled, but the bottom was stuck fast. He hunched down farther. There was a lock, a deadbolt that dropped straight into the floor. The latch to pull it open had broken off long ago, leaving only a jagged ledge so thin he could scarcely get his fingers around it. As he yanked it upward, it cut into his fingers, leaving thin red lines. The bolt stayed fast in place.

"Jessica, you try," he said, turning to look at her. Her eyes were on the wall of televisions; they were all showing static, but every now and then one flashed a picture. "Never mind," John said. "Keep watching." He bent his head again and went back to the deadbolt.

In the bathroom, Charlie was silent. She paid attention to each breath she took, each inhale and exhale a slow, deliberate process. She had tried meditating once; she had hated it, but now the intense focus on her breathing was calming. *I guess I just needed the right motivation*, she thought. *Like staying alive.* The stalls rattled briefly, and there was a distant booming sound that went on for several seconds. *It's storming outside.*

She kept her eyes trained on the floor. The light overhead was so dim it scarcely illuminated her stall. She held her breath. The light flickered and let out a brief hum, then was silent. The toilet tank she sat on felt unstable; she scooted to the edge of it to quietly let her foot down. Just as the tip of her shoe touched the tile, the wide bathroom doors opened with a thunderous bang.

Without thinking she jerked her foot up, and the lid of the porcelain tank clanged like pots clattering together. She held herself perfectly still, her shoe suspended in the air, then carefully pulled her foot back into place on top of the toilet seat. *That was too loud*, she thought. Carefully, she leaned forward and reached up with one hand to grasp the stall divider. She pulled herself up to stand slowly, the toilet seat rocking on its hinges beneath her feet.

She peered out over the top at the two stalls next to her. It was too dark to see beyond the metal stalls, and the whole row of them swayed gently from her weight.

There was a shuffling sound; something wide and heavy was sliding across the floor, not trying nearly as hard as she was to be quiet. Her eyes darted from the stall door beside her to the bathroom door. The shuffling continued, but she could not tell where it was coming from; the sound filled the room.

Suddenly the nebulous sound resolved: It was crisp, and it was nearby. The wall she clung to trembled slightly. She panned her gaze around the room, hoping her eyes would adjust a little more. She could make out a trash can by the door and the outline of the sinks. Apprehensively, she looked back at the door of her stall, letting her focus creep along the edges until she set her eyes on the inch-wide gap along the door. A large plastic eye stared back, unblinking and dry, fixed directly on her. Two large and unnatural rabbit ears hung over the top of the door.

Charlie clasped her hand over her mouth and jumped to the floor as fast as she could, dropping to her stomach and scooting along the floor into the second stall. She heard Bonnie rattle the door of the stall she had just left, but the shuffling feet did not move. She crawled under the next divider and into the stall nearest the entrance. This time her foot bumped the toilet behind her, and the lip dropped down with a loud clank.

Charlie froze. The shuffling thing did not move. For what felt like an age, Charlie held her breath. *He heard, he must have heard!* But Bonnie still made no sound. Charlie held still and listened, waiting for another sound of movement to mask her own. Her breathing seemed louder than before. She lowered her head, trying to make out shapes along the floor.

The shuffling sound resumed, and now, without warning, it was directly in front of her. She held her breath, desperately trying to make out any forms in the darkness. *There he is.* A large, padded foot was just outside the door, as if it had stopped midstep. *Is he leaving? Please leave*, Charlie pleaded. There was a new sound: stiff fabric, softly crunching. *What is that?* The foot outside the door had not moved. The noise grew louder, the sound of fabric and fur twisting and stretching, tearing and popping. *What is that?* Charlie dug into the floor with her nails, holding down a guttural scream. *He's bending over.* A large paw touched down gently in front of her, then another shape: the creature's head. It was massive, filling the space under the door. Gracefully, Bonnie lowered himself to the floor and turned his head sideways until his eye met Charlie's. His giant mouth was open wide with a ghoulish excitement, as though he had found someone in a game of hide-and-seek.

A warm burst of air rolled in under the stall door. *Breath?* Charlie clasped her hand over her nose and mouth; the stench was unbearable. Another wave of it hit her face, hotter and more putrid. She closed her eyes, on the point of relinquishing the hope of escape. Maybe if she kept her eyes closed long enough, she would wake up. Another gust of hot air hit, and she jerked back, hitting the back of her head on the toilet. She recoiled with pain and threw her arm in front of her, shielding her face against attack. No attack came. She opened one eye. *Where is he?*

Suddenly the metal walls around her swayed with a resounding bang. Charlie startled and covered her head as Bonnie struck again. The stalls rocked on their legs, and the bolts screeched as they were yanked free from the floor, the whole assembly seeming ready to collapse. Charlie scrambled under the last divider and climbed to her feet, grasping for the door handle to pull it shut as she ran out.

She ran back into the main dining area, darting toward the control room. Her eyes no longer adjusted to the light, she ran with her hands in front of her, unable to see farther than her next steps.

"John!" she cried, grabbing the doorknob and yanking at it, pushing. Nothing happened.

"Charlie, it's stuck!" John shouted back from inside. As Charlie struggled with the door, she glanced up at the stage.

Chica was gone.

"John!" Charlie shouted in desperation. Without waiting for a response, Charlie took off again, running for a hall to her left, trying to get as much distance from the bathroom as possible.

The hall was almost completely dark, and as she ran, open doorways yawned at her with wide black mouths. Charlie did not stop to look inside any of them, instead only praying that nothing jumped out at her. She reached the last door and paused for a brief moment, hoping against hope that it would be unlocked. She grabbed the knob and twisted. Thankfully, it fell open easily.

She slid through the door, then closed it rapidly, trying not to make a sound. She stood watching the door for a long moment, half expecting it to be flung open, and then finally she turned. It was only then that she saw him: Carlton was there. His eyes widened in surprise when he saw her, but he did not move, and after her eyes adjusted to the dim light she understood. He was trapped, wedged somehow into the top half of one of the animatronic suits, his head poking out from the wide shoulders of the costume. His face was white and exhausted, and Charlie knew why. *The spring locks.* She heard her father's voice for a moment. *It could snap off your nose!*

"Carlton?" Charlie said cautiously, as if her voice alone might set off the mechanisms.

"Yup," he said, with the same faltering tone.

"That costume is going to kill you if you move."

"Thanks," he wheezed, half attempting a laugh. Charlie forced a smile.

"Well, today is your lucky day. I'm probably the only person who knows how to get you out of that thing alive."

Carlton exhaled a long and shaky breath. "Lucky me," he said.

Charlie knelt at his side, studying the costume for long moments without touching it. "These two spring locks at the neck aren't holding anything back," she said at last. "He just rigged them to snap and pierce your throat if you try to move. I have to undo those first, and then we can open the back of the costume and get you out. But you can't move, Carlton, seriously."

"Yeah, serial killer man explained the not moving to me," he said. Charlie nodded and went back to looking at the costume, trying to devise an approach.

"Do you know who I'm wearing?" Carlton asked, almost casually.

"What?"

"The costume, do you know what character it was supposed to be?" Charlie studied it, then looked around until she saw the matching head.

"No," she said. "Not everything he built made it to the stage." Her fingers suddenly stopped working. "Carlton." Charlie carefully surveyed the array of costumes and parts that lined the walls in varying stages of completion. "Carlton," she repeated. "Is he in here?"

With a new sense of dread, Carlton struggled to get a look behind him without moving. "I don't know," he whispered. "I don't think so, but I've been kind of in and out."

"Okay, stop talking. I'll try to work fast," Charlie said. She had the mechanism figured out, or at least she thought she did.

"Not too fast," Carlton reminded her.

Carefully, slowly, she reached into the costume's neck and took hold of the first spring lock, maneuvering it until her fingers were wedged between the lock and Carlton's neck.

"Careful with that artery; I've had it since I was a kid," Carlton said.

"Shh," Charlie whispered. When Carlton spoke, she could feel his neck move; he was not going to set off the locks by talking, she thought, but the feeling of his tendons moving under her hands was unsettling.

"Okay," he whispered. "Sorry. I talk when I'm nervous." He clamped down his jaw and bit his lips together. Charlie reached down farther into the costume's neck and found the trigger. With a stinging snap, the lock sprang against her hand, so hard that it numbed her fingers. *One down*, she thought as she pulled it, harmless, out of the neck of the costume. She flexed her fingers until the feeling came back into them, then crawled over to Carlton's other side and began the process again. She looked over her shoulder from time to time, making sure every costume was still in its place against the wall.

His skin was warm under her touch, and even though he was not speaking, she could still feel movement, feel the life in him. She could feel his pulse against the back of her wrist as she worked, and she blinked back unexpected tears. She swallowed hard and focused on the task, trying to ignore the fact that she was touching someone who would die if she failed him.

She worked open the spring lock again, taking the impact on the palm of her hand and pulling the disabled device free of the costume. Carlton took a deep breath in, and she startled.

"Carlton, don't relax!"

He stiffened and exhaled slowly, his eyes wide and frightened.

"Right," he said. "Still a death trap."

"Stop talking," Charlie pleaded again. She knew exactly how much danger he was still in, and she could not bear to hear him speak now, if he was about to die. "Okay," she said. "Almost there." She crawled around behind him, where a series of ten leather and metal fasteners held the back of the costume together. She considered it for a moment. She needed to keep the costume still, exactly as it was, until the last moment. She sat down behind him and bent her knees, positioning herself so that she could hold the costume in place with her legs as she opened it.

"I didn't know you cared," Carlton muttered as though attempting to put a joke together but too tired and too scared to finish it. Charlie didn't answer.

One by one, she worked the fasteners free. The leather was stiff, the metal tightly fitted, and each one fought back as she worked, clinging together. When she was halfway up the back of the costume, she felt its weight begin to shift. She gripped it tighter with her knees, holding it together. Finally, she undid the last one, at the nape of his neck. She took a deep breath. This was it.

"Okay, Carlton," she said. "We're almost done. I'm going to open this and throw it forward. When I do, you pull out of it as fast as you can, okay? One . . . two . . . three!"

She yanked the costume open and thrust it away with all her strength, and Carlton jerked back from it, toppling roughly into her. Charlie felt a sharp, quick pain on the back of her hand as she pulled free, but the costume skittered halfway across the room, leaving them clear. A series of snaps sounded, making a noise like fireworks, and they both cried out, leaping back and banging into a heavy metal shelf. Together they watched as the empty costume writhed and twisted across the floor, the animatronic parts snapping violently into place. When it came to a stop, Charlie stared, fixated. The thing was just a torso, just an object.

Beside her, Carlton let out a low, pained groan, then turned and vomited onto the floor beside him, heaving and retching like he would be turned inside out. Charlie watched, unsure what to do. She put a hand on his shoulder and kept it there as he finished, wiped his mouth, and sat gasping for breath.

"Are you okay?" she said, the words sounding small and ridiculous.

Carlton nodded wearily, then winced. "Yeah, I'm fine," he said. "Sorry about the floor. I guess it's your floor, kind of."

"You might have a concussion," Charlie said, alarmed, but he shook his head, moving more slowly this time.

"No, I don't think so," he said. "My head hurts like somebody hit it really hard, and I feel sick from being stuck in this room and pondering my death for hours, but I think I'm okay. My mind is okay."

"Okay," Charlie said doubtfully. Then something he had said finally registered. "Carlton, you said 'serial killer man explained' for you not to move. You saw who did this to you?"

Carlton got to his knees carefully, then stood, bracing himself on a nearby box. He looked at Charlie. "I was trapped in that thing for hours; I'm all tingly." He shook out his foot as if to make the point.

"Did you see who it was?" Charlie repeated.

"Dave, the guard," Carlton said. He sounded almost surprised that she did not know. Charlie nodded. She had known already.

"What did he tell you?"

"Not much," Carlton said. "But . . ." His eyes opened suddenly, as if he had just remembered something of grave importance. He looked away from Charlie and slowly dropped to his knees.

"What is it?" Charlie whispered.

"Do you want to hear?" he said. He seemed suddenly calm for someone who had so narrowly escaped death.

"What is it?" she demanded. He glanced nervously at her for a moment, then took a deep breath, his face draining to white.

"Charlie, the kids, all those years ago . . ."

Charlie snapped to attention.

"What?"

"All of them, Michael and the others, they were taken from the dining room when no one was looking, and they were brought here." Carlton suddenly recoiled and moved toward the doorway, watching the walls as though they were crawling with invisible creatures. "He—Dave, the guard—he brought them here . . ." Carlton rubbed his arms like he was suddenly cold and squinted in pain. "He put them into suits, Charlie," he said, his face twisting in sorrow or disgust. "Charlie." He stopped abruptly, a faraway look in his eyes. "They are still here."

"How do you know that?" Charlie said in such a soft whisper that she was almost inaudible.

Carlton motioned toward the far corner of the room. Charlie looked; a yellow Freddy costume was propped against the wall, the costume all fitted together, as if he were about to walk onstage for a show.

"That's the one. That's the bear I remember from the other restaurant." Charlie clasped her hand over her mouth.

"Other restaurant?" Carlton looked puzzled.

"I don't understand." Charlie's gaze was still fixed on the yellow costume. "Carlton, I don't understand." Her tone was urgent.

"Michael."

Charlie stared at him. *Michael?*

"What do you mean?" she said in a level voice.

"I know how it sounds," he said, and then his voice dropped to a whisper. "Charlie, I think it's Michael in that suit."

"I still can't get this thing out!" John sighed in frustration and rubbed his hand; the lock was leaving harsh red imprints

312

on his fingers. Jessica murmured something sympathetic, but she did not take her eyes off the screens.

"I can't see anything!" she burst out after a moment.

The radio squawked, and then Marla's voice came, calling to them from the control room in Pirate's Cove.

"Both of you, be quiet and don't move." They froze, hunching down in their places. Jessica looked at John, a question in her eyes, but he shrugged, as at a loss as she was.

Something thudded against the door. John jumped away, almost falling.

"Marla?" Jessica said with a pale expression. "Marla, that's you out there, right?" The thud came again, more powerful than before, and the door shook under it.

"What is that, a sledgehammer?" John whispered hoarsely. The door pounded in again and again, dents appearing in the metal door, which had looked so solid. They huddled back against the control panel with nothing to do but watch. Jessica grabbed the back of John's shirt, knotting the cloth between her fingers, and he did not shake her away. The door rocked in again, and this time a hinge unfolded slightly, exposing a thin crack between the door and the frame. The door still held, but it would not hold for long. John felt Jessica's fingers tighten on his shirt; he wanted to turn and give her some kind of comfort, but he was mesmerized, unable to look away. He could almost see out through the little open space, and he craned his neck. Another blow came. The crack widened, and on the other side he saw eyes peering in, calm and expressionless.

"Get out, get out!" Marla shouted, waving her hands at the security monitor as if John and Jessica could see her, as if it would do any good if they could. Lamar had both hands clapped over his mouth, his eyes wide, and Jason was sitting on the floor, waiting nervously as though an attack on their own door might begin at any moment. The monitors were dark, but it was clear that something large was lurking in front of the main stage, a black static shape that prowled back and forth, momentarily blocking the entire picture.

"Marla," Lamar whispered, hoping to quiet her. "Marla, look—" He pointed to the monitor showing Pirate's Cove, just outside their door. Marla looked over his shoulder at the other screen. The curtain was pulled back, and the space was completely empty. The OUT OF ORDER sign hung perfectly straight across the platform, untouched.

"The lock, we didn't . . . ," Marla said feebly, realizing now the magnitude of their mistake. Marla turned to Jason, then let out a panicked whimper—the door behind him was slowly opening.

"Shhh." Lamar quickly flipped a small switch, killing the light in the control room, and backed against the wall next to the door. Marla and Jason mimicked his motions, flattening themselves against the wall across from him. The monitors still flickered with static, illuminating the space in oscillating grays and the occasional flash of white.

The small door creaked outward at an excruciating pace, a gaping black void widening until the door stopped, fully open.

"Marla!" a static-laced voice called from somewhere on the floor. Lamar shot out his foot across the narrow carpet, trying to catch the walkie-talkie.

"Shhh, shhh . . ." Marla closed her eyes, pleading in her mind for Jessica to stop talking.

"Marla, where are you?" Jessica's voice called again. Lamar managed to flip the walkie-talkie onto its side, and with a *click* it went silent. He didn't know if he had jostled a battery out of place or somehow managed to flip the switch, but it didn't matter.

There was nowhere to hide in the tiny room. The ceiling was too low to stand, and even with their backs against the wall their legs stretched under the doorframe. The ledge under the door was high enough to hide their legs from anything outside, but not from anything that managed to get in.

As one, they stopped breathing. The room was no longer empty; something was entering the space. As it pressed forward into the room, they saw a snout and the scratchy gloss of two unblinking eyes staring straight ahead. The monstrous head threatened to fill the room.

"Foxy," Jason mouthed, making no sound. The plastic eyes clicked left and right with unnatural motions, searching but not seeing. The jaw twitched as though about to open, but never did.

The dim light from the monitors gave his face a reddish hue, leaving the rest of him shrouded in darkness. His head slowly moved backward, his ears moving up and down at random, programmed as an afterthought a decade before. As Foxy backed away, his eyes thrashed back and forth, one partially hidden under a rotting eyepatch. Marla held her breath, dreading the moment when the eyes would fix on her. The head was almost out the door when the eyes clicked to the right and found Marla. The head stopped, its jaw frozen, slightly open. The plastic eyes remained on Marla, who sat in terrified silence. After a moment, the head retreated, leaving a black and empty space.

Jason darted forward to find the door outside and shut it, and Marla made a weak grab at him, trying to stop him. He brushed past her, then stopped, kneeling in the doorway. He looked into the darkness, only now afraid of what must be there. He crawled slowly forward, his torso disappearing temporarily as he reached outside for the doorknob, then pulled himself back in and gently closed the door. Marla and Lamar closed their eyes and let out a deep breath at the same time.

Jason looked at them; he was almost smiling when, in a blur, the door burst open again and an ugly metal hook sank into his leg. He screamed in pain. Marla leaped to grab him, but she was too slow. She watched helplessly as Jason was dragged through the doorway.

"Marla!" he cried, clawing futilely at the floor, and she howled in despair as he was taken from her again, nothing visible of his assailant but the awful glimmer of the hook.

Marla dove toward the door after him, falling to her knees and crawling toward the thing, but Lamar grabbed her shoulder and yanked her back, taking hold of the door. Before he could pull it shut, it was ripped from his hands with an inhuman strength. Suddenly Foxy was there before them, coming inside.

He was full of life, a different creature, and he turned to look at Marla, his silver eyes appearing to comprehend. His face was a canine rictus, the scrappy orange fur insufficient to cover up his skull. He looked between them, turning his ghoulish smile first on Lamar, then on Marla. His eyes flared and dimmed, and he snapped his jaws with a sound like something breaking. They stared, backed up against the control panel, and then Lamar realized suddenly what he was looking at.

"He can't fit all the way in," he whispered. Marla looked. It was true—Foxy's shoulders were jammed in the doorway, his head the only part he could wedge through the door.

Lamar lunged forward and kicked the animatronic, bracing himself against the wall and striking out with his foot three times before Foxy gave a low whine, a sound more machine than animal, and slunk back out into the dark. Lamar snapped the door shut behind him and slid the deadbolt into place. They stared at each other for a long moment, breathing hard.

"Jason!" Marla screamed.

Lamar put his arms around her. She let him hug her, but she did not cry, just closed her eyes.

"What do you mean, it's Michael in the suit?" Charlie said softly, as if she might be talking to someone who had gone mad, while also desperate to hear the answer. Carlton looked at the yellow bear for a long moment, and when he turned back to Charlie, his face was calm. He opened his mouth to speak, and Charlie put a finger to her lips. Something was coming; she could hear footsteps out in the hall, moving toward them. Deliberate, heavy steps, the approach of someone who did not mind if anyone heard. Charlie looked wildly around the room and spotted a pipe in a corner. She grabbed it and hurried to stand behind the door, where whoever opened it would not see her. Carlton picked up the torso, as though to use it as a weapon somehow. He looked confused, like he was not thinking clearly.

"Don't," Charlie warned in a low voice, but she was too late. Something snapped inside the suit. Carlton dropped it and stepped back, a shimmer of blood on his hand.

"Are you okay?" Charlie whispered. He nodded, and then the doorknob turned.

Dave appeared in the doorway, his head held high and his face grim. It should have been imposing, but he just looked like a man walking through a door.

"Now you've done it," he announced to the room in general, then his eyes lit on Carlton, unfettered. His face darkened. Before he could move, Charlie raised the pipe high, stepped forward, and swung it down on his head with a sickening *thunk*.

Dave turned, shock on his face. Charlie lifted the pipe, ready to attack again, but the man just stumbled backward against the wall and dropped into a sitting position.

"Carlton! Come on," Charlie said urgently, but he was looking down at his injured hand. "Carlton? Are you hurt?"

"No," he said, shaking off his reverie and wiping his hand clean with his black shirt.

"Come on," Charlie said firmly, taking his arm. "Come on, we have to get out of here. I don't know how long he'll stay out." *You're awfully calm for just having knocked a guy out cold*, she thought wryly.

They crept out into the empty hallway, lit only by the dim glow of light from the other rooms. Charlie hustled them through the swinging doors to the kitchen, where the dark was total. The air was thick with a blackness that was almost tangible; it was as if they had been swallowed. She turned to look at Carlton, but only the faint sound of his breathing told her that he was still beside her. Something touched her arm, and she stifled a scream.

"It's just me," Carlton hissed, and she let out a sigh.

"Let's just make sure that we aren't being followed, then we can find the others and get out of here," she whispered. Charlie glanced back at the door, and the last spots of light peeking under it. She scooted herself a little closer to it and got to her feet to peer through the round window, careful not to touch it.

"What do you see?" Carlton whispered.

"Nothing. I think it's safe."

Just as she finished speaking, a form passed by, darkening the window. Charlie jumped back, almost falling over Carlton. They stumbled forward, rushing to get away from the door.

Suddenly two beams split the darkness, illuminating the room in a harsh yellow light. Chica loomed there, almost on top of them. She stretched up to her full height, growing taller still. *She must have been hiding here all along*, Charlie thought. The dark recesses of the kitchen could be hiding anything. Chica looked at both of them in turn, the beams of light shifting dizzyingly as her eyes snapped mechanically from one side to the other. Then she paused, and Charlie grabbed Carlton's arm.

"Run!" she screamed, and they took off, looping around the prep table, the metal furniture clattering as they rushed clumsily past it. Behind them, Chica's steps were long and slow. At last they reached the door, and they burst out into the hall and ran for the main dining room.

John and Jessica were silent, listening to the clamor outside. John was resting his hand on the door of the control room; whatever had been on the other side was gone, or at least was pretending to be. The lock had been wrenched out of the floor. John tried the knob, but the door, twisted out of shape, still stuck.

"Are you crazy?" Jessica exclaimed, alarmed.

"What else are we going to do?" John said calmly. Jessica didn't answer.

John backed up against the control panel and gave the door a calculated kick, moving it an inch closer to opening.

"Here, let me," Jessica said, and before he could reply she had delivered a kick of her own, the door again moving just a little.

They took turns, not speaking, until finally John kicked

and the top hinge broke. John quickly wrestled the door the rest of the way off until they could crawl out.

They hurried out and stopped, exposed in the main dining room. Jessica looked at the main stage in misery. It was empty.

"I don't know how this is safer," she said, but John was not listening.

"Charlie!" he cried, then covered his mouth with his hand, too late. Charlie and Carlton were running from the dark hallway at a furious pace.

"Come on!" Charlie yelled at them, not slowing down as she passed, and John and Jessica ran after them as Charlie led them out of the dining room into the opposite hall, toward the storeroom they had come in through.

Charlie ran down the hall with a purpose, stopping in front of a closed door and trying to get it open. Behind them loomed the open mouth of a pitch-black party room, a wide, empty space that could have hidden anything. John turned his back to the group, keeping an eye on the abyss.

"Is it locked?" Carlton asked, an edge of rising panic in his voice.

"No, just stuck," Charlie said. She forced it, and the door popped open. They hurried inside, John lingering until the last moment, his eyes still on the darkness behind him.

When the door was shut, Charlie reached for the light switch by the door, but John put a hand on her arm.

"Don't turn the light on," he said, looking back for a moment. "We have enough light; let your eyes adjust."

There was a window high up on the door, thick glass with a bubbling frosted pattern that let a trickle of light and color into the room from the hallway.

"Right," Charlie said. A light on in here would have marked them out clearly. In the semidarkness, she surveyed the room. It had been an office, though not one she remembered visiting often; she was not sure who had used it. There were cartons here and there on the floor, overstuffed to bulging with papers, their lids perched sheepishly on top of the mess inside. There was an old desk in the corner, a grayish-blue metal with visible dents in the surface. Jessica boosted herself up to sit on it.

"Lock the door," Jessica said in an irritated tone, and Charlie did. There was a button set into the knob, which she knew would be useless, and a flimsy bolt lock, the kind in bathroom stalls and on picket fences.

"I guess it's better than nothing," she said.

CHAPTER ELEVEN

They sat silently for a few minutes in the little office, everyone eyeing the door, waiting. *It's just another place to be trapped*, Charlie thought.

"We have to get out of here," Jessica said softly, echoing Charlie's thoughts. Suddenly Carlton made a small sound of distress. Spasmodically, he grabbed a cardboard box, tipping it over to dump out some of the contents, and vomited into it. His stomach was empty; he retched futilely, his guts clenching and seizing to no effect. At last he sat back, gasping. His face was red, and there were tears in his eyes.

"Carlton? Are you okay?" John asked, alarmed.

"Yeah, never better," Carlton said as his breathing returned slowly to normal.

"You have a concussion," Charlie said. "Look at me." She

knelt down in front of him and looked at his eyes, trying to remember what the pupils were supposed to look like if someone had a concussion. Carlton waggled his eyebrows.

"Oh, oh, *ow!*" He ground his teeth and ducked his head, clutching it as if someone might try to take it away from him. "Sorry," he said after a moment, still bent over in pain. "I think it was all that running. I'll be okay."

"But—" Charlie started to protest, but he cut her off, straightening with a visible effort.

"Charlie, it's fine. Can you blame me for being a little out of sorts? What about you?" He pointed at her arm, and she looked down, confused.

There was a small, bright red patch leaking through the bandage on her arm; the wound must have opened while they were fleeing.

"Oh," Charlie said, suddenly a little nauseated herself. John moved toward her to help, but she waved him away. "I'm fine," she said. She moved the arm experimentally; it ached with the same dull pain that had been radiating through it for the last few days, but it did not seem worse, and the spot of blood wasn't growing very fast.

There was another rumble of thunder outside, and the walls trembled.

"We have to get out of here. Not out of this room, out of this building!" Jessica exclaimed.

"Carlton needs a doctor," John added.

Jessica's voice rose in pitch, sounding frantic. "We're *all* going to need a doctor if we don't leave!"

"I know," Charlie said. She felt a rising irritation at the self-evident statement, and she tried to tamp it down. They were scared, and they were trapped; sniping at one another would not help. "Okay," she said. "You're right. We need to get out. We could try the skylight."

"I don't think we'll be able to get out that way," John said.

"There's got to be a ladder in this place somewhere," Charlie replied, her fear receding as she considered the options. She sat up straighter, gathering herself together.

"It won't help," Jessica said.

"Air vents," John said hastily. "The ones Jason got in through were too small, but there have to be others. Windows—Freddy's had windows, right? They have to lead somewhere."

"I think it's safe to say that they've all been bricked up." Charlie shook her head and looked at the floor for a moment, then she met John's eyes. "This whole place has been sealed."

The walkie-talkie crackled to life, and they all jumped. Lamar's voice came over the radio.

"John?"

John grabbed the radio.

"Yeah? Yeah, I'm here, and I'm with Charlie, Jessica, and Carlton. We're in an office."

"Good," Lamar said. "Listen—" There was a brief scrabbling noise, then Marla's voice came through.

"Good," she said. "Listen, I'm looking at the monitors, and it looks like all the robots are on the main stage again."

"What about Pirate's Cove?" Charlie put in, leaning over John to talk into the receiver. "Is Foxy there, too?"

There was a brief pause.

"The curtain is closed," Marla said.

"Marla, is everything okay?" Charlie said.

"Yeah," she answered shortly, and the background static vanished abruptly—she had turned the walkie-talkie off.

Charlie and John exchanged a glance.

"Something's wrong," Carlton said. "Other than the obvious, I mean." He gestured in a vague circular motion, indicating everything around them.

"What are you talking about?" Jessica was losing her patience.

"With Marla, I mean," he said. "Something's wrong. Call her back."

John pressed the call button again. "Marla? What's going on?"

There was no reply for a long minute, then Lamar replied, "We don't know where Jason is." His voice began to break. "He's in danger."

Charlie felt a jolt through her stomach. *No.* She heard John take a deep breath.

There was a shuddering sound from the other end of the radio: Marla was crying. She started to speak, broke off, and tried again.

"Foxy," she said, her voice a little loud as she forced the words out. "Foxy took him."

"Foxy?" Charlie said carefully. *The figure standing in the front hallway, the rain whipping past it, the silver eyes, burning in the dark.* She took the walkie-talkie from John's hand; he gave it up without protest.

"Marla, listen, we're going to find him. Do you hear me?" Her bravado echoed emptily, even in her own ears. The walkie-talkie made no sound. Agitated, needing to move, to *do* something, Charlie turned to the others.

"I'm going to check out the skylight one more time," she said. "Jessica, come with me; you've got the best chance of fitting."

"Right," Jessica said reluctantly, but she got to her feet.

"You shouldn't go alone," John said, standing to go with them. Charlie shook her head.

"Someone has to stay with him," she said, gesturing at Carlton.

"Hey, I'm a big boy. I can stay by myself," Carlton said, speaking to a shelf.

"Nobody is staying by themselves," Charlie said firmly. John gave her a brief, precise nod, something just short of a salute, and she returned it. She looked back at Carlton, whose face was drawn, tight with pain. "Don't let him fall asleep," she told John in a low voice.

"I know," he whispered.

"I can hear you, you know," Carlton said, but his voice was flat and fatigued.

"Come on," Jessica said. Charlie shut the door behind them and heard John slip the lock back into place.

Charlie led the way. The closet with the skylight wasn't far, and they crept down the hallway and through the doors without incident.

"The skylight. Look, there's no way to climb out through it, even for me. To get to the roof, I would have to put all my weight on the glass; it would break. Even if we had a ladder, this isn't the way out," Jessica said.

"We could take the skylight window off," Charlie suggested weakly.

"I guess we could break out all the glass. But that just brings us back to the ladder question. We need to look around."

A sudden knock on the door caught John's attention, and he sprang to his feet and listened carefully. Charlie knocked again, briefly regretting that they had not come up with some sort of signal. "It's me," she called softly, and the lock slid back. John looked worried.

"What is it?" Charlie said, and he cast his eyes in Carlton's direction. Carlton was huddled on the floor, his knees drawn up tight to his chest, and his arms were wrapped oddly around his head. Charlie knelt down beside him.

"Carlton?" she said, and he made a small whimper. She put a hand on his shoulder, and he leaned in to her a little.

"Charlie? Sorry about all this," he whispered.

"Shhh. Tell me what's going on," she said. She had a sick feeling of dread. Something was really wrong, and she did not know how much was his injury and how much was just exhaustion, pain, and terror. "You're going to be okay," she said, stroking his back and hoping it was true.

After a long moment, he pushed at her, and she drew back, slightly hurt, until she saw him pitch forward over the cardboard box, retching again. She looked up at John.

"He needs a doctor," he said in a low voice, and she nodded. Carlton sat up again and wiped his face with his sleeve.

"It's not that bad. I'm just so tired."

"You can't go to sleep," Charlie said.

"I know, I won't. But I didn't sleep last night, and I haven't eaten since yesterday—it just makes everything worse. I had a bad moment, but I'm okay." Charlie looked at him dubiously but did not argue.

"Now what?" Jessica said. Charlie didn't answer right away, even though she knew the question was for her. She was picturing the guard, his eyes rolling back in his head as

330

he collapsed, his thin face going slack as he fell. They needed answers, and he was the one who had them.

"Now let's hope I didn't accidentally kill that guard," Charlie said.

"I don't want to go back out there," Jessica said.

"We have to go back to where I found Carlton."

"Hang on," said John, pulling out the radio again. "Hey, Marla, are you there?" There was a blip of static, then Marla's voice.

"Yeah, we're here."

"We need to get to the supply room. It's off the main dining room, past the stage. Can you see the area?"

There was a pause as Marla searched her screens.

"I can see most of it. Where are you? I can't see you."

"We're in an office. It's—" John looked at Charlie for help, and she took the radio.

"Marla, do you see another hall leading from the main room? Sort of the same direction as the closet, but next to it?"

"What? There are too many hallways!"

"Hang on. Can you see this?" Over the protests of the others, Charlie opened the office door and poked her head out cautiously. When she saw that the space was clear—or at least she was fairly sure it was clear—she stepped out into the open, looked up, and waved. There was nothing but a quiet, steady static from the walkie-talkie, then Marla's voice came through, excited.

"I see you! Charlie, I can see you."

Charlie ducked back into the little room, and Jessica caught the door and shut it behind her, double- and triple-checking the lock.

"Okay, Marla," Charlie said. "Follow the cameras. You can see that hall. Can you see the main dining room?"

"Yes," she said instantly, "most of it. I can see the stage and the area around it, and I can see the second hallway, the one parallel to yours."

"Can you see the door at the end?"

"Yes, but Charlie, I can't see into the supply room."

"We'll just have to take our chances with what's in there," Charlie answered. "Marla," she said into the receiver, "are we clear to get to the dining room?"

"Yes," Marla said after a moment. "I think so."

Charlie took the lead, and all four of them made their way slowly down the hall. Jessica hung back a little with Carlton, staying so close to him he almost tripped over her feet.

"Jessica, I'm fine," he said.

"I know," she said quietly, but she did not move away, and he did not protest again.

When they reached the end of the hallway, they stopped.

"Marla?" Charlie said into the radio.

"Go ahead—no, stop!" she cried, and they froze, pressing their bodies up against the walls as if it might make them invisible. Marla whispered over the walkie-talkie, her hushed tones distorting her voice even more.

"Something—stay quiet—" She said something else, but it was unintelligible. Charlie craned her neck to see out into the room and what might be lurking there, some murky form, lumbering heavily in the shadows, poised to attack. There was a long rumble outside, and the panels on the ceiling rattled as if they were about to fall.

"Marla, I don't see anything," Charlie said into the walkie-talkie. She looked at the stage, where all of the animatronics were still in position, staring sightlessly into the distance.

"Me neither," John whispered.

"Sorry," Marla said. "Not to overstate the obvious, but it's creepy in here. It feels like it's been midnight for hours. Does anyone know what time it is?"

Charlie checked her watch, squinting to see the little hand. "It's almost four," she said.

"A.m. or p.m.?" Marla said. She didn't sound like she was joking.

"P.m." Lamar's voice came over the radio, hard to hear, like he was not close enough to the receiver. "I told you, Marla, it's daytime."

"It doesn't feel like daytime," Marla sobbed, shrieking as the building shook with a crash of thunder.

"I know," he said softly, and the radio clicked off. Charlie looked at the walkie-talkie for a moment with a sense of emptiness. It was like hanging up the phone, knowing the person on the other end was still there but feeling a loss anyway, as if they might be gone for good.

"Charlie?" John said, and she looked at him. He cast a nod back at Carlton, who was leaning against the wall, his eyes closed. Jessica was hovering worriedly, not sure what to do. "We have to get him out of here," John said.

"I know," Charlie said. "Come on. That guard is our best chance of getting out alive." With one more look at the open space in front of them, she led them out into the main room.

Crossing in front of the stage, she saw John and Jessica glancing upward, but she refused to look at the animals, as if that would stop them from looking at her. It did not help; she felt their eyes on her, taking her measure, waiting for their moment. Finally she could not stand it—she snapped her head around to look as they passed. She saw only the inanimate robots, their eyes fixed on something that no one else could see.

They paused again at a hall entrance, waiting for Marla to guide them, and after an anxious moment her voice came over the radio, calm again.

"Go ahead, the hall is clear."

They went. They were almost there, and Charlie felt a tightness in her stomach like a living knot, something snakelike that was fighting to be free. She thought of Carlton, retching on the floor of the office, and she felt for a moment like she might do the same. She stopped a few feet from the door, holding up a hand.

"I don't know if he's in there," she said in a low voice. "And if he is, I don't know if he's—awake." *Now let's hope I didn't accidentally kill that guard*, she had said. She was only kidding, but now the words came back, unsettling her. It had not really occurred to her that he might be dead until the words were out of her mouth, and now, as she stood in the hall, about to find out, the idea took hold.

As if he knew what she was thinking, John said, "Charlie, we have to go in."

She nodded. John moved as if to take the lead, but she shook her head. Whatever was in there, it was her doing. Her responsibility. She closed her eyes for a brief moment, then turned the knob.

He was dead. He was lying on the floor, on his back, his eyes closed and his face ashen. She felt herself put a hand over her mouth, but it was as if someone else were moving her body. She felt numb, the knots in her stomach gone still and dead. John pushed past her. He knelt and slapped the man's face.

"John," she said, hearing a note of panic in her voice. He looked up at her, surprised.

"He's not dead," he said. "He's just out cold. He can't tell us anything like this."

"We have to tie him up or something," Jessica said. "Don't wake him up like this."

"Yeah, gotta agree with that," Carlton said. His eyes searched the room for devices, tools, or costumes—anything that Dave could—and probably would—use against them, given the opportunity.

Charlie just stared, the numb feeling lingering. *He's not dead.* She shook herself all over like a dog, trying to rid herself of the remnants of shock, and cleared her throat.

"Let's find something to tie him up with," she said. "This place seems to have everything." Jessica headed to the back of the room, where costume pieces were piled haphazardly, empty mascots' heads staring out from odd angles with ghastly eyes.

"Careful touching the costumes," Charlie called toward Jessica.

"We could always put him in one of them, like he did to me," Carlton said. There was an uncharacteristic edge to his voice, something hard and painful. Charlie didn't think it was from his injury. He sat down on a box, his face strained and his arms wrapped around his body like he was holding himself together.

Suddenly Carlton's face lit up with alarm.

"Don't touch—" he shouted and pushed Charlie out of the way. He stumbled past Jessica, who was searching through the clutter, and started tearing his way through the mess, picking up boxes and pushing things out of his way, scrambling in a desperate search.

"Charlie, where is it?!" he demanded, his gaze roaming around the room futilely. Charlie went to him, following where he looked, and realized what was missing: the yellow bear suit that had been slouched in the corner.

"What?" John said, confused.

"Charlie, where is it? Where is Michael?" Carlton sat with a thud on a cardboard box that sagged a little but held his weight. He was only looking at Charlie, as if they were the only people in the room.

"Michael?" John whispered. He looked at Charlie, but she returned his gaze silently; she had no answers to offer him.

"Michael was there." Carlton pressed his lips firmly, rocking himself back and forth.

"I believe you," Charlie answered calmly, her voice quiet. John put his hands on his knees and let out a breath.

"I'm going to go help Jessica," he muttered and stood up with resignation. "There has to be rope around here somewhere."

"Be right there." Charlie smiled at Carlton, hoping to reassure him, then joined the others, heading for the boxes in the corner beside the door.

The first just held more paperwork, official forms with tiny print, but underneath was a box of tangled extension cords.

"Hey, I found something," Charlie said, but she was cut off by a banshee scream.

Charlie was on her feet instantly, ready to run, but everyone else was still. Jessica was pointing to something in the corner, almost shaking. John was behind her, his eyes wide.

"What is it?" Charlie demanded, and when they did not answer, she rushed over and looked down at the pile of empty costumes to where Jessica was pointing.

It was hard to sort out what was what in the pile of mascots. She stared blankly at the jumble, seeing nothing but fur and eyes and beaks and paws, and then it resolved before her eyes.

A dead man.

He looked young, not much older than they were—and he looked familiar.

"That's the cop, the one from the other night," John said, recovering his voice.

"What?" Carlton said, snapping to attention. He came over to look. "That's Officer Dunn. I know him."

"Your dad sent him to look for you," Charlie said quietly.

"What do we do?" Jessica said. She had been inching slowly backward, and now her foot bumped against Dave, and she jumped, stifling another scream. It pulled Charlie's eyes away from Dunn, and looking away was enough to recall her to their task.

"There's nothing we can do," she said firmly. "Come on, we don't know how much time we have before he wakes up."

John and Jessica followed her across the room, Jessica catching up and keeping close to Charlie as if afraid to get too far away from her again. Charlie grabbed a handful of cords and tossed it to John.

It was a long and tedious process. They propped Dave up into a sitting position against the wall, but he kept sliding sideways until John took hold of his shoulders. John bent him forward as Charlie tied his hands behind his back. She finished and looked up to see John with a faint smile on his face.

"Do my knots amuse you?" she said as lightly as she could manage. The feel of Dave's flesh, alive yet limp and heavier than it should have been, was disturbing, and as she let go of him, she could still feel the traces of his clammy skin on her palms.

He shrugged. "All those times we played cops and robbers seem to have paid off."

"I forgot about that." She laughed. He nodded sagely.

"And yet I still bear the scars of the rope burns you gave me." John smiled.

"And that was before I was even a Girl Scout," Charlie said. "Stop complaining and pick up his feet. Let's hope my skills haven't atrophied."

She finished tying up Dave, pretending a confidence she did not really have. The cords were thick and stiff; they were hard to manipulate, and she was not sure how long they would hold. When she was as sure as she could be, she stepped back.

John looked around for a moment as though searching for something, then slipped out through the door without a word.

Carlton was on his knees, and he walked toward Dave without standing, a clunky, unsteady walk—he looked like he might tip over at any moment. "Wakey, wakey, sleepy head," he whispered.

"We've got this, Carlton, thanks. You just relax." Charlie rolled her eyes toward Jessica, then turned her attention back to Dave, slapping his face lightly, but he remained inert.

"Hey, dirtbag. Wake up." She slapped him again.

"Here, try this." John reappeared with a can of water. "Water fountain," was the only explanation he offered. "The can didn't hold much," he added.

"That's okay," Charlie said. She took it from him and held it over Dave's head, letting the small streams of water dribbling from the holes in the tin fall on his face. She aimed for his mouth, and after a few moments, he spluttered, his eyes opening.

"Oh, good, you're awake," Charlie said, then dumped the rest of the water on his head.

He said nothing, but his eyes remained open in a stiff, unnatural stare.

"So, Dave," she said. "How about you tell us what's going on?"

His mouth opened slightly, but no words came out. After a moment he became still again, so still that Charlie reluctantly pressed her fingers to his neck to check for a pulse.

"Is he alive?" John said, creeped out by what seemed to be an on-again, off-again animated corpse. He moved closer to the man, kneeling so their eyes were level, and looked at him gravely, searching for something.

"His pulse is normal," Charlie reported. She pulled her hand back, more startled than if he'd been dead.

"Charlie, there's something different about him," John said urgently. He reached out and grasped Dave's chin, turning his head back and forth. Dave did not resist; he just kept staring without expression, as if the world around him were not really there.

"What do you mean?" Charlie said, though she saw it, too. It was as if the guard, the man they had met, had been stripped away, and what sat before them was nothing but a blank canvas.

John shook his head and released the guard's chin, wiping his hands on his pants. He stood and stepped back, putting a distance between them.

"I don't know," he said. "There's just something different."

"Why don't you tell us about the kids?" Carlton was leaning back against the wall, emboldened but still not completely balanced. "The kids you killed, you stuffed them into those suits out there." Carlton motioned toward the stage outside.

"Carlton, shut up," John said angrily. "Everything you're saying is nonsense."

"No, it's true," Charlie whispered. John gave her a searching look, then turned to the others, who had no more answers than Charlie. He looked back at Dave with an expression of renewed disgust. Seeing John's face, Charlie was suddenly struck with the weight of memory. Michael, who had been a cheerful, careless little boy, Michael who had drawn portraits of them all, passing them around with a solemn pride. Michael who had been killed, whose final moments must have been all pain and terror. Michael, who had been killed by the man before them. She looked to the others, and on each of their faces she saw the same single thought: *This was the man who killed Michael.*

Without warning, John's arm shot out like lightning and struck Dave across the jaw with a loud crack. Dave slumped back, and John lunged and almost fell from the impact of the strike. John regained his posture and bounced a little on the balls of his feet, alert, waiting for a reaction, or a chance to strike again. Dave's body moved upward, straightening, but the movement was too smooth. He seemed to make no effort, use no muscles, and exert no energy. Slowly, his posture corrected, unfolding to his slumped state, his mouth hanging open.

Carlton stumbled forward. "Take that, jackass." He swung his arm into the air and swayed on his feet. Jessica leaped forward just in time to catch him in her arms.

Dave continued to stare, and it was only after a moment that Charlie considered that he might actually be staring at something. She turned, following his line of sight, then suddenly she recoiled. On the table along the wall sat a rabbit's head.

"That's it? You want that?" Charlie stood and approached the mask. "You need this?" she added in a whisper. She picked it up carefully, the light catching the edges of the spring locks that filled the mascot's head. She picked it up and carried it almost ceremoniously to Dave, who tipped his head down in a barely noticeable fashion.

Charlie placed it over his head, not being nearly as cautious as she had been with Carlton. When the mascot's head was fully resting on his shoulders, the large face raised itself until it was almost completely upright. Dave's eyes opened steadily, glassy and without emotion, like the robots on the stage outside. Lines of sweat began to trickle down from under the mask, a stain darkening the collar of his uniform shirt.

"My dad trusted you," Charlie said. She was on her knees now, looking intently at the rabbit's face. "What did you do to him?" Her voice broke.

"I helped him create." The voice came from inside the mask, but it was not Dave's, not the pitiful, sour tone they would have recognized. The voice of the rabbit was smooth and rich, almost musical. It was confident, somehow reassuring—a voice that might convince you of almost anything. Dave cocked his head to the side, and the mask shifted so that only one of his bulbous eyes could peer through the sockets.

"We both wanted to love," he said in those melodious tones. "Your father loved. And now I have loved."

"You killed," Carlton said, then burst out with something that sounded like a laugh. He seemed more lucid now, as if anger was focusing his mind. He shook loose of Jessica's hands on his arms and knelt down on the floor.

"You're a sick bastard," Carlton sputtered. "And you've created monsters. The kids you killed are still here. You've imprisoned them!"

"They are home, with me." Dave's voice was coarse, and the large mascot's head slid forward and tilted as he spoke. "Their happiest day."

"How do we get out?" Charlie placed one hand on the mascot's head and pushed it back into position on Dave's shoulders. The fur felt wet and sticky, as though the costume itself were sweating.

"There isn't a way out anymore. All that's left is family."
His round eye reappeared through one of the sockets, glimmering in the light. He locked eyes with Charlie for a moment, struggling to lean in closer. "Oh," he gasped. "You're something beautiful, aren't you?" Charlie recoiled as if he had touched her. *What's that supposed to mean?* She took another step back, fighting a surge of revulsion.

"Well, then, you're trapped, too, and you're not going to be hurting anyone else," John said in response to the veiled threat.

"I don't have to," Dave answered. "When it gets dark, they will awaken; the children's spirits will rise. They will kill you. I'll just walk out in the morning, stepping over your corpses, one by one." He looked at each of them in turn, as if relishing the bloody scene.

"They'll kill you, too," Jessica said.

"No, I am quite confident that I will survive."

"Really?" John said suddenly. "I'm pretty sure they're the spirits of the kids *you killed*," he all but spat. "Why would they hurt us? It's you they're after."

"They don't remember," Dave said. "They've forgotten. The dead do forget. All they know is that you are here, trying to take away their happiest day. You are intruders." He lowered his voice to a hush. "You are *grown-ups*."

They looked at one another.

"We're not—" Jessica began.

"You're close enough. Especially to a vengeful, confused, and frightened child. None of you will survive the night."

"And what makes you think they won't kill you?" John said again, and Dave's eyes took on something shining, almost beatific.

"Because I am one of them," he said.

CHAPTER TWELVE

They all stood staring at the man on the floor. Jessica took an involuntary step backward. Charlie was glued to the spot; she could not look away from him. *Because I am one of them.* As if he could tell what she was thinking, John stepped up beside her.

"Charlie, he's insane," he said quietly, and it was enough to break her away from that dreadful, ecstatic gaze. She turned to John.

"We have to get out," she said. He nodded, turned back to the group, and gestured to the walkie-talkie in his hand.

"I'm going back to the control room," he said. "These things are police radios; there has to be a way to get them to reach the outside. Maybe I can use the equipment in there to get a signal somehow."

"I'll go with you," Charlie said instantly, but he shook his head.

"You have to stay with them," he said, barely audible. Charlie looked over at Jessica and Carlton. He was right. Carlton needed someone with him, and Jessica—Jessica was holding it together, but she couldn't be left alone in charge of the safety of both of them. Charlie nodded.

"Be careful," she said.

He didn't answer; instead he tucked the walkie-talkie into his belt, gave her a wink, and left.

Clay Burke was in his office, reviewing the week's case files. There was not much: traffic violations, two petty thefts, and one confession to the murder of Abraham Lincoln. Clay shuffled through the papers and sighed. Shaking his head, he pulled open the bottom drawer of his desk and removed the file that had been plaguing him all morning.

Freddy's. When he closed his eyes, he was there again, the cheerful family restaurant, its floor streaked with blood. After Michael disappeared, he had worked fourteen-hour days, sometimes sleeping in the station. Every time he came home he went to look at Carlton, who was usually asleep. He wanted to grab his son and hold him close, never let him go. It could have been any of the children there that day; it was blind, dumb luck that the killer had spared his own.

At the time, it was the first murder that the department had dealt with. It was a sixteen-person department, usually charged with small thefts and noise complaints, and to be handed a gruesome murder made all of them feel a little like kids whose toy guns had suddenly turned real.

Clay opened the file, knowing what he would find. It was only a partial report; the rest of it was in a storage room in the basement. He scanned the familiar words, the bureaucratic language that tried but failed to obscure the point: There had been no justice done. *Sometimes the guilty get away with terrible things, but it is the price we pay.* He had said that to Charlie. He cringed a little now, realizing how that must have sounded, to her of all people.

He picked up the phone, calling the front desk in a moment of urgency rather than walking the twenty feet to ask in person.

"Has Dunn reported back from Freddy's?" he asked before the officer on the other end could speak.

"No, sir," she said, "I'll—"

He hung up, not waiting for her to finish. Clay stared restlessly at the wall for a long moment, then grabbed his coffee cup and headed to the basement.

He didn't have to search for the box of evidence from the Freddy's disappearances; he had been here before. There was no one around, and so instead of taking it upstairs to his office, Clay sat down on the concrete floor, spreading papers and photographs around him. There were interviews, witness statements, and reports from the on-scene officers, Clay included. He sifted through them aimlessly. He didn't know what he was looking for; there was nothing new here.

There was nothing to find, really. They knew who did it. At first he had suspected Henry, just like so many others around town. It was a terrible thought, but it was a terrible crime; there was no solution that would not be shocking. He had not been the one to question Charlie's father, but he had read the transcript. The man had been almost incoherent, so shaken that he could not give straight answers. He sounded as if he were lying, and to most people that was proof enough. But Clay had resisted, had delayed having him arrested, and sure enough they came to William Afton, Henry's partner. Afton seemed like the normal one in the venture, the businessman. Henry was the artist; he always seemed to be off in another world, some part of his mind thinking about his mechanical creatures even when he was holding a conversation about the weather or the kids' soccer games. There was something off about Henry, something almost shell-shocked; it seemed like a miracle that he could have produced a child as apparently normal as Charlie.

Clay remembered when Henry had moved to town and begun construction of the new restaurant. Someone had told him that Henry had a kid who had been abducted several years prior, but he didn't know much else. He seemed like a nice enough guy, though he was obviously terribly alone, his grief visible even at a distance. Then Freddy Fazbear's opened, and the town came alive. That was also when Charlie appeared. Clay hadn't known Henry even had a daughter until that day.

William Afton was the one who made Freddy's a business, as he had the previous restaurant. Afton was as robust and lively as Henry was withdrawn and shadowy. He was a hefty man who had the ruddy geniality of a financially shrewd Santa Claus. And he had killed the children. Clay knew it; the whole department knew it. He had been present for each abduction, and he had mysteriously and briefly vanished at the same time as each child went missing. A search of his house had found a room crammed with boxes of mechanical parts and a musty yellow rabbit suit as well as stacks of journals full of raving paranoia, passages about Henry that ranged from wild jealousy to near worship.

But there had been no evidence, there had been no bodies, and so there could be no charge. William Afton had left town, and there was nothing to stop him. They did not even know where he had gone. Clay picked up a picture from the pile; it had been taken, framed, from the wall of Henry's office at the restaurant. It was a picture of the two of them together, Henry and William, grinning into the camera in front of the newly opened Freddy Fazbear's. He stared at it; he had stared at it before. Henry's eyes did not quite match his smile. The expression looked forced, but then, it always did. There was nothing unusual here, except that one of the men had turned out to be a killer.

Suddenly, Clay felt a shock of recognition, something indistinct he could not quite catch. He closed his eyes, letting his mind wander like a dog off the lead: *Go on, find it.* There was something about William, something familiar, something *recent*. Clay's eyes snapped open. He shoved everything back into the evidence box, cramming it in messily, keeping out only the photograph. Clutching it, he took the stairs up two at a time, almost running by the time he got to the main floor of the station. He headed straight for a particular filing cabinet, ignoring the greetings of his startled officers. He tore open the drawer, pawing through it until—there it was, employee background checks requested by businesses from the last six months.

He pulled out the stack and flipped through it, looking for photos. In the third folder, he found it. He picked up the picture and held it up next to the one of Henry and William, turning so his body did not block the light.

It's him.

The background check application was labeled "Dave Miller," but it was unmistakably William Afton. Afton had been fat and affable; the man in the picture was sallow and thin, his skin sagging and his expression unpleasant, as if he had forgotten how to smile. He looked like a poor facsimile of himself. Or maybe, Clay thought, he looked like he had dropped his disguise.

Clay flipped the page back to see why the check had been requested, and his face drained white, his breathing stopping for a moment. Clay stood, grabbing his jacket in the same motion, then stopped. Slowly, he sat, letting the jacket fall from his fingers. He took the partial file back out of its drawer, and delicately he lifted one of the photos out. It had been taken in the aftermath, when the place was no more than a crime scene. He paused for a moment and closed his eyes. Then he looked again at the picture, willing himself to see it as if for the first time.

There was a glimmer of light he had never noticed before. One of the animatronics on the stage, the bear, *Freddy*, was looking toward the cameraman, one of his eyes illuminated with a smear of light.

Clay put the picture aside, moving to the next one. This one was from a different angle, but the side of the main stage was still in the frame. Chica's body was facing away from the camera, but her face was turned directly toward it, and another smear of light streaked across her left eye. Clay rubbed it with the tip of his finger, making sure it wasn't a defect in the paper. The next photo showed Bonnie in the darkness behind the chairs. A pinpoint of light, like a star, shone from one of his eyes as though reflecting a spotlight that wasn't there. *What is this?* Clay could feel his face flush;

he realized he hadn't been breathing. He shuffled his hands on the desk like a conjurer calling forth a picture to reveal itself. One did. The last picture had been taken in Pirate's Cove. Tables had been disturbed, he remembered. The scene was chaotic: the tables and chairs in disarray, clutter strewn through the halls. But unlike so many other times he had stared at this picture, he ignored the disorder and focused only on the stage. The curtain was pulled back slightly, a figure barely visible in the recesses behind it, one eye presumably illuminated by the flash of a camera. Clay studied the rest of the pictures, looking for more reflections, but found none. *There was no flash.*

Jason opened his eyes. His leg hurt; it was a steady, dull pain. He flexed it tentatively and found he could move easily; the injury could not be too bad. He was lying on something lumpy, and his whole body felt stiff, like he had been asleep on a pile of—he looked at what he was lying on—a pile of extension cords and wires. He sat up. It was dark, but he could dimly see what was around him. He bent over to examine his leg. His jeans were ripped where Foxy's claw had gouged him, and the gash in his leg was ugly, but it was not bleeding badly. The hook had mostly got hold of his jeans. Jason felt a little relief. Satisfied, he began to examine his surroundings. He was in a corner, and there was a heavy black curtain strung from one wall to the other, cutting the space off from the room outside. He crawled forward over the cables cautiously, careful to make no sound. He made his way to the edge of the curtain, where there was a tiny sliver of a gap between it and the wall. Jason took a moment to steel himself, then peeked out, conscious of his every movement.

He was on the small stage in Pirate's Cove, behind the curtain. He could hear something moving out there, something large, but from his position he could see only an empty room. He pushed his head out a little farther, craning his neck to look. He couldn't tell where the sound was coming from, but with each second he grew bolder, readying himself to leap from the stage and run. A light was pulsing in the main dining room, illuminating the hall for brief seconds at a time with bright, dizzying carnival colors. It wasn't much, but it gave Jason a direction to run. He watched it intently until it was all he could see, and then it stopped. The room was dark, darker than it had been before—his eyes had adjusted to the light and now he was nearly blind. The shuffling sound went on, and Jason pulled the curtain open farther. This time he moved too fast, and as the curtain was drawn, the metal rings that held it clinked together.

The light above Pirate's Cove went on.

Foxy was there, right in front of him, his face so close to Jason's that they could almost touch. Jason scrambled back through the curtain, pulling it closed again, trying to escape the small alcove, but there was nowhere to run. He crawled backward, staying against the wall, hoping that the curtain would somehow shield him from Foxy.

At once, the curtain began to open, not by force, but as if a show were about to begin. Lights and color flashed in silent patterns, and the glittered front curtains rolled back in grand fashion to reveal the stage, with the beast standing patiently at its base.

Foxy cocked his head to the side as if considering something, and then he began his approach. He climbed the stairs to the stage one by one, each step a whole series of disjointed movements, as if each piece of his metal body maneuvered itself individually. Jason watched, struck with horror, yet some small part of him was enthralled; it was like nothing he had ever seen. Foxy reached the stage and took two more large, deliberate steps, until he was standing over Jason. Jason stared up at him, too afraid to move, frozen in place like a mouse beneath a diving falcon. His breath was shallow; his heart beat so fast his chest hurt. Foxy raised his hook again, and Jason threw himself down on the floor in a ball, protecting his head with his arms, waiting for the blow to come.

It did not come.

Jason did not move. He waited, and waited, wondering if time had slowed down as he approached the moment of his death, his mind trying to give him refuge, making the last moments feel as long as possible. But not this long. He opened his eyes and turned his head a little, keeping his arms in front of his face. Foxy was still there, not moving. Despite himself, Jason met the creature's eyes. It was like looking into the sun—Foxy's burning gaze made Jason's eyes tear up, made him want to look away, but he could not. It was the animatronic who looked away. As Jason watched, peering through the afterburn that clouded his vision, Foxy turned to face his absent audience. His hook fell slowly to his side, his head tilted forward, and he went motionless. The sounds of whirring machinery and clicking parts came to a stop, and the curtains drew closed again.

"Ready?" Lamar said. Marla nodded curtly.

"I'm ready," she said. She threw open the door, fists clenched, and they climbed out, facing opposite directions, preparing for an assault. Marla was breathing heavily, her face furious. The darkness was thick, almost tangible, and she could barely make out what was around her. She could see Lamar, but if they drifted three feet apart they would be lost to each other. The lights above them flickered, but only for a moment; the brief illumination ruined what little night vision they had, making the dark impenetrable.

"Anything on your side?" Marla whispered. Lamar looked toward her voice, distressed.

"No, anything on your side?"

"Light, please," Marla whispered. Lamar held up the flash-light as though aiming a weapon and turned it on. Above them, the lights sputtered.

Jason could see their flashlight waving back and forth, filter-ing through the slightly transparent curtain. *Oh no.* The light fell on the animatronic, just for a moment, and there was a clicking noise. Jason looked up. Foxy was not moving. The light swept across him again, and again the mechanical sounds came, this time unmistakable, though he still did not move. Jason scooted forward, around Foxy's foot, and looked up at the animatronic's face as the light struck him again. Again the clicking noise came; something inside him was readying itself, but his eyes stayed dark. Jason crawled as far forward as he was willing to venture, trying not to cross into Foxy's line of sight. He made it to the edge of the curtain and reached his arm out to wave a warning.

"Jason!" He heard his sister's voice, and then a quick shushing from what must have been Lamar. The flashlight swept up, trained on the stage, and Foxy's eyes lit up. His head swept toward the light with a predatory precision, and Jason, panicked, reached for the pile of cords and grabbed a cable. Foxy lifted a foot, and Jason threw the cord around it and yanked with all his strength. Foxy pitched forward, grabbing at the curtain with his hook. It caught, ensnaring him, and he ripped through the cloth with a vicious tearing noise, falling to the ground in a tangle of cloth and metal limbs. Jason scrambled past the struggling creature and ran toward the light.

Marla reached for him, but he brushed her aside.

"Run," he panted, and the three of them took off down the hall. They turned a corner, and as one they stopped, Jason skidding against Lamar and grabbing him for support. At the end of the dark hall stood another figure, too large to be a person. The top hat was unmistakable.

Freddy Fazbear.

His eyes were illuminated, their piercing red glow consuming the space around him. They could hear the brittle notes of a song, mechanical and thin like a music box, coming from Freddy's direction. They stared, mesmerized, then Jason found himself and pulled at Marla's arm.

"Come on," he hissed, and they followed him, running back the way they had come. When they reached Pirate's Cove they slowed; Foxy had thrown off the curtain and was beginning to right himself. The three exchanged glances, then ran past him. Jason held his breath until they were through to the next doorway, invoking some old superstition.

Lamar motioned to one of the party rooms, and they ducked inside. He switched off the flashlight, and they stood still for a moment, their eyes adjusting. The room had three long, cafeteria-style tables, each one still set for a party: Metal folding chairs were lined all up and down them, and each place was set with a party hat, a paper plate, and a plastic cup. By wordless agreement, each hid beneath a different table, leaving themselves as much space as possible. They crouched low, hoping to be lost behind the chair legs, and together they stared silently into the vacant hall and listened.

"Hello? Anyone?" John repeated into the radio, but there was only static. He had managed to hook the walkie-talkie into the sound system, but getting a signal to the outside seemed impossible—Freddy's was sealed off from the world. He looked at the monitors again. On one screen he could see three figures crouched under tables. Marla, Lamar, and Jason, he thought. *They found Jason*, he realized with profound relief, letting go of a tension he had not known he felt. Everything on-screen was lit with unnatural grays and whites. "These must be night-vision cameras," he said to no one, squinting to see through the static. He watched the blurry figures crawl and come to a stop beneath the long party tables, then movement from another screen caught his eye.

There was a figure in the hallway, moving steadily toward the room they were in. John could not tell what it was, but the way it moved wasn't human. It stopped beside a doorway, and with a sudden jolt of realization John looked again at the party room where his friends were hiding. He grabbed the walkie-talkie and flipped the speaker system on, jamming the volume control as high as it would go.

"Lamar," he said calmly, trying to sound commanding. He heard the reverberation of his own voice through the walls of the control room. "Lamar, don't move."

John's voice blared over the speaker, blurred with static but intelligible.

"Lamar, don't move."

Lamar, Marla, and Jason looked at one another across the distance between the tables. The room lit up with a burning red glow, and they watched, as still as they could be, as Freddy Fazbear entered the room. His movements were mechanical and graceless as he walked with deliberate steps to the middle of the room and stopped between two tables; Marla on one side, Jason on the other. Jason looked at his sister, and she put a finger to her lips. Jason hadn't realized that there were tears on his cheeks until now.

He watched as Freddy surveyed the room. His head, with eyes like spotlights, whirred to one side, stopped with a click, and then turned to the other side. There was a long pause. The two padded feet were motionless, the legs like black trees in a forest. There was a sound of twisting fur and crinkling fabric, and the feet began to pivot. Freddy turned around and headed for the door, each step shaking the floor beneath him. As Freddy passed by, Jason shrank back instinctively, his foot hitting one of the metal chairs. It made a scraping sound. Jason's heart raced. Frantic, he looked across the space at Marla, who beckoned to him urgently. Freddy had stopped, but they could still hear the sound of fabric and fur scrunching and moving. Freddy began to bend down. His motions were slow, and in those precious few seconds Jason pushed the two chairs in front of him apart, making a gap just wide enough for him to be able to crawl behind Freddy as soon as he had the chance. The light of Freddy's eyes came into view under the table, illuminating the space beside Jason, and he quickly but quietly crawled between the chairs to where Marla was hiding. Freddy stood again, training his eyes on the floor just as Jason pulled his foot out of sight.

Freddy began to pivot toward the table they were under. Marla put a hand on Jason's arm, steadying him. There was another pause. Lamar, under the table opposite them, beckoned to Marla and Jason, urging them to his own table, farther away from Freddy. Marla shook her head, not wanting to risk making noise. *Maybe he's leaving*, she told herself. Jason was beginning to breathe normally again when it struck them: Freddy was ducking down again, this time silently. His eyes had gone dark, but as soon as they spotted him, his gaze lit up again, illuminating the room. Marla and Jason scrambled around the metal chairs as fast as they could without touching them. They crawled across the thin carpet between tables until they came across an opening in the chairs and crawled under the table beside Lamar. Marla and Lamar looked at each other, at a loss; Freddy was straightened up again and beginning to circle around to the third table.

"We have to run for the door," Marla whispered. Lamar nodded, then motioned for them to follow his lead. He watched, waiting until Freddy was bending down once again, and then gestured to the middle table. They caught their breath, trying not to gasp, and Lamar looked toward the door. Could they make it? Marla put a hand on Jason's shoulder, and he started to shrug her off, but she was gripping him tightly, her fingers digging into him. He moved to brush her away, then looked at her. She was terrified, even more than he was. He let her hold on to him while keeping his eyes on Freddy, waiting for their next opening.

It didn't come. As they waited, poised for flight, Freddy turned away, his deliberate steps taking him to the doorway. The room went dark, and Jason's heart skipped before he understood what had happened. The lights were gone because Freddy was gone.

"Marla," he whispered, his voice little more than a breath of air. "He's gone." Marla looked at him and nodded, but she did not let go of his shoulder.

"Are you okay?" she asked in the same almost soundless way. He nodded, then pointed to his leg and shrugged theatrically. She smiled at him and took her hand from his shoulder to muss his hair.

Suddenly Lamar was tapping Marla's arm. He pointed to his ear, and she gave him a puzzled look. Jason stiffened, realizing what it was, and in a second Marla did, too. There was music in the room, a tinny, labored sound like a music box, the gaps between the notes just a little too long. The room lit up again, a drowning red, and before they could move, the table was wrenched away. Freddy stood over them. He shoved the table aside, almost hurling it. They screamed— not a scream for help but the last, futile act of defiance. Jason clung to his sister, and she pulled his head down against her, shielding his eyes so he would not have to see.

Suddenly, Freddy stumbled off-balance and lurched to the side. He tried to right himself, but another jolt from behind sent him flying forward, falling face-first into the tables. Marla, Lamar, and Jason looked up to see Charlie and John, their faces flushed with effort.

"Come on," Charlie said. "Let's go."

★   ★   ★

Dave shrugged out of his bonds quickly; the knots were sturdy, but the cords had too much give—a few twists and turns and he was free. He crawled to the door on hands and knees and held his ear to the crack, careful not to jostle the door and give himself away.

The loudspeaker blared, and then the sound he had been waiting for: footsteps, running away.

He waited just until the sound faded, then got purposefully to his feet.

"Where are we going?" Marla panted as they raced back toward the main dining room.

"The office," Charlie called. "It's got a real door; we can barricade ourselves in." She glanced at John, who nodded shortly. What they would do once they were barricaded inside was another question, but they could worry about that once they were safe. They ran through the dining room; Charlie glanced at the stage, blurred in passing, but she saw what she knew she would: It was empty.

They reached the narrow hall that led to the office, and Charlie's heart lifted when she saw the door, light shining from its small window like a beacon.

Wait, light?

She slowed her pace; they were ten feet from the door. She lifted a hand, signaling the others to stop, and they approached the door slowly. Steeling herself, Charlie grabbed the knob and turned. It was locked. She looked helplessly at the others.

"Someone's in there," Jason whispered, moving closer to Marla.

"There's no one else here," Marla said softly, but it sounded like a question. Charlie was about to try the door again, but stopped herself. *Don't draw their attention.*

"He got loose!" Jessica said, her voice hoarse, and Charlie felt a chill. *She's right.* She didn't say it.

"We have to go back," she said. Without waiting for a response, she turned, pushing between Lamar and John to take the lead. She took two steps forward, then stopped dead as she heard the others gasp.

It was Chica, her eyes like burning orange headlights.

She stood at the other end of the short hall, blocking their only way out. Her body filled the space; they could not even try to run past her. Charlie glanced behind her, even though she knew there was no other way out. Before she could react, John was running at the animatronic. He had no weapons, but he hurtled himself toward the thing and leaped up, trying to grab hold of her neck. He caught it briefly, struggling to hold on as Chica thrashed her head back and forth. Chica bent forward and swung to the side, slamming John into the wall, and John let go, crumpling to the floor. The cupcake on Chica's platter snapped its mouth as if laughing, its eyes rolling in their tiny sockets.

"John!" Charlie cried as she thrust the flashlight back for someone else to take. She felt its weight leave her hands, but she didn't look back to see who took it. She looked up; there was an electrical cord dangling above their heads. Parts of the rubber had worn away, exposing stretches of bare wire. Chica was slowly advancing. Charlie jumped up, but she could not get high enough to reach it. She looked to either side. *Is it narrow enough?* She glanced at Chica. She was moving slowly, with measured steps; they were trapped, and she did not need to hurry. Charlie planted one foot against the wall, then stretched her leg across the narrow hallway and did the same on the other side, bracing between the walls to climb. She inched upward, her legs shaking with the effort. She looked up, struggling to retain her balance as she reached for the cord. Careful to touch only the rubber, she closed her fingers around it and dropped to the ground. Chica lunged forward, her arms extended and her teeth contorted in a mechanical smile.

Charlie sprang up, the electrical cord brandished in front of her, and she shoved it into the space between Chica's head and her torso. Chica jerked backward, sparks flying, and for a horrible moment Charlie could not move. Her hand throbbed with the electric current, and she was caught there, unable to make her hand let go of the wire. She stared down at it, willing her fingers to open. *Is this how I die?* Lamar grabbed her and pulled her away, and she looked up at him wide-eyed. The others were already running. Chica was deactivated, or so it appeared, slumped forward, her eyes dark. Lamar gave her arm a tug, and they took off after the others.

With a pleased smile, Dave watched the confrontation through the window in the office door. *Just a matter of time now*, he thought. The girl had been clever, climbing the walls like that, but she had almost killed herself. They could not last much longer. All he had to do was wait.

Suddenly, the room was lit with an ethereal blue. He froze, then slowly turned. *Bonnie*. The animatronic towered over him, close enough to touch. Dave fell back against the door and screamed.

There was a scream from the direction of the office. The group paused for a minute and looked nervously at one another.

"It doesn't matter," Charlie said. "Come on."

She took a quick look back at Chica, who was still slumped forward, inert. Charlie led them into the main dining room. As they emerged, there was a sudden movement. Foxy was there.

He leaped onto a table in front of them, looking among them until his silver eyes lit on Jason. He crouched as if he were about to jump on the boy, and Charlie grabbed a napkin dispenser and threw it as hard as she could. It struck Foxy's head, glancing off with little effect, but it was enough to get his attention. He turned to her and pounced.

Charlie was already running, racing to lure him away from the others. *Then what?* she thought as she ran furiously out of the dining room and down the hall. *The arcade.* It was dark; there were things to hide behind.

She kept running full-out until she reached the door, then turned so fast she almost fell, hoping to give Foxy a moment's disorientation. She looked around frantically. There was a row of arcade machines at the back of the room, set out just a little from the wall. She heard footsteps behind her and dove for it.

The space was so tight she could barely squeeze herself into it. Her sides were pressed between the consoles and the wall, and there were thick, coiled wires beneath her feet. She took a step back, moving deeper into the crawl space, but her foot slipped on a cable, and she barely kept from falling. Movement in the room caught her eye, and she saw a flash of silver light.

He sees me.

Charlie dropped to her hands and knees. She crawled backward, scooting inch by inch. Her foot caught on a cable and she stopped to free it, twisting into an impossible position to quietly dislodge it. She moved back farther, and then her foot bumped against another wall, and she stopped. She was closed in on three sides; it almost felt safe. She closed her eyes for a moment. *Nothing here is safe.*

There was an awful sound, a clash of metal hitting metal, and the console at the far end of the row rocked on its foundation, banging back against the wall. Foxy leaned over it, and now Charlie could see him as he smashed the display, spilling shards of plastic onto the floor. His hook caught on something inside the machine, and he yanked it out again, trailing bits of wire.

He moved on to the next game, smashing the screen and throwing the console against the wall with a casual brutality. Charlie felt the impact of it echoing through the wall as he moved closer.

I have to get out. I have to! But there was no way out. Now that she was sitting in one place, she realized that her arm was stiff with pain, and only now did she look at it. The bandage was soaked through with blood; the wall beside her was streaked with a line of it where her arm had pressed. She wanted to cry suddenly. Her whole body ached. The wound in her arm, the constant tension of the last day or so—who could tell how long it had been?—was draining her, taking all she had.

The next console crashed against the wall, and Charlie flinched. It was only two away. He was almost to her. She could hear his gears working, humming, grinding, and sometimes screeching. She closed her eyes, but she could still see him: his matted fur, the metal bones showing through, the searing silver eyes.

The console beside her was wrenched away and tumbled to the ground like it weighed nothing at all. The cords beneath Charlie's hands and knees jerked forward with it, and she slipped, grabbing at nothing, trying to regain her balance. She caught herself and looked up just in time to see the downward swing of a hook.

She moved faster than she could think. She hurled herself at the final console with all her strength, and it balanced precariously, then fell, knocking Foxy to the ground and trapping him. Charlie started to run, but his hook shot out and snared her leg, cutting into her. She screamed, falling to the ground. She kicked at him with her other foot, but his hook was stuck deep in her leg; every time he jerked back she felt the impact. She kicked him in the face, and his hook tore free, slicing open her leg. She screamed again, instinctively grabbing the wound, and then Foxy was on top of her, snapping his jaws and clawing her as he tried to free his legs from under the console. She fought back, struggling to get away. His hook slashed at her again and again as she tried to block the blows, screaming for help.

Suddenly John was there. He stood over Foxy and stomped down hard on the creature's neck, holding his foot there. Foxy flailed but could not reach him.

"Charlie, get up!" he called. Charlie just stared at him for a second, too shaken to register the question. He stamped his foot on Foxy's neck repeatedly, and then in one quick movement, he grabbed Charlie's hand, heaved her up, and started to run, pulling her along behind him. They made it to the main dining room, where the rest of the group was huddled in the middle of the room. Relieved, Charlie rushed to join them. She could tell she was limping, but she did not feel any pain, which, she realized somewhere dimly in the back of her mind, was not good. When they got to the others, her heart sank. Their faces were grim. Lamar was holding the flashlight out in front of him, but it rattled in his trembling grip.

Marla gestured quickly to the entrances. Freddy stood in the hall to the storage room, while Bonnie now blocked the hallway to the office. Chica, reanimated, stood on the stage, looming over them. Charlie glanced back the way they had come.

Foxy was approaching; he had freed himself. He stopped in the doorway as if waiting for a signal. There was no escape. Suddenly acutely aware of everything around her, Charlie noticed the sound of a music box, as if she had, unconsciously, been hearing it all along. She took a deep breath. The moment seemed to go on forever. It had come to this; they were trapped. They waited. Now, perhaps, for the animatronics, there was no hurry. Charlie cast her eyes around futilely for a weapon, but there were only party hats and paper plates.

As one, the animatronics started their approach. Charlie grabbed the back of a metal folding chair, not sure how she could even use it. The animals were moving faster now, coming in unison, as if this battle were a choreographed dance. Marla took Jason's hand and whispered something in his ear. Whatever it was, he shook his head, set his jaw, and balled his hands into fists. Lamar glanced at him for a moment but said nothing. Jessica had her hands stiffly at her sides, and she was murmuring something to herself inaudibly. The animals were almost on top of them. Freddy's trundling walk was predatory, and the music box notes were coming from Freddy's direction—from *inside* Freddy, she now realized. Chica leaped from the stage and took small, bouncing steps toward them as if excited but holding herself back. Bonnie's big, paw-like feet slapped the ground like a challenge, and Foxy slunk forth with a malevolent grace, his eyes fixed on Charlie as if she were the only thing he saw. She gazed into his silver eyes. They filled her vision, crowding out everything else until the world was silver, the world was Foxy's eyes, and there was nothing left of her.

John squeezed her hand. It broke the spell; she looked at him, her vision still cloudy.

"Charlie," he said haltingly. ". . . Charlotte—"

"Shh," she said. "Later." He nodded, accepting the lie that there would be a later. Foxy crouched down again, and Charlie let go of John, her heart pounding as she braced for it. Foxy's joints shifted in their sockets as he prepared to spring—then he stopped. Charlie waited. There were no screams from behind her, no sounds of fighting; even the music box was silent. Foxy was motionless, though his eyes still glowed. Charlie looked around, and then she saw.

It was Freddy. Not the one they all knew, not the one who stood less than a foot away from Marla, his mouth open as if poised to bite. It was the other one, the one she remembered, the yellow Freddy from the diner. The costume her father used to wear. It was looking at them, staring from the corner, and now she heard something. It was indistinct, just whispers in her head, a gentle susurrus, blowing through her conscious mind without taking hold. She looked at the others and knew they heard it, too. It was indecipherable, but the meaning was unmistakable.

Carlton was the one to say it:

"Michael?"

The sounds they heard grew warm, an unspoken confirmation, and together they approached the golden bear. Marla brushed past brown Freddy as if he were not there, and Charlie turned her back to Foxy, unafraid. There was only one thought in her mind: *Michael. It's you.*

They were almost to him. All Charlie wanted to do was fling her arms around him, hold him close, and to be again the little girl she was so long ago. To embrace him again, this beloved child who had been ripped from their lives on that carefree afternoon. To do it all over, and this time to rescue him, this time to save his life.

"Michael," she whispered.

The yellow bear stood motionless. Unlike the others, there seemed to be nothing inside of it; it stood of its own accord, by its own will. There was nothing to hold the costumed jaw closed, and its eyes were empty.

Suddenly aware that their backs were to the other animals, Charlie startled and turned, apprehensive. Freddy, Bonnie, Chica, and Foxy stood at rest, almost as if they were back on their stages. Their eyes were locked on Charlie, but they had halted their approach.

"It's the kids," Carlton whispered.

"Foxy wasn't attacking Jason," Marla gasped. "Foxy was trying to protect him."

John took hesitant steps toward the middle of the dining room, then approached more boldly, looking at each of the robots in turn. "It's the kids," he echoed. "All of them." Their faces were no longer animalistic, no longer lifeless, as if some spirit inhabited them.

Suddenly, there was a crash from the sealed exit door.

They all startled, turning as one as the wall beside the welded entrance shook with the force of a dozen blows.

Now what? Charlie thought.

The bricks broke and fell, scattering in pieces across the floor, dust filling the air in rusty clouds. A figure stepped through the hole wielding a massive sledgehammer, and as the air slowly cleared, they saw who it was: Clay Burke, Carlton's father.

His eyes set on Carlton, and he dropped the hammer and ran to his son, sweeping him into an embrace. Clay stroked his hair, gripping him like he would never let go. Charlie watched from her distance, relief touched by a stiletto edge of envy.

"Dad, I'm gonna puke," Carlton murmured. Clay laughed but leaned back when he saw that Carlton wasn't kidding. Carlton bent over, hands on his knees, fighting the urge to retch, and Clay's face took on alarm. Carlton straightened. "I'm good."

Clay was not listening anymore. He was looking around the room, at the animals. All of them were frozen in time, displaced.

"Okay, kids," Clay said, his voice low and his words careful. "I think it's time for us to go." He started toward the exit he had made.

They glanced at one another. The whispers were gone. Whatever he had been, the yellow Freddy was slouched again, an empty suit, though no one had seen it move. Charlie nodded toward Clay, and the rest started forward, heading almost reluctantly to the hole in the wall. Charlie hung back. John stayed beside her, but she gestured him forward, taking up the rear.

She had barely had time to take a step when something took hold of her throat.

Charlie tried to cry out, but her windpipe was being crushed. She was whipped around as if she weighed nothing, and she found herself face-to-face with the yellow rabbit. Dave's eyes were shining through, triumphant. He had his arm around her neck, squeezing her throat so tightly that she could scarcely breathe. He held her so close it was almost an embrace. She could smell the costume, stained fur and years of putrid sweat, blood, and cruelty.

He spoke, still staring at Charlie.

"You are staying."

"Absolutely not," Clay said, taking on the group's authority.

Dave dug his fingers deeper into Charlie's neck, and she made a strangled sound.

"I will kill this one, right here, while you watch, unless you do as I say," he said, and his voice was almost pleasant. Clay looked at him for a long moment, calculating, then nodded.

"Okay," he said, his voice calm. "We'll do as you say. What do you want?"

"Good," Dave said. He relaxed his grip on Charlie's neck, and she took a shaky breath. Clay began to move toward them, and the others followed. Charlie looked up at the man in the rabbit suit, and he met her gaze. *It was you. You killed Michael. You killed Sammy. You took them from me.* His eyes should have held something fierce and dangerous. They should have been windows to the rotten core inside. But they were only eyes, flat and empty.

Charlie plunged her hands into the gap beneath the costume's head. Dave drew back, but she held on.

"If you want to be one of them, then *be* one of them!" she shouted, and she tripped the spring locks. Dave's eyes widened, and then he screamed. Charlie jerked her hands free, barely evading the locks as they snapped open and plunged into his neck. She took a step back, watching as Dave crumpled to the ground, still screaming as the costume released. Part by part, the animatronic insides pierced his flesh, ripping up his organs, tearing through his body as if it were not even there. At some point he stopped screaming, but he still writhed on the floor for what felt like long minutes before he was still.

Charlie stared, breathing hard as if she had been running. The form on the ground seemed unreal. John was the first to move. He came beside her, but, still staring down, she waved him off before he could touch her. She could not bear it if he did.

Jessica gasped, and they all looked up. The animatronics were moving. The group drew back, huddling together, but none of the animals were looking at them. One by one they took hold of the broken body on the floor and began to drag it away toward the hall to Pirate's Cove. As they disappeared down the hallway, Charlie noticed that the yellow Freddy was gone.

"Let's go," she said quietly.

Clay Burke nodded, and they filed out of the restaurant for the last time.

CHAPTER THIRTEEN

The sun was rising as they emerged into the open air.

Clay put his arm around Carlton's shoulder, and for once Carlton didn't brush him away with a joke. Charlie nodded absently, blinking in the light. "Carlton and I are taking a drive to the ER," Clay continued. "Is there anyone else who needs a doctor?"

"I'm fine," Charlie said reflexively.

"Jason, do you need to go to the hospital?" Marla asked.

"No," he said.

"Let's see your leg," she insisted. The party stopped as Jason held his leg out for Clay to examine. Charlie felt an odd relief wash through her. A grown-up was in charge now. After a moment, Clay looked up at Jason with a serious face.

"I don't think we're going to have to cut it off," he said. "Not just yet." Jason smiled, and Clay turned to Marla. "I'll take care of him. It might leave a scar, but that'll just make him look tough."

Marla nodded and winked at Jason, who laughed.

"I need to change my clothes," Charlie said. It seemed like a petty thing to be worrying about, but her shirt and pants were wet with blood in some places, dry and stiff in others. It was beginning to itch.

"You're a mess," Carlton pointed out redundantly. "Will she get a ticket if she drives like that?"

"Charlie, are you sure you don't need to go to the hospital?" Marla said, turning her laser-like concern on her friend now that her brother had been declared safe.

"I'm fine," Charlie said again. "I just need to change my clothes. We'll stop at the motel."

When they reached the cars, they split into what had become their habitual groups: Marla, Jason, and Lamar in Marla's car; Charlie, John, and Jessica in Charlie's. Charlie opened the door to the driver's side and stopped, looking back at the building. It wasn't just her; out of the corner of her eye she could see them all gazing at it. The empty mall was dark against the pink-streaked sky, long and squat, like something brutish and slumbering. They all turned away, getting into the cars without speaking. Charlie kept her eyes on it, watching as she started her car, waiting to turn her back to it until the last possible moment. She pulled out of the lot and drove away.

Along the road, the cars split off. Clay and Carlton took the other turn out of the parking lot, heading to the hospital, and Charlie turned off toward the motel while Marla continued to the Burkes' house.

"I call first shower!" Jessica said as they got out of the car, then, seeing Charlie's face, "I'll make a special exception in your case. You go first."

Charlie nodded. In the room, she grabbed her bag and took it into the bathroom with her, leaving John and Jessica to wait. She locked the door behind her and undressed, deliberately not looking at the gashes on her arm and leg. She didn't need to see what was there, just to clean and bandage it. She got into the shower and let out a quiet yelp as the stinging water hit her open cuts, but she gritted her teeth and cleaned herself, washing her hair over and over until it was rinsed clean.

She got out and toweled herself dry, then sat down on the edge of the tub, put her face in her hands, and closed her eyes.

She was not ready to go out yet, not ready to face whatever aftermath, whatever discussion there might have to be.

She wanted to walk out of this bathroom and never speak again of what had happened. She rubbed her temples. She didn't have a headache, but there was pressure inside there, something that had yet to emerge.

You can't stay here forever.

Charlie still had the gauze and tape from the first time around, so she took it from her bag, wiped both wounds clean with a hotel towel, and bound up her arm and leg, using all the gauze. *I probably need stitches*, she thought, but it was only an idle thought. She would not do it. She got up and went to look in the mirror. There was a cut across her cheek; it had stopped bleeding, but it was ugly. She didn't know how she could cover it, but she didn't really want to, for the same reason she didn't want stitches. She *wanted* them to heal wrong, wanted them to scar. She wanted proof, displayed on her body: *This happened. This was real. This is what it did to me.*

She dressed quickly in her jeans and her last remaining clean T-shirt and emerged from the bathroom to find Jessica and John carrying suitcases out to the car.

"I figured there was no point leaving stuff here," Jessica said. "We're all going in the morning; we may as well bring it all to Carlton's." Charlie nodded and grabbed Jason's backpack, taking it out to the car along with her own.

★   ★   ★

Carlton and his father were already back by the time they arrived, and again they entered Carlton's living room, now almost familiar. Carlton was curled up in an armchair by the fireplace, where someone had lit a fire, and Marla and Lamar were on the couch. Jason sat right in front of the fireplace, staring in at the licking flames. Charlie sat down near him, arranging herself stiffly. John joined her, looking at her with concern, but she ignored him, and he said nothing.

"Are you okay?" Charlie asked, reaching up and rubbing Carlton's arm for a moment. He looked at her sleepily.

"Yeah, it's a mild concussion," he said. "I'll be fine as long as no one else tries to murder me."

"So . . . now what?" Jessica asked as she took the chair beside Carlton. "I mean—" She paused, searching for words. "What happens?" she said finally. They looked at each other; it was the question they all had. *What do you do after something like this?* Charlie looked at Clay, who was standing in the doorway, only half in the room.

"Mr.—Clay, what happens now?" she said quietly. He looked off into the distance for a minute before answering.

"Well, Charlie, I'm going to go back to Freddy's. I have to get my officer," he said gravely. "I won't go alone." He forced a smile, but no one joined him. "What do you think should happen?" he asked. He was looking at Charlie, asking her this impossible question as if she could answer it. She nodded, accepting responsibility.

"Nothing," she said. "It's over. I want to leave it that way."

Clay gave her a nod, his face impassive. She could not tell if it was the answer he was looking for, but it was all she had. The others were silent. Marla and Lamar were nodding, but Jessica looked like she wanted to protest.

"Jessica, what?" Charlie said gently, realizing with unease that her friend wanted her permission to disagree.

"It just seems wrong," she said. "What about . . . everything? I mean, people should know, right? That's how it works. That guard, he murdered all those kids, and people should know!"

"No one will believe us," Jason said without looking up.

"Officer Dunn," Jessica said. "Officer Dunn, he *died* in there! What will you tell his family? Will you tell them the truth?" She looked at Clay.

"Officer Dunn died at the hands of the same man who killed your friends. I can prove that now." A silence fell over the room. "It won't bring them back," Clay said softly. "But maybe it will give them some rest."

Clay turned his eyes to the fire, and a few minutes passed before he spoke again.

"You kids have been carrying Freddy's with you all these years. It's time you left it behind," he said. He was stern, but his commanding tone was reassuring. "I'm going to see to it that Officer Dunn is given a proper burial." He paused, collecting himself, as though what he said next required effort.

"Your friends, too." His brow furrowed. "I have a few favors to call in, but I can make this happen quietly. The last thing I want to do is disturb that place, or desecrate it. Those kids need rest."

The next morning they began to go their separate ways. Marla offered to drive Lamar and Jessica to the bus station, and they said their good-byes with hugs and promises to write. Charlie wondered if any of them meant it. Marla probably did, at least. They pulled out of the Burkes' driveway.

"So my bus isn't till later," John said as Marla's car disappeared around a bend in the road.

"I wouldn't mind a few more hours in Hurricane," Charlie answered. To her surprise, she realized it was true.

John flashed her a quick, almost nervous smile.

"Okay, then," he said.

"Let's get out of there. Let's go somewhere, anywhere."

When they were alone in the car, John gave her a sideways glance.

"So," he said, "are we ever going to see each other after this?" He tried to say it lightly, but there was no way to lighten it. Charlie stared straight ahead.

"Maybe," she said. She could not look at him. It wasn't the answer he wanted, she knew that, but she could not give him what he wanted. What could she say by way of explanation? *It's not you, it's the weight we both bear. It's too much. When you are here, I can't ignore it.*

But something in her thoughts felt off, not quite right, as if she were speaking by rote, thinking off a script. It was like flinching instinctively to protect an injury before remembering it had healed. She finally looked at John beside her. He was staring through the windshield, his jaw set.

"I have somewhere I need to go," she said abruptly, then made a slow U-turn. She had never gone to visit the place, but now, without warning, her mind was consumed by it. Aunt Jen had never suggested it; Charlie had never asked. She knew where it was, though, and now she headed there with a singular sense of purpose. *I need to see.*

Charlie pulled to a stop in a small gravel parking lot beside a low fence of short white posts, chains swinging between them.

"I just need a minute," she said. John gave her a concerned look.

"Are you sure you want to do this now?" he said softly. She did not answer, just got out of the car, closing the door behind her.

The graveyard before them was almost a hundred years old. There were hills of lush grass and shading trees. This corner was at the edge of the cemetery; there was a small house only a few yards past the edge of the fence. The grass was trimmed neatly, but it was patchy and yellowing. The trees had been pruned too far so the lower branches were bare, too exposed.

There was a telephone pole set just inside the fence, barely on the cemetery grounds, and beside it were two headstones, plain and small. Charlie stared at it for a long moment, not moving. She tried to conjure up the right feeling: grief and loss so that she could mourn. Instead, she just felt a numbness. The graves were there, but the sight did not touch her. She took a deep breath and started toward them.

It was such a small memory, one of those moments that meant nothing at the time, just one day in a series of days, the same as all the others. They were together, just the two of them, and it must have been before everything, before Fredbear's went wrong, before anyone was dead.

They were sitting out back behind Fredbear's, looking out over the hills, and a crow landed and began pecking in the dirt, looking for something. There was something about its sharp, darting movements that struck her as the funniest thing she had ever seen. Charlie began to laugh, and her father looked at her. She pointed, and he turned his head, trying to see as she did, but he could not tell what she was pointing at. She could not get it across to him, she did not know the words, and just as her excitement was about to turn to frustration, he saw it, too. Suddenly he laughed and pointed to the crow. Charlie nodded, and he met her eyes, looking at her with an expression of pure, boundless delight, as if it would fill him to bursting.

"Oh, Charlotte," he said.

About Scott Cawthon

Scott Cawthon is the author of the bestselling video game series Five Nights at Freddy's, and while he is a game designer by trade, he is first and foremost a storyteller at heart. He is a graduate of the Art Institute of Houston and lives in Texas with his wife and four sons.

About Kira Breed-Wrisley

Kira Breed-Wrisley has been writing stories since she could first pick up a pen and has no intention of stopping. She is the author of seven plays for Central New York teen theater company the Media Unit, and has developed several books with Kevin Anderson & Associates. She is a graduate of Cornell University and lives in Brooklyn, NY.